Since a young age, [author] loved to read and write. A few years a[go her] parents moved from the family home where they had lived for almost half a century, she came across a book she had penned aged seven and three quarters. It started off with impeccably neat handwriting and childish illustrations, then became increasingly untidy until it fizzled out altogether. She vowed there and then to finish her next one.

After qualifying as a management accountant and enjoying a varied career in Finance and HR, she gave up work in 2018 to focus on her other interests, including creative writing. She lives in Monmouthshire with her husband Andy and their two lassie collies.

Her first book *I'm Going to Find You* was published in 2021 and had great success in New Zealand, Canada and Australia as well as the U.K. This, an independent sequel, is her second.

https://www.jdpullan-author.com
LinkedIn: Justine Pullan
Facebook and Instagram: J D Pullan Author.

Also by J D Pullan:

I'M GOING TO FIND YOU

What readers are saying...

"An outstanding debut from an author to watch."

"J.D.Pullan's debut novel is better than anything by the authors who have found fame in her chosen genre. She has an extraordinary talent."

"Another book from this author can't come soon enough."

"Dripping with tension and suspense from the very beginning!"

"One of my favourite books this year!"

"A brilliant first book."

"An intriguing and memory-jerking novel which keeps your attention all the way."

"It was so riveting and enticing I read it in one sitting, practically consumed until the end. And what an end!"

"The labyrinthine plot shifts backwards and forwards between the heatwave of 1976 and the summer of 2010. Both eras captured with perfect precision."

"Fascinating… A beautiful story that captures your attention and your heart from beginning to end."

I Know You Were There

J D PULLAN

Copyright © 2024 J D Pullan

The moral right of the author has been asserted.

Apart from any fair dealing for the purposes of research or private study, or criticism or review, as permitted under the Copyright, Designs and Patents Act 1988, this publication may only be reproduced, stored or transmitted, in any form or by any means, with the prior permission in writing of the publishers, or in the case of reprographic reproduction in accordance with the terms of licences issued by the Copyright Licensing Agency. Enquiries concerning reproduction outside those terms should be sent to the publishers.

This is a work of fiction. Names, characters, businesses, places, events and incidents are either the products of the author's imagination or used in a fictitious manner. Any resemblance to actual persons, living or dead, or actual events is purely coincidental.

Troubador Publishing Ltd
Unit E2 Airfield Business Park,
Harrison Road, Market Harborough,
Leicestershire LE16 7UL
Tel: 0116 279 2299
Email: books@troubador.co.uk
Web: www.troubador.co.uk

ISBN 978-1-83628-028-6

British Library Cataloguing in Publication Data.
A catalogue record for this book is available from the British Library.

Printed and bound in Great Britain by 4edge Limited
Typeset in 10.5pt Minion Pro by Troubador Publishing Ltd, Leicester, UK

For everyone who bought, enjoyed, borrowed, shared or recommended my first book. Your wonderful reviews and kind messages of support mean the world to me and inspire me to keep writing.

1

SATURDAY 19 MAY 2012

EMILY

A beautiful, vibrant double rainbow arches over the horizon as Emily cruises along the motorway. Surely that must be a sign of good fortune. She is looking forward to her weekend plans – and life in general – for the first time in months and the radiant glow of the early afternoon sun illuminating the clouds fills her with hope.

'It's just ten weeks to the opening ceremony of the London 2012 Games and the Olympic Torch has arrived in the UK!' the radio host proclaims, as excited as she is. 'The traditional lighting ceremony took place in Greece just over a week ago and it was officially welcomed by the people of Cornwall this morning…'

Emily glances in the rear-view mirror, relieved to see Molly and Jack are settled. More often than not they are fidgety after five minutes and she smiles to herself, contentedly. Molly is so like Marcus, with dark curls framing her face and brown eyes that always glint with mischief. Jack, two years younger, is the complete opposite. A smattering of freckles on his nose and blonde hair shining like a halo in the watery sunshine.

Checking no vehicles are approaching from behind, she pulls out to pass a slow-moving lorry and her windscreen wipers swoosh, like an overactive metronome, to clear the spray of dirty water thrown up by the huge wheels. With her foot pressed hard on the accelerator, she makes good progress towards a gap in the traffic further ahead. Gaining on the lorry, she hears a loud beep and jumps, wondering why someone has tooted their horn at her. Then her car shudders violently and, simultaneously, a flashing red triangle appears on the dashboard, advising her to stop immediately. She panics. She isn't speeding, but how can she possibly stop in the middle lane on a busy motorway?

Molly and Jack had been chattering away but are now silent as the ear-piercing alarm fills the air between them and the huge lorry dwarfs her car. A delivery van races past on her other side, followed far too closely by three more vehicles, and Emily grips the steering wheel; she's trapped in the middle, with nowhere to go. *Damn.* Another red light has appeared. *Shit.* The tyre pressure. All four wheels. The engine shudders again, making the steering wheel snatch and, as the car skews across the lane, it takes all her strength to keep it centred and not lose control.

Emily feels sick. Jack is whimpering and she has to resist her maternal instinct, an overpowering urge to turn around and comfort him. Survival mode takes over. She needs to get to the safety of the hard shoulder, and she needs to get there as quickly as she can.

Drawing level with the lorry, she becomes aware the driver is looking in her direction. He seems to sense her predicament and slows down, flashing his lights. Her heart thumps in her chest and Emily isn't sure what he means. Does he want her to move out of his way or is he letting her in? Undecided, she indicates to let him know her intentions and to double check she hasn't misinterpreted. He flashes his lights again, and again, then hangs back, freeing up space for her to move in front of him. 'Thank you,' she says out loud, then repeats. 'Thank you, thank you.' Normally she would wave, to show her appreciation, but her hands are glued to the steering wheel.

For a little while, the lorry follows immediately behind; far enough not to be intimidating whilst close enough to protect her from other vehicles and to make sure she is okay. Then, as Emily reduces her speed and indicates again – ready to manoeuvre her car onto the hard shoulder – the thoughtful lorry driver signs a thumbs up, toots his horn gleefully and pulls out around her, once again throwing dirty spray across her car.

Giddy with adrenaline and more-than-ever thankful to be alive, Emily's brings her car to a kangaroo halt at the side of the motorway and watches the truck, her guardian angel for today, roar off into the distance.

2

SATURDAY 19 MAY

EMILY

The thunderous noise of traffic is deafening and Emily's knees are painfully stiff as she crouches at the top of the steep embankment. An overwhelming smell of exhaust, lingering in the low cloud, is nauseating and Molly's hairclip cuts into her skin. She knows it is her daughter's favourite but, right now, the plastic unicorn is razor-sharp as Molly and Jack cling to her, too frightened to let go. As if that's not enough, the rough grass is scratching the back of Emily's legs and she flinches every time a lorry roars past. The earlier sunshine proved to be short-lived and rain from her sopping fringe runs in rivers down her forehead, dripping off the end of her nose and onto her clammy, wet jeans.

Molly and Jack tremble with a mixture of fear and cold, as she strains to make herself heard on her mobile phone. Even at maximum volume the voice at the other end is nothing more than a whisper. She thinks the girl said her name was Sabrina, but it could have been Katrina. Or Davina. Emily senses whatever-her-name-is has had exactly the same conversation numerous times already today as she attempts to reassure her that help is on its way and encourages Emily to "remain calm" in a disingenuous, monotone voice.

'I've registered your call as a priority and our expert vehicle technician should reach you within forty-five minutes, he is just completing another call-out.'

Emily sighs. So much for a relaxing, idyllic weekend in Devon. She can tell the girl is reading from a script.

'Please ensure you remain a safe distance from any passing traffic and keep your phone with you in case we should need to call you back. Please note all calls are recorded for training and monitoring purposes. Is there anything else I can help you with today?'

She has got to be joking, thinks Emily. Is she really going to discuss insurance, or anything else as banal, when she is stuck at the side of a manic motorway with two terrified children?

'Er, no, that's fine,' she replies politely, biting her lip. 'It's just my car I need to get sorted today. But thanks for the offer.'

'No problem, thank you Mrs Harrison. Rest assured you're next on the list and I wish you a good day.'

Emily puts her phone in her pocket, making sure it is on vibrate. There is no way she'll hear it ring. Her eyes are watering but she's not sure if it is her sodden hair, which desperately needs a trim and keeps getting in her eyes, or the fumes. Or the sadness that still engulfs her whenever anyone calls her Mrs Harrison.

She kisses Molly and Jack in turn, gently brushing her lips on the top of their heads. Resting her chin on Jack's soft hair, she shuts her eyes to stem the flow of tears she knows will follow if she doesn't pull herself together.

'How about a chocolate biscuit?' she asks in the most upbeat voice she can muster. She mustn't let them know she is anxious. At least she had the presence of mind to get some food out the car in case they had a long wait.

Still in shock, she shivers at the thought of what could have happened to them and silently prays there is nothing seriously wrong with her car. She isn't hungry but nibbles on a sandwich purely to persuade Molly and Jack to have something too or they will be ravenous.

Her phone twitches in her pocket and she can see it is Mitch calling. Talk about timing. She lets it go to voicemail then plays it back on speaker, holding it close to her ear.

'Hi Emily, it's me. I got a lift into town, so if it's okay with you I'll walk to where you're staying and meet you there, then you can drop me back at my mum's a bit later on.'

She looks at her phone in disbelief. Who does he think he is? She isn't making the trip down especially for him, yet he is already taking over. It's a weekend break for her, Molly and Jack. To recharge their batteries. Okay, so it was his idea initially – he came down for a school reunion and his mum told him about the newly renovated holiday cottages – then, when Emily spotted the special offer for the first three months, it seemed too good an opportunity to miss. So, yes, he did have *something* to do with it, but that was all. Now he's telling her what to do and where to be.

Emily inhales deeply, then has a moment of remorse; it's not his fault. Just because she is having a bad day there is no reason whatsoever to take it out on Mitch. He doesn't actually know she has broken down yet and he is only trying to be helpful by letting her know what time he will get there.

Lost in her thoughts, she tries to evaluate what she *really* thinks of Mitch. He is actually quite pleasant but she simply isn't interested in him as anything more than a friend. Her mind wanders back a few months, when her colleague Jo introduced them to each other. They aren't dating, they never have been. Just thinking about it scares her. How does it work these days? No, Jo had simply persuaded her, talking in hushed tones over their desks, that what she needed was a bit of friendship and a bit of fun. Nothing more, nothing less. Mitch wasn't looking for anything serious either. 'You've got nothing to lose by going out for a harmless drink with him,' Jo had said. 'It'll do you the world of good to have a bit of a laugh again.'

'Who was that, Mum?' asks Molly kindly. She can tell her Mum is preoccupied.

'Just Mitch.'

'Mitch the Itch!' adds Jack.

'Stop it Jack, you know you're not meant to say that,' Molly nudges him in the ribs to shut him up.

'Where on earth did you get that expression from?' Emily asks.

'Dad,' they reply in unison, before Molly explains further, in a very matter-of-fact way. 'Dad says he is an irritant. An itch. He says he's not good for you and he can't see what you see in him.'

Well, hats off to Molly, thinks Emily. She certainly says it as it is. Marcus obviously thinks there is far more to their friendship than there actually is. They've been out a grand total of three times – twice for a drink after work and once for a coffee after Jack's football on a Sunday morning. Then she bursts out laughing at their childish innocence and the tears she has been fighting for the last twenty minutes roll uncontrollably down her cheeks. The three of them giggle and her heart bursts with love for them both. It's not only what Molly said about Mitch that made them dissolve into fits of laughter, but hysteria at the ludicrous situation they are in, sat at the side of the motorway in the pouring rain watching the monotony of the traffic whizzing past.

Just as they are about to regain control Molly knowingly winks at Jack and they erupt with laughter again. Emily wipes her tears away with the back of her hand and hugs them both as tight as she can.

'He says he still loves you Mum and he wants you back,' Molly continues, eventually catching her breath.

'Oh really, when exactly did he tell you that?' Emily asks, as she stares through watery eyes at the distant, rolling hills that are fuzzy-edged in the grey, overcast sky.

'Well, Mum, it's complicated,' Molly explains candidly and with a clarity that is significantly beyond her eight short years. 'He didn't really tell *me*. Dad was talking to his friend; they were watching the telly and I couldn't sleep. So, anyway, I crept downstairs to ask Dad for a glass of water but he didn't know I was there and that was when I heard them talking.'

'Oh, I see, and did your dad say anything else?' Emily can't help but ask.

'He said he still loved you, then his friend said "I would too, if I were you". Something like that, I can't remember *exactly*.'

Emily shakes her head and shuts her eyes. That is the sweetest thing she has heard in ages. It is music to her ears even if, at this moment, they are about to burst with the horrendous noise of the traffic.

Three solid lanes of cars, lorries, vans and motorbikes on both carriageways. Everything going in different directions, coming from different starting points and heading for different destinations.

Her eyes glaze over with the hypnotic effect of the vehicles. How apt. *An accurate reflection of her life*, she muses. *Chaos*. Why does life have to be so complicated? She has known all along that she wants Marcus to come home and for the four of them to be a proper family again.

A feeling of dread runs down her spine. All of a sudden, Emily knows she has made a terrible mistake coming away for the weekend with Molly and Jack.

Not only is she driving one way when what she genuinely wants is to be heading in the opposite direction. No, it is worse than that. A thousand times worse.

At this moment in time, she is stalled, broken and deflated

at the side of the motorway. If only she could see into the future and know which way she will be going when everything is mended.

3

SATURDAY 19 MAY

MITCH

Mitch sits on the wall by the bus stop on the edge of town and scrolls through the messages on his mobile phone. It's been buzzing all day – and pretty much non-stop – since he went to his school reunion the previous weekend. Facebook notifications mostly. Old school friends sharing photos and gossip on the TavyStars1987 group they set up to celebrate the 25th anniversary.

A few of them are meeting up again this evening to watch the football, although he unexpectedly bumped into Trev and Ian last night and a 'swift pint' turned into a full-on session, so he may take it a bit slower tonight. He flicks through the notifications and hopes he isn't featured in any of them. He hates having his photo taken at the best of times and the thought of sharing a selfie on social media horrifies him.

Open to the elements, the bus shelter has definitely seen better days. The plastic windows are grimy, smeared with dirt and covered in graffiti. They mirror how he is feeling. Rough. Seriously rough. It is the worst hangover he has had in ages, and second thoughts about the weekend only make his head hurt more. What had seemed an excellent idea, when he mentioned to Emily about the newly opened holiday cottages, now seems fraught with problems.

Mitch hangs his aching head and looks at the ground through the gap between his knees. The tarmac sways from side to side and, for now at least, he's content to rest his legs and not move his head any more than he needs to. Enjoying a moment of solitude, he quietly watches a few pedestrians going about their business, interspersed with a lycra-clad runner pushing her slumbering baby in a bouncy, three-wheeled pushchair, and two teenagers trying to control a young puppy. It looks like a labradoodle. Then a bespectacled, elderly gentleman wearing a showerproof, plastic poncho appears from nowhere, motoring along at a breakneck speed on his mobility chair with little regard for other road users.

Mitch checks his watch. Three o'clock. He will give Emily a call to see what time she expects to arrive. Hopefully not just yet as he still has some distance to walk. Emily inadvertently gave him the entry code for where she's staying – it was in an email she sent him with the directions – so he could go on ahead, but it would be wrong to let himself in without her permission, given it is booked in her name. To be fair, he's a little confused about Emily. When Simon, his badminton partner, said his wife knew someone who was looking for a bit of company it had seemed a nice thing to do, given that was what he needed too while his divorce was going through and custody of Olly was being sorted.

And she is nice. But that's it, just nice. He's never felt any real spark between them, or that she is particularly bothered about him at all. She is always busy, either at work or with the kids. Or this, or that. He's never entirely sure whether she uses it as a smokescreen, to keep him at a distance, or whether she is genuinely busy.

That's why this weekend had seemed such a good idea. He thought it would be an opportunity to be more relaxed with each other, to see if there is anything there. The only trouble being his mum is reading far more into her visit than she should. Plus, he is definitely getting cold feet about introducing Emily to his pals later on. He will die on the spot if anyone mentions what happened at the reunion, although Trev and Ian didn't say anything last night, so maybe he's fretting unnecessarily.

Mitch watches the elderly gentleman brake hard as he negotiates a narrow ramp leading up to the corner shop and feels another, even more painful, pang of regret. He is too far past the point of no return to change his plans now; Emily is almost here and he agreed with his friends to meet them at the pub to watch the football. It will look odd if he isn't there, his absence would only create more speculation.

He will just have to grin and bear it. Hopefully both the evening, and the weekend in general, will go significantly better than he expects and no one will mention what happened last week.

SATURDAY 19 MAY

EMILY

Emily doesn't have to wait long. They've barely finished their make-do picnic as the technician emerges from the stream of traffic. He certainly looks the part with a smear of engine oil across his forehead and a big smile. He shouts as he makes his way up the embankment, his voice barely audible above the cacophony of the traffic.

'Where are you heading?' he asks as he borrows her car key and Emily tells him all about their weekend plans. 'Wow, it sounds great. You stay right where you are, Mrs Harrison, and I'll get you on your way as soon as I can.'

Having retrieved a bag of leads and a small hand-held computer from his van, it is not long before he is climbing back up the slope, his boots sliding on the wet grass.

'The engine's running fine now – I found the problem and the tyres are all top-notch too. You're good to go.'

'That's such a relief, thank you!' smiles Emily. 'It freaked me out to be honest. I was scared stiff.'

'Just a loose connection on one of the wires, they're very sensitive. Nothing at all to worry about,' he replies, smiling, and then shakes her hand to reassure her further. 'I hope you have a great weekend – the place where you are staying sounds fun. I've never heard of it before but my kids would love it, I'll definitely have to check it out.'

'Oh, I will, and thank you again,' Emily laughs, her relief palpable 'Not far to go now and it'll be a day or two before we need to drive home again. That will give the car a rest, as well as the driver!'

*

Emily checks the sat nav as she pulls away: forty-eight miles, estimated time an hour and twenty-five minutes. It seems far too long for the distance and it's already much later than planned but, once they get there, she will be able to relax.

The Cowshed had looked fabulous on the website, set in the grounds of an old mansion. Four of the original estate buildings have been renovated and are now wonderful places to stay. Even better, a craft gallery is opening soon in a converted barn, with dozens of local artists displaying their work. Emily can't wait to have a proper look around. She is certain both Molly and Jack will adore the tiny cottage, tiny being the operative word. The others – The Piggery, The Chicken Coop and The Dovecote – look amazing too.

She thinks they sound like something out of a fairy tale and absentmindedly crosses her fingers on the steering wheel, wishing for the next two days to live up to her expectations of an idyllic weekend.

Emily checked the details carefully before making a reservation, to make sure it would be suitable. The Cowshed has an open-plan downstairs with a comfy lounge and kitchen area, leading to a bathroom with a roll-top bath. Wooden stairs take you up to a mezzanine floor with a double bed and two pull-out beds, ideal for Molly and Jack. It looks perfect in the photos. Just perfect. It means Mitch won't be able to invite himself round either, she isn't ready for that. Even if she was, Emily is convinced he is still not over his first wife. The divorce isn't sorted yet, or the custody arrangements for his son, and his soon-to-be ex is always hassling him. Or he her. It could very easily be too much, too soon for him.

The traffic is light and although Emily still feels jittery about the earlier breakdown, her car is running smoothly and she, once again, allows herself to get excited about their plans for the weekend.

Magic FM plays quietly and 'Unchained Melody' with Robson and Jerome pulls at her heartstrings. It was the song she and Marcus chose for their first dance and had been number one in the charts for months before their special day. *1995. Wow. Almost seventeen years.* How Emily wishes she could go back and do it all again.

Yet again her mind wanders. She knows she still loves Marcus. In her heart, she is Mrs Harrison and always will be. How on earth did they manage to get into this ridiculous situation? She knows she was foolish not to tell him when she became obsessed with Cerys, the girl who went missing in Cornwall, but that was almost two years ago. Plus, he knows she was only doing it for all the right reasons, to help Cerys's elderly parents get the closure they so desperately needed. She's explained so many times now. Even if she made some poor decisions, her intentions were good and it doesn't make her a bad person. Surely?

*

The motorway is superseded by rolling hills and Emily imagines the road to be a giant, silver-grey snake slithering across the countryside towards Okehampton. The farther they travel, the wilder the scenery becomes and, when she turns south towards the moor, the old-fashioned, black and white signs to Tavistock take her down the narrowest of roads. A cattle grid shakes the car violently as they enter the national park, making them laugh out loud, and all three of them take delight in the rugged, expansive views across Dartmoor.

Emily pulls over at a small layby and switches off the engine to fully appreciate the beautiful scenery opening up before them. Craggy, granite tors fill the skyline and the bright yellow flowers of the windswept gorse glisten after the earlier rain. The wonderfully small, yet strong, eponymous ponies – in every shade of black, grey and brown – graze happily, wandering from one patch of green to another, completely oblivious to anything around them. Now and then, they glance towards their car with huge, expressive eyes, shaking their long, wild manes and whinnying loudly, making the children squeal with delight.

In the distance there are stone farmhouses, standing proudly among fields of sheep and cattle. Small columns of smoke rise from their ancient hearths, even though it's now late spring. To complete the panorama, a derelict tin mine serves as a bygone reminder of more industrious times on the moor, its tall, slender, tapering chimney like a finger pointing to the sky. It may not be far from home, in terms of distance, but it feels like a totally different world.

Excitement building, a buzzard swoops overhead as Emily looks forward to meeting Lady Allington and exploring her estate. Then she thinks about the Olympic torch procession on Monday; the grand finale of their weekend trip and an extra day off school for Molly and Jack. Not that their headteacher had minded – he had waved his arms in the air with infectious enthusiasm when she asked his permission. "Of course, it is unlikely we will host the Olympics again anytime soon!"

Next week, Molly and Jack will watch the torch when it is transported by powerboat across Bristol Harbour and then head to Cheltenham Racecourse to see it paraded on horseback. All part of a school project they are doing on the history of the Olympics. Emily is sure Lady Allington mentioned her granddaughter is training with Team GB too, she can't remember precisely but thinks it is the modern pentathlon. Perhaps Molly and Jack could meet her. That would be incredible, a *real* Olympic athlete.

Emily is brought back to earth with a bump as her phone vibrates.

'Hi, Mitch! Yes, everything is fine, thanks – we've just pulled over to admire the lovely view, so not far to go.'

'That's great. I should get to Allington House about five o'clock.'

'Perfect,' Emily replies. 'We'll be just after... if I can find it!'

*

Continuing their journey, the alarmingly narrow lanes offer few passing places and Emily slowly weaves her way through a herd of cows and squeezes past a tractor. No wonder the sat nav said it would take so long, it must be programmed to know.

With just a few miles remaining the high Devon hedges, at least fifteen foot high, tower over them and after a hairpin bend – endorsed with a warning that oncoming cars may be in the middle of the road, which may also be liable to flooding – Emily is relieved when a large entrance appears in front of her.

Turning through the ornate metal gates, she is stunned by the grandeur as a Georgian mansion comes into view at the end of a long drive, the landscaped grounds in stark contrast to the winding lanes of the moor. Tall, symmetrical windows surround the pillared entrance porch and a low, unpierced parapet almost hides the roof-line from view at eye level, giving the building a simple, yet formidable, appearance.

Further along the drive, flanked by rhododendron bushes holding on to their shocking pink spring blooms as long as they can, a small sign indicates a right turn to the holiday cottages. Emily follows this and passes a row of three attached houses where a carving, embedded in the dry-stone wall, reads Meadow View. How bucolic, it would be impossible to think of a more suitable name.

Behind the houses she can see long, narrow rear gardens. They must be permanent residences. Scattered toys and a well-used trampoline feature at number one, where a tired but well-used lawn bears the hallmarks of children playing, although there are none to be seen or heard at the moment. The middle cottage is dark and empty; old, torn curtains hang untidily at dirty windows. In the garden of the third chickens cluck contentedly and an early climbing rose adorns a trellis, laden with buds about to burst open. Beneath it a handmade notice offering "Local Honey and Free-Range Eggs" is propped up against an ancient, metal milk churn and an honesty box.

Emily can't believe it. At long last they have arrived and it looks just as perfect as she imagined, if not more so.

SATURDAY 19 MAY

EMILY

The Cowshed and The Piggery each have large nameplates to avoid any confusion and a narrow path leads from the shared front garden to the back of the cottages via a small metal gate. The Dovecote and The Chicken Coop look to be works-in-progress and a skip piled high with builder's rubbish has been positioned carefully behind a hedge so it doesn't spoil the façade.

Mitch is already there and hears her arrive, his breath steaming up the glass as he leans forward to peer through one of the windows with his hand over his forehead to shield the light. 'Hi there, how are you?' he smiles, spinning around.

'I'm fine, thanks – apart from having the fright of my life on the motorway. Although the mechanic arrived pretty quickly so I can't complain.' Emily is flattered that he cares. 'Well, I don't know about you, but I'm gasping for a cup of tea and Molly and Jack are desperate to see inside. I wrote the code for the key box on my hand to save time, so what are we waiting for?'

'How very organised! At your service, m'lady – call the

numbers out and I'll do the honours,' Mitch replies with a mock salute.

He fiddles with the combination lock, lining up the numbers until the tiny door pings open.

'Hmmm,' he mumbles. 'There doesn't seem to be anything in here. There's definitely no key.'

'What do you mean there's no key?' Emily pushes him aside and scrapes around to make sure it's not hidden at the back. 'I don't believe it. I just don't believe it.'

'Hey, hang on, don't panic, I'm sure the key is in there somewhere,' Mitch tries to reassure her, although it clearly isn't.

'Seriously Mitch, this isn't funny. Not after the day I've had. Please tell me you're joking and you're hiding it up your sleeve or something?'

'Nope. Afraid not. Sorry.'

'This is utterly ridiculous. Honestly, I don't believe it. All I wanted was a fun evening with the kids; to relax in the cottage, maybe stroll around the grounds before a few bedtime stories and a soak in the bath. Is that so much to ask?' Emily shakes her head with disappointment.

All Mitch can do is shrug his shoulders, adding to Emily's frustration and she shuts her eyes, not wanting Molly and Jack to see how upset she is.

'It's not fair, Mitch. It's just not fair. Why does *everything* have to be so complicated?'

After a lengthy silence Mitch is the first to talk. 'Hey, come on, don't be like that. The code worked perfectly so there *must* be a logical explanation. The key has to be somewhere.'

'I know, I'm sorry. But what do we do now? I'm desperate for a cup of tea… and the bathroom!' she laughs, trying to ease the atmosphere.

'Let's look around, maybe there's another box,' Mitch suggests as she follows him around the side of the cottage.

Despite the urgent need to find the key, Emily is awestruck. The steep back garden is delightful, verging on wild, compared to the highly manicured front garden. A table and chairs, deliberately placed to command the best view over the surrounding countryside, sit adjacent to a small meadow bursting with ox-eye daisies, purple loosestrife and yellow rattle. Just beyond, next to a sprawling oak tree, a rickety gate leads to a large, kidney-shaped pond.

'God, this is such a pain,' Emily groans, flopping herself onto one of the chairs. 'After all the trouble with my car the last thing I need is to be sat here, admiring this incredible view *and* the lovely cottage, when we can't get inside.'

'What are we going to do, Mum?' asks Molly, picking up on her unease.

'I don't know sweetheart, but we will think of something.'

Emily puts a reassuring arm around Molly and Jack as she and Mitch sit in silence, both knowing the other is thinking the same thing. As they do, a black and white cat nonchalantly saunters past, rubbing its hind quarters against the table leg and miaowing gently. Molly puts her hand out to stroke it, but the nervous animal takes flight and disappears as quickly as it arrived.

*

'Are you alright?' Emily asks, ending the hiatus as Mitch yawns noisily.

'Yeah, late night that's all. I'm not used to it anymore.' Mitch grins half-heartedly. 'I bumped into some old mates and ended up staying for a few drinks. Some of them are meeting up again tonight, I said we might join them if that's okay with you.'

'Oh, I don't know, Mitch. It's kind of you to ask, but after breaking down and the awful journey we've had I was looking forward to a relaxing evening with Molly and Jack… if we ever get this sorted, that is.' Emily tries to sound interested, although organising their social life isn't her main priority at the moment. 'God, I'm sorry Mitch. Look at me. Look at us. This is meant to be a fun weekend away and we're sat here like a pair of old codgers. Let's try again, the key *must* be somewhere or how else does *anyone* get in?'

She stands up, drawing on all her reserves of positive energy and strains her eyes up against the glass to look inside. The lounge looks *so* cosy and inviting, which simply makes the situation worse, given they can't actually get in. She pulls at the patio door in frustration, then jumps back in surprise as it slides open a few inches.

'Mitch, it's not locked! Maybe the key is in here after all.' She is inside before she can think what she is doing, then leaps back out. 'Gosh, do… do you think we should?' she stammers, turning around to look at Mitch, who has jumped out of his chair and is right behind her.

'Should what?'

'Go inside… you know… do you think it's okay, without a key?' she clarifies.

'Yes, Mum, yes!' screeches Molly.

'Well, you've paid to stay here so I can't see why not.'

'That's very true.' Emily smiles. 'Come on you two, our holiday starts right now!'

And, taking them both by the hand, she steps into the cottage.

SATURDAY 19 MAY

EMILY

'Wow. This is amazing! Everything looks brand new, we might even be the first people *ever* to stay here!' Emily's excitement more than compensates for the difficulty they had getting in.

Immaculate furniture and the pleasing aroma of old-fashioned, citrus polish welcomes them. The flagstone floor is topped with a soft rug in a stunning combination of autumnal colours, adding to the overall cosiness. Mitch nods in agreement and explores the kitchenette, opening and shutting a random selection of drawers and cupboards.

Emily listens to him muttering compliments under his breath as she stands motionless in the centre of the lounge, awestruck. 'Honestly Mitch,' she continues 'this is *incredible*.'

Having feared their weekend was over before it had even begun, Emily sinks into an armchair, plumping up a large bolster cushion behind her back as Molly and Jack disappear, their feet noisy on the wooden stairs, to the mezzanine floor. Excited voices fill the air as they unpack their toys and Molly's favourite teddy bear, Peanut, takes up residence on the bed she has chosen. Letting the children enjoy the moment, Emily unlocks her phone to check her emails, wondering if Lady Allington sent other instructions she has forgotten about. She immediately spots an unopened message.

'Oh. My. God.' Emily claps her hand over her mouth. 'Mitch, come here, quickly. You won't believe this!'

'What now?' Mitch is still preoccupied, inspecting every inch of the kitchen.

'Lady Allington emailed me earlier, while I was driving. She's made a mistake with my booking. She says she is away at the moment and was checking the outstanding admin tasks for the estate when she realised that she had my reservation in the diary for *next* weekend.' Emily continues to read silently, shaking her head in disbelief, as she absorbs the impact of the words. 'Oh no… Mitch, listen to this, Lady Allington says, *"it wouldn't normally be a problem, but my housekeeper is also away, so there is no one available to make sure the cottage is ready for you. I am terribly sorry. It is completely my fault for misreading the dates of your reservation and I would like to offer you a free upgrade to the larger cottage – The Piggery – next door on another date. If you would like to accept this offer, please let me know and I will reschedule your booking as soon as possible."* Oh my god, Mitch. It's a disaster.'

'She can't be serious!' Mitch has reappeared and is, finally, listening to her.

'Bloody hell Mitch, what am I going to do? We've only just got here.' Emily glares at him, panic-stricken.

'Hey, steady on, it's nothing that can't be sorted.' Mitch gently rubs her shoulder, to calm her down. 'You can always stay with my Mum, I'm sure she won't mind,' then adds for extra persuasion '… plus she'd love to meet Molly and Jack.'

Emily isn't convinced. She stares at the message in front of her, as if it might change into something more positive if she looks at it long and hard enough. She hasn't yet met

Mitch's mother. To descend on her at short notice, with two children – who will be devastated when they find out they can't stay in The Cowshed *and* grouchy after their long journey – might not be the Saturday night his mother had planned for herself.

'Look, I can see what you're thinking. But it's going to be hard to find somewhere else this late in the day. Mum has a spare room she rarely uses and it would be great for her to have some company for a change.'

'I don't know Mitch; it doesn't seem fair on your mum.'

Mitch shrugs. 'Honestly, it's okay. I'll call her now.'

'As long as you're sure,' Emily appreciates his help and knows he is probably right. She doesn't have the energy right now to search for alternative accommodation. 'We'd better get out of here, though. I don't want either of us to get into trouble. Do you think it's okay for me to use the bathroom?' A rhetorical question, she must be quick, Molly and Jack are still upstairs and she needs to tell them what's happened.

Separate to the main bathroom the room is tiny and, like everything in the cottage, seems newly decorated with stylish Italian marble tiles and a Lilliputian corner handbasin. It's spotless, apart from a few dead insects on the windowsill, but then Lady Allington did explain her housekeeper is away for the weekend and couldn't prepare it for her guests like she normally would. Then Emily remembers, strictly speaking, they are not guests. They are trespassers.

A vanilla-scented reed diffuser and the most sumptuous hand towel she has ever seen complete the luxurious effect. Drying her hands, she momentarily puts the towel next to her cheek, just to relish the softness of it, and catches her reflection in the mirror. What a mess. The cream-coloured towel only accentuates her skin, flushed a deep pink, and her unkempt hair. Her blonde highlights are dull, damp and ridiculously frizzy after sitting in the rain at the side of the motorway.

*

'What did your mum say?' Emily asks, hoping for a positive response.

'Uh…'

'Bloody hell, Mitch, what's wrong?' Emily reels back in horror.

Mitch stumbles across the room, clutching his chest and gasping for air.

'Mitch, talk to me. What is it?' She reaches out as Mitch falls towards the settee and leans over, gripping it with both hands, to steady himself. 'Are you okay?' She rubs his back, desperately trying to work out what is going on.

Without a word, Mitch pulls himself up and puts one arm around Emily's shoulders, then forcibly pushes her towards the half open patio door. 'Don't look… just don't look,' he mumbles.

'What is it?' she starts to panic; her brain is automatically reacting to the situation and yet she doesn't understand what. She strains her neck, turning around to see what is going on. Then, knowing the children are in earshot she adds more quietly and calmly. 'Molly, Jack, I'm really sorry but can you come back down. Now. Please. Bring your bags and toys with you.'

'I said don't look Emily.' Mitch is agitated but clearly trying to keep his voice low because of the children. 'Just grab the kids and get in the car.'

'Don't tell me what to do! I said *what is it*, Mitch? What have you done?'

'Just get out. Honestly Emily, I mean it. I will tell you in a minute but, for now, just do as I say.'

Ignoring his advice, Emily twists around angrily and extracts her elbow from his grip. She looks back over her shoulder, which only makes him push her harder. The bathroom door is half open; all she can see is another fluffy towel hanging over the edge of a roll-top bath. The same colour as the one she has just used. It must be a matching set.

Baffled, she has no idea what he is making such a fuss about and yet, at the same time, senses something is seriously wrong and a hundred alternative scenarios spin in her head. Perhaps he's thrown up in the bathroom and made a mess in a cottage they're not meant to be in. Could that be it? He's still badly hungover and knows she will lose her deposit if anything gets damaged. That *must* be it.

However, as much as Emily tries to convince herself, she has a feeling deep in her gut that something much worse has triggered his pale face and urgent instructions. Mitch continues to push her towards the sliding door, his hand forceful in the small of her back, and Emily's heart beats so rapidly she can barely breathe. Molly and Jack are now at the bottom of the stairs, bewildered. She grabs them both by the hand and pulls them with her.

'Get in the car and don't worry.' Mitch speaks softly, Emily can tell it's fake; that he's trying not to scare the children. 'Honestly, I mean it. Leave this to me, I'll sort everything out, then I'll shut the door and be right behind you.'

Numb and confused, Emily does as she is told.

'What's going on, Mum?' asks Jack.

'Can we go back in, Mum?' Molly asks, clearly confused. 'Pleeeeease Mum? I bagsied the bed by the window!'

7

SATURDAY 19 MAY

LEXIE

'Just here will be great,' Lexie points at the T-junction next to a small grass triangle. 'And thank you so much, you've saved my day.'

'It's been a pleasure. Look after yourself Lexie, it's been lovely to hear all your news, say hello to your grandmother from me too.'

Lexie shuts the door firmly and breathes in the familiar air with a broad smile as she waves goodbye. She's thumbed a lift many times but is wary of doing so these days. It was fortunate that Miss Tucker, her former history teacher, came along at precisely the right moment.

Desperate to come home after the disappointment of the championships in Rome, Lexie decided she needed to talk to her grandmother. Her confidante. So, when she spotted the two-day rest period in her training schedule, she immediately decided to travel home. Technically, the athletes should request special permission to leave training camp, but Lexie isn't one for sticking to the rules, so she bought a return rail ticket on the spur of the moment and headed straight off. Bumping into her former teacher has just added to her excitement; the likelihood of getting a suitable lift on the main road from the station had been next to zero but, for once, serendipity was on her side. She can't remember the last time she saw Miss Tucker, but guesses it must be ten years ago.

Anna, her coach, will no doubt be disappointed – and furious – when she finds out, but Anna is one of the things Lexie wants to talk about. Plus, she just wants to be with her grandma, the person she loves most in the world. To eat her favourite home-cooked food, rather than the meticulously planned menus prepared by the stern dieticians and, most importantly, to sleep. Sleep. Who would have thought she would be excited about getting some decent sleep at the grand old age of twenty-five? It will be a treat not to have the alarm going off at some ridiculous hour of the day.

She hasn't yet told her grandmother she's coming to stay, although Lexie knows she won't mind, quite the opposite. Her grandmother loves a bit of company and will be thrilled at the surprise of it all.

8

SATURDAY 19 MAY

EMILY

After what seems like an eternity, yet is probably only seconds, Mitch joins Emily in the car. 'Drive back the way you came,' he mutters, almost inaudibly.

She nervously presses the accelerator, still shaking, and the car jerks forward.

'Mum, what is it? Where are we going?' Molly's voice wobbles. 'Has something bad happened?'

'Not now love, we need to sort something out,' Emily replies, trying not to let the children know she is frightened, or let Molly's disappointment make her feel even worse.

Mitch points at a layby appearing on their left. 'Pull in here,' he clears his throat and whispers. 'We need a quick chat.'

Emily bites her lip. The whole world around her is blurred; moving in slow motion. The wonderful birdsong, so lyrical when they arrived, is now muffled and distorted. She brings the car to a halt and gently releases her seatbelt. Climbing out, she moves away from the car to lean against an old, stained rubbish bin. The stale stench of trash hits the back of her throat with a punch but her legs are weak and there is nothing else around to offer any viable means of support.

'Okay, I'm not exactly sure how to say this, so I'm just going to blurt it out whichever way it comes,' Mitch stutters, still a sickly shade of green.

'Bloody hell, Mitch. Whatever it is, you have completely freaked me out. Completely. Freaked. Me. Out,' Emily hisses back, desperate for him to explain what happened.

'Honestly, you won't believe it... you really won't...'

'Just tell me. Stop messing me around.'

'There... there... there was a body in the bath.' Mitch retches as he says it, making the veins in his neck bulge.

'WHAT?!' Emily waits for him to elaborate then sneers angrily in his face when he doesn't reply. 'If this is some sort of sick joke it has gone too far. Way, way, way too far.'

'Listen to me. Why would I make it up?' He turns away and then back again, looking Emily straight in the eye as he wipes spittle from the corner of his mouth.

'Seriously Mitch, that's ludicrous! Totally and utterly bonkers!' Emily is fuming and Molly and Jack are watching, their little faces open-mouthed and fearful.

Mitch, says nothing; he stares at the ground, silent.

'We need to call the police.' Emily says matter-of-factly. 'RIGHT NOW. Where's your phone?'

'I don't see how we can.' Mitch shakes his head, still not looking up.

'Why not? Surely, if you call the police and explain to them what you saw, they will deal with it?'

'Are you insane? Just stop for a second Emily and *think* about it.'

'What do you mean *think* about it? Of course, we do. That's what normal, rational people do.' Emily sighs loudly, as Mitch ignores her. 'Well, if you won't, I will.' Emily puts her hand out. 'Give me your phone.'

Mitch moves closer but rather than offer his phone he gently holds both her shoulders, hangs his head and closes his eyes, as if praying for inspiration. Then he rests his forehead against hers.

After what seems an eternity Mitch starts to speak. 'I'm sorry Emily, I really am, but let's just think it through before we rush into anything we regret.'

Emily can feel his heart beating, the rapid rhythm coursing through his body.

'What do you mean, why would we regret it?'

'We let ourselves into a property where we weren't meant to be. Well, you did maybe, not me. It was booked in your name.'

'WHAT?!' Emily screeches as loud as she can without scaring the children any more than they already are, and pulls her head away, prodding him roughly in the chest. 'So, what you mean is, you're basically saying it's *my* problem and *I've* got to deal with it?!'

'No. Hear me out. All I'm saying is that we shouldn't have been there.' He holds her more tightly to stop her waving her arms about. 'How can we go to the police if we were trespassing ourselves?'

'You can't be serious!'

'Just listen to what I'm saying Emily, for Christ's sake. They might think we have something to do with it and then we'll be in even deeper trouble. Plus, I've got two really big contracts coming up and custody of my son to think about. It would ruin everything. I can't risk it.'

'Shit. Shit. Shit,' Emily repeats under her breath.

'Stop saying that, it really isn't helping.'

'Oh, so what is? Us, stood in a layby arguing, with nowhere to stay, two tired and hungry children and what you think is a dead body. Oh, and come to think of it, the two of us likely to get a criminal record for breaking and entering?' Emily snarls angrily.

'Don't be angry with *me* Emily, I'm just trying to help,' Mitch pleads.

'Well, try a bit harder. Why did I ever agree to this weekend, staying in the middle of bloody nowhere?' she replies, unable to stop herself flying off the handle.

Mitch holds her tight again.

'I'm sorry Emily,' he says gently, trying to calm her down. 'I really am. But... I... I think I know what we need to do.'

'So do I – it's simple. You call the police.'

'No. Honestly, Emily, that isn't going to work. No. Trust me. I think we just have to forget we ever went there.'

'What do you mean? How exactly is *that* going to help?'

'We weren't there Emily. We never went. The place is exactly as we found it. No one will ever know.' Slowly, he continues. 'You never went because you read the email earlier in the day and knew not to. Lady Allington said she is away – and her housekeeper is away too – so you didn't go. Like I said, no one will ever know.'

He pauses to let her digest what he has said. Emily is not convinced.

'Do you see what I mean?' he coaxes. 'We simply pretend nothing happened and let someone else discover the... the... bod...' Mitch can't say it out loud. Coughing, he continues. 'We just let someone else find it in their normal course of business, whoever that might be. It might be the housekeeper or, maybe, even Lady Allington herself. Then they deal with it in the appropriate way and contact the relevant emergency services.'

'Is that really going to work?' Emily silently mulls over the implications.

'I don't know what other option there is.'

'Call an ambulance?' Emily suggests.

'But that'll only involve the police as well once they arrive, if the person is already dead.'

*

Emily stands motionless. She runs over his proposition in her mind, still acutely aware that Molly and Jack are watching their every move. It seems to make sense. If they hadn't been there – which they *shouldn't* have been – then none of this would have happened. And, if they hadn't been there, they wouldn't actually know whatever it was, whoever it was, was even there. Which means they aren't hurting anybody by pretending they didn't go, as it would have been what would have happened anyway. *There's logic in there somewhere*, she tells herself convincingly.

But then she backtracks. What is she thinking? If Mitch really did see a dead body, then of course he *must* tell the police.

'I can see what you mean. Nobody else will ever know. But...' she carefully considers what he has suggested, talking it through out loud helps her think more clearly. 'It's wrong, Mitch. Whether you have new contracts and a custody review coming up or not. There's no other word for it. It's wrong – morally wrong – not to do something.'

'But what do we say?'

'You tell them exactly what it is you think you saw.'

'What about Mum, we can't keep her waiting any longer, she'll be wondering where we are.'

'Did you tell her where we were when you called her?'

'No. I just said you'd been let down. I mentioned to her a while back that you were staying at Allington House, but she didn't know that's where we were when I called. She thought I was meeting you in town.'

'Well, why don't we go to your mum's house and you call the police from there? It'll make it easier for you, give you time to calm down after the shock.'

'Hmmm.' Mitch is still not convinced.

'Honestly Mitch, you've got to. Please… *please* Mitch,' she begs, taking his hand. 'There's no point in *me* phoning as I didn't see anything. All I can tell them is that *you* said *you* saw something and they will ask to speak to you anyway. Please Mitch. PLEASE.'

Mitch rubs his eyes as he pulls away from her. 'Okay. I'll give them a ring when we get to Mum's house.'

'Promise?'

'Promise.'

9

SATURDAY 19 MAY

EMILY

Mitch's mum, Yvonne, is a treasure. Not only does she have a huge pot of tea waiting for them, there is a plate piled high with warm, freshly baked chocolate brownies. As she welcomes them, Mitch provides a brief but plausible explanation why Emily couldn't stay in the cottage as planned and without the need to mention they had actually been *inside* The Cowshed uninvited. Fortunately, Yvonne is less concerned with the details and more intent on pouring out the tea.

'There's been a lot of development down on the Allington Estate, no wonder it's not quite ready.' Yvonne nods her head as if in agreement with herself. 'Nice lady though, very kind. My mam used to work at the big house when we were kids, a bit of cleaning and the like. Of course, it was her mother who was the lady then, really down to earth she was, then the current Lady Allington inherited it all. Lovely family, my mam said. Such a shame about her husband.'

'Oh, that must have been interesting for your mother.' Emily leans in to listen, after the trauma of her car breaking down and their hasty exit from the cottage, she is thankful to sit on a comfy sofa with a cup of tea and some friendly chat, and Yvonne clearly has lots of stories she wants to share.

'Well now, where do I start? She's the lady you know, it's her family's estate. Her husband was a lot older and married into it, that's why he was never officially a lord or anything – although he acted like one!' She laughs at her own joke. 'Always lording it about from what my mam said. Rumour was they couldn't have kids then, after years of trying, lo and behold, Lady A found she was pregnant.'

'Oh?' Emily is fascinated, Yvonne is a natural storyteller.

'Yes, anyway, she – the current Lady A – is a wee bit older than me, but her Penelope was born the same year as Rodney. Sweet little kid, but they packed her off to some posh boarding school so she never really mixed with the locals. Maybe a bit in the summer holidays, at the tennis club, but that was it.' Yvonne takes a breath. Emily senses the main bit of the story is yet to come. 'Well, they only had the one child and then her husband went and died, when they were away skiing. Had a stroke up on the mountain and they couldn't get him back down in time. Awful it was.'

'Goodness,' Emily is surprised. 'Poor Lady Allington, what a life, I had no idea.'

'But that's not all.' Yvonne clearly isn't ready to stop. 'Her daughter was the complete opposite. I mean, it caused quite a stir at the time, when Penelope went and got herself pregnant when she was still a teenager. After they had spent a fortune on her private education and all that. Well, she had a baby girl – Alexandria, I think she called her – then Lady A looked after her granddaughter for a few years so she could go to university and then, when she – Penelope that is – got married, her husband took her daughter in as his own.'

'Wow, that's amazing, what a family. It's like something out of a TV drama.' Emily is enthralled.

'Sounds like you two are having a good old gossip,' Mitch

laughs as he comes back in the room. He excused himself from the conversation a few minutes earlier to make a call, Emily assumes *the* call, in the kitchen. 'I know we've only just arrived, but what do you want to do tonight, Emily?'

Yvonne grabs her by the arm. 'Now, my love, after the day you've had with your car and everything else, if you want to join Rodney this evening I'll happily look after these two little ones for you, I've brought up three of my own and five grandchildren so I know what I'm doing.' Yvonne's shoulders tremble as she laughs and Emily feels like she has known her forever.

'I can't get used to you calling Mitch by his proper name, Rodney,' Emily says, smiling. The earlier events seem unreal as the normality of Yvonne's front room with a myriad of family photos and memorabilia make her feel more grounded. 'I'm not sure he even looks like a Rodney.'

'Call him what you like, but he'll always be Rodney to me, my dear. Rodney John Mitchell. Same as his father and his father before that.' Yvonne winks.

'Well, if you really are sure.' Emily thinks out loud, the offer is extremely tempting. 'Mitch, what do you think… did you manage to get hold of the other people you talked about earlier? You know, the people you said you were going to call, are they coming tonight too?' she adds, cryptically, willing him to understand the subtext, as she looks at him with knowing eyes. She doesn't want Yvonne to think anything strange is going on, or Molly and Jack given they are now settled again.

'Oh, yes… yes, I did.' Mitch raises his eyebrows as the penny drops and he considers carefully what to say and how to say it. 'They're caught up with something in Plymouth at the moment, probably for another hour or two, but they know where it is and said they will definitely come along as soon as they can.'

'Oh, that's great, Mitch. I'm so glad you got hold of them.' Emily's cup rattles loudly on the saucer and she puts it back on the tray so her nerves don't get the better of her. 'How about you go along and I'll drop by later? It'll be great to meet your friends, but I'll give your mum a hand first.'

'Sounds good. It's The Moody Ram on the edge of town, we passed it earlier, give me a ring when you're on your way and I'll keep an eye out for you.'

*

After a quick shower, change of outfit and a squirt of perfume, Emily is refreshed and ready to go and Molly and Jack are settled in their pyjamas with Yvonne reading them bedtime stories. She'll give Mitch a ring to let him know she's on her way.

Retrieving her handbag from under her jacket, where she hung them both on a coat hook in the hall, Emily rummages around inside. That's strange. Her keys are lying right at the top, next to her purse, yet she always leaves them in the zipped inner pocket with her mobile phone, so they can't fall out without her knowing. Perhaps she just threw them in loose when they got to Yvonne's house. It's been such a chaotic day nothing would surprise her anymore. She opens her bag as wide as it will go, to peer inside more closely.

It's infuriating. Her phone must be hiding at the bottom. She feels around with her hand. Lots of tissues, a pen and a screwed-up wrapper from the chocolate biscuit she ate while waiting for Molly to finish her dance class last week.

She tries to recall when she last had it. Certainly not in the car, or when she and Mitch stopped in the layby. Her heart sinks. The last time she definitely remembers using it was to check the email from Lady Allington. The email she read out to Mitch while she was sat down, on the armchair, just before she went to the bathroom.

At The Cowshed.

They rushed off in such a stupid hurry she must have left it behind.

Emily is frantic; feeling faint, she leans with one hand on the wall to steady herself. When they were chatting with Yvonne, she had managed to relax, confident Mitch had called the police and everything would be resolved. With a sense of dread, she checks her bag one more time despite knowing there is only one possible option. She will *have* to go back to The Cowshed to retrieve her phone. On her own. What's more, she had better be quick, otherwise the police will get there first. An hour or two. That's what Mitch said. And the clock is already ticking.

Yvonne is reading to the children and her gentle voice permeates softly from the other side of the living room door as the urgency – and gravity – of the situation hits home. Emily grabs her bag, her hands clammy on the leather strap.

'I won't be long.' She smiles, desperate to appear calm, and gives both Molly and Jack a kiss. 'Make sure you do as you're told and don't play Yvonne up, I will be checking later!'

Yvonne smiles, looking at Emily over the top of her glasses. 'Have a lovely time dear, and don't worry about these two, we've got plenty more stories and some hot chocolate to get through yet and I've jotted your mobile number down on a bit of paper, just in case I need it.'

10

SATURDAY 19 MAY

LEXIE

Lexie strolls happily along the footpath without a care in the world. The mud has been churned up by the earlier rain, but she doesn't mind. It will be quicker and more scenic than the alternative, which is at least a mile along the lane and up the winding drive. Tying her long blonde hair into a ponytail to stop the wind blowing it in her face, she crosses the meadow and the brooding outline of the moor beckons her faster.

Climbing over the stile, she pauses for a moment to enjoy the wonderful view and then follows the hedge adjacent to the holiday cottages. The summer party music playing in her headphones matches her carefree mood and she notices a parked car and the outline of two people in the lounge at The Cowshed. They must be guests, making the most of their weekend break the same as she is, their dark silhouettes like ghostly shadows of times gone by. Lexie briefly imagines that's what they are. Ghosts. The buildings had always felt haunted when she played there as a child; these days they are barely recognisable as the crumbling, derelict ruins she once knew.

*

'Hey Grammie, surprise, it's me!' Lexie shouts into the handset, her excitement palpable. She's called her by that name since she was a toddler and knows it still makes her grandmother smile every time. It's been a long day but, as Lexie turns the final corner and the mansion comes into view, her tiredness evaporates and she breaks into a run.

'Lexie darling, this *is* a surprise. How lovely to hear from you, I thought you were still in Rome?'

'We flew back on Wednesday and our coach has given everyone a two-day rest from training so I'm looking forward to a relaxing weekend. How are you? Are you at home tonight?' Lexie decides to keep her grandmother in suspense just a little bit longer, she wants to see the surprise on her face when she opens the door.

'Oh, didn't I tell you love? I'm in Kent. Cousin Edwina's funeral is on Monday and it's such a long way I didn't want to travel at the last minute.'

Lexie stops in her tracks. Her eyes sting with tears and a sensation of emptiness fills her stomach. She had completely forgotten. Flight delays after the physically, and emotionally, exhausting competition in Rome have taken over her thoughts the last few days.

'You still there, love?' Lady Allington says kindly.

'Yes… yes… still here.' Lexie replies quietly. She's devastated. She can't possibly tell her grandmother what her plans were for the weekend now. If she does, Lady Allington will only fret about her being in the house on her own. She'll have to think of a plan B. Quickly.

*

Having managed to complete the conversation without making it obvious where she was, or that she was overcome with

42

disappointment, Lexie sits on an old wooden bench while she gathers her thoughts. Covered in lichen, and decidedly rickety, it's been in the same position next to the back entrance for years. A perfect resting place for removing muddy boots after walking the dogs or digging the garden. Lexie feels foolish. It's early evening and she needs to make a decision about what to do. It hadn't occurred to her for a moment that her grandmother may not be at home.

Looking around, she sees the old, weather-worn window of the pantry with its damaged pane. The one she accidentally broke after throwing a ball against it when she was nine years old. It was one of the few times her grandmother raised her voice to reprimand her, but it must have worked as she never did it again.

Lexie has a thought. Knowing her grandmother rarely sets the alarm, if she carefully removes the triangle of glass below the crack, she could, with an enormous stretch, reach in and unhook the old-fashioned latch and let herself in.

She stands up and peers into the darkened room. The glass is covered in years of dust and despite the dense, opaque cobwebs, she can see the deep shelves, still with their original tiles, overflowing with an assortment of packets and tins.

*

The glass is surprisingly easy to dislodge. Using an old trowel she found in the rhubarb bed, Lexie knocks it firmly until it relents. Then she leans in, stretching as far as she can. With a sharp tug, the latch releases, but she loses her balance and catches her forearm on the jagged edge of the broken window. Swearing under her breath, she retracts her arm as blood runs down to her wrist. On closer inspection, the wound appears superficial and Lexie pulls a paper tissue from her pocket and wraps it tightly around the cut, holding it in place with the cuff of her sweatshirt. It's the best she can do for now. She can clean it up properly once she is inside.

Climbing in through the small window is tricky, and she decides feet first is the answer. Lexie hauls herself up into a sitting position on the window ledge then gently pulls her knees to her chin, before swinging her legs into the dark void of the pantry, trying to find something solid on which to land the other side. She can feel a chair with her foot and, holding on tightly to the sill behind her, uses all her strength to get sufficient traction to pull it closer. Finally, with her toes between the vertical spindles, the wooden legs scrape noisily on the stone floor as she nudges it into position.

Her feet safely on the ground, she retrieves her bag from the window sill and sits on the chair to get her breath back. She might be an Olympic athlete, but that took some doing. After a few minutes, she can't resist taking a closer look at the shelves. Even in the shadows it is obvious some of the tins have been in the pantry for decades. It might not be the home cooking she was looking forward to, but at least she will be able to eat.

Contemplating what to do, she finds a packet of biscuits to enjoy in the drawing room at the front of the house while she mulls things over. It'll be more comfortable and has a lovely view across the moor, especially now the clouds are clearing. She fleetingly considers calling her grandmother again to let her know what she has done, but decides not to. No, her decision is made. If she stays for one night, she can return to training camp tomorrow and tell her grandmother after the funeral. She'll just have to work out how to get back to the station in the morning.

Grabbing the biscuits, Lexie pauses for a moment to admire the grand entrance hall where the magnificent oil paintings never fail to impress her, despite their familiarity.

However, with a mouth full of chocolate digestive and the beady eyes of her ancestors gazing down upon her, the thrill of being home disappears in an instant as the intruder alarm springs into action, screeching at full volume.

11

SATURDAY 19 MAY

EMILY

Emily's knuckles are white where she grips the steering wheel. Troubled about what happened at The Cowshed, she wasn't concentrating when Mitch provided directions to his mother's house and she can't remember the way. The light will be fading soon and everywhere looks completely different as twilight beckons. Plus, she mustn't draw attention to herself by driving inconsistently, or looking lost.

Recognising a junction, she turns down what she thinks is the valley road she took earlier, but soon realises her mistake. This is *not* good. She tries to find a gateway in which to safely turn around, but they are few and far between. She's scared. Extremely scared. She is miles from anywhere and totally lost, billowing cow parsley, heavy with rain, slaps against the side of her car and the high hedges are overpowering; they're like dark, menacing dragons, threatening to gobble her up and swallow her whole.

After three more false turns Emily is completely disorientated and beads of perspiration roll down the back of her neck. She continues to follow the winding lane, desperately hoping nothing will come the other way, and that she will stumble across a turning she remembers.

Eventually, she recognises the small hump-backed bridge with the sign warning motorists the road is liable to flooding and turns into the sweeping drive. Relieved, she momentarily stops to catch her breath and reset her headlights so they don't alert the residents of Meadow View, but then her heart pounds even faster when she notices a van, a ladder tied to the roof, parked by the main house. A cloud of fumes billow from the exhaust pipe as if someone has just started the engine.

With the radio on mute, she edges forward and the scraping sound of the tyres on the gravel is amplified. Keeping one eye on where she is going and the other on the van, she sees it follow an arc around the fountain, directly in front of the main entrance, and make its way back down the drive. Emily swears under her breath as it heads towards her, and she turns along the track towards the holiday cottages just in time. Relieved to be out of sight, she manoeuvres her car so it is facing in the right direction, fearful she might need to leave in a hurry. The gravel is less crunchy here, compacted by the numerous vehicles that have no doubt come and gone, but still every sound seems to echo back and forth across the valley.

She shuts the car door as gently as she can and stands still for a moment, trying to hold her nerve. Strangely, despite the noisy road surface testing her resilience, the silence that now surrounds her is even more deafening. Then a pair of blackbirds call to each other, their raucous squawk startling her as they settle down for the night, always the last ones to roost.

Pulling up the hood on her long, woolly cardigan, Emily shivers. It's her favourite for keeping warm on cooler evenings, but doesn't seem to be working tonight. The atmosphere is damp from the earlier rain and the smell of smoke, she assumes from a distant bonfire, hangs in the air as she creeps along the path, around to the back of the cottage, and tentatively looks through the glass of the patio door. In the dimness she can just make out her phone, wedged down the side of the armchair. The protective cover is the same colour as the cushion and well camouflaged. That's one good thing, at least she has found it. Emily pulls the handle of the sliding door, she'll nip inside quickly, grab her phone and be on her way.

The door doesn't move.

She tries again.

Nothing.

With both hands she pulls again, and again, then shakes it as hard as she can. It doesn't budge.

Emily slumps down in a heap, her hooded head in her hands and her back leaning against the cold, glass door. The police will be here any minute. So much for embracing her independence, getting out and being more adventurous again.

Emily is desperate. She dreams of being at home, snuggled up on the settee with Molly and Jack, watching a film and eating popcorn. What was she thinking, coming away for the weekend?

Frightened and alone, she stares into the nothingness. The late afternoon sun, having chased away the earlier rain, has now fallen from the oppressive, monochrome sky and the evening chillness of the glass is like a sheet of ice on her back. The blackbirds squawk loudly once more and something twists painfully in her gut.

Something is wrong. Very wrong indeed.

12

SATURDAY 19 MAY

EMILY

Emily shivers, her fingers numb where she has both hands jammed under each arm. How long has she been slumped against the patio door in this catatonic-like state?

What a complete mess of a day. She is desperate to run away, but can't. Her phone is taunting her from the other side of the glass. Less than two metres away and yet unreachable.

Then she has a brainwave. She still has the code for the key safe written on her hand. Drained and exhausted, she is simultaneously consumed with hope that the key will now be there, and yet semi-paralysed with fear that it won't. She studies the faded, four-digit number and silently, chronologically, works through her logic.

Firstly – if the patio door is now locked – then *someone else* must have locked it, because she and Mitch certainly didn't. The thought process makes her head hurt. She rubs her forehead and takes a moment for the idea to sink in. If someone else has locked the door, they *must* have had a key. So, maybe, just maybe, that someone has put the key back in the box where it should be. Emily looks up at the nebulous, broody sky, praying this might be a tiny bit of good fortune in an otherwise completely crappy day. So much for the double rainbow she saw earlier.

Slowly she pulls herself up, aware someone may see her, and tip-toes to the box. Her trembling hands make co-ordination almost impossible but she eventually rotates the combination lock to line up the correct numbers. The door springs open and she nearly screams with joy as a small brass key on a red leather fob falls out. There is a tiny, plastic cow hanging on a chain from the key ring, to remind visitors which cottage they are renting. Normally Emily would laugh out loud, but she barely notices.

Entering through the front door, the layout is unfamiliar as she approaches from a different direction. Fumbling through the darkness, she almost knocks over a large urn containing two wooden-handled umbrellas. It is so large it fills the small entrance vestibule, next to a row of coat hooks and a shoe rack for muddy boots. Before her, a solid oak door leads into the lounge and she slowly opens it. Immediately, she sees the armchair on the far side of the room and she moves furtively, like a shadow, until she is close enough to pull her phone from behind the cushion. The instant she does, it shines brightly with numerous missed calls and text messages.

Talk about drawing unnecessary attention to herself. She hides behind the nearest door, her heart racing. There are at least three missed calls from her mum. Emily gulps. Her mum will be worried sick by now, wondering whether they have arrived safely.

Then she becomes aware of something else, with a gut-wrenching realisation. She is in the bathroom where the stunning roll-top bath sits majestically in the centre of the room. Bile rises uncontrollably at the back of her throat and Emily does a double take. *The* roll-top bath. The amazing roll-top bath that had been a selling feature in the marketing brochure with its beautiful, ornate taps standing proudly over the side and a sparkling cascade of water as it fills. The bath she had *so* looked forward to, indulging in a deep, luxurious, scented soak after putting the children to bed.

The bath with the body in it.

Except, the bath is empty. No towel. No dead body. *Nothing*.

That's it. Emily cannot stay in The Cowshed a moment longer.

Holding her phone tightly shut, so it can't light up again and trying not to panic, she inches slowly back the way she came, steadying herself as a folded over corner of the rug catches on her heel and almost trips her up. As she nears her escape, she has a thought. Her fingerprints will be all over the place. She darts back to where she spotted a box of expensive looking floral tissues, pulls out a handful and quickly wipes down all the door handles.

Bloody hell, what else have I touched? She can't think straight. *Patio doors. Key box. Front door. Armchair.*

She works her way around the cottage. Her inner counsel guides her; keeping her calm as she silently works through a list of all the items she needs to clean, to eliminate any trace of her having been in the building. Emily methodically checks each room, running her eyes, now accustomed to the darkness, over all the furniture; the floors, the handles. She spots a button on the rug in the lounge, half hidden between the woven wool, and picks it up. It's definitely not one of hers, but it could be from Mitch's jacket. She puts it in her pocket, just in case.

Her heart beating like a drum, she cautiously makes her way back across the room and exits through the front door, locking it behind her with a reassuring click. Replacing the key in the box, Emily exhales deeply. It feels like she has been holding her breath for the last half hour and a rush of blood surges to her head, making her dizzy.

Using her hood to obscure her face, she looks from side to side and heads towards her car. An upstairs light has been switched on in the end cottage and the flickering light of a television illuminates a downstairs window at number three. Then she hears it. A rustle. A crunch. Footsteps on old, dry leaves. She darts around to the back of the cottage and hides behind a tree. The old oak she admired earlier, with its beautiful, gnarled trunk so wide she wouldn't be able to get her arms around it however hard she tried. A wooden swing squeaks softly in the breeze where the ropes dig into the bark.

There's a splash. Something has fallen in the pond. Emily shuts her eyes and listens carefully, blood pumping in her ears. After a couple of minutes, she decides whoever it was, whatever it was, must have gone. Perhaps it was a squirrel scavenging for something to eat.

She decides to count to fifty and – if she hears nothing more in that time – she will make a move towards her car. But, before she can even start, an owl, sitting high up in the oak tree, hoots noisily. The wise old bird has been watching her every move and is advising her to leave. Immediately. Without hesitation, Emily runs on tip-toe, grabs the handle of her car door and jumps in.

Starting the engine, she sits motionless for a few seconds to make sure she hasn't been seen or heard; the moonlight is barely sufficient but she won't switch the headlights on until she is far enough away not to arouse suspicion. The gravel starts to crunch beneath the wheels and she is startled as a pair of eyes shine in the dark, before she recognises the black and white cat from earlier. It scoots under the bonnet, disappearing for the second time today, and then leaps on to the stone wall, thankfully unscathed.

She tentatively presses the accelerator and the speedometer dial starts to move. Ten miles per hour… twelve… fourteen. That will do for now. Moments later, and relieved to be back on the sweeping drive, Emily double-checks her phone is on the central console, where she put it, just to be sure.

It is only a fleeting glance but, as she does, something in the distance catches her eye. Blue flashing lights. Her body reacts, shaking with terror before her brain has time to compute what it means.

Barely aware of her actions, she pulls sharply into a gateway, behind a trailer loaded high with hay bales, praying she won't be seen, and sinks into the driver's seat, as low as she can whilst still able to watch what unfolds. The approaching vehicle is obscured by the high hedges but the lights illuminate the sky, like a spectacular laser show. The blue fluorescence blinding through her windscreen.

She mustn't move. Resting her forehead on her steering wheel as the vehicle roars through the entrance gates, she stares open-mouthed as a police car screams past, the passenger gripping the bar above their door to hold themselves upright. *Of course. Mitch said an hour or two, that would be about right.*

Frozen to her seat, Emily watches in the wing mirror, expecting it to turn towards the holiday cottages. But it doesn't. It continues at a hair-raising speed, gravel flying everywhere, up to the main house, then screeches to a halt as both officers jump out and run around to the back of the building.

Panicking, Emily restarts her car. She wrenches the gear stick and the wheels spin as she accelerates from behind the trailer. The police car is now stationary, parked in front of the main house, and fear, mixed with relief, makes her feel light-headed. As the engine growls comfortingly, she exits the wide gates and opens the window to let in some fresh air. Emily's nostrils are immediately filled with the sweet smell of the moonlit meadows and freshly cut hay, and her ears with the sound of the breeze in the high beech trees. Normally she would savour both but, tonight, her senses are numb.

The name might not do it justice but, at this very moment, The Moody Ram sounds like the most welcoming place in the world.

13

SATURDAY 19 MAY

TANYA

Tanya watches in disbelief from behind the gate as the mahonia bush catches on her wide hood, pulling it down and obscuring her vision. She flicks her head to straighten it, then regrets doing so as water drips down her neck.

She shuts her eyes, fearful the stranger will have heard the rustle of the rough, spiky leaves. As the uninvited visitor moves out of view, Tanya unhooks the rusty latch and the wooden gate, always stiff to open, creaks.

She stands bolt upright. For an awful, fleeting moment she thought they would turn around and see her, but the blackbirds, equally disturbed, do her a favour and disguise the noise with their raucous squawks.

Settling into a more covert position, Tanya is not sure what to do. There definitely isn't a booking at The Cowshed this weekend and Lady Allington is at a family funeral in Kent, so it can't be her popping down to check everything is okay, like she sometimes does. Tanya feels guilty for misleading her. It was only a white lie; she didn't want any extra work while Lady Allington was away, so she told her she had a trip planned too.

Walking in the Cotswolds with friends from the village where she used to live. Not a complete untruth as she does plan to visit them, just not this weekend.

Tanya watches silently from the shadows as the clandestine visitor pokes around. Intrigued, she strains her neck to watch them creep along the path to the back of The Cowshed and hears them tugging at the patio door. Then it all goes quiet. Extremely quiet.

Tanya waits. They must be loitering in the back garden, unless they have jumped over the hedge and into the adjoining field, but that would be impossible with all the brambles.

Leaning against the gate, to take the weight off her legs, Tanya hears a tiny crackle-like noise and detects a flicker of movement in the side window. They're coming back, sidling along the path with their back against the wall.

Tanya holds her breath. There's definitely something not quite right and, as they look at their hand and head for the key box, Tanya is equally fascinated and fearful; their behaviour is extremely odd, yet she doesn't want to confront them and put herself in a potentially dangerous situation. Nor does she want to call the police. It would be a disaster to have them snooping around with Lady Allington away, and she has got far too many other things to worry about at the moment.

Convincing herself that taking no action is the best course of action, she watches aghast as they let themselves in the building. She may recognise them when they switch the lights on. Perhaps it's Norman the builder, he is still working at the cottages and has keys to all the buildings. He laughed when Lady Allington gave him a snagging list as long as her arm but, surely, he can't be working on "War and Peace" as he called it at this time of day, or at the weekend?

Thank goodness The Cowshed is clean and tidy, Tanya thinks to herself. Now she is familiar with the layout in both cottages it takes her half the time it did. She knows which socket to plug the hoover in to reach all the rooms in one go and, if she does them in a methodical order, the floor tiles in the kitchen are just about dry as she finishes off the bathroom. And the bathroom, well that is a joy to clean with the beautiful tiles. She thought Lady Allington had completely lost her mind choosing such an expensive décor but she can see why she did now.

Tanya can't move from where she is to get a better look without being visible and decides to stay behind the slightly ajar gate to observe what happens next. Her mind begins to wander as, despite the intruder being inside the cottage for what seems like ages, it's still in darkness and impossible to see what they are doing, or even which room they are in.

While she waits, she thinks about her stand at the craft gallery and how best to move all her artwork there in time for the opening without damaging anything. She will need to have a plan in place soon. The last few weeks have been chaotic, too many other time-consuming priorities, yet she is delighted, and extremely excited, about having her own exhibition.

*

Tanya is brought back to the present with a jump as the visitor reappears at the front door. She doesn't know for certain how long they were inside snooping around, but she watches incredulously as they doublecheck they have locked the front door and then silently return the key to the box on the wall, then doublecheck they have locked the key box too. Whoever it is, they are meticulous. Or paranoid.

Tanya gently pushes the gate until it is almost shut. At the same moment, the visitor darts into the shadows of the back garden. Whatever disturbed them, it must have been on the other side of The Cowshed as Tanya heard nothing. She patiently awaits their return, then sees them tip-toe to their car as Cleo runs out from next door's garden. Just in time, she manages to stop herself calling out to her cat. She is not sure who is more worried about being seen or heard, but she isn't going to take any chances.

An owl hoots and makes her jump, but the sound is dulled by the whirr of the engine and the car inches forward, without lights. Common sense tells Tanya to check The Cowshed; if they have damaged anything she will need to let Lady Allington know.

She waits until the car has disappeared around the corner and along the main drive, then dashes across the track to retrieve the key. It is still warm. But, at the very same moment she steps foot inside the cottage, she hears the roar of an engine. It's revving hard and getting closer. They must be coming back. Panicking, she slams the door and clumsily throws the key in the safe, then darts behind her gate.

The mahonia bush is, yet again, determined to add to her agitated state of mind and drops water down her neck for the second time, but Tanya holds her nerve and moves defiantly to shut the gate. As she does, a police car, blue lights flashing, screeches past the turning to the cottages and up the drive towards the main house.

14
SATURDAY 19 MAY

EMILY

The Moody Ram is an eclectic mix of old and new. A beautifully handcrafted, thatched roof sits proudly above whitewashed walls and cottage windows juxtaposed with an ultra-modern outdoor seating area, boasting a huge barbecue, pizza oven and patio heaters.

The interior looks cosy and inviting, but Emily's whole body is still trembling. She can't think straight, let alone spell, and struggles to co-ordinate her fingers with her phone to send a text message.

Outside – on my way in :)

She waits briefly for a reply while watching a group of people through the window; they laugh and joke as one of them carries a tray, laden precariously with drinks. It looks noisy. Mitch will probably be deep in conversation so she decides, still shaking, to just go in.

Then she remembers, it's the final of the European Cup – Chelsea versus Bayern Munich – and the kick-off was at quarter to eight. They'll all be glued to the screen.

She's correct. The whole pub is engrossed in the match and she's shocked to see it's already gone nine o'clock. She must have been at The Cowshed for much longer than she thought.

'Hi stranger. What took you so long?' Mitch shouts above the din as he waves her over, then looks concerned. 'Bloody hell Emily, you look like you've seen a ghost – are you alright?'

'Oh, I'm fine, thanks... hello everyone... I didn't realise the time,' Emily flusters, waving her hand and trying to be friendly, her cheeks burning with embarrassment. She can barely hear anything above the chanting and no one seems remotely bothered by her arrival. She is not sure if it makes her feel better or worse. 'I didn't want to abandon your mum so soon after we arrived, so I helped her for a bit with Molly and Jack...' she continues, raising her voice for Mitch to hear, whilst battling against the noise.

Shouting only exhausts her further and her explanation fizzles out, as the entire building erupts. People are jumping around. They're cheering, high fiving and glass clinking, as Drogba equalises for Chelsea late in the second half.

'No worries, you're here now, what can I get you?' Mitch shouts back through the din, squeezing her shoulder to reassure her and completely unconcerned about her tardiness. 'You look like you could do with a drink and I'm on orange juice after yesterday's overindulgence, so I'll drive us back to Mum's.'

Emily smiles and nods to confirm acceptance of his offer. It's easier than shouting. How lucky Mitch is, to be able to forget about the traumatic events of the afternoon so easily.

Mitch eventually reappears from the scrum of bodies, still consumed with glee about the equalising goal, and his friends shuffle up the reclaimed church pew to let Emily squeeze in. The noise, though deafening, is soothing. It is so loud it completely fills her head, making it physically impossible for any other thoughts about her chaotic day to edge their way in.

Thank goodness for the football; it means there is no need to make any sort of sensible conversation. She has never been so relieved to be amongst a bunch of friendly faces but, at the same time, not have to talk.

Emily leans back and tries to relax. The pew may be aesthetically pleasing but it is extremely uncomfortable and digs sharply into her vertebrae, with no give. However, despite the searing pain, she is happy to just be in the moment. To be among fellow, human beings and do nothing other than listen to their banter without having to contribute.

Mitch squeezes her spare hand as she takes a long, satisfying sip of wine. The peachy flavours remind her of summer holidays; warm sunshine and more restful times. He winks at her kindly, and she knows he is just checking – as best he can in a room full of people – that she is okay after their crazy afternoon. She smiles back, just as someone knocks her elbow, which she had rested on the arm of the pew to make it slightly easier on her back. Wine slops down her front and over the table although the culprit is completely oblivious to what they have done. At least it is white, not red.

Having had years of wiping up after Molly and Jack, Emily automatically deals with the puddle on the table and pulls a paper towel from her pocket. She instantly recognises the pattern. It is the handful of tissues she grabbed at The Cowshed to get rid of her fingerprints. Immediately, her mind returns to what she has done. Within a millisecond it is overflowing with creeping shadows, roll-tops baths and non-existent dead bodies, all interspersed with flashing blue lights, owls hooting and revving engines.

Mitch squeezes her hand again, after jokingly rolling his eyes at the person who knocked into her, but Emily is eviscerated. She has no capacity left whatsoever to be able to have any meaningful discussion, so she simply laughs an empty laugh and smiles.

*

The commentator shouts in delight as the teams reappear and the whole pub erupts in football mania once again. They were level after ninety minutes of play and Emily is grateful for extra time; it will give her at least another half an hour before she needs to do or say anything. Longer if it results in penalties.

'Has anyone seen Chas since the reunion – I thought he was coming tonight?' asks Trev, his voice overly loud, in a brief lull before they kick off again.

Emily has no idea who they are talking about.

'No, I haven't, I thought old Dodders the biology teacher would be here too. All he could talk about last week was his beloved Chelsea,' replies another.

'Gosh, yes, you're right. Although I'm not *really* surprised about Chas not being here, after what happened,' Trev adds.

'What do you mean? I thought he had a good time. You should have seen him on the dancefloor, he was hilarious.'

'Bloody hell, didn't you see it all kick off? I'm sure Mitch will fill you in…'

'Sorry, what's that?' Mitch asks, too focused on the football, as he hears his name mentioned.

'Yeah. Tanya was there too, I think,' Janine chips in. 'Didn't they have a thing going once, her and Chas? Not sure what happened, they always seemed so right for each other.'

'God, yes, they did!' says Trev, his voice increasing to a shout as the referee blows his whistle and match excitement erupts again. 'You're right. I seem to remember she moved away all of a sudden, after our exams?'

His question is left hanging in the air unanswered; every person in the building jumps back to their feet, straining to get the best view. Every square foot of carpet is occupied. The noise level goes up and down as the ball goes from one end of the pitch to the other, then back again. The match is frenetic;

dramatic and daring as both teams desperately try to take the lead.

The thirty minutes of extra time is over all too quickly and the score remains one goal each.

Wonderful. Penalties. Although Emily is grateful for the additional extra-time, the atmosphere is beginning to overwhelm her. Completely exhausted, the ever-increasing volume and commotion from the football crowd are becoming too much to bear. All of a sudden, as it reaches a peak of crescendo, she relishes the opportunity to join in.

'AAAAAGGGGGHHHHHHHH!' Emily screams at the top of her voice, with no inhibitions and as loud and as long as her lungs will permit.

The sense of release is enormous, yet not one person has heard her outburst. All the people around her are too busy laughing, clapping or jumping up and down; making their own hellish noise.

The only difference being that Emily's screams are absolutely nothing to do with the football. They are her release mechanism, like a pent-up pressure cooker. Enabling her to let go of all the trauma and distress of the preceding twelve hours, before she explodes.

SATURDAY 19 MAY

EMILY

'God, that was a game and a half!' Mitch talks excitedly as they drive back to his mother's house. 'Sorry you didn't get much chance to talk to everyone, I think we were all a bit preoccupied.'

'It doesn't matter, I have never been so happy to see a football match.' Emily laughs, not fully explaining her reasons why.

They carry on, driving in silence. Whereas initially, she had been desperate to tell Mitch she had gone back to The Cowshed without him, now she is not so certain. While they were watching the football, she thought she ought to let him know that – whatever it was he thought he saw – he *must* have imagined it because there had been nothing there when she went back. But now she is wondering, does she need to tell him? What difference will it make? Either way he called the police and she saw them arrive. They will have dealt with it by now.

Emily watches idly through the windscreen as football revellers stagger along the pavements, still on a high from the match. Mitch carefully negotiates around a group of young lads, who look dangerously close to stepping, or falling, in the road. Letting him concentrate on his driving she is back with her thoughts. Does it really matter to Mitch what she did earlier that evening? Perhaps it would be better to wait until the morning; either way, he isn't going to absorb much information at the moment, with the excitement of Chelsea winning the title.

The further they get from the town centre the quieter the roads become and she stares at the moon. It stares back, teasing her as it plays peek-a-boo between the clouds. Every now and then Mitch mumbles something else about the match and she nods and smiles in agreement, although her mind is in turmoil.

'Hey!' he jokily squeezes her leg, making her flinch. 'What's up? You've gone all quiet on me?'

'Oh nothing. I was just thinking what an amazing match that was, who would have thought Chelsea would come back on penalties after being one nil down?' Emily hopes her fake enthusiasm will work.

'Too right. Bloody hell, what a weekend, seeing Chelsea win the European Cup.'

'I'm hurt,' she retorts. 'What about me? I came all this way to see you, sat on the edge of the motorway for hours, helped your mum and *all* you can talk about is a bloody football match.'

'Hey, I'm sorry. I think it's great you came this weekend and I know my mum will enjoy it too. You've got to admit it was a brilliant match though, it certainly helped to take my mind off everything.' He looks at Emily, then his voice wavers as he continues. 'You're going to have to make sure you don't say anything to anyone though… you know… about earlier on?'

'What do you mean? Why should *I* say anything?' Emily is annoyed. 'And anyway, if you called the police, they'll have sorted it out by now.'

'Of course, they will. It's just, I know it sounds harsh, but I don't want you to get me in any trouble. It wouldn't be good for business. I think I mentioned earlier, I've got two important contracts coming up.'

Emily says nothing.

'… and, after all, the cottage was booked in your name, not mine.' Mitch continues, glancing at her again and desperate for confirmation. 'Promise me?'

Emily is deathly quiet; she can't even look at him. Who the bloody hell does he think he is. How dare he say that. Get *him* in trouble? What about her, it was all *his* idea to go in. All of a sudden, the turmoil in her mind has vanished. Emily silently, but resolutely, makes up her mind.

'Promise,' she says sternly.

She definitely isn't going to say a word. Not a single, solitary word – and that includes telling Mitch she went back to The Cowshed on her own to retrieve her phone, and there was nothing there.

That'll teach him.

16
WEDNESDAY 30 MAY

EMILY

Shiny, wet bubbles float around the bathroom and the children's laughter is infectious. Emily has soap in her eyes but she barely notices how much they are stinging. She loves this time of day as much as they do. For a little while each evening, it feels like the insurmountable problems seeping into every other corner of her life disappear.

Not long after, Molly and Jack drop off to sleep while she reads *The Singing Mermaid* by Julia Donaldson. It was Molly's choice today. Emily savours the moment as she watches their young, innocent faces, slumbering without a care in the world. More than a week has passed and Emily, still traumatised by what happened, hopes the all-too-vivid memories of their fateful weekend on Dartmoor will fade into the distant past as they revert to their normal daily routine.

With Molly and Jack settled, she makes herself a cup of decaf coffee and flicks on the television in the hope there might be something half decent to watch. She shudders as she remembers her shocking behaviour a couple years earlier.

Thankfully she has managed to break the habit of having a large glass of wine, or two, every evening. It was all too easy; a form of escapism when her life fell apart due to her obsession with establishing what happened to Cerys, the girl who vanished without trace in Cornwall.

Scrolling through the channels, she can't decide what to select. She never used to miss an episode of *Grand Designs*, but not anymore. Now the programme is just a painful reminder of the dream she and Marcus once had to buy a plot of land and build their own home. She dreads to think what would have happened if they had been half-way through a stressful project like that when all their other problems started. Plus, it had been so exciting to buy a brand-new house that no one else had ever lived in and she loves it here. *Their house*. She thinks to herself. Hopefully it will be again, sometime soon.

She decides to watch *Silent Witness* – anything to keep her mind fully occupied – and puts her feet up on the settee, fighting the urge to close her eyes. Hopefully she will stay awake long enough to get to the end of the episode.

Barely ten minutes in and, just as the story line is getting interesting, her phone buzzes. Emily is in two minds whether to answer, but it might be her sister grabbing a quiet moment for a chat after putting her nine-month-old twins to bed. Disappointment kicks in as she realises it's not. Instead, it's an email from Mitch. She hasn't heard or seen anything of him since she returned home nine days ago and was hoping to keep it that way.

From: Rodney Mitchell *30 May 2012 21:11*
To: Emily Harrison
Subject: Hello

Hi there,

Thought this might be of interest, Mum spotted it in the local paper.

POLICE CALLED OUT TO SUSPECTED BREAK-IN

Police were called to Allington House, the ancestral home of Lady Allington-Thorpe on the evening of Saturday 19th May when the intruder alarm was activated while the building was unoccupied.

Police found a window had been forced open at the rear of the mansion house and carried out a full internal search of the property. No one was found and the building was made secure.

A police spokesperson said they are currently following up a number of lines of enquiry but are unable to provide any further details at this present time. A member of the public also reported seeing an unfamiliar, dark blue estate car in the vicinity earlier that evening.

If anyone has any information, they are asked to contact Crimestoppers and quote reference 1103.

Emily reads it twice. That must have been why the police car was in such a hurry when she hid behind the trailer loaded up with hay. She reads it for a third time, it definitely says the incident was at the mansion house not the holiday cottages. Her phone pings again, this time it's a text.

I KNOW YOU WERE THERE
YOU WILL PAY FOR WHAT YOU DID

It must be Mitch, but what does he mean, has he found out she went back to The Cowshed? She's about to reply to his email to ask him, then decides to call instead.

'Hey Mitch, it's me. Just thought I'd phone to say hello. Thanks for the email… do you think they went there after you called them?'

'What do you mean?'

'The police and the break-in at the mansion house, that's the same day we were there and you called them, from your mum's house. Did you ever hear back from them afterwards?'

'Sorry, I was miles away. Yes, you're right… it was.' He coughs. 'And no… not really… they said there was nothing more I could do, that I should leave the matter with them.'

'Oh, I see. Fair enough. What's with your text though?'

'What text?'

'The weird text you sent a moment ago, straight after the email?' Emily doesn't elaborate with any details.

'No. Not me, I'm afraid. Must be from someone else.'

Emily checks again. He's correct, it's not his number. It isn't even a number from her list of contacts. She finishes the conversation with Mitch as quickly as she can, without being rude, then immediately calls the number to find out who sent it.

She waits for the ringtone, but there is nothing. After a pause, there is a recorded message saying the number is unavailable and a deep shiver runs down Emily's spine.

All of a sudden, watching *The Silent Witness* has lost its appeal.

17

THURSDAY 31 MAY

MITCH

The shrill noise grates on his ears and Mitch can't work out where it is coming from. Eventually realising it's his alarm, he rolls over, presses the snooze button and pulls a pillow over his head to block out the light which is bursting through a gap in the curtain. Then he remembers with a jolt, he is meeting a potential new client at half past seven. A breakfast meeting at the coffee shop near the station for convenience; easy parking for Mitch and his companion will be travelling by train from Cardiff before continuing their journey for another meeting in London.

Just as he relishes a few extra moments in bed, the room once again fills with loud, electronic beeps, and the alarm abruptly reminds him he really does need to get up.

Half past six. He stumbles into the shower, rubbing his eyes and ignoring his phone which has been buzzing continuously on the shelf where he left it charging overnight.

A few minutes later, and a little more awake, he pulls his face to the left and then to the right, determined to finish shaving as quickly as he can and slaps on a bit of cologne. The moisture from his breath masks his reflection in the mirror. If he's missed any whiskers he will never know, but his skin feels smooth as he runs his fingertips over his chin and contemplates the day ahead.

*

His phone continues to vibrate as he unlocks his car, then he remembers it's Thursday. He has to go straight from work to badminton practice with the juniors tonight, it's his turn to coach. *Damn*. He needs to fetch his kit bag. That's another five minutes wasted and if he gets delayed, or stops to look at any social media, the traffic will be horrendous. He dashes back inside, up the stairs two at a time and grabs his holdall. Throwing it on the passenger seat, he can still get to the station in plenty of time and check all his messages once he's in the carpark.

The seven o'clock pips announce the hourly news on Radio Two and he listens briefly before changing channels. He's not sure which radio station he has landed on but they are playing music so it will do for now. The news is far too depressing these days. A bus crash in Cameroon with at least thirty fatalities and more on the vast oil spill in the Gulf of Mexico. Why can't they report on something happy for once.

*

The motorist behind him hangs back, just long enough for him to reverse into a parking space. Luckily, he manages to centre his car perfectly between the white lines on his first attempt, he knows how impatient people can be when they have left too little time to catch their train, especially in rush hour when every second is critical.

Turning down the radio to aid his concentration, he picks up his phone. Nineteen minutes past seven. Perfect. Ten minutes to spare, he scrolls through his texts to find out what the constant buzzing has been about. He's normally had at least one from his ex-wife by now, but nothing as yet this morning, perhaps it's going to be a good day after all.

There are two WhatsApp messages from his badminton club, one asking him to confirm he is still okay to coach this evening and the other with information about the league matches this week. He smiles to himself as he sees he's been drawn against the player who is third from the bottom and sends a 'thumbs up' in reply to both.

He opens Facebook and is stunned to see he has eighty-three notifications. With the exception of two, they all relate to the TavyStars1987 group. Mitch clicks on the link. It takes him to a black and white photo of a smiling, heavily bearded Charles Webber, dressed as if he is on an arctic expedition, with a huge, bulging backpack towering over his head.

Umran S – Admin
Chas is missing. If u know where he is plz comment below or DM me and I'll pass on to Annabel his sister. Thank u. Plz don't speculate, useful info only.

Top Comments:
Umran S – Admin
Further to the comments below plz can you share any sightings. This is really important. Thank u.

Fiona Jones
Will do, hope he's OK

TaxiMumSue
OMG... WTF

Tracy Soames
Saw Chas at the reunion but not since. Is he OK? Someone must know where he is?

BuzzKid
Great guy, knew him at school

Doug Taylor
Didn't see him at the do myself, but I woz late so maybe that's why

Sammy Philpot
Saw him Tues before last, not since. Sorry cant help.

Biker05
Yea, I saw him about then too.

BuzzKid
Didn't see anyone with a beard like that

Umran S – Admin
Old photo. Only one we've got.

BuzzKid
Anyone got a recent photo then, give us a clue what he looks like now?

Biker05
Jeez, Buzz you'd know if you saw him, just help if you can

BeasBees
I haven't seen him

Oliver White
He was chatting to a few people early on at the reunion, didn't see him leave. Where's he been since?

DaisyWheel
Yea – saw him too – talking to one of his old teachers, don't know his name as woz not my class

Mikey
Was it Mr Davis? Science teacher?

DaisyWheel
Don't know

BuzzKid
Don't remember a Mr Davis

Sammy Philpot
Davis was geography

Mitch is barely a quarter of the way through the comments when there is a tap on his driver's window. *Shit*. How unprofessional, he'll be lucky if he wins this contract. He was so absorbed in seeing what the others are saying about Chas he has completely lost track of time. It's twenty to eight and his client is stood on the other side of his car door, tapping his watch and glaring at him through the glass.

FRIDAY 1 JUNE

EMILY

The weekend can't come soon enough for Emily as she glances out the office window and watches a queue of people jostle to board a double decker bus. She is consumed with worry about the anonymous text and her schedule today is non-stop. She reluctantly increased her hours after Marcus moved out and her new manager, recently promoted, is out of his depth. He doesn't have a clue how to organise the team. Or motivate them. Or appreciate anything they do. Instead, as she and Jo are the most experienced, he throws *everything* in their direction instead of delegating properly and, as a result, she regularly has to cram five over-full days of work into four and this week has been no exception. Fortunately, to date she has kept her cool and counted to ten, or twenty, when needed, otherwise she might have told her manager politely where to go by now.

Today, sadly, the office banter which usually lifts her spirits is not having the desired effect. Trying her hardest not to drag everyone down, she calls Jo, her job-share, to update her for the following week. It was Jo that introduced her to Mitch a few months ago. "A friend of a friend of a friend" she had said, or something like that.

'Oh my god, Emily, I had no idea. It sounds like you had the weekend from hell!' Jo exclaims, it's the first time Emily has mentioned anything to her, yet she doesn't know the half of it. 'It was really good of Mitch's mum to let you stay though.'

'I know, she was *so* kind and it was great watching the Olympic torch. I think Mitch and I might have come to a natural end though,' Emily adds, thinking Jo ought to know.

'Look Emily, it makes no difference to me whatsoever, I just thought he would be good for you,' Jo replies. 'He was going through a rough patch and he sounded nice. I was worried about you, after you and Marcus split up. I just wanted you to have some fun again. I missed the old Emily.'

Emily smiles gratefully and realises how much she herself misses the old Emily too. She'd do anything to get her back. To get Marcus back too. He's visiting again this weekend and she can't wait to see him.

*

Emily checks the clock. Ten to four. The weekend is beckoning. Molly has a friend's birthday party on Saturday and Jack goes to football club every Sunday morning, so she needs to be organised this evening, to prepare for their busy social diaries. They go out more than she does these days.

Her thoughts return to Mitch. She's relieved about having told Jo and, after the traumatic events at The Cowshed, she thinks the easiest way for them both "never to say anything" is simply not to see each other anymore. Mitch is never going to say anything because – as far as he's concerned – it was nothing to do with him and he wasn't even there and Emily's never going to say anything because she didn't actually see anything.

The more she thinks about it, and she has thought about it a lot, she only has his word for it that there was a body in the bath. She thought she saw a towel hanging over the edge but, when he rushed her out the door, she didn't get another opportunity to have a proper look. It all happened so quickly her memory is nothing more than a blur and she will never know for certain.

She's grateful though, in a perverse sort of way, that the peculiar afternoon at the cottage did happen because, as frightening as it was, it has given her a natural form of closure with Mitch. She just needs to tell him now.

Lost in her thoughts she tidies up loose ends, ready for the weekend and, as if he knew she was thinking about him, a surprise email arrives from Mitch. It's another article his Mum has seen in the local paper.

From: Rodney Mitchell   *01 June 2012 16:18*
To: Emily Harrison
Subject: Weird stuff

This is strange, went to school with Chas, nice guy. Saw him at the reunion. Weird.

LOCAL MAN REPORTED MISSING BY SISTER

Freelance journalist Charles Webber, who went to school in Tavistock and recently attended a reunion, has been reported missing by his sister Annabel Tait.

She last saw him at 4pm on Friday 18th May when Annabel and her children left to visit a friend in Somerset for an overnight stay. They returned home the following afternoon to find him gone and she has not heard from him since.

Charles is known to travel widely for his job but his family say it is totally out of character for him not to let someone know his plans. Police are concerned for his safety and have asked anyone who thinks they may have information regarding his whereabouts to contact them on Crimestoppers quoting reference 1295.

From: Emily Harrison *01 June 2012 16:21*
To: Rodney Mitchell
Subject: Re: Weird Stuff

Gosh, how awful. Feel sorry for his sister. Hope they find him.

From: Rodney Mitchell *01 June 2012 16:23*
To: Emily Harrison
Subject: Weird stuff

Knew him well at school. It's the same weekend we were there, what if it's connected?

From: Emily Harrison *01 June 2012 16:25*
To: Rodney Mitchell
Subject: Re: Weird Stuff

Connected to what?

From: Rodney Mitchell *01 June 2012 16:27*
To: Emily Harrison
Subject: Weird stuff

Sorry. I get what you mean, we said we wouldn't discuss it. Won't do it again.

Emily sighs. She has no idea who Charles Webber is, but vaguely remembers someone called Chas being mentioned during the football match at the Moody Ram. Whoever he might be, she has a strange feeling in her stomach and deletes the email trail. Better safe than sorry and it doesn't seem like a very good idea to keep it.

19
FRIDAY 1 JUNE

LEXIE

'Grammie, it's me,' shrieks Lexie into her handset. 'You'll never guess what!'

'Lexie darling, what a lovely surprise,' Lady Allington laughs, despite being in the middle of a fraught discussion with Norman the builder about the latest timescales for the overdue renovations at the gallery.

'I've done it Grammie. I've only gone and bloody done it!' Lexie continues, out of breath with excitement. 'The final places were allocated today based on the current world rankings. Oh my god, it's unreal. The competition was unbelievably tough and I honestly thought I had messed up, but I've just found out a moment ago that I'm in Team GB.'

'Lexie...' Lady Allington, turning her back on Norman, can't get a word in edgeways.

'I just had to tell you; I am *so* excited. I can't believe it. I really, truly, honestly can't believe it!'

'Lexie, darling, I am over the moon for you. I always knew you would.' Lady Allington turns back to look at Norman, silently mouthing "bear with me" and waving her hand to apologise for interrupting their conversation. 'Have you told your mother yet? We've got our tickets you know; we never doubted you for a second.'

'Oh Grammie, you're so sweet but I never dared to hope it would actually happen. I have never felt as nervous as I was this morning. The running and swimming in Rome were okay, *sort of*, but the pistol shooting trial was the hardest, like, *ever*.' Lexie catches her breath noisily. 'All the other athletes were amazing but then, somehow, I managed to pull it back a bit in the fencing and the show jumping was just, like, *the* best. All those riding lessons you gave me on Tarquin have definitely paid off!' Lexie is beyond excited; her words spill out so fast she is barely making sense.

Lexie's energy and excitement are palpable and, in return, she can feel the overwhelming sense of pride in her grandmother's voice. It is her dream come true. The modern pentathlon at the London Olympics. She and Lady Allington have always had a special relationship; she spent most of her formative years with her dear Grammie. When she was thirteen, she was diagnosed with dyslexia and struggled at times with academic subjects, but they both shared a love of riding. Riding and pretty much all country sports. Becoming a pentathlete was the most natural thing in the world and meant she could do all the things she loved and not have to choose just one sport to specialise in.

'So, what happens next, my love?' Lady Allington finally manages to be heard. 'Where will you be, when can we see you?'

'It's full on, Grammie. The training schedule is serious stuff, like, *every* day, *all* day. We're moving to the Olympic village because the opening ceremony is only eight weeks away and then the pentathlon starts on the eleventh of August.' Lexie is short of breath from talking so fast. 'But I'll let you know – I am sure we can meet up somewhere. It'll be so lovely to see you. I've got to go now though, our coach is calling everyone over, I just had to call you straightway to tell you the news. I love you Grammie.'

*

Lexie hopes her grandmother's pride will make up for the disappointment she is going to feel when she admits to what she did two weeks earlier. When the intruder alarm finally stopped, after twenty arduous minutes, Lexie found a key and let herself out the back door, then retraced her steps along the footpath next to the holiday cottages. There she had clambered over the stile to sit in the summerhouse by the pond, next to the field where she used to keep her beloved horse, Tarquin. She had used her coat as a cushion, to protect her jeans from the damp, and listened to the breeze whispering through the old oak trees and the birds settling down for the night; waiting until darkness completely set in and she had only the moonlight shining on the water for company. Just like she used to as a teenager.

There had been a discarded teddy bear, probably left behind by one of the guests, lying in a puddle and she rescued it, hugging it tight. Two lost souls together. The soft fur and squidgy innards comforted her as she sat there, lonely and lost in her muddled thoughts, planning what to do and what to say. Little did she know the police had already contacted Lady Allington and were racing down the country lanes.

The following morning, she realised she had left her coat behind and retraced her steps; luckily, someone had found it and placed it on the stile. Three days later, having deliberately waited until after the funeral, Lexie was mortified when Lady Allington told her about the break-in. Her grandmother explained, although the officers did not find anyone inside the building, they carried out all the usual forensic tests, including fingerprints and a blood sample where a window had been broken and it looked like the intruder had cut themselves. Plus, she had given clear instructions that, when they found the perpetrator, she would be pressing charges.

Lexie was struck mute. She had been blissfully unaware the police had been called while she sat by the lake, cuddling a child's teddy bear. She lost her nerve and all her good intentions about confessing to her grandmother evaporated into thin air. Everything she had planned to say felt too trite. She couldn't drop a bombshell like that over the phone, her words would all come out wrong. No, the police would never work out it was Lexie who had broken in, so she decided to leave it until another day.

When she next sees her grandmother in person, she will admit to everything she did that evening.

SATURDAY 12 MAY

THE REUNION

Mitch inhales deeply. He never thought he would be the sort of person who would go to a reunion and is surprised to feel excited, as well as a teeny bit nervous. He tries to recall who, out of all his former school mates, he has seen in recent years but soon realises there are none. When he relocated to Bristol, with his then wife, he gradually lost touch with all his former friends. The ensuing six years quickly vanished, along with the love he and Melissa had shared, and the responsibilities of setting up his own business, bringing up a young son and everyday life simply took over.

Trying not to let negative thoughts win, he runs his fingers over his scalp and grins to himself. At least he still has a full head of hair, unlike some of his peers. Feeling more upbeat, Mitch adjusts the neck of his shirt to a more comfortable position and checks his watch. Ten past eight, just about right. The invite said "Eight 'til late" and he hates to be the first to arrive.

'Oh my god, is that you Mitch?' a voice screeches from the other side of the car park and whoever it is grinds a cigarette butt into the tarmac with her platform sole. 'Oh my god, it is. Bloody hell, it's been years... decades! Come on in, you really must meet everyone...'

Before he can work out who it is they grab him by the elbow and sweep him along at speed to the main entrance where the sound of Prince singing 'Little Red Corvette' is already blasting from inside. Bunting adorns the building and a huge banner, in the school colours of navy blue and orange, hangs over the porch, emblazoned with "Class of 1987".

'Janine... oh no, don't say you've forgotten my name?' The woman laughs then puts on a fake, disappointed look as she points a highly manicured finger nail, painted deep scarlet and finished off with silver glitter, at the homemade badge pinned to her blouse. She runs the same finger methodically along the rows of badges displayed on the reception desk as she continues to talk without taking a breath. 'I'm one of the organisers along with Sue Williams – you must remember Sue, surely? She changed schools halfway through, joined us in the third form... played the clarinet?' Janine looks up to make sure Mitch is listening. 'Well, *she* said she went to a reunion for her *other* school and she would have been completely flummoxed without them... name badges I mean ... aha... here you go...'

Mitch is relieved. At least that particular conundrum is solved. JANINE EDWARDS is written in bold capitals on the small rectangle of turquoise blue cardboard with "Falcon 2" underneath. How thoughtful, not only have they included the class she was in they have also used former surnames where needed, as he's sure she is now Janine Morris.

Janine voluntarily pins Mitch's badge to his shirt, without asking, and he tries to relax. He would prefer not to have pin holes in the material but she will think him rude if he makes a fuss, so he keeps quiet. She is so close he can smell her perfume. He thinks it is Angel, or Alien. Either way, it suits her. Her dark hair is elegantly tied up in a chignon bun, held in place with diamante pins, a small lock of which has escaped and curls over her face as she concentrates on fastening the badge without stabbing him in the chest. Mitch silently ponders how many others he won't recognise and how long he should wait before he admits he can't remember their name or, alternatively, feign recognition with gusto, saying 'of course, you haven't changed a bit' when they introduce themselves.

Badge fixed in place, he thanks Janine as two other party goers, laughing loudly and clinking their prosecco glasses, push past.

'Cheers! Oh, I know, who would have thought it and look at them now...'

Mitch has no idea who they are, or who they are talking about, and strains to read the names on their badges, but they disappear too quickly. Instead, he tries his best to keep up with Janine. She is making a bee-line for the welcome table laid out with glasses of bubbly and he follows her into the function room at the back of the building. He is immediately transported back in time. It's a psychedelic grotto of noise, sparkle and an effervescent fizz of anticipation. The walls are plastered with hundreds of old school photos and 80's disco glitter balls spin overhead, sprinkling flashes of gold and silver like fairy dust across the already half-full dancefloor. Balloons float in the air and crowds of people are silhouetted against multicoloured spotlights that create more optical treats as he shouts above the hubbub, trying to continue their conversation.

Fighting their way through, the animated DJ introduces Madness. The way he shouts and whirls his arms above his head reminds Mitch of the noise and thrill of a childhood fairground; the screams and sirens of the exhilarating rides.

Then, as the intoxicating beat of 'Our House' takes over and the whole floor vibrates beneath his feet and through his body, any nerves Mitch had previously felt yield instantly to the power of the music and, before he knows it, he is in the middle of the thong of dancers waving his glass around and doing his best Suggs impression.

SUNDAY 3 JUNE

EMILY

Wind and rain lash against the window and the forecast is for half a month's worth of precipitation in one day. Emily is at her wit's end trying to keep Molly and Jack amused after his football club was cancelled, and her heart goes out to the organisers of the Queen's Diamond Jubilee. One thousand boats are taking part in the celebratory pageant on the River Thames and it does not look fun at all. Choppy, mud-brown water and spectators, soaked to the skin, hidden beneath an array of umbrellas.

Molly and Jack are still enthralled by the Olympics. The excitement of watching the torch relay at the end of their unexpected weekend with Yvonne, and witnessing the dramatic scenes first-hand as the flame accidentally went out while passing through Great Torrington has not left them. The entourage, highly trained for all manner of unexpected situations, sprang into action and quickly relit the torch, but the drama of it grabbed their imagination and they have enjoyed the daily updates on television ever since.

Emily makes a cursory glance into the lounge to check

they are both playing quietly while she sorts out some washing in the kitchen and lets her mind wander. It's now fourteen days since their fateful weekend and she still hasn't seen anything of Mitch, although he sent a third, even more disturbing message, early this morning. On a Sunday. On an extended bank holiday weekend. He certainly knows how to choose his moments.

It was yet another article his Mum had supposedly spotted in the local paper.

Emily is uneasy; she is becoming increasingly concerned about Mitch's odd behaviour. He seems to be thinking far too much about what he saw in The Cowshed that afternoon. Or what he *thinks* he saw. It's crossed her mind that he may have been so badly hungover from the drinking session with his mates the night before that he imagined it. After all, she didn't see anything herself and she still only has his word for it. It would certainly explain why there was nothing there when she went back to retrieve her mobile phone.

No mess, no blood, nothing at all that would suggest something grisly had happened. Certainly, no dead body. Emily bitterly regrets not asking him more questions at the time now. She opens up the latest message and reads it again.

From: Rodney Mitchell   *03 June 2012 06:38*
                              To: Emily Harrison
                          Subject: More weird stuff

This is getting really weird. What if it's Chas? Mum says there's all sorts of talk going round the town.

P.S. Promise me you haven't told anyone about what I saw.

BODY FOUND NEAR PUBLIC FOOTPATH

A body, believed to be male, has been found near a public footpath connecting the riverside walk by the River Tavy with the Allington Estate. The footpath had been temporarily closed whilst development work was being undertaken.

Local builder, Norman Weatherby, who is said to be traumatised by the find, has been renovating derelict buildings on the estate where four new holiday cottages have been created and the Allington Barn Craft Gallery is due to open next month. He made the gruesome discovery when a lorry driver, Alistair Morris, arrived to collect a skip.

A police spokesperson confirmed the skip, which was leased from Morris & Sons Skip Hire of Yelverton had been in the same position for two months and it is not currently known how long the body had been there, although it is not thought to be suspicious. Identification has not yet been possible and a post-mortem will be carried out.

From: Emily Harrison   03 June 2012 10:53
To: Rodney Mitchell
Subject: Re: More weird stuff

Why are you sending me this stuff? PLEASE STOP.
P.S. No I haven't.

Why is Mitch over-analysing everything? She can't handle it. The trouble is, the more he sends her these unsettling newspaper clippings, the more she thinks he is genuinely worried about something from that weekend. Plus, he still doesn't know she went back to The Cowshed without him and she wants to keep it that way. Mitch's behaviour is worrying enough in itself without the weird text she also received last Wednesday. Fortunately, she hasn't had another one, so is trying to convince herself that, whoever sent it, they did so in error.

Emily boils the kettle and pours two small glasses of milk, one each for Molly and Jack. They love having "levenzies" as Jack calls it and seeing who can dunk a biscuit for the longest time without it collapsing. Molly and Jack giggle as she blows her coffee to cool it down and she joins in, despite her thoughts being elsewhere. She knows she is probably just being paranoid about Mitch being paranoid, but everything about that awful weekend is niggling away at her. It's also bringing back difficult memories of the time she spent obsessively researching Cerys, the girl who went missing in Cornwall. It's all flooding back. The same rollercoaster of emotions.

Emily shivers, despite the hot coffee she is drinking. She wants to be back in control; to forget about the weekend with Mitch and everything that happened. The implications of the latest email are only just beginning to register and now a body has been found in such close proximity to The Cowshed it makes her feel sick.

Molly and Jack, oblivious to her thoughts, chat away happily at the kitchen table before Jack reverts to a virtual battle with his toy soldiers. He's lost in his own imagination as much as Emily is in hers. When she went back to The Cowshed there was nothing there; it certainly wasn't a gory crime scene. *So, what is the problem?* She asks herself over and over. *The body on the footpath must simply be an unfortunate coincidence.*

Coffee break finished, Emily keeps herself busy and promises Molly and Jack they can do some baking in the afternoon. Fruit scones sound like a fun way to spend a rainy

Sunday. Washing up their cups, she realises she too is in danger of over-analysing the news report, which isn't going to help with anything, least of all her own sanity.

However, as much as she tries, Mitch has definitely unnerved her by sharing the newspaper articles. Since reading about someone breaking into Allington House and the dark blue vehicle that had been seen by "a member of the public" she has been feeling deeply troubled.

She needs to change her car.

WEDNESDAY 6 JUNE

MITCH

Mitch pulls up outside the bleak, grey, single-storey building. The cracked concrete path leading to the double doors is littered with deep, muddy puddles from the weekend rain and he carefully steps around them, not wanting to spoil his leather shoes. Four of the eight parking spaces are taken and he wonders if any others from the reunion are also here today.

Umran, the admin on their Facebook group, posted a few days ago to ask everyone to co-operate, so that is what he is doing. Co-operating.

Apparently, the police have asked anyone who saw Chas at the reunion to get in touch, to help with their enquiries. They want to know what time he arrived, what time he left, what he did, who he spoke to. To help them piece together a timeline for the evening and, if possible, what has happened to him since. Umran's post was before Mitch's mum sent him the article about the body on the footpath, so he guesses they are now investigating that as well. *Kill two birds with one stone,* Mitch thinks, then cringes at how inappropriate the saying is in this context.

Whether the police did, or didn't, know about the body on the path when they asked the TavyStars1987 Facebook group to help, Mitch decided, after much deliberation, that it was the best thing to do. The *right* thing to do. At least his mother is happy; he stayed over and told her all about his appointment while she sipped her morning tea. It was better she knew. If someone were to see him at the police station it would spread like wildfire and there is nothing worse than small town gossip or idle speculation. His mum would be distraught. Instead, she said she was proud. Proud her son was being a good, moral citizen. He hasn't told Emily though; what she doesn't know about she can't worry about.

*

So here he is. Ten o'clock on a dreary Wednesday morning after a wet bank holiday summoning up the enthusiasm to enter the stern-looking building. The sooner he gets it over and done with, the sooner he can be on the road back to Bristol.

A notice in the porch welcomes visitors, with a photo of the neighbourhood policing team, covering two hundred and fifty square miles between four of them. Underneath are more generic notices about the Crimestoppers service and a Victim Care support line. Mitch sighs as he tentatively pushes the swing door into the main reception area. He has never visited a real-life police station before and isn't sure what to expect.

It's deserted. An oversized arrow points to a large red button on the wall instructing visitors to ring the bell to get attention. He nervously does as asked and a buzzer echoes around the building. Within seconds a uniformed, world-weary officer appears, shirt sleeves rolled up to his elbows. He places a clipboard and pen on the front desk and peers through the glass screen.

'Morning sir, how can I help?' Mitch recognises the familiar South Devon accent.

'Good morning. My name is Rodney Mitchell – I have an appointment with PC Clayton at ten fifteen.'

'Ah, yes.' He's officious. 'I'll let her know you're here, do take a seat.'

Left alone, Mitch prefers to stand and a clock on the wall ticks noisily. He shifts from foot to foot, reinforcing his desire to get this ordeal over as soon as possible when, at last, another human being emerges.

'Good morning, Mr Mitchell.' PC Clayton appears with a surge of energy and a far more welcoming manner. 'Sorry to keep you waiting, I was just finishing a phone call.' She opens a door and holds it open for Mitch to enter as a strip-light flickers into action. 'Do sit down,' she continues. 'I won't take up any more of your time than is absolutely necessary.'

Mitch takes a seat. It is hard and uncomfortable and reminds him of school. The formica-topped table is bare and the room sparse; as he tries to pull his chair forward, he realises it is screwed to the floor and then spots the table is too, acutely aware not all visitors might be as co-operative as he is.

PC Clayton doesn't look much more than twenty-five but has a confident air about her as she opens up a file of untidy papers and sits down directly opposite him, crossing her legs.

'You will know by now that we have a person reported as missing – a Mr Charles Webber – who we believe was last seen on the evening of Friday the eighteenth of May, having attended a school reunion six days earlier.' She briefly looks at Mitch. 'We also believe there may have been events that took place during, or after, the reunion which have a bearing on his current situation. You are therefore here today, Mr Rodney Mitchell, as a possible witness, to provide details of anything which you think may be relevant to the said individual.'

'Yes, that's correct.' Mitch confirms politely as she looks up again.

'Mr Mitchell, I need you to explain, in your own words, what happened during the evening of the reunion, or any days since, that may be of relevance to Mr Charles Webber's disappearance.' PC Clayton takes a deep breath. 'Then, when you are sure you have nothing further to add, I will ask you to read through your witness statement and sign it, to confirm you agree with all the details.'

Mitch nods.

'Mr Mitchell, I hope that is clear. Do you have any questions before we begin?'

'No – I mean no questions – and, yes… yes, it is clear.' Mitch replies meekly. Unusually for him, he feels nervous and doesn't want to be ambiguous.

*

Forty-five minutes later, Mitch reads PC Clayton's notes and silently reviews his recollection of the evening.

WITNESS STATEMENT
Name: Mr Rodney John Mitchell

I arrived at The Moon and Sixpence Inn in Tavistock at 20:10 hrs on Saturday 12th May 2012. The reunion was in the function room at the back of the building. I didn't immediately recognise anybody; however, it was a large school so I wouldn't have known everyone. A little while later others, who had been in the same class as me, started to arrive and I mingled a little more. It was fun, with lots of drinking and dancing to 1980's music. I do remember seeing Charles Webber in conversation with a former teacher whose name I don't recall at about 21:30 hrs but I didn't speak to him myself during the course of the evening.

I saw Charles Webber again at approx. 22:45 hrs. He was with a small group of people, none of whose names I recall for certain although one was, possibly, Janine Edwards who I had spoken to earlier in the evening. After that I saw him chatting with people, both in the garden and on the dance floor. I stayed at the event until about 23:30 hrs and do not recall seeing Charles Webber again at any point after that or in the days since.

Mitch reads through the witness statement three times to be sure of what he has said then, taking the pen off the table, adds his signature.

23
MONDAY 11 JUNE

EMILY

The radio is playing 'Somebody That I Used to Know' and the remix by Gotye resonates around the lounge as Emily rushes around, picking up toys. She loves seeing the house neat, even if it only lasts a few hours, but – despite searching high and low – she still can't find Peanut, Molly's teddy bear, anywhere. The lyrics pull on her heartstrings. They seem so apt. Marcus has been visiting more frequently of late but she still misses him terribly. The more she sees him, the more she would do anything for them to get back together. To be a normal family again.

It's almost time for the afternoon school run. Molly and Jack reluctantly returned this morning after a fun-filled half term. Given their noisy protests when she was desperately trying to get the three of them dressed and out the door by half past seven, she was mightily relieved to find they were far less upset when she actually dropped them off.

It's probably because they had such a wonderful time staying with her parents during half-term. Emily did too, so much so, she almost told her mother about the possibility of her and Marcus getting back together, then decided not to tempt fate when the conversation naturally moved on. Her parents had been devastated when everything blew up so spectacularly two years ago, and she doesn't want to give them false hope, just in case it all goes wrong again. However, strange as it might be, the disastrous weekend with Mitch has only served to intensify her emotions; she is more determined than ever. Determined for her and Marcus to get back together. She just needs to plan carefully how – and when – she will broach the subject so she doesn't scare him off. And she doesn't want anything from the horrible weekend with Mitch to get in the way or spoil their chances.

She flops down on the settee, leaning back against the squidgy cushion she has just plumped up, and screams silently at the ceiling. She has five minutes; if she leaves it any longer, she'll get caught in the traffic and Jack panics so easily these days. Separation anxiety, the doctor called it. She knows exactly how he feels. She would love to tell Marcus just how much she wants him back but she is petrified about getting it wrong. Saying the wrong thing. Doing the wrong thing. Making their situation even worse.

Much of her anxiety stems from her preoccupation with the random messages she still keeps getting from Mitch. Despite having asked him, at least twice, to stop. Mitch promised faithfully he would but then another one arrived almost immediately.

Sometimes he texts, sometimes he emails. Sometimes at work, sometimes at home or, if she is *really* lucky, it's both. True to form, another text message arrived five minutes ago telling her to check her emails and, when she did, there was yet another link to yet another unsettling report.

As much as she tries, Emily cannot get the newspaper articles Mitch has been sending out of her head. Two days ago, it was nothing gruesome, just a little snippet about the

Olympic Torch Relay and a local athlete who took part. Whoever it was, Mitch thought he knew their grandmother, or something equally tenuous. Today it reverts to the morbid theme.

From: Rodney Mitchell *11 June 2012 14:38*
To: Emily Harrison
Subject: In the paper

I know we said we wouldn't discuss it but you have to admit this is odd.

BODY IS NOT MISSING MAN

Police have confirmed the body of a man found near a public footpath by the River Tavy is not that of Charles Webber who has been reported missing by his sister Annabel Tait.

Formal identification is yet to take place; however, a police spokesperson confirmed the next of kin have been informed and the family of the deceased are being supported by specialist officers. As reported two days ago, the footpath had been temporarily closed whilst development work was undertaken at Allington House and it is not known how long the body had been there.

Why is he getting himself so worked up about all of this? She wasn't going to respond but now decides she will. With her shoulders hunched and her brow furrowed deep, she stabs at the keys.

From: Emily Harrison   *11 June 2012 14:48*
To: Rodney Mitchell
Subject: Re: In the paper

WHY ARE YOU DOING THIS??? I asked you to STOP sending me this stuff. It is NOT of interest to me. We discussed and agreed. We DID NOT do anything wrong. We WERE NOT THERE. Remember???

I can't take any more. I am sorry to do this by email, but I think it is better if we stop contacting each other. WITH IMMEDIATE EFFECT.

She presses send, almost breaking the button on her keypad, as if the extra pressure will make her reply travel faster to its destination.

The instant it disappears from her screen she feels as if a huge weight has been lifted from her shoulders.

24
TUESDAY 12 JUNE

EMILY

There is a light-hearted, summery buzz in the office and Emily is beyond excited. Finishing things with Mitch has been liberating, plus she and Marcus are both taking the afternoon off work so they can go together to watch Molly and Jack in their school sports day. She has also resolved to tell Marcus what happened when she was in Devon. He's helping her choose a new car and she doesn't want any secrets if – when – they get back together. Or anything that will make him change his mind, or risk everything going wrong. Maybe tonight she will get the opportunity.

Marcus already knows she broke down on the motorway and that she had to call for help, although Emily didn't elaborate too much about their wait on the hard shoulder as she didn't want him to worry about it, or to know how long the three of them were stuck there, crouching in the rain. He also knows she met with Mitch while she was there, even though they weren't staying together. She also managed to tell him she received a last-minute email from Lady Allington about the mix up with the dates which meant she and the children ended up staying with Yvonne. Mostly they have chatted about the Olympic Torch Relay and how much Molly and Jack enjoyed it. After all, that had been their main reason for going.

She runs through it in her head – the bits he doesn't yet know are that she was already at The Cowshed – *no,* she corrects herself she was already *inside* The Cowshed when she got the email – as she had let herself in without a key. He doesn't know that Mitch was also there. He doesn't know anything about what Mitch saw. He doesn't know she went back again later, on her own. Likewise, he doesn't yet know about the man who has gone missing, or that a body that has been found on the footpath that runs across the Allington Estate. Basically, he doesn't know much at all. The enormity of it hits her and a lump forms at the back of her throat. She can't do this. She can't hide things from him all over again.

Emily's phone pings. It's almost half past twelve so it's probably Marcus checking she is ready to leave. But it's not. It's a text, from the same number as before.

I KNOW YOU WERE THERE
YOU WILL PAY FOR WHAT YOU DID
I AM GOING TO TELL

Emily bolts upright in her chair. It must be some kind of sick joke. She calls back immediately. What's the worst that can happen – someone answers? Even if she doesn't know who it is they will have to talk to her. She calls the number and waits for the ringtone.

Nothing. It's exactly the same as before.

'The number you have dialled is not available,' says the harsh, computer-generated voice.

WEDNESDAY 13 JUNE

EMILY

Emily stares across the open-plan office, quietly fuming at her desk; her colleagues are gossiping about a television programme from the night before. How dare they. She knows she took the afternoon off yesterday but she hasn't got time to talk, let alone laugh, about inane topics, so why have they?

All her plans had been going so well until the text arrived yesterday. It's spoiled everything and she hates feeling this way. She had just about put the worry about the weekend with Mitch behind her, convincing herself the first text had been sent by mistake. Now it feels as if the last three weeks of festering anxiety have all resurfaced at once.

Seething, she fakes a dramatic sigh and looks back at her laptop screen. Trying hard to concentrate, she is so distracted by the office banter she can't even remember what she was doing two minutes ago. In her peripheral vision, she catches them rolling their eyes, amused at her behaviour, which only annoys her further. Emily knows she is completely over-reacting and her colleagues must think she is losing the plot. She usually takes everything in her stride but, since the awful weekend with Mitch, she has struggled. She has also promised Molly and Jack they can go swimming this evening. It will do her good to exercise but, if she is honest with herself, it is the last thing she feels like doing.

Emily glances at the old-fashioned calendar hanging on the wall with a different breed of cat featured every month; an unwanted Christmas present someone brought in to brighten up the office. Even that makes her angry, then ungrateful too. She would have much preferred a dog-themed one. Either way, she is shocked to see it will be two weeks tomorrow since she dumped Mitch.

It feels odd in some ways, an invigorating release in others. Her immediate concern – that he would continue to send inappropriate messages about missing people and dead bodies – has relented but, annoyingly, it has been superseded by her own anxiety about what really did happen. She still only has Mitch's word for it that there was a body in the bath, yet she saw nothing. There was no crime scene. No blood, no gore, no mess. Nothing. So, from her perspective at least, it is all hearsay. There is nothing substantial for her to be worried about. And yet she is. She's worried sick. Why? None of it adds up.

Her mind wanders back to the trauma of that weekend. Not so much her car breaking down, that was bad enough, but the rest of it. Emily knows she let herself into The Cowshed when, strictly speaking, she shouldn't have. However, it was just an innocent error and she is certain Lady Allington would understand if she were ever to find out.

Narrowing it down, it's the menacing texts that are keeping her awake at night. She has gone over them both so many times in her mind. Were they meant for someone else, or are they something to do with that awful afternoon?

She bitterly regrets not pressing Mitch for more information. However, there was nothing to be seen when she went back to get her phone which means he *must* have imagined it. So why can't her brain let go of the annoying conundrum that keeps circling and spinning in her head, every waking hour?

Her vibes were in overdrive at the Moody Ram too, when she looks back. Just mundane stuff. Like when Mitch's friends were chatting about the reunion. Who had talked to who – or *not* talked to who – who had upset who and who had stormed off. That sort of thing. Idle gossip that would have only been important to people who were there but, clearly, something happened that Mitch knew about because his friends alluded to this more than once. She didn't absorb any details and now wishes she had, even though at the time she was incapable of doing so. Her head had been in turmoil after her traumatic day.

The million-dollar question has to be why someone who went to the reunion is now missing? Plus, the discovery of a body on the footpath. Are the two connected and, if so, how? Emily's gut twists. She remembers seeing a skip piled high with builders' debris and, from what she read in the paper, it sounds like it – he – was found just behind it. Whoever sent the text must think she is something to do with it.

The office is relatively quiet at the moment; her team are all in a meeting, so Emily convinces herself to recover all Mitch's messages from her trash file. If she reads them again, extra thoroughly, she may spot something. Scrolling through she recalls some of the names. Annabel Tait, she remembers, is Charles Webber's sister and it was she who reported him missing. She'll have a quick look online, see if she can find her.

A general google search produces dozens of possibilities, so she narrows it down by adding 'Devon, UK'. Immediately there are more promising entries.

"Annabel Tait, mother of Jessica, Scott and Toby, wins the egg and spoon race at St Cuthbert's Primary School annual sports day," reads one from 2009.

"Annabel Tait and Monica Williams celebrate the Devonshire Building Society's centenary with customers at their local branch," reads another from 2005.

"Annabel Tait has asked that her family's privacy be respected at this difficult time" reads a third dated 2011.

Emily reads on, biting her lip. "Julian Tait passed away on Monday 11th April aged thirty-nine after being diagnosed with an aggressive brain tumour in January. His family were at his side. Julian will be greatly missed; he had been a popular member of both the local football team and cricket club for many years. Julian had worked for the Allington Estate since leaving school and leaves a widow, Annabel, and three young children."

Emily's eyes fill with tears. The poor lady, not only is her brother missing, she lost her husband just over a year ago. Her children are the same age as Molly and Jack. How awful. He was so young.

Then a fourth article grabs her attention. A photo shows a young girl, her face beaming with happiness, standing next to her mum, two brothers and a towering sunflower. The caption reads, "Jessica and the Giant Beanstalk!" Evidently, she won first prize in a competition to grow the tallest sunflower in the village in August 2011. She planted it in memory of her father and the winning bloom was so incredibly high the photographer could barely fit the little girl and the flowerhead in the same shot.

Emily peers closer, then realises why it looks familiar. The houses in the background are the row of terraced cottages on the Allington Estate. *Of course*, she nods to herself. *Meadow View*. The house with the trampoline in the garden. So that must have been where Charles Webber was staying when he went missing.

How peculiar, thinks Emily, her brain now in overdrive. Surely Mitch would have known that, especially given his mum used to work for Lady Allington.

Why didn't he say something?

FRIDAY 15 JUNE

MITCH

The shuttlecock squeals past Mitch's ear and he and his doubles partner, Jo's husband Simon, punch the air after clinching the neck-and-neck match, elevating them to second position in the league.

*

'Cheers! Not a bad way to start the weekend.' Mitch takes a large swig from his celebratory pint of beer then screws up his face. He's aching after the tense game of badminton and he hopes he hasn't pulled a muscle. 'If we can just keep it going for two more matches, we could be in with a chance of winning the cup.'

'And pigs might fly, especially with that shoulder!' Simon replies, not convinced, before changing the subject. 'What are you up to this weekend, are you still seeing Jo's friend?'

'Not really. Started off okay, but we cooled things off a few weeks ago.'

'Sorry mate, wouldn't have said anything if I'd known.'

'It doesn't matter. Work is pretty busy at the moment,

there's lots of new tenders on the go plus I'm still getting tons of grief from the ex-missus, so I'm probably better off getting that sorted first anyway.'

Simon nods vacantly into his pint as Mitch wipes the condensation on his glass with his thumb. The downbeat topic of conversation has taken the edge off their earlier jubilation.

'So, have you heard any more about the bloke who went missing after your school reunion?' Simon asks. 'Sounded really weird.'

'No, he's not been found yet. Loads of us have given witness statements, including me. I'd never been inside a police station before, so that was an experience.'

'God, I have. Had to take my licence in for speeding. Got off with a caution, thankfully. Jo would have gone ballistic.' Simon laughs at the memory.

'I had to sign a full statement,' Mitch explains. 'I'm not kidding. The police officer went through everything in the minutest detail... and I hardly spoke to Chas that evening.' Mitch doesn't know why he added that bit, Simon doesn't even know the guy. He just doesn't want anyone thinking he has anything to do with it.

'Jeez, I guess they have to check out all sorts of stuff... bank cards, CCTV. Wonder if they'll find him.'

Mitch's phone buzzes on the table and he picks it up, expecting it to be yet another pre-weekend text from his ex-wife reminding him to pick up Olly in the morning. But it's not. There's an email relating to a recent tender document and another cluster of Facebook notifications from TavyStars1987.

'Sorry Si, just need to check this, looks important.'

Umran S – Admin
URGENT – PLEASE READ.
Devon and Cornwall Police have asked me to close

down this Facebook Group until further notice. This is while they complete their investigation.

They have asked me to thank everyone who has provided them with information from the evening of the reunion. The Facebook Group will be suspended and no further posts or comments will be possible with effect from 2100hrs tonight.

If anyone does have any information which they think may be useful they are asked to contact Crimestoppers and quote ref 1347
20 mins ago

Top Comments:

TaxiMumSue
OMG. Sounds serious.
14 mins ago

BuzzKid
WTF?
5 mins ago

Mitch checks the time. Three minutes past nine. He clicks on the link to see if he can type a reply. Not that he intends to, he's just curious. Immediately he receives the following message.

TavyStars1987not found

TUESDAY 19 JUNE

EMILY

A colleague's shrill voice demands Emily's attention and she jumps; the project meeting must have finished and she hadn't noticed. 'Sorry, I was miles away,' she offers by way of apology, but they are clearly frustrated with her.

'What is it, Emily? You're on a different planet to the rest of us today.' Outwardly a gentle question, but with just enough of a barb of annoyance to get the message across. 'I was going to update you on the agenda for the marketing conference tomorrow but let's get a coffee first and see if a bit of caffeine does the job. You look like you need some.'

Emily glances at the clock. It's half past eleven and she's barely ticked anything off her to-do list, having been far too engrossed in the articles she has found.

'Oh yes please, that would be great,' she stutters, aware she's hit a nerve but grateful for her colleague's thoughtfulness. 'Jack didn't sleep at all well last night and I'm exhausted.'

It is true Jack had a fitful night. However, it is not only the lack of sleep that is making her appear so vacant. She is desperate to find out more about what has been going on at the Allington Estate before she arranges her next visit. Lady Allington promised to send her some alternative dates to compensate for the mix-up and Emily is keen to book them in as soon as possible, to make sure she doesn't lose out financially. It wasn't just the hefty deposit; she paid the balance in full, three days before her fateful trip.

'Thank you, this is perfect.' Emily smiles gratefully at her colleague as she sips her drink. At least she got away with it this time.

Emily is paranoid about people checking up on her, even though everyone takes a few minutes break at some point during the day to look at the latest news headlines, or the traffic updates before they head off home. There's one girl who is on eBay every time she passes her desk and nothing has *ever* been done about that. So, it isn't like she is doing anything wrong, with a few innocent searches on the internet. She'll concentrate on what her colleague has to say for now but after discovering so much about Annabel Tait she is desperate to see what she can find out about Charles, Annabel's brother, later on.

*

There's a lull between meetings in the afternoon and Emily makes a tray of tea for the team. It's her turn on the rota and she bought a box of doughnuts in her lunch break to share with everyone, to make up for being a little preoccupied. Despite being cleared of any serious wrongdoing at her HR disciplinary two years earlier she still senses some of her workmates are wary of her. A tiny swell of an undercurrent she picks up on, every now and then. Even though she told them the details as soon as it became public knowledge, gossip had been rife and she thought it was the best thing to do; to avoid any malicious office rumours getting out of hand. Instead, they had all been fascinated; they had not realised the full extent of her involvement in solving the decades-old mystery of the tragic disappearance of a girl in Cornwall. Two years on, even though she was acquitted of any wrongdoing by HR, she still feels the need to be scrupulous in everything she does. The team secretary now knows *all* the details of *all* her meetings, and she shares everything in her fortnightly one-to-one sessions with her manager. Plus, she and Jo, her job-share, are closer than ever before. Emily confides in her about everything and wishes she had always done so. Whereas Emily gets so easily caught up in everyone's problems and always wants to help, Jo has an innate ability to cut through the emotion. Not that she doesn't care, she just doesn't let 'nonsense' as she calls it, get in the way. Jo concentrates on the things she *can* do something about, not the things she *can't*.

Emily certainly isn't going to fall into the same trap she did before; she may be intrigued about both the missing man and the dead body, but she won't let herself become compulsive about either mystery. Definitely not.

The combination of milky tea and doughnut hits the spot and the delectable, sweet smell disseminates to every corner of the open-plan office. There is going to be a serious sugar rush this afternoon. Laughing with them as they choose their favourites, Emily swallows the last of her drink and reassures herself that, if she is fully up to speed on the latest news *before* she, Molly and Jack stay at the Allington Estate again then she won't inadvertently get herself – or them – embroiled in another convoluted police investigation.

She has a brilliant idea. Finding the contact page on "Devon Live", she subscribes to the website encompassing all the local papers, where it proudly states a mission of "Bringing you the latest news, sport and events from around Devon, including live blogs, pictures and videos." *Perfect*. Why hadn't she thought of that before? Now she'll automatically receive email updates, and there is nothing suspicious about her doing that, thousands of people must be signed up.

She also makes a mental note to check out Charles Webber, the missing man; Norman, the builder; and the skip company.

That will be it. Nothing more. Nothing less. And, most importantly, nothing that will stop her doing her job or cause any problems.

Absolutely nothing.

SATURDAY 12 MAY

THE REUNION

The reunion is overflowing with laughing, jostling people and Mitch is deep in conversation with Trev and Ian; shouting over the music and reminiscing about when their football team won the under sixteens' cup. Mitch is sure Ian didn't score the hat-trick he seems to be intent on telling everyone about, but he won't make an issue of it. Whether he did or not, they had been the best team the school had produced for many years.

Mitch glances around to see if he recognises anyone else. It's ten to ten and the room is packed as he leans against the frame where the bifold doors leading to the garden have been opened as wide as they will go, to let in some cooler air. Pots of half-dead tulips, dotted around the patio, have seen better days and spiders' webs, hanging underneath the picnic tables, glisten as they catch the flashes of colour from the disco balls, like luminous trapeze artists. Mitch savours his pint and wonders who to talk to next as a familiar face appears from the other side of the room.

Chas.

He looks exactly the same as he always did, admittedly a little older, but in a good way. Gone are the slightly goofy smile and messy hair, replaced with a well-groomed beard and a sense of style he must have learnt after leaving school, given he had the reputation for being the scruffiest lad in class, despite being the most handsome and the boy *all* the girls fawned over. Even after twenty-five years Mitch is familiar with the sharp pang of envy, deep in his chest. Like the serrated edge of a knife. As a teenager it had always been there whenever Chas was around. And even worse when Chas *and* Tanya were around.

Tanya.

He hasn't spotted her yet. He hasn't actually looked – he assumed she wouldn't come, despite desperately hoping she would. He will check in a bit. It would be good to see her again. No, he silently corrects himself, it would be *brilliant* to see her again. He wonders, subconsciously, if she is the reason why he came. Why he had been so excited earlier.

Chas catches his eye and nods his head. 'Mitch! How are you doing mate?'

'Long time, no see! Hey, I'm just getting some drinks in, what can I get you?' Mitch offers, fighting the ache inside.

'Good timing – I'll have a pint of the local beer, whatever's on draught – thanks.' Chas slaps his back. 'Good to see you, what have you been up to?'

After returning from the bar, which is now six deep, the conversation reverts to sport. Olympic fever is starting to build and Southampton beating Coventry City four nil a few hours earlier and securing their promotion to the premier league has been mentioned at least twice.

Then Mitch sees her. Tanya. Tanya Symonds. Still as petite as ever in a midnight blue shift dress and her hair in the same short bob that suited her heart-shaped face so perfectly when she was at school. Mitch can't take his eyes off her. She has her back to the wall and is chatting with one of the girls he remembers from his French lessons. He studies her closely. She looks nervous; like she always did if she was asked to read her homework out loud in class, or a teacher picked on her to answer a question. Always willing to help anyone else and never one to argue, she was always happier to sidle in the background than be the leading lady. Mitch's heart races as he watches her, fascinated. He can see her gently biting her lip as she laughs and crosses, then uncrosses, her ankles. The general unease of someone who hates walking into a room full of people, having to make small talk, until they find a group they can relax with.

Mitch stands back and listens to Chas telling the others about his latest project. He's to be a presenter for a TV documentary to be filmed on a 'desert island'. A remake of the one he did before, somewhere off the UK coast, but he is forbidden to say where. *Yeah, right.* Mitch thinks to himself as he sips his beer. *Same old Chas, always wanting all the attention and always having to be so much more exciting than anyone else.*

'... we'll be living completely off-grid without any modern technology or contact with the outside world for eight weeks, maybe longer depending on how it goes. There's fifteen of us altogether – young and old, all different backgrounds. A reality-show-come-human-experiment to see what impact it has on our mental and physical wellbeing.'

'Sounds like hell to me,' says one of the crowd that is rapidly forming around him. 'What if one of them is a murderer or a psychopath? If you're on an island in the middle of nowhere you're not exactly going to stand much chance of escaping a lunatic.'

Mitch doesn't think he can stand much more of this. He likes Chas but, at the same time, he still finds him incredibly irritating. Maybe he's just jealous. He wanders away, gradually working his way across the room to where Tanya is now standing near the exit. Ready to beat a hasty retreat should she need to, no doubt.

Mitch accidentally knocks against someone and a slop of beer lands on his sleeve. He mutters annoyingly under his breath just as Tanya spots him and catches his eye. He immediately laughs instead as she joins in, hiding her mouth with her free hand.

Before he knows it, she is walking towards him. 'Still as clumsy as ever, then Mitch.' she touches his arm, ever so gently. 'How the devil are you, old boy?' She laughs again.

'Less of the "old boy" if you don't mind. If I remember correctly, you are *at least* six months older than me and I was one of the youngest in the class as my birthday is at the end of August.'

'Ooooh, get you! I can't honestly remember the last time I saw you, but it must have been just after we finished our exams, all those years ago.' Mitch's arm tingles where her hand is resting, now more tightly, and she moves in closer to him. 'Oh my god Mitch, this is amazing. I wish I had known you were coming, we have *so* much to catch up on.'

TUESDAY 19 JUNE

EMILY

It turns out to be a very interesting afternoon and Charles Webber a very interesting man. According to Wikipedia, he is an investigative journalist who graduated with honours from Cambridge in 1990, then spent a year in the States after winning a scholarship at Stanford University in America before returning to the UK to freelance for the Times and other publications. It all sounds incredibly impressive, and it doesn't take long for Emily to get drawn in.

"Five students achieve their dreams of going to Oxbridge" the headline sings in an article in the local paper from 1987, before listing the exam results for each of the students from all the schools in the area. There are pages and pages of them. His headmaster is quoted as saying "I am extremely proud of Charles and his peer group for their record-breaking exam results. They have worked incredibly hard and are a credit to our school, I wish them every future success."

Emily leans forward and scans the names. They are in alphabetical order and it doesn't take her long to find both Charles Webber and Rodney Mitchell. The M's are just a few lines above the W's. So, he and Chas definitely attended the same sixth form, although the only subject they had in common was mathematics. Another extract, on the same topic, is a short caption inserted below a black and white photo of Chas with his mother, father and sister. All four of them looking rather sombre, in contrast to the upbeat words. "Charles Webber celebrates his exam results with his parents. George, originally from Jamaica, and his wife Sybil say they are immensely proud of their son."

Emily is absorbed and carries on searching. "Local man delighted to be part of team exploring island life." Yet another article, this time from 2004; a television programme he was involved in, alongside a photograph of a heavily bearded man with a broad smile who bears little resemblance to the younger, rather more serious-looking schoolboy. Then, a blog for a travel magazine in which he retraced the steps of Alfred Wainwright MBE. Headed up as a "candid and eye-opening diary" Charles followed the very same route the famous fell walker wrote about in his Pennine Way Companion in 1968, to see how his modern-day experience compared with that of the iconic adventurer.

Emily is enthralled. Mesmerised by what she has found, it has made her yet more curious. Mitch clearly knew Chas – knew him well – so why hasn't he said more about him? Chas was definitely at the reunion and it is not like Mitch to have forgotten. He chatted at length about the others he knew from school, who had far less exciting back stories, and he must know some of the work Charles has been involved in.

*

Putting her investigation to one side, Emily checks she has all the information she needs for her marketing meeting the following morning. She really mustn't let her personal research get in the way of her professional responsibilities or she'll make big problems for herself. Although she can't help but wonder what Charles' disappearance is all about. Meeting notes ready, she decides to look up the builder. Strike while the iron is hot, but that will be it. No more of this while she is in the office.

Scrolling through Mitch's emails she soon locates his name. Norman Weatherby. She jots it down next to Alistair Morris, the driver of the skip lorry. Perfect.

A Google search brings up a link to the builder's very basic, one-page website, introducing members of the team underneath a family photo. Norman Weatherby is the elder of two boys, both sons of John Weatherby. The other son, his brother, is called Nicholas. Established in 1967 by his grandfather, Norman seems to be the boss these days. Emily's eyes scan up and down the screen, programmed to automatically spot anything that may be interesting or unusual and her brain continues to work furiously as she goes back to the original results page and flicks through the various articles. *Hang on, this could be something.* Tavistock Magistrates Court 2007. Reported in the Western Morning News: "Builder Norman Weatherby was sued by an elderly customer for whom he had built a new garage. The client claimed the builder had deliberately misled her with his quote, then blatantly overcharged her and was aggressive when challenged. When she wrote a letter of complaint, the builder and his apprentice turned up on her doorstep and threatened her." Maybe not such a nice man.

Morris Skip Hire is also a family run business. No website but they do have a business page on Facebook with contact details, hours of business and a few posts. They raise thousands of pounds every year for the local children's hospice, decorating their yard with a magical display of Christmas lights to attract hundreds of visitors. There are numerous festive photos, all of which feature a very jolly, and very huge, inflatable Santa Claus on an even more giant sleigh overflowing with sparkling gifts.

Emily sighs, none of this helps. Once again, her thoughts run away with her and she shudders at the thought of the two men finding the dead body. Shutting her eyes, she recalls the events of that afternoon for the umpteenth time. Maybe someone else had been there all along, watching her with Mitch. Then, when she went to retrieve her mobile phone, they saw her again and would have known who she was. Hence the texts. That must be it. She was tired and hungry after breaking down but, even if Mitch *imagined* what he saw, someone *must* have been in The Cowshed after they drove to his mum's house as the patio door was locked when she returned on her own. It didn't budge an inch, and she gave it a good shake.

She rubs her forehead as if it will help her solve the problem. None of it makes sense. Even if she is correct, why would anyone be there? What were they doing? Then the terror, that completely overwhelmed her at the time, comes flooding back. She had been so dizzy and weak her legs could barely hold her up and her heart was racing so fast it actually made her chest hurt. That is not normal.

There was definitely something wrong about that weekend. Something very wrong.

FRIDAY 22 JUNE

LEXIE

Lexie stretches her weary body. Never have her muscles ached as much, yet she can't stop pushing herself harder and further. For as long as she can remember she has dreamt of being in the Olympics and it still hasn't sunk in. She's in the Team GB squad. She's a pentathlete at the London Olympics.

Six months ago, she had been at Allington House celebrating Christmas. Eating turkey and mince pies. Singing carols and playing charades. Talking excitedly about the year ahead. She remembers how, completely out of the blue, she had suddenly felt completely lost. As if all her dreams were too epic. Too challenging. Too ridiculous. The qualifying rounds had been much harder than she had anticipated and the championships in Rome, the last opportunity to gain a place on the team, had seemed an impossible task. Her grandmother had consoled her, like she always did; listening to her worries and eliminating her fears. She guided her through her emotions, helping Lexie to make sense of it all. Without her dear Grammie, and her constant encouragement, she would never have had the determination to keep going.

Now, with the opening ceremony imminent, Lexie wants to repay her grandmother by winning a medal. To make her proud. She still hasn't confessed about breaking in to Allington House, or told her Grammie anything about what happened that weekend, but it hasn't been mentioned lately. She assumes that means the police haven't made any progress with their investigation. She will wait for a suitable moment when her grandmother comes to visit and tell her then. Lexie has had too much else to think about lately. And dream about.

Recently, whenever she does dream about being in the Olympics, all she can imagine is the competition itself; the stadium, the shooting arena, the swimming pool. Now she is actually here, living the dream, the experience is on a whole different level. East Village, designed to house sixteen thousand athletes is almost full, with more arriving every day. There's noise, hustle and bustle and an intoxicating buzz of excitement around the clock. All day, every day. Athletes from every corner of the globe and from every discipline. She read somewhere that the eleven accommodation blocks, specially designed for the games, will be converted into almost three thousand apartments and homes after it is all over. Stratford in East London is suddenly the hippest, coolest place to be and Lexie loves it.

She's sharing with three others – her coach Anna, another pentathlete called Bev and Louise the sprinter. She's quite happy with the arrangement and they all get on well, most of the time. Bev is the moody one but Lexie is getting used to her ways which are, basically, that Bev likes to get her own way. With everything. Lexie, who will do anything for an easy life, does her best to let it wash over her. She prefers to focus on her training.

Lexie is obsessive about her sport and Anna is the best coach she could ask for. They've worked together for eighteen months and hit it off from the instant they met. If she didn't know better, she would say she actually has a crush on Anna. Anna knows everything about Lexie, she has to. What she eats, her daily routines, her sleep patterns, biometric tests for this and that, blood tests for something else, what motivates her, what annoys her, how to get her to go faster, shoot on target or be more strategic with her fencing. You name it, she has a special knack of knowing what makes Lexie tick, and making her strive for a place on the podium more than she ever thought was humanly possible. Lexie doesn't just want to get a medal for her own sense of achievement, she wants to win gold. And to win gold for her Grammie and Anna too.

It's not all hard work, they do socialise, in moderation. They can save the crazy stuff for when the Olympics close, although that seems like another world at the moment. Every second of every day is taken up thinking about her diet, her training, her rest, her mindset, her performance. Then she goes to sleep, wakes up and does it all over again.

Tonight, they're meeting up with other Team GB athletes. It will be fun to let her hair down a little and, with so many venues in the village to explore, she's looking forward to immersing herself in the once in a lifetime opportunity. Well, maybe two if she's lucky enough to get selected again in four years' time.

'Hey, are you three ready yet?' Anna shouts up the stairs. 'They'll be starting without us if we don't get a move on!'

'Thirty seconds,' Lexie replies, pulling on a sweatshirt over her jeans and stuffing her purse into her bag.

Lexie, Bev and Louise emerge from their rooms at the same moment and after joining Anna, the four of them link arms as they walk up the road. There are still five weeks before the games open but the air is already filled with the heady euphoria of the Olympics.

31

MONDAY 25 JUNE

MITCH

Mitch looks up and smiles from behind his desk as Gabriella taps on his door and, opening it a fraction, tentatively peers in. A freelance PA, she works two afternoons each week; it's almost the end of her first month and she probably wants a chat about her contract. That's less than thirty hours, if his mental arithmetic is correct, and already she has transformed his office, reorganised his diary and generally made everything far more efficient. She has been a godsend.

'Mr Mitchell,' she says, her Italian accent making his name sound far more interesting than it is. 'There is a gentleman here to speak to you. He says he doesn't have an appointment but he would very much like to speak with you this afternoon. Would you like me to show him in?'

Without looking up, Mitch nods his approval 'Yes please Gabriella, that would be great, do you have a name?'

'DS Chandler. He has a card.' Gabriella disappears again and ushers the visitor in.

Before Mitch has time to interpret what Gabriella has said, DS Chandler is in his office, stood over his desk and extending his hand. 'Good afternoon, Mr Mitchell, I hope I haven't disturbed you.'

Mitch jumps to his feet. 'Well, if I'm honest this is a surprise but, no, not disturbed *as such*… what can I help you with?' Mitch indicates to DS Chandler to take a seat and returns to his own leather chair behind the desk. With one elbow leaning on the arm rest he rubs his chin, trying not to appear flustered.

'I'll explain.' The plain clothes detective continues. 'As your PA said, my name is DS Chandler and I am a detective on the local CID team based in North Bristol. I understand that you recently talked to our colleagues in Devon and Cornwall Police and provided a witness statement regarding a school reunion you attended in May this year at The Moon and Sixpence public house in Tavistock.'

'Yes, indeed I did. Has there been some news? Has Charles been found?' Mitch automatically assumes there must be an update, but is bewildered why DS Chandler should need to visit him in person to let him know.

'No, sadly not. There have been no formal sightings since his sister reported him missing. That is why I am here today.'

'Oh… oh, I see. Then what is it I can do?' Mitch is confused.

'I need to ask you to accompany me to the local police station Mr Mitchell and I would be most grateful if you would co-operate. I am not arresting you, but I do need to explain carefully that you will be questioned under caution.'

'Excuse me? I don't understand.'

'We believe the witness statement you provided, and signed, on Wednesday the sixth of June does not fully align with other evidence we have subsequently received and now have in our possession.' DS Chandler looks directly at Mitch, his face devoid of emotion. He must have rehearsed these words many times before.

'Oh… oh, I see,' replies Mitch, unnerved and aware he is

repeating himself, not sure what else to say. 'Am I allowed to ask what that evidence is?'

'Indeed. I would like you to attend an interview at Thornbury Police Station at 18:00 hours this evening with myself and DC Smale. I need to let you know that although you are not being arrested, you are entitled to a solicitor, whom you can arrange yourself or request the duty solicitor to be in attendance when we reconvene.'

'A... a... a solicitor?' Mitch is completely thrown.

'Yes, you are entitled to have a solicitor join you.' DS Chandler glances at the expensive looking watch on his wrist. 'It's 15:00 hours at the moment so you have a few hours to think things through. If you have any questions, we will discuss them when we meet.'

'Thornbury Police Station. 18:00 hours. Okay,' Mitch repeats, nodding his head as the DS stands up to leave and shakes his hand firmly.

'Thank you, Mr Mitchell, I'll show myself out.'

Immediately after DS Chandler leaves his office, Mitch tells Gabriella she can finish early. A thank-you for all the hard work she has done for him over the last month. She is delighted that he is pleased with her diligence, but clearly hasn't realised the significance of DS Chandler's visit and is determined to stay for her allotted time. Mitch repeatedly insists she leave, explaining he will pay her in full, and is relieved when she finally accepts his offer.

Once he is alone, Mitch Googles what it means to be questioned under caution. Should he have a solicitor? How serious is it? He decides he won't. He has nothing to hide. He provided a witness statement of his own volition and he hasn't spoken to anyone else about anything that happened. What possible evidence could they have to indicate he was involved? If he agrees to have a solicitor present it might make him look guilty of something and he certainly doesn't want that. He decides to keep calm and carry on. He will go home, have a shower and put on some fresh clothes. Then he will answer all their questions and co-operate as asked.

*

The butterflies in his stomach are worsening with each passing minute and as Mitch approaches the police station an unmarked car screams past, exiting the gates with sirens blazing and lights flashing on the front grill. He pulls over to let them through and, despite continually telling himself to keep calm, he is now feeling decidedly uncomfortable. He was supposed to be taking Olly to the cinema, but instead he's visiting his second police station in as many weeks, on top of which he had to provide a barely plausible explanation to his ex-wife for not sticking to their arrangement. Needless to say, she was not happy. Not happy at all, but then she rarely is these days. If she knew the real reason, she would be even less happy.

The custody sergeant records his arrival in the log and, at 18:00 hours precisely, Mitch is ushered into a room at the back of the station by DS Chandler. DC Smale is waiting for them and nods politely. The windowless room smells of stale sweat mixed with pine disinfectant. It's as if the table and chairs have been wiped down quickly with some sterilising liquid since the last occupant and the unpleasant odour, coupled with his nerves, is nauseating.

'Interview commenced 18:02 hours.' DS Chandler wastes no time. 'Thank you for your co-operation in joining us this evening Mr Mitchell. We have asked you to attend this interview under caution because we believe there are grounds to suspect that you have committed a criminal offence.'

Mitch is silent. He rubs the back of his neck with his hand and loosens his collar a little. He wishes he hadn't worn a suit and tie now.

32
WEDNESDAY 27 JUNE

EMILY

Emily runs between meetings, trying hard to remember what else she has to do before she leaves the office today. Her previous conference call over-ran by twenty minutes and now she has no time available to catch up on anything before the next one.

She nods hello to a lady from finance and, as they pass in the corridor, a notification appears on her phone. Her colleague jumps and Emily apologises profusely, not sure if it was the *Mission Impossible* ring tone Jack installed on her phone that startled her, or something else. This time it's a reminder to leave five minutes early to pick the children up from school, roadworks caused mayhem yesterday and she was late getting there. Poor little Jack was in tears and it had broken her heart to see him so distraught. She swipes her screen to delete it and, as she approaches the meeting room, she can see a dozen or so people are waiting for her.

Flustered as the music sounds again, she sees another notification appear on the screen. It's from the newspaper website she subscribed to. She dithers and then, despite her better judgement, lets curiosity gets the better of her and opens it, hovering outside the door to read it.

** DEVON LIVE – BREAKING NEWS **

Devon and Cornwall Police have confirmed the body of a man found on a public footpath adjacent to the Allington Estate in Devon last month is retired school teacher Mr Timothy Dodds. A post-mortem has been carried out and it is thought he died of natural causes, most likely a heart attack whilst out walking. An inquest will be held.

Bloody hell. Emily screams silently to herself and covers her mouth with her hand in shock. *That's the teacher they were talking about when the football match was on. You stupid idiot. Why did you open it before the meeting?*

Taking a deep breath, her cheeks burn red with embarrassment as she takes her seat, acutely aware that everyone is staring at her.

33
SATURDAY 12 MAY

THE REUNION

Revellers at the reunion have formed a chaotic conga as Diana Ross singing 'Chain Reaction' blasts through the speakers. The manic, dancing snake has already jigged across the function room and meandered around the garden three times, and with each lap it increases in length and absurdity. Mitch and Tanya attempt to converse over the hubbub as they get jostled by straggling dancers who pull on their arms, trying to persuade them to join in, but they are happier chatting. That is, until Chas rudely interrupts and the conversation automatically moves on so he is, yet again, the centre of attention.

Mitch immediately stops talking. Why is it that everyone gets taken in by Chas and it is only he who can see through his façade? All show and no substance. He and Tanya had been perfectly happy catching up, why couldn't Chas leave them alone, just for once? Nothing has changed. Twenty-five years have passed and everything is the same as it always was. He should have known tonight would not be any different.

The whole room tremors as the crazy conga disintegrates

and the dance floor once again overflows, this time to Rick Astley singing 'Never Gonna Give You Up'. All the while Tanya hangs on to Chas's every word and Mitch is on the sidelines, watching helplessly. He takes a swig of his beer; it now tastes flat and bitter. Like his mood. The reunion he had so eagerly anticipated, and which had got off to such a good start, is rapidly going downhill.

As he watches Chas and Tanya, his mind wanders back to when they were in the sixth form. If only he could turn back time, he would do it all differently. How he had loved Tanya. With her delicate, heart-shaped face. Petite and perfect. Kind and caring. She was beautiful inside and out. Quieter and more reserved than the other girls, but still fun to be around. She wasn't brash like some, or over the top with make-up and short skirts. She was natural, unspoilt. Totally Tanya. He had been the typical gangly, socially awkward teenager who compensated for his lack of self-confidence by acting the clown and messing around with his mates. Relentlessly teasing others, purely to conceal his own shortcomings. He never told anyone about his feelings for Tanya because he knew Chas liked her too and, out of the two of them, Chas was far more appealing as boyfriend material.

Instead of risking defeat in a rutting match, Mitch opted to watch, and love, Tanya from the side lines. As a friend. They chatted easily and would share class notes and homework, laugh on the bus about the latest episode of *The Young Ones*, or disagree about what was the best new music on *The Tube*. It was only when Chas and Tanya started dating that he realised how much she meant to him. He had never felt such excruciating pain inside and, as the relationship between Chas and Tanya became increasingly intense as each term passed, Mitch felt completely inadequate. Yet, all the while, he pretended to be ultra-cool about it. To anyone observing it was obvious Chas and Tanya were crazy about each other and no-one noticed as Mitch retreated into self-isolation, punishing himself for being so boring and uninteresting.

Mitch always knew that he would be second best unless Chas did something really stupid. Over time he learnt to accept this, enjoying Tanya's platonic friendship and doing his utmost to concentrate on his exams instead. His plan was to smash his predicted grades and forget all about his secret, unrequited love when he went off to university.

Everything was on track until that fateful day in 1987. The day he will never, ever forget. Friday the thirteenth of March. How apt. The image still as vivid now as it was then. Having borrowed some past exam papers from Ian, he needed to photocopy and return them intact, before the weekend. He would then repeatedly practise old exam questions in the hope that, if he did a sufficiently large number of iterations, a familiar question would come up in the actual exam and improve his chances of getting top grades.

The month of March had been unseasonably wet and Friday the thirteenth was no different. The wind was howling and the rain horizontal as he made his way to the only photocopier the students had access to, located in the science block. With his head bowed down against the elements he sped across the campus, glad of his parka anorak and trying not to get soaked through. The upper-sixth enjoyed a free period last thing on a Friday for private study so he planned to get his photocopying done and start the weekend early.

The room was deserted and the biology teacher nowhere to be seen so Mitch, shaking himself dry, duly put his twenty pence in the honesty jar to cover the paper costs and let himself into the print room. Bursting through the door, the sight that met him was horrific. He knew she and Chas had been close but this was something else. Tanya's skirt was up around her waist and she had her back against the roller door of the paper store, which rippled almost to the point of collapse as she writhed and pressed the full weight of her body against the metal slats. He held her arms tightly behind her back with one hand and her hair with the other. Her eyes were closed as her face nuzzled in his neck and shoulder. Mitch could see her long, dark eye lashes contrasting with the soft skin of her flushed pink cheeks.

Frozen to the spot, Mitch's brain tried to compute the image before him. The acrid smell of hot ink and the rhythmic, cranking whirr of the photocopier filled his senses as sheet after sheet of paper emerged from the machine. The collecting tray was overflowing and each new sheet fluttered haphazardly down to the floor. A radio, balanced precariously on the top shelf, was playing at maximum volume. He remembers Steve Wright in the afternoon introducing 'Invisible' and Mitch has never been able to listen to any Alison Moyet track since. Fortunately, the overloud music, coupled with the mechanical sound of the printer, had blocked out the scrape of the door opening, although it was painfully clear to Mitch that the two of them were oblivious to anything else that was going on around them.

Desperate to get away, Mitch's hand felt clammy on the cold metal of the doorhandle. He shot out the room as quickly as his legs would carry him and, stuffing the exam papers in his rucksack, he leapt down the concrete stairs three at a time and pushed his way through the heavy double doors to the staff car park.

'You alright Mitch?' Ian shouted across to him. 'You catching the bus or walking today? Look like you're in a hurry.'

'You go ahead, think I'll walk today mate,' Mitch replied, catching his breath and leaning on the bonnet of the nearest vehicle, even more grateful than usual it was the weekend.

34

FRIDAY 29 JUNE

EMILY

The early morning drizzle is cold on Emily's face and it doesn't feel like June, let alone her birthday. Forty-two years old.

Many Happy Returns, she thinks with a deep sigh, and flashes her pass at the electronic card reader, which seems to be taking forever to turn green. Waving her arms in frustration, she realises the security guard, who covers the reception desk through the night until the day staff take over at seven o'clock, is giving her a strange, sideways look.

'Morning!' she calls out, not wanting to appear rude, as the lock eventually releases. He probably hasn't seen anyone for hours and will appreciate a friendly greeting.

'Morning ma'am, early today.' He nods his head gently and Emily realises she has never heard him say anything else. Exactly the same four words whenever she is in at daybreak.

She takes the stairs, running up to the fourth floor will be quicker than waiting for the ancient, juddery, elevator to make its way down to reception and back up again. Plus a few flights of stairs will get her energised for the day ahead.

Another week gone and another week closer to the school holidays. Molly and Jack stayed with Marcus last night, so she grabbed the opportunity to start work early and catch up. Both home and work have been hectic lately and she still hasn't heard from Lady Allington.

Her stomach flutters as she sits down at her desk and gets her breath back, while deciding which of her tasks need to take priority. She is changing her car this weekend too. The cumulative worry from reading Mitch's messages slowly ate away at her and, after much deliberation, she decided the only way to eliminate her fear was to get a new one. She spent last weekend traipsing around garages and settled on a nearly-new, bright orange Toyota Avensis. She and Marcus are collecting it tomorrow and it's a cheerful change from her navy blue Volkswagen Passat. Not only has it eased her worries about breaking down again it will stop the newspaper report about someone at Allington House seeing a "dark-coloured estate car" preying on her mind.

She is thrilled that Marcus helped her choose it. He was horrified at the thought of them huddled on the hard shoulder and it has been a brilliant opportunity to do things together again, as a family. It gave them an excuse to stop for lunch *and* take Molly and Jack to see the latest Spiderman film as a special treat. Yesterday's visit was his eighth in two weeks and it definitely feels like they are getting closer. Ironically, the car going wrong has made their relationship better. It has been a catalyst. It prompted Marcus to think about everything from a different perspective. To be grateful that he has a wife and family, rather than continually punishing Emily for what she did. It's as if he has started to, very gradually, release all the pain and suffering he has held inside for the last two years. Emily feels she is healing too, although she still can't forgive herself for becoming so obsessed with Cerys, the missing girl in Cornwall. She lost his trust and now things are improving she won't ever take him or her children for granted again.

Molly and Jack are delighted too. Marcus had got into a habit of just picking them up and dashing off, but lately it has been different. They spend time together, all four of them, as a family. It feels wonderful. Marcus has even hinted a few times about something more permanent but Emily, so far, is taking it very slowly. Baby steps in the right direction. She doesn't want to ruin the progress they have made but, at the same time, she is becoming desperate to ask him if he will ever be ready to stay over or, even better, move back in.

*

Later in the day, after another round of meetings, teleconferences, staff interviews and reports, she writes detailed notes for her job-share, Jo, to get up to speed when she is next in. Half past four and counting. Emily is definitely clock watching when an email pops up on her screen.

Dear Emily,

I trust this message finds you well and please accept my sincere apologies for taking so terribly long to get in touch, however, it has been an extremely busy time.

The building work at Allington House is behind schedule and causing a lot of angst but, on a more positive note, my granddaughter has been selected for the Team GB Olympic Squad, representing the modern pentathlon so we have all been rather excited as you can imagine. To say I am a proud grandmother simply doesn't do it justice!

Anyway, that aside, I also want to apologise again for the unfortunate confusion with your reservation for The Cowshed a few weeks ago. Although I know I cannot rectify any inconvenience this may have caused you at the time, I would very much like to offer you the opportunity to stay in the other cottage (The Piggery, which is more spacious and sleeps up to six people) for the same number of nights at no extra cost.

If this is acceptable, please do let me know. Due to a cancellation The Piggery is available for the weekend of 13th to 15th July by which time the new craft gallery will also be open and you are very welcome to stay then. Alternatively, if you cannot make these dates, I would be happy to find another time to suit you and your family. If you could let me know as soon as possible it would be much appreciated.

Thank you again for your custom and I look forward to welcoming you to Allington House sometime very soon.

With best wishes,
Lady Henrietta Allington-Thorpe

Oh my god, thinks Emily. *What a lovely, generous offer.* She was hoping to reschedule her stay but this opportunity is even better and it's only two weeks away.

Before Emily is aware of what she is doing, she is texting Marcus to ask him if he would like to have a weekend in Devon with her, Molly and Jack. She even broaches the subject of a reconciliation, calling it a trial 're-coupling' as the celebrities might say. It would give them chance to talk, to work things through, in a neutral environment. Isn't that what all the marriage counsellors advise? It was such a beautiful place to stay plus it will be fun to take her new car on a longer journey, give it a good run.

She shuts her eyes, crosses her fingers and presses send, then has a rush of nerves. What if he says no? She continues to pack up for the weekend, not anticipating a quick response, but her phone vibrates with a resounding ping almost immediately.

16:48
Would love to. Googled it. Looks great. C U tomorrow to pick up the new car.
Mxx

Emily's eyes well up with happiness, then she punches the air, oblivious to the others around her. What a brilliant way to celebrate her birthday *and* end the week.

The weekend has most definitely started.

35

SUNDAY 1 JULY

TANYA

Ethereal wisps of mist rise gently from the serene landscape. Tanya loves this time of day and the eagle-eye view from the top of Sheeps Tor is sublime. The granite speckled moorland falls away beneath her feet and she can see for miles and miles across the rolling countryside. The beautiful Burrator Reservoir surrounded by forest in one direction and, in the other, she can just make out the city of Plymouth glistening in the early morning sun with the English Channel, just beyond, shining a pale, watery blue.

Always an early riser, Tanya runs at least twice a week. Two days ago, the view had been monochrome, the resplendent hills a grey, fuzzy silhouette. Today the air is fresh and the miniature animals in the far distance are crisp and clear, their colours vivid. It inspires her art, the refreshing energy of a new day dawning recharges her soul, from the inside out. Like a battery.

Simultaneously meditative and invigorating, Tanya will stand and contemplate for as long as she needs. She relishes the shapes and colours, the sounds and scents, the light and the shadows; embracing the cool breeze as it contrasts with the stillness. Her senses overflow with the very essence of life in everything around her. The majestic, ancient grandeur of the moor. A landscape that has existed for millions of years and she, a mere mortal, a temporary visitor. She is awestruck at the power and energy it holds; from the weather-beaten shrubs, lopsided from the relentless pounding of the prevailing wind, to the tiny dew drops on the grass. Today the delicate balls of water reflect the golden sun as it glides ever higher, giving the whole world a gilded feel.

As Tanya makes her way back to Meadow View the fieldfares flit to and fro. She thinks field flares would be a far more suitable name, the flashes of red under their wings shining bright. She will make a mental note of everything she sees and enjoy the thrill of what transpires when she is in her studio. The shapes, colours and textures of her creations all inspired by the wonder of nature and her observations.

*

Her cafetiere fills the air with the delicious smell of freshly made coffee and once she has cooled down from her run and performed a few stretches to relax her muscles, she will check her bees. It's high summer so they should be at their happiest; long, warm days and surrounded by acres of wild flowers in every direction, all bursting with pollen for them to collect. It was her life-long ambition to keep bees and a trial run as an apprentice apiarist with a local club a few years ago whetted her appetite more. When a nearby bee keeper offered her a hive, complete with colony, she immediately knew her move to Meadow View was always meant to happen. It had been her destiny.

She has been stung, but it wasn't their fault. She had moved too fast and surprised them. No, her bees are calm and fascinating; their exquisite beauty more enchanting the closer you get. Sometimes to relax she will pull up a chair and sit, motionless, next to the hive. Quietly and reverently observing them going about their business, in and out the tiny entrance.

Last year she had one hive, now she has two. They swarmed about six weeks ago when a new queen hatched out and, having learnt the theory, she placed a spare wooden box nearby to attract the original queen as she flew off with her worker bees in search of a suitable new home. It worked faultlessly. Knowing her bees had decided to stay with her at Meadow View made it even more special and she has carefully positioned both hives facing east, to catch the morning sun as it rises over the meadow; exactly how they like it.

*

Tanya sips her coffee and plans her day. Norman is dropping by later to help her move her crates. She always dreamt of having her own gallery, with visitors admiring her work and asking lots of questions while she works on her latest creation in a clay-smeared apron. She's never had the chance before. It's a vicious circle. She needs to sell enough – and get sufficient interest in her work – to be able to afford to rent premises. However, until she has somewhere to exhibit her creations properly, she won't ever get the level of sales she needs to pay for a suitable building. When Lady Allington offered her a stand in the long-awaited gallery it was too good an opportunity to miss.

She looks at her work, a collection of ceramics and handmade candles, lip balm and soap all crafted from beeswax and honey. An eclectic mix, but it was popular with tourists when she experimented at the spring show in the pannier market earlier in the year. Lady Allington has kindly given her a thirty per cent discount on the rent for her stall to help her get up and running. "Just for the first season mind," Lady Allington had been quite clear, "there's a lot of interest and I can't give them away you know." Tanya had laughed but was extremely grateful and the grand opening is only nine days away. Fingers crossed sales will be good.

Tanya starts wrapping various pieces in bubble wrap. She mustn't overfill the crates or they will be impossible to move and she can't risk dropping one and damaging her stock. She meticulously prepares an inventory for the contents of each so she doesn't forget what she has or hasn't packed. Always a perfectionist, she examines each artifact carefully, holding them up to the light and dusting them off.

*

Norman arrives five minutes early. She jumped at the chance when he offered to help. The gallery is just around the corner and she had planned to use her trusty sack trolley, the one she uses for moving heavy clay to her studio at the bottom of the garden, but it will be much easier with two pairs of hands and a large van. Tanya likes Norman, she thinks of him as a gentle giant; his powerful six-foot-four frame is as broad as it is high and he's as strong as an ox, although nimble on his feet when he needs to be.

'Not today, Bea,' he says, turning down the offer of a cup of coffee as he loads all the boxes into the back of his van in the blink of an eye. He and Lady Allington are the only people to call her that and she likes it. 'I need to get back to The Chicken Coop to check the floorboards I laid yesterday.'

'It must be looking lovely in there now,' Tanya replies as she gives the passenger door a powerful tug, before noticing an old towel in the footwell has caught in it. She pulls it out. It's the same colour as the towels in The Cowshed but it can't be one of those, more likely an old one he uses as a dust sheet.

'Lady Allington has guests booked in for September so not long to go now.'

'Jesus, not you as well.' Norman tips his head back and laughs his deep, belly laugh. 'She's reminding me every day at the moment. Don't tell her, but I've given Alistair the skip man a set of keys and he's been helping me to clear the debris from inside to speed things up a bit. We promised Hattie we would get everything off site before the gallery opened.'

It is only a sixty-second drive around the corner and Norman pulls out slowly. Tanya is trying to work out what it is in front of them, then it dawns on her. The overhang of his ladder, secured to the roof rack, is casting a deep, dark shadow over the ground. It makes her shiver. A reminder that she mustn't let her own secrets from the past cast a shadow over her new life. Lost in her thoughts as they pull up outside the entrance she returns to the present; to more positive thoughts. The craft gallery looks amazing, a hive of activity with stall holders dropping off all manner of wonderful pieces of art and setting up their stands. Waiting their turn, they sit in Norman's van with the radio playing softly in the background.

'So how are you anyway?' Norman interrupts her silent thoughts as they wait patiently for the van in front to free up a space so they don't need to double park. 'I expect you've heard about the missing man and the dead teacher bloke? Gave me and Alistair the fright of our lives finding him there like that. How about you, did you see anything strange going on around here that weekend?'

Tanya gulps. She is about to reply with something noncommittal, then she remembers. She told Lady Allington she was away that weekend so she can't let Norman know she was at home and saw someone snooping around or he might give her away.

Tanya feels flustered. The back of her neck prickles. She looks the other way, towards the mansion house. She always thinks it looks like a happy face but, today, it looks puzzled, disappointed even. The front door a straight-lipped mouth and the glassy-eyed windows almost tearful. She needs to think of something. Quickly.

'Oh, here we go.' Norman breaks the slightly-too-long silence as the vehicle in front indicates to pull out. 'Thought they were never going to finish unloading their stuff, I'll get as close as I can.'

Phew. Saved by the artist in front just in time, Tanya thinks to herself as she unclips her seatbelt ready to jump out.

'So did you?' Norman asks again, pulling up the handbrake with a jolt and looking around to meet her eye.

Unnerved, luckily the extra few seconds have given Tanya the opportunity to compose herself. 'No, I didn't. I was away that weekend.' She smiles at him, trying not to let her voice wobble. 'But it must have been a terrible shock for you both.'

36

THURSDAY 5 JULY

EMILY

Emily is relieved when the perfect opportunity presents itself for her to tell Marcus more about what happened at The Cowshed. After accepting her invitation last Friday, they had a brilliant weekend picking up her new car and tonight they've had a fun evening ten-pin bowling with Molly and Jack. The young waiter has just wandered off to put their remaining, cold, slices of pizza in a cardboard box and she seizes the moment.

'There's something else I need to tell you before we go to Devon next week,' Emily says quietly, not wanting to procrastinate any longer.

'Sounds interesting!' Marcus replies, one eyebrow up and the other down. Emily loves the way he does that without realising. 'I know you were worried about letting yourself in the cottage, but you really didn't do anything wrong. It was a mistake anyone could have made.'

Emily leans back, thankful for his understanding. She gently strokes Molly's hair as her daughter makes a loud noise, sipping the last of the lemonade from the bottom of her glass.

'I know, and it was really kind of Yvonne to let us stay. It's just that it seems like other stuff was happening while we were there too...' she continues, aware she is waffling. 'It's difficult to explain. I wasn't going to say anything, but it's all a bit weird and I don't want us to have any secrets.'

'What secrets?' He frowns.

'I was browsing a news website the other day and, apparently, a bloke that went to Mitch's school reunion has gone missing and, not only that, one of the teachers has been found, you know,' Emily lowers her voice and mouths the final word so the children don't hear, 'dead.'

'You're joking. That's awful.' Marcus is taken aback. 'But what's that got to do with Lady Allington or your weekend away?'

'He – the teacher – was found on her estate, on a footpath. Next to the cottage.'

'Hang on a minute, what do you mean, while you were there? did you see anything?'

'No, nothing. The whole place was deserted when I was there. I think the body was found a day or two later, so who knows.'

'Why are you worrying then?' Marcus rubs her arm. 'It sounds like a coincidence. You're feeling bad about going in without a key, that's all.'

'I know I'm being daft. Except, I don't know, it's just I've had a couple really strange text messages lately and I don't know who's been sending them.' Emily bites her lip.

'What do you mean by strange?'

'Well, basically, saying "*I know you were there*" and "*You'll pay for what you did*" and horrible things like that. Except, when I tried calling the number back, there was a recorded message saying it was unavailable.'

'Hey guys, how are you doing? We haven't seen you in ages!' both Marcus and Emily spin around in surprise, distracted by a booming voice. Their former neighbours, from long ago and pre-children, when they lived in their tiny apartment on the waterfront in Bristol, have spotted them and come over to say hello.

Shaking their hands and slapping Marcus on the back, they proceed to talk noisily over one another and cram ten years of family, work and other news into a rapid-fire conversation. Emily can't believe it. Just as soon as she has started the difficult explanation, it comes to an abrupt halt.

Finally, their ex-neighbours realise they are getting in the way of the waiting staff, who are politely squeezing past them, when their youngest child knocks over a bottle. A fountain of brilliant red tomato sauce lands on everything and everyone within a two-metre radius, followed by ear-piercing screams as his embarrassed parents reprimand him. A member of staff hastily brings the card machine over, eager for both families to leave, and by the time they make it back to their car Emily has lost her train of thought. Not that it matters as Marcus, now intent on getting home, has completely forgotten about their half-finished chat.

As he drops them off at home Marcus gives them each a kiss. 'Sorry Ems, I wish I could stay for coffee but I've got an early start and my laptop and work stuff are all at the flat. Don't worry though, I'll see you at the weekend and I promise we'll sort everything out next week on our mini-holiday.'

Emily gives him a hug. She's not sure if he is referring to her anxiety about the texts and their earlier discussion or their marriage, but she would be happy for it to be either. Even better if it was both.

Shutting the front door, she watches the children run up the stairs. Emily's excitement is building at the thought of their weekend away as a family. Just one more week to go.

Her phone buzzes in her pocket, probably Marcus calling to say good night. He's got into the habit of doing that lately.

Somehow, she manages to balance her phone on the pizza box to sneak a look and is aghast to see it is yet another text from the same, unknown, number as before.

I KNOW YOU WERE THERE
I MEANT WHAT I SAID
I'M GOING TO TELL

Emily feels sick. Dropping the greasy box, she immediately calls back, determined to catch them out this time.

But once again there is nothing.

37

MONDAY 9 JULY

EMILY

The light has faded fast and Emily is surprised to see it is almost ten o'clock. She's been chatting with her mum and had no idea it was so late. Balancing the phone under her chin, she pulls the curtains and returns to the settee, putting her weary feet up while she continues to talk. The moment she does, her doorbell rings.

'Mum, I'm sorry, but I need to go. I think Sian my neighbour is at the door, she said she'd drop a book round. It looks a great read – I'll let you know!'

Her mum laughs, 'No problem, I remember you saying she asked you to join her book club. Bye for now love, look after yourself and I'll ring again in a day or two.'

The doorbell rings for the second time. *Patience*, thinks Emily, as she opens the door and jumps with surprise to find a pair of strangers looking straight at her. The shorter of the two flashes a warrant card.

'Mrs Harrison?" she asks politely. 'I'm DI Julie Sands from Devon and Cornwall Police and this is my colleague DS Darren Fuller.'

'Yes, that's me,' Emily replies nervously. Her brain springs into overdrive. They're not in uniform. What does that mean? Are they genuine? Has something awful happened to Marcus?

'Mrs Harrison. We're very sorry to trouble you this late on a Monday evening but would it be okay to come in for five minutes?' DI Sands explains. 'We need to ask you a few questions, it won't take long.'

'Of… of… course. Yes, please, do come in,' Emily garbles, her cheeks flushed as she leads them into the lounge. She put Molly and Jack to bed before she called her mother so they should be asleep by now. Hopefully they won't wake up.

Emily chooses the armchair as they sit down at opposite ends of the settee, declining politely when she offers them a cup of tea and reiterating, they won't be long.

'Mrs Harrison, we just need to ask a few routine questions. It is absolutely nothing to be concerned about, however, we think you may be able to help regarding a case we are currently working on, and which our colleagues at Avon and Somerset have been helping us with.'

DS Fuller doesn't speak but nods at Emily, to reinforce what his colleague has said, as DI Sands continues.

'We believe you visited Dartmoor during the weekend of Saturday the nineteenth of May. Following a police incident in the area, we put out a public request for information and received a number of responses. In particular, a car mechanic claims he remembers you talking about the property known as the Allington Estate when he fixed your car at the side of the motorway.'

'Uh…' Emily tries not to looked shocked. She had been secretly hoping it would be about something completely different. Something she could honestly say she knew nothing about. But it's not. The fateful weekend with Mitch continues to haunt her.

'Can you confirm that you did indeed visit Dartmoor that day?'

'Yes… yes, I did.'

'And did you visit the Allington Estate?'

She hesitates. Her stomach is turning somersaults. What does she do? She can't lie.

'Yes,' Emily answers quietly. 'Why? Has something happened?'

'What time did you arrive at the estate?' DI Sands continues, ignoring her question.

'I don't know precisely; I think it was about quarter past five. I had a reservation to stay at one of the holiday cottages.' Emily takes a breath as she considers what to say next. 'I planned to get there sooner but my car had a fault on the motorway. A mechanic came out to fix it, that must have been who spoke to you.'

'I see,' DI Sands nods. 'What did you do when you arrived?'

'I checked my messages, to get the code for the key safe. That was when I noticed an email from Lady Allington that she had sent earlier in the day.'

'Thank you. What did the email say?'

'It said she, Lady Allington, was sorry. That she had made a mistake.' Emily looks up at the detective; the DI makes no move to speak and obviously wants her to continue. 'She had got confused with the dates, or words to that effect. Basically, it was telling me it was not possible for me to stay there after all.'

'I see. What did you do next?'

'A friend of mine, who was there waiting for me, called his mother and asked if we could stay with her instead.' Emily fiddles with her sleeve, twisting the material between her finger and thumb.

'Please can you tell me the name of your friend?'

'Yes. It's Mitch. Sorry, I mean Rodney Mitchell, we call him Mitch for short.'

'I see. And when you say "we" who else was with you?'

'My two children; Molly and Jack. They're asleep upstairs at the moment,' she adds, pointing to the ceiling for some absurd reason, then feeling embarrassed for doing so. 'The three of us were meant to be staying there, mainly to watch the Olympic Torch Relay for a school project, but also for a relaxing weekend away. Mitch is just someone I know and had come over to say hello.'

'How long did you remain at the Allington Estate?' DI Sands continues to ask questions as the DS scribbles in his notepad.

'Not long at all. Molly and Jack were hungry and tired. I didn't want to keep them waiting any longer than was necessary.'

'So how long, in hours and minutes, did you remain at the Allington Estate?' she repeats, a little more sternly.

'Uh… twenty minutes? Half an hour? Not long.' Emily doesn't mention going inside. DI Sands hasn't asked what she did, just how long she was there, so that's all she needs to say.

'I see. What car were you driving that day Mrs Harrison?' she tries a different question.

'A Volkswagen.'

'What colour and model was it?'

'A dark blue Passat estate.'

'I see. Can you confirm the registration of the vehicle please Mrs Harrison.'

Emily's heart sinks. Every time the DI says "I see" she wonders if she actually means "I know". And the newspaper article Mitch sent her is still etched on her brain.

"A police spokesperson said a member of the public reported seeing an unfamiliar dark blue estate car in the vicinity earlier that evening."

*

'I'll just recap, Mrs Harrison, to make sure I've recorded everything correctly.' The DI is formal but not intimidating. Emily, distinctly uneasy now, leans back in her chair. Hopefully they will be finished soon. 'You, along with your two children, booked to stay in one of the holiday cottages at the Allington Estate for the weekend. On the way your car developed a fault and a mechanic came and fixed it for you. On arriving at the Allington Estate you found an email from the owner explaining your booking had been cancelled, or words to that effect, meaning you had nowhere to stay.'

'That is correct.' Emily nods.

'Please can you confirm which cottage you had planned to stay in?'

'The Cowshed.'

'And what did you do after your friend, Rodney Mitchell, called his mother?'

'She agreed we could stay with her and we drove to her house.'

'And you went straight there?'

'Yes. Mitch came with me and the children in the car to show me where to go.'

'Did you see anyone else while you were at The Cowshed?' She checks her radio briefly as it beeps, before pressing a button and looking back at Emily.

Emily returns her gaze. 'No one at all, I was amazed how quiet it was.'

'I see. And what did you do after arriving at Mr Mitchell's mother's house?'

'She gave us a cup of tea and cake and we chatted for a bit. She was very kind.' Emily recalls sitting in Yvonne's lounge, looking at all her family photos and thinking how surreal the events of the afternoon had been.

'And after you finished your tea and cakes?'

'Mitch had arranged to meet some former schoolfriends

and he asked me to join them. Yvonne – Mrs Mitchell – offered to look after Molly and Jack but I didn't want to leave them so soon after arriving so I stayed for a bit and then popped out later while she read them a story.' Emily is flustered. So many questions. At point will she stop asking?

'Where did you join Mr Mitchell that evening?'

'At a pub called The Moody Ram.'

'What time did you get to The Moody Ram?' she deliberately emphasises the word 'moody' for some reason, making Emily feel uncomfortable again. It has been a long five minutes.

'It had gone nine by the time I got there.' Emily's cheeks feel hot. 'The football final with Chelsea was on the television and it was almost the end of the second half.'

'Can you remember who else was at The Moody Ram that evening?'

'Not really. It was packed. Other than Mitch, I didn't know anyone. He introduced me to some of his friends but it was noisy and I barely heard what he said.' The DI raises her eyebrows and Emily assumes she wants her to elaborate further. 'To be honest, they were more interested in the football match than me. Mitch bought me a glass of wine, they all shuffled up to let me sit down and then we watched the football match. That was pretty much it.'

'What time did you leave the pub?'

'Shortly after the match finished. It went to penalties so I guess about half past ten, maybe quarter to eleven.' Emily realises she had better clarify she didn't drive after drinking. 'Mitch drove my car as he had orange juice after overindulging the night before. We went straight back to his mum's house but there were loads of people around, all celebrating Chelsea's win.'

'Was Mr Mitchell with you the whole of the time you were there?'

'Yes, he was.' What a strange question thinks Emily. 'Like I said, we were all watching the football.'

'Did you return to the Allington Estate at any point during the remainder of the weekend?'

'No.' Emily answers truthfully. After all, she did not return *after* the football match.

'Thank you, Mrs Harrison. Just one more question and then we will leave you in peace.'

Emily nods, silently willing them to finish their questioning.

'Can you confirm when you returned home?'

'I drove back with Molly and Jack after we had seen the Olympic Torch Relay on the Monday. We got back early evening.'

'Thank you again Mrs Harrison, we do appreciate you helping us with our inquiries.'

The pair get to their feet and head towards the front door, both shaking her hand in turn.

As soon as they are gone Emily locks the door and takes a long, deep breath. The house is eerily silent and, as the unmarked police car pulls away, she realises she is exhausted.

FRIDAY 13 JULY

EMILY

It is just like old times. Molly and Jack laughing with Marcus while Emily fusses over the three of them. Dragging their enormous amount of luggage down the stairs, along the hall and squeezing it into the boot of the car, anyone would think they were holidaying for a month not two nights.

Molly and Jack are excited. More excited than they have been about anything since Marcus decided that he needed space to think "for a few days". Then never came back. Until now. Emily is just as bad, since Marcus agreed to join them, she has been meticulously planning everything about their weekend trip. Over and over in her head. What to wear, where to go, what to take, where to eat, what to say, what to do. How to be how they used to be.

She watches them, remembering how they were when they set off to Cornwall two years ago. They had been blissfully unaware how much their life was about to change. To be turned upside down and inside out. Emily often wonders if they hadn't gone on that holiday what would have happened instead. Would they still be in this situation?

So much is exactly the same and yet so much is completely different. Molly cuddles her new teddy bear, having still not found Peanut, and Jack has his favourite blue blanket tucked under his arm. Her heart melts. Hindsight is a wonderful thing but, looking back, she knows she lost all sense of reason. All she had wanted was to help Cerys's parents get closure. If only she were able to rewind the clock, she would do it all differently.

*

It's another week to go before the official school summer holiday but you wouldn't think it, given the nose-to-nose traffic. After making slow progress, the tortuous journey is offset a little by countless games of 'I-Spy' and 'Count the Caravan'. With just twenty miles remaining, Emily tries to remember the directions but it all seems so unfamiliar. The lanes are narrower and more twisty and the towering hedgerows even higher. Perhaps her brain is subconsciously blocking out her memories of that awful weekend with Mitch.

The foxgloves, red campion and hawthorn blossom of late May have been replaced by the midsummer madness of white daisies and pink clover. The heady scent of pollen and the buzz of insects fills the air. Emily watches in delight as swallows swoop across the fields, narrowly missing the cows while they munch contentedly on the grass in the late afternoon sunshine. A rural idyll if ever there was one. So many people are superstitious about Friday the thirteenth but she doesn't think it applies today.

The one thing that is familiar is the cattle grid. Their car judders and rattles as they drive over it; with the wonderful view of Dartmoor to the right and an ancient, thatched inn to the left. They are tempted to stop but the car park is already overflowing so decide to keep going, only to gawp at a slow-moving herd of cattle as they wantonly block the road. Looking through the windscreen with huge brown eyes as if to say 'we were here first' and blatantly ignoring the toots from an antique camper van which looks like it might not survive another hill start.

*

'Wow!' exclaims Marcus as they finally turn up the gravel drive and Allington House appears before them. 'I can see why you wanted to come back.'

'I know, it's really special, isn't it. There's the craft gallery too, it looks amazing. It wasn't quite finished when we came before, there was a skip and lots of builder's rubble still lying around, it's completely different.'

A skip. Emily inhales deeply. She had forgotten about the skip outside the craft barn and immediately wonders if that is where the body was found, rather than by the skip next to the holiday cottages. Luckily the moment is soon gone and the cheerful chit-chat of customers enjoying cream teas in the outdoor café takes over as they turn up the track and past the terraced cottages of Meadow View.

Emily takes it all in; the neglected trampoline is now overgrown with bindweed and the home-made sign offering eggs and honey for sale is still propped up against the milk churn. Her throat tightens as they pull up outside The Piggery and Emily tries to push all thoughts of her previous visit from her mind.

Marcus jumps out to open the boot and she is about to help him unload their luggage when her phone buzzes on her lap. It's Jo calling from work. She knows instinctively that she will be wanting to check the notes Emily left her about a client meeting.

'Hi Jo, how is it going?' Emily smiles at Marcus through the window, expecting it to be a thirty second conversation. 'Everything ready for Monday morning?'

'Hi Emily, yes all good, your notes were very comprehensive, although that isn't actually what I was calling about… are you okay to talk?'

'Yes, of course.' Emily is curious. 'What is it?'

'It's sort of difficult, I wasn't sure whether to tell you or not. I presume you haven't heard anything?'

'I guess not, as I have no idea what you are talking about. Has something happened in the office?'

'No… gosh no, works okay. It's Mitch.'

'Mitch? What's happened?' Emily talks more quietly so Marcus, who is lining their bags up on the path ready for them to get the key, can't hear.

'I'm sorry, Emily, I don't really know what to say. Mitch has been arrested.'

'Arrested? What for?'

'Well, they say it's on suspicion of murder… or manslaughter… or something. I'm not sure of the details…'

'WHAT?!' Emily clasps her hand over her mouth as Marcus starts walking back to the car. Jo doesn't know the police visited Emily on Monday night. Then Emily remembers she told them Mitch's name. She told them he was at the Allington Estate with her. It must be her fault he's been arrested.

'Look, I'm really sorry Emily, I just thought you ought to know. I know it's your special weekend away with Marcus, but I thought you would be annoyed if you came back next week and I hadn't told you.' Jo's voice trails away as Emily's head fills with dread.

'No, you're right, thank you for telling me.' Emily is stunned. She knows Jo will have agonised over telling her. 'I'm just gobsmacked.'

'Well, I do know a little bit more…' Jo whispers down the phone, as if she is trying not to let anyone else hear. 'Apparently – and I don't know for certain, I am just repeating what I have been told – he gave a witness statement a few weeks ago, then they took him in for questioning again in June but he was released on bail. Something like that. Anyway, now, he's been *properly* arrested. On Tuesday this week.'

'Shit.' Emily suddenly realises what she has said and looks around to check Molly and Jack didn't hear. Or Marcus. Tuesday. The day after Monday. The day after the police came and asked her questions. 'Bloody hell Jo. I haven't seen him for weeks so I had no idea. I really don't know what he has been doing, or where he has been.'

'It's something to do with a school reunion he went to… I think…' Emily doesn't hear the rest of the sentence as the phone falls from her hand. Emily stares at the footwell, her eyes blurred. Was it something she said? Did she inadvertently tell the police something that has landed Mitch in trouble? Retrieving her phone slowly she hears Jo continue. '… anyway, I think that's it. I'm so sorry Emily, but it's better you know.'

Emily doesn't ask Jo to repeat what she missed of the conversation. She has already heard enough. There is a loud knock on the passenger window; Marcus smiles as he points at the luggage and then the door, clearly wanting Emily to end her conversation and help out.

She nods and smiles back at him. 'Look Jo, honestly, it's fine, you have done the right thing but I'm sorry, I really need to go now. Let me know if you hear any more though.' Then adding, as Marcus opens her door, '…thank you again Jo, I really appreciate you telling me. Hope it all goes well on Monday. See you soon, bye.'

She puts her phone away and gets out of the car as quickly as she can. 'Sorry Marcus, Jo was just double-checking all the details for Monday. She is such a worrier.'

'No problem, but are you sure everything is okay?' Marcus asks, looking concerned. 'You look like someone just walked over your grave.'

39

SATURDAY 12 MAY

THE REUNION

Mitch sits in the beer garden, having a quiet moment to himself. He watches the dancing silhouettes through the window, still angry with Chas for interrupting his chat with Tanya. 'You Win Again' echoes in his ears, the Bee Gees' lyrics taunting him. Mocking him.

Laughing, noisy revellers follow him outside. They pour through the door and onto the grass and Mitch tries not to get wound up further as Chas also reappears. The music changes and a video of Limahl singing 'Never Ending Story' flickers on the supersized screen as enthusiastic dancers continue to gyrate, while Mitch watches them in silence. The DJ has certainly kept the party atmosphere going.

Minutes later he downs the last of his beer in one gulp and decides not to let Chas annoy him any longer. He came here to enjoy himself, to catch up with old friends and have a good time, and that is *exactly* what he is going to do. Slamming down his empty glass he heads back inside and joins the horde of dancers, hurling himself around to Wham!'s 'Wake Me Up Before You Go-Go'.

*

'Ten minutes to go before last orders folks, get your drinks in while you can!' the DJ announces, the party still in full swing. 'I'll be playing some more gentle tracks shortly too, so if you're feeling nostalgic do let me know if you have any special requests...'

Thirsty after all his exertion, Mitch considers getting another drink, but he can see Tanya standing on her own near the exit and hopes she isn't thinking of leaving just yet. It would be good to have at least one dance together for old times' sake.

As he makes his way towards her, Janine reappears. 'Hey Mitch, how's it going?' she asks, completely blocking his view of Tanya.

'It's great, crazy seeing everyone after all this time.' He smiles, panic-stricken he may miss his opportunity then immediately placated as Janine is dragged away by another acquaintance to sing karaoke-style to the music.

Tanya is still alone and Mitch grabs his moment as the hauntingly accurate REO Speedwagon song 'Can't Fight This Feeling Anymore' fills the room. He moves swiftly, not wanting to waste any more time.

'Fancy a dance?'

'I'd love to!' Tanya replies and gently takes his hand.

'Not so fast, Mr Mitchell, I think the young lady owes me this dance.'

Before he knows it, Chas has swept Tanya away and Mitch is left standing, his arm outstretched. To pour salt on his wounds, Mr Dodds the biology teacher, laughs out loud at him from where he has been watching, one elbow leaning on the bar.

'Your face, Rodney, it's a picture,' he taunts. 'Just like you were as a teenager. Incompetent. Useless.'

'Fuck off, Dodds. What's it to do with you anyway?' Mitch spins round.

'Nothing really. It's just hilarious watching you again, after all these years. He's always had one over you, hasn't he. You were never going to be able to compete with the likes of him, didn't you ever realise?'

'Oh really? Is that what you think? You're an arsehole Dodds. You always were. Well, I'll show you.'

Their voices raised, a crowd starts to gather, wondering what the commotion is about. But Mitch is undeterred. Fuelled by alcohol and years of envy, he charges towards Chas on the dancefloor and punches him in the face. Chas staggers away holding his bloodied nose, not willing to be drawn into a fist fight, while Mitch is pulled in the opposite direction by Ian and Trev.

'C'mon Mitch, lay off. Don't ruin the evening for everyone.'

Irate, Mitch snatches his arm away and strides past onlookers towards the door, well aware Tanya is right behind him and doing her best to pacify him.

'Mitch, *please*, calm down.' He hears her call. 'Chas didn't mean anything. He didn't mean to upset you.'

'He might not have, but Dodds did!' he shouts back, then throws his head back in laughter. 'There. I've said it now. Chas never knew, did he? No, but *I* did. *I* saw you. I know you were there… by the photocopier. What a sight. Little Miss Perfect wasn't quite as perfect as she liked everyone to think, was she now?'

Mitch immediately regrets what he has said. The words spewed out of his mouth before he could stop them.

Tanya is motionless, the colour drains from her cheeks and she turns away, unable to look at him. For a moment he thinks she is going to collapse. Then she swings around, the pain and anger in her voice unfettered.

'You little shit. You always were an idiot, Rodney Mitchell, why did I ever think you were my friend.'

'I'm so sorry, I really am…'

'Too bloody little, too bloody late.' She throws her words at him with pure venom and pummels him in the chest with both hands to make sure he gets the message. 'I thought you were my friend. Why did you have to go and say something now, after all these years? Why didn't you do something at the time?'

FRIDAY 13 JULY

EMILY

The key box is identical to the one before, only this time it does have a key. The dangling plastic pig amuses Molly and Jack but only serves to remind Emily of the toy cow on her previous visit. Trying to push it from her mind, she struggles to hold the door open as they dump all their luggage in the lounge and Emily catches sight of someone rushing towards them. Immaculately presented in a tweed skirt, an open-necked blouse with a neatly tied silk scarf and a wicker basket over her arm, she knows immediately who it is.

'Hello, you must be Emily, it is *so* lovely to meet you at last. I am Lady Allington but everyone calls me Hattie for short so you must too!' the well-spoken lady extends her free hand for Emily to shake and then, putting down the basket, continues to hold Emily's hand gently in both of hers before explaining. 'My full name is Henrietta Allington Thorpe which is far too much of a mouthful for anyone.'

Lady Allington laughs loudly as Emily agrees. 'Hattie it is then!'

'I was just popping over to check everything is ready for you so this is perfect timing. I was in the gallery and saw you arrive. It's been such a busy day but it is wonderful to see it open at long last. The planning permission took forever and was a *complete* nightmare and then, with the monstrous building delays, I wondered if it might not happen at all – and I am not getting any younger.'

'Well, it all looks fabulous to me Hattie,' enthuses Emily, eventually managing to retract her hand. 'I'm not sure two days are going to be enough and we must definitely try some of the local honey while we're here.'

'Oh, my dear, you simply must. Bea's Bees. She looks after the cottages for me and it is the best, and I mean the *very* best honey you could *ever* eat. The eggs are amazing too, look – I've just collected some for myself – all different colours and sizes, your children will love them, if they like eggs that is, I know how fussy some children can be.' She laughs again, revealing the contents of her basket which are hiding under a red and white checked tea towel. 'Oh, I'm sorry, there I go, I can't stop talking once I start. Let me leave you in peace to unpack, there's a folder full of information on the coffee table. Oh, and don't go leaving anything lying around outside if you can help it, Cleo the cat has a habit of running off with things.' She is about to head off when Marcus reappears. 'Oh, my goodness, you must be Marcus, it's a pleasure to meet you too, welcome to Allington.' Hattie continues, then spots the children who, too shy to talk, are hiding behind their father. 'Oh my, how lovely, you must be Jack and Molly. Well, please don't let me hold you up, I am sure you have loads you want to do. If you have any questions at all please don't hesitate to ask and have a fabulous weekend.'

Before Marcus can reply, the whirlwind that is Hattie rushes off as quickly as she arrived, clearly an energetic septuagenarian. Her pixie-cut, silver-grey hair perfectly frames her delicate face and turquoise-blue eyes. Adjusting her scarf as it blows in the wind and, checking the eggs are safely positioned, she heads back up to the main house with the basket swinging on her arm. Emily recalls Yvonne saying how Hattie is a little older than she is, even though her daughter was born in the same year as Mitch, but she doesn't seem her age at all.

*

Later in the evening they stroll around the estate. Walking past the now-closed gallery, they admire the mansion house then wander down the footpath to the stile by the meadow. The shimmering reflections on the pond next to the summerhouse, with its wooden decking jutting out over the deep water, are beautiful. Sheep bleat in the meadow and Emily remembers the cattle two months earlier, in the spring. How everything has changed. Allington House looks warm and inviting, the elegant windows shine like mirrors in the early evening sun. Quite different to the damp, chilly night when she hid behind the trailer full of hay bales, shivering with fear as the police car screamed up the drive.

Making their way back to The Piggery, Molly and Jack chat incessantly, skipping and jumping as they both hold her hand. As they stroll, the black and white cat that made a brief appearance at The Cowshed spots them and saunters over for a bit of attention. It must be Cleo. Molly and Jack are enthralled. They shriek with delight and the animal follows them, less nervous than before.

'At least the ghost person isn't here this time,' Molly says innocently.

'What do you mean the ghost person?' replies Marcus, smoothing her hair back where it has fallen out her slide and is hanging over her eyes.

'The ghost person. They were really weird, with the black and white cat. That's what reminded me. Jack saw them too, when we were here before with Mummy.'

'Yes, they were *really* weird,' agrees Jack. 'When we got back in the car; they were all white and had no face. They were scary.'

Marcus, puzzled, meets Emily's gaze.

'They disappeared behind the gate… that gate over there.' Jack adds, pointing at the terraced cottages opposite.

41

SATURDAY 14 JULY

EMILY

Emily wakes up in the middle of the bed, confused. The wardrobe has moved to the other side of the room and, from downstairs, she can hear the muffled sounds of Molly and Jack chatting and cereal packets being shaken. She rolls on to her side as her eyes come into focus; a dormer window looks out over acres of green pasture. Apart from the roof of a summerhouse, which is just visible through some trees, there are no other buildings in sight.

Then she remembers. She's in The Piggery. She's with Marcus and the children and it's their special weekend. If it all goes well, they may even get back together.

And Mitch has been arrested.

Shit. There it is again. She lies on her back, gazing up at the ceiling. Initially, she had been pleased that Jo told her. Now, she wishes she hadn't. She ought to tell Marcus, she promised not to have any secrets, but she doesn't want to spoil their weekend. If only Jo had waited until Monday.

'Morning!' Marcus appears with two cups of steaming hot coffee and sits down on the edge of the bed.

Emily pulls herself up, plumping the pillows to make them comfortable, and savours the moment, trying to push any thoughts of Mitch from her mind. 'Wow, thank you.' She smiles. 'I'm in heaven with this view *and* a delicious coffee before I've even got up.'

'Well, we are on holiday and you were sleeping so soundly I thought it better to leave you there. Plus, look what I've found on the doorstep,' Marcus continues. 'It's Peanut. There was a message tucked under his collar.'

'What do you mean it's Peanut? We've been searching for him for weeks.'

'Well, Molly must have dropped him last time you were here and someone found him.'

Emily reads the note. *"I know you were there. In The Cowshed."*

Emily chokes on her coffee. Whoever has returned Peanut knows she was here before. They must have seen her, recognised her, and returned her daughter's teddy bear while they were asleep. 'Oh my god, that's really creepy Marcus. Who would have known it was Molly's?'

'Don't ask me, but I wouldn't read too much into it. Hattie said Cleo the cat is in the habit of running off with things. I think it's really kind of whoever it is to return Peanut. Molly's delighted.'

*

The craft gallery has the untapped energy of a newly opened venture. Solid, oak frames support the upper floor and a spiral, wooden staircase leads Emily's eyes up to the rafters, which compels her to investigate further. There is so much to see and it's helping to take her mind off Mitch being arrested and the disturbing reappearance of Peanut. Paintings adorn the walls alongside textiles and sculptures, surrounded by stalls laden with sparkling jewellery, delicate raku pottery, beautiful watercolour landscapes, dazzlingly bright knitwear and wooden bowls made from ash, beech, oak and walnut. Emily imagines the thousands upon thousands of hours of creativity, toil and dedication contained within the building, if she were to tot it all up.

At the bottom of the stairs, Emily admires a display of beautiful pottery interspersed with handmade soap and candles made from beeswax. They smell divine; floral, honey scents emanate from the tabletop. It's clearly popular as nearby is a sack trolley, laden with crates, ready to replenish stock and the stall holder is deep in conversation with browsers, explaining her products. Emily would like to stop and chat but it would be rude to interrupt, so she picks up the stallholder's business card and wanders to the next table to view some stunning wildlife sculptures, each made out of scrap metal.

*

Wandering around the town centre a little later is equally interesting. The historic pannier market bustles with more stalls, this time an eclectic mix of antiques, pre-loved books and hand-made bird tables and everywhere is bedecked with bunting to celebrate the Queen's Jubilee and the Olympic Games. They pass a statue of Sir Francis Drake and, as Emily explains to Molly and Jack how he circumnavigated the world over four hundred years ago, she spots The Moon and Sixpence and realises it's where Mitch attended his reunion.

'Look, Mum,' Molly says impatiently, tugging at her arm. 'Mum, look who's over there.'

Emily turns to see a familiar face. It's Yvonne. She is not sure if Yvonne has recognised her or not, but if she has there is no hint of acknowledgement. Emily wants to say hello, but then panics. Does Yvonne know her son has been arrested?

If she does, what will she think if she suddenly bumps into Emily, especially as she is now with Marcus? She ducks behind a rotating stand of postcards, leaning in to pretend she is looking at them, while mulling over what to do.

'Don't think we'll be here long enough to send any cards.' Marcus appears beside her, curious to know what she is looking at.

'Oh, I was thinking, maybe, for our parents?' Emily replies, trying to buy some time. She discreetly watches over his shoulder as another woman, walking in the opposite direction, grabs Yvonne's attention and stops to chat, making it an easy decision for Emily. 'No, you're right. We can just show them our photos when we get back.' Emily stands back up. 'C'mon Molly and Jack, let's see if we can find the swings in the park.'

She swiftly walks them through the small souvenir shop and out another door, hoping to avoid Yvonne and her friend. They are deep in conversation so Emily should be able to escape, even if she does feel guilty ignoring her. Yvonne was so welcoming that weekend, but she can't risk her saying anything about Mitch being arrested in front of Marcus, not until she has told him first.

'But Mum, why don't you want to say hello?' Molly asks innocently.

'I would normally, Molly love, but not today.' Emily looks over one final time. 'She looks busy, she's chatting to her friend and I don't want to interrupt them.'

But it's too late, Yvonne has clearly seen Emily and recognised Molly and Jack. She fires them a look of disgust and then grabs the other lady's arm, pointing her finger at them.

'That's her, the one I told you about,' Emily hears as she turns away, walking as fast as she can without making it obvious to Marcus what is going on. Molly and Jack can barely keep up, but she bribes them with an ice cream if they speed up and, before she is out of earshot, Emily can't avoid eavesdropping.

'Oh yes, it's her alright. What a bitch. Treated my son like dirt, she did. Used him for her own purposes. Whatever went on that weekend it was all her fault and now he's paying for it.'

SATURDAY 14 JULY

TANYA

Tanya picks up the envelope from her doormat and immediately recognises Lady Allington's handwriting. It must have been delivered while she was working in her studio. The paper is smooth and glossy to touch; embossed with the Allington coat of arms in gold at the top and Hattie's flamboyant signature at the bottom.

> Dear Tanya,
>
> I am writing with much regret to ask you to move your stand at the craft gallery to a different location. Unfortunately, I completely overlooked that I had promised another exhibitor the space at the bottom of the stairs (Pitch 2) and they were most upset when they came to set up this week and found it was being used by Bea's Bees.
>
> In view of the timescales, I need to ask you to move urgently and a space has been prepared for you on

the upper floor in the far right-hand corner (Pitch 31). Given the gallery has now opened it will only be possible to do this when it is closed to visitors. Therefore, please do let me know which evening will suit you best and we can make the necessary arrangements.

I am so very sorry and apologise profusely for any inconvenience. However, as I am offering you a stand at a significant discount – whereas the other exhibitor will be paying the full fee – I am sure you will understand that I must honour my commitment.

Thank you as always for your support Tanya, I know this will come as a terrible disappointment for you.

Yours faithfully,
Lady Henrietta Allington-Thorpe

Disappointed? Inconvenient? Too bloody right. Who the hell does she think she is? Tanya is fuming. How could Lady Allington do this? She is always helping her out – deliveries, plumbers, guests, you name it – and this is how she repays her. What a nerve. And she can't even do it in person. Tanya spent days deciding how to display all her ceramics for maximum impact and now she will have to do it all again, and Norman gave up his Sunday morning to help. She doubts he will have the time to do it again.

Pitch 31 as well. The worst possible place. Hardly anyone will pass by if she's stuck upstairs *and* right at the back and, even if they do, they won't spend as much time looking at her exhibits. The spot at the bottom of the stairs had been perfect. It is the first place people are drawn to as they come in through the main entrance and they wander past *at least* twice more on their way to the cafe or up the stairs and back down again.

What a kick in the teeth. Tanya is stunned.

She won't respond just yet. She'll think about it. Mull it over. Take her time. She certainly won't be rushing to move her stand any day soon. Lady Allington owes her that.

43

SATURDAY 14 JULY

EMILY

The Moody Ram is completely different to how Emily remembers it. Last time, despite being packed to the rafters with excited football fans inside, the atmosphere outside had been dark, damp and distinctly chilly. She recalls two people loitering by the porch, hunching their shoulders against the evening draught as they sucked with hollow cheeks on their cigarettes. Tonight, the evening sun coats everything in a warm, golden glow and the al fresco pizza oven is in full demand.

'So where are you staying?' asks the friendly landlady as she takes their order.

'The Piggery at Allington House – it's wonderful!' replies Emily.

'Oh yes, it is and Hattie's great – have you met her yet? Quite a character, you'll know when you do.' She laughs as she pulls a pint.

'We certainly have, we had a good look around the craft gallery too, it's fabulous.'

'I know, it's been really good for business in the town and she's done it all on her own since her husband died. That was sad. Far too young.' The landlady places the glass on the bar mat as beer dribbles down the side. 'The barn was derelict, ivy and brambles were growing up through the roof, you wouldn't recognise the place now. Really strange about all the police stuff going on down there though, have you heard?'

'Oh?' Emily pretends not to know, worried it might look odd as she isn't local.

'Yes, some chap went missing after a school reunion and then a body was found too. Mind you, turns out the dead bloke isn't the missing one, like everyone expected, but one of the teachers.'

'Really? Do the police know what happened?'

'Not yet. Natural causes they're saying. Keeled over on the footpath while out walking, but even so they seem to be asking everyone lots of questions.'

'Gosh, that's odd. What about the missing guy, does anyone know where he is?'

'Not officially, but someone said they thought he had been found. He was staying with his sister down by the big house, in one of the cottages, that's why I mentioned it. As if Hattie doesn't have enough going on.'

Emily smiles to herself but doesn't reply. The landlady is a hub of local gossip.

'Plain weird if you ask me. He's a bit of a TV personality, apparently, had only been here for a few days when he vanished. Puff. Into thin air. Must be some explanation though, there always is. I'm sure we'll find out soon enough.' The landlady animates the word 'puff' with her hands in the air, then rolls her eyes before moving some empty glasses that have been left on the counter.

Emily gathers up their drinks, intending to move away as the landlady, with no one waiting to be served, rests her elbow on the bar and leans towards Emily, clearly wanting to talk some more. Intrigued to know what scandal is coming next, Emily lingers just long enough for the landlady to continue.

'Brilliant news about her granddaughter though.'

'You mean about her being in Team GB?' Emily enquires. 'Hattie is incredibly proud.'

'Oh, she is, it's wonderful. A remarkable turnaround, if you ask me.' She shakes her head in disbelief, then leans in even further forward, glancing around, as if not wanting anyone else to hear. 'Don't say I said it but – rumour has it – she's more than a bit of trouble that one. Always getting into scrapes. Got a frightful temper too. Hattie won't hear any of it though, she's the apple of her eye.'

'Gosh, I won't say anything. Hattie thinks the world of her. She can't wait to go to the opening ceremony.' Emily smiles.

'Sport has been her saviour. Mind you, again, don't go saying it was me who told you but one of my regulars said it was her that broke into the house while Hattie was away, you know, a few weeks back. Police were called and everything.'

'Really? Why?'

'Don't ask me. Surely, she could have asked her grandmother for a key, don't you think?' She frowns, as if Emily should know the answer, and shrugs her shoulders. 'Chip off the old block I guess, it was her father, Hattie's son-in-law, who left the PTA under a cloud a few years ago. Caused a storm that did. He was chairman but, allegedly, had some massive argument with the teacher that's just turned up dead. So *that's* all a bit peculiar too if you ask me. They kept that hushed up at the time too. Weird.'

'Goodness.' Emily can barely keep up; she doesn't know what else to say.

'Anyway, here's your receipt. Table fifteen. One of us will shout the number and bring your order over when it's ready. Make sure you listen out, it's pretty busy in here tonight. Thanks again my love, mind how you go.'

*

'What was the landlady chatting about, you were gone for ages when you went up to the bar?' Marcus asks later, as they drive back to The Piggery.

'I know – where do I start! Apparently, the missing man may have been found – you know, the one I told you about after our pizza the other day? Well, that, and a bit of gossip about the teacher *and* Hattie's granddaughter.'

'What teacher?'

'You know, I told you about him as well,' Emily checks the children can't hear then looks at Marcus as she mouths the words '… the dead teacher.'

'Oh, yes. How could I forget.'

'So yes, anyway, the teacher incident isn't thought to have been suspicious. Natural causes she said. But, *apparently*, rumour has it, that Hattie's granddaughter broke into the mansion house when Hattie wasn't there a few weeks ago.'

'Really? Why would she do that?' Marcus is sceptical.

'Don't ask me, I'm just repeating what I was told.' Emily laughs, whilst her mind spins into a maelstrom of possibilities and the weekend with Mitch once again fills her head and the vision of the police car racing past her. 'Just town gossip, I expect.'

'As they say, now't as strange as folk,' Marcus replies, then feels someone kicking the back of his seat. 'Hey you two, what are you doing?'

'Nothing!' Molly and Jack say in unison followed by childish giggles.

Emily's phone pings and, stupidly, she ignores her inner counsel telling her not to look. Immediately she wishes she hadn't. It's a text from Mitch. It's five weeks since she told him she wanted no further contact and she wants to keep it that way. What could he possibly want at this time on a Saturday evening? Masking the screen with her bag, she reads it.

**Sat 14 Jul 22:05
Need to talk. When r u free?**

Emily's heart sinks. The conversation with Jo the previous evening is still raw. The vision of Mitch in a police cell, being cross-examined by some fearsome detective over what they did back in May has been tormenting her all day. For him to have got in touch again means it must be serious. It must also mean he has been released, surely? Or would he be allowed to send messages while he is being detained? Emily has no idea.

'Everything alright?' Marcus glances in her direction, they don't have far to go now.

'Yes,' Emily says quietly, before adding the first explanation she can think of. 'Just a diary reminder about something. Nothing important.'

SUNDAY 15 JULY

EMILY

'I want this weekend to last forever.' Emily dries up their breakfast bowls, determined to leave The Piggery clean and tidy.

'Me too, it's been brilliant and the kids have loved staying here,' agrees Marcus as he retrieves a jar she has inadvertently put away. 'Make sure we take our honey home, it's too good to leave behind.'

Emily smiles to herself. Marcus is calling home precisely that. Home. She decides to grab the moment. 'How about you Marcus? Can I take you home too?' she kisses his cheek and gives him what she hopes is a persuasive hug, before rubbing his nose affectionately with the soggy, wet tea towel.

'Well, I was hoping we could, maybe, talk about it,' he glances through the door to the lounge.

Jack is playing with his favourite toy dinosaur, making gruff noises as he pretends it is flying around the room. Molly is in the bathroom cleaning her teeth, but mostly spitting toothpaste all over the basin, having been promised her pocket money if she does everything without being asked twice.

'Do you think it would be better to discuss it when we are on our own?'

'That depends on whether it could be a "yes"?' Emily holds him tighter.

'Maybe.' He laughs, poking her in the ribs. 'But I don't want to raise their hopes if you then decide to turn me down.'

'Why on earth would I do that?'

'I don't take anything for granted anymore.' Marcus looks her in the eye. 'I thought you would want to talk it through properly, before we make the jump. Make sure we don't leave anything in the way between us that could make things difficult again. I'd rather get it all out in the open once and for all. For good.'

'Me too.' Emily smiles. She hasn't heard Marcus talk like this since before it all went so wrong, so badly. He has obviously put a lot of thought into them getting back together.

'For one thing, I need to know Mitch is definitely off the scene,' Marcus continues.

'Oh, he is. He most definitely is.' Emily looks straight back at him, not wanting to ruin this opportunity.

'What about that weekend? What really happened when you stayed with his mum?'

Emily swallows hard. What does Marcus mean? Has he heard something about Mitch being arrested and just been too polite, or unsure, to say anything?

'Nothing happened, that's just it,' Emily whispers. 'It was all a mistake. I wish I had never gone.'

An awkward silence. Emily doesn't know whether to continue or not. She may end up digging a bigger hole for herself.

Then Marcus steps in. 'Hey, don't be like that. Molly and Jack got to see the Olympic Torch and they loved it.' He gives her a hug. 'It's just what they said yesterday about the ghost person. What was that all about?'

Emily bites her lip. She can't throw away this opportunity or he may never come home for good. She will tell him everything, one more time. She thinks of all the times she got interrupted or something stopped her. This is her chance to make sure he knows everything.

'I honestly don't know who the ghost person was, but it was a really weird afternoon. You know we accidentally let ourselves in, well, when we did, Mitch thought he saw something odd in the bathroom. I don't know what it was because he wouldn't let me look,' Emily explains. 'But whatever it was, he was so worried that when we got to his mother's house, he called the police.'

'The police?'

'Yes. It was the same day the mansion house got broken into, because I saw that in the paper too, so I guess whatever it was Mitch thought he saw, the two things were connected.'

'Did the police find anything?'

'Not that I know of. I haven't spoken to Mitch for ages but I am sure he would have told me if they had.'

'Did Molly and Jack see any of this?'

'No. Nothing. They were upstairs.'

'So, what was so weird about it? Are you worried about the dead guy?'

'Not really. The landlady said it was natural causes, he keeled over while out for a walk. He must have been found a few days later, so I guess it is just an unfortunate coincidence.'

'Oh, at least that's one good thing. Sort of. Not for him I guess.'

'None of this will change things, though, will it?' she rests her head on his shoulder. 'For us, I mean?'

'No, of course not. Why should it? None of it was anything to do with you. It's all just a coincidence, like you say.'

'Jo did tell me Mitch has been helping the police with their enquiries though. Apparently, he knew the missing man from school and spoke to him at the reunion, but so did lots of other people and they've been helping too. I guess it's routine investigation work for them. Plus, he called the police that night and they would need to follow it up properly, they must have set processes to follow.'

'I don't think you should worry yourself about it; there's nothing you can do. You weren't at the reunion, you just happened to be in the area the following week, for one afternoon. If that.'

'I know. I could have done without the joke texts though.' Emily can't think what else to call them. She doesn't find them remotely amusing. 'I mentioned them when we were out for our pizza?'

'God, I'm sorry, I'd forgotten about those – have you had any more?'

'Not for a while. I've had three in total now, I thought it was Mitch winding me up to begin with, thinking he was being funny, only he says they weren't from him.'

'How do you know for sure?'

'I guess I don't, but it isn't his number. I thought if I ignored them, they would go away. The last one was ten days ago so, fingers crossed, they've stopped. It was odd though, whenever I called the number back it was unavailable.'

'Bloody hell, you don't half get yourself into some awkward situations, Em,' Marcus kisses her cheek. 'Look, if you get any more of these texts, you're to tell me straight away, okay?'

'Yes. Promise.' Emily's sense of relief is enormous. Telling Marcus about the texts has immediately made them feel less terrifying. 'But you still mean it, don't you, this doesn't change anything for us?'

'Most definitely not.' Marcus pulls her in with an enormous hug and holds her tight. 'Come on, Mrs Harrison, let's find Molly and Jack and start making tracks. We need to let them know and do some serious planning about me moving back in.'

FRIDAY 20 JULY

LEXIE

Tears stream down her cheeks as Lexie races up the stairs, locks her room and pushes a chair against the door for extra protection, wedging it under the handle so it can't budge. She doesn't want anyone to know where she is. To speak to her. To console her. To do anything. Why had she been so unlucky to end up sharing accommodation with Bev? She is the most conniving, deceitful person she has ever met. She simply can't accept that Lexie's training is going better – much better – than hers, or that she and Anna the coach get on so well.

Lexie had noticed Bev becoming increasingly jealous of the time she and Anna were spending together; only last week Bev repeatedly said that Anna was not giving her enough focus, or enough motivation. "A coach should be equally interested in *all* their athletes" she proclaimed loudly, in front of everyone at the warm-up session, and then followed up with how Anna was "spending too much time with her little favourite" while looking directly at Lexie. When Lexie protested, Bev had waved her pistol in the air at Anna saying "…this is ridiculous. How am I meant to be at my peak performance if you don't actually spend any time coaching me? I demand more attention."

Lexie kicks the wall in anger. It *must* have been Bev who reported her. Who else could it have been? She is such a drama queen. No one else would be that evil, that cruel. To file an official complaint, just one week before the opening ceremony, knowing the Olympic standards committee would be unable to ignore it. It is her way of getting even after Lexie lost her temper with her; that and finding out she had broken the rules to travel home to Devon for the weekend back in May.

Just a few days ago Bev had deliberately taunted her, when they were out in the evening. Taking care so no one else noticed, but more than enough to make it abundantly clear to Lexie that she knew what she had done. Bev had then seen Lexie's hand resting on Anna's thigh under the table and the touchpaper had been lit. Ever since it has been snide comments and gestures. To others they have probably seemed amusing, comical even, but Lexie knows better. Bev has continually insinuated she is only on the team because of her special relationship with the coach.

The final straw was on Tuesday afternoon when Bev arrived home and found Anna with Lexie in her room. It had only been the second time. The first time they just chatted. They had talked for hours about all sorts of stuff and it was the most relaxed Lexie had felt in months. They talked about topics no one else would have found particularly interesting, but they were fascinated with each other. It was so easy. The second time it went further. The attraction between them had been too great; was it the extra thrill of being at the Olympics and the constant and contagious atmosphere of the athletes' village where they were staying, or would it have happened anyway? Lexie isn't entirely sure. All she does know for certain is that it had felt like the most natural thing in the world.

They hadn't heard the front door opening, or Bev walking up the stairs. All of a sudden, she appeared in the doorway holding her mobile phone. Filming them. Laughing and mocking them. Saying Lexie should have known better than to lash out at her the other day. Saying she had evidence of Lexie assaulting her on the way home a few nights earlier and Lexie leaving the athletes' village without permission. That she would have no choice but to report her.

Lexie throws herself down on the bed, shoves her face in her pillow and sobs. She knows she can file an appeal but with so little time left before the games open it will be too late for the paperwork and bureaucracy to be completed. They had thrown the entire code of conduct at her. Inappropriate behaviour towards other team members. Harassment. Bullying.

Then the worst word of all.

Suspension.

That was when her world collapsed around her.

'Suspension pending further investigation,' the woman had said, her jet-black hair pulled tightly back into a knot at the base of her neck and fixed with a scarlet red band. That's all Lexie could focus on as she uttered the dreaded word. The scarlet band, like a red light at a traffic junction. Stop. No entry. You cannot proceed any further.

Then the lady with the red band added, without even looking at her, 'Please report back to the committee for a special hearing on Tuesday 24th July at ten o'clock. You are permitted to bring a representative with you. The relevant papers will be issued and delivered to your accommodation within the next twenty-four hours.'

46

FRIDAY 20 JULY

EMILY

Emily paces up and down, barely able to contain her excitement. Marcus isn't due for another ten minutes and she has surprised herself by being ready early.

She hears laughter in the lounge. Molly and Jack are cosied up in their pyjamas with Helena the babysitter deciding which bedtime story to read. Emily smiles as she watches them and thinks how lucky she is, then tries to move Marcus's bulging suitcase to a more convenient place in the hall. She can barely lift it and puts it back down; he'll have to carry it upstairs himself. They have a busy weekend lined up, moving all his stuff back in.

To kill time and keep herself occupied while she waits, she tidies up the shoes in the hall, matching up the pairs. Her heart misses a beat. She still loves how small their feet are. Not the exquisite tininess of a new born baby's bootee, she has those framed upstairs, but still unbelievably cute. School shoes, sandals, trainers, football boots. How is it possible to have so many pairs at their age?

A car drives past, slowly, towards the top of the cul-de-sac, and she glances through the patterned glass of the door to see if she can work out who it is, even though she instinctively knows it isn't Marcus from the sound of the engine.

Tonight, they are celebrating. Celebrating everything. Getting back together, the start of the school holidays and Emily's birthday, which was actually four weeks ago but, with one thing and another, they haven't had chance to mark the occasion until now. Marcus has booked a trendy, new restaurant on the outskirts of town and they were extremely lucky to get a table. It's been getting rave reviews since the chef was a finalist in a TV competition and she is starting to feel hungry, having deliberately saved her appetite by missing lunch. Emily empties the dishwasher, to pass a few more minutes, and the tempting smell of the children's fish finger tea lingering in the kitchen makes her look forward to their special meal even more. She's told Helena they won't be late back, not that she minds if they are. She's the elder daughter of Sian, her neighbour who runs the book club, and Molly and Jack love her. Normally she brings revision to do once they are in bed but, having just finished her exams, she's in no rush this evening.

Emily hears a car pull up outside. It must be Marcus this time and she absentmindedly checks her reflection in the hallway mirror, adjusting her hair slightly. A habit that she simply can't break. She waits for the front door to open but instead the doorbell rings.

She opens the door, laughing. Marcus always does that, pretending he can't find his key, all the time knowing it is pure laziness really.

Emily jumps back in shock as she finds two stern-faced police officers standing in front of her. 'Oh, please God, no.' Emily can't look at them. 'Not Marcus. Please, please tell me no.'

Immediately fearing the worst, she clasps a hand over her mouth and grabs the doorpost as her legs give way beneath her.

FRIDAY 20 JULY

MITCH

Mitch pushes his pillow to one side and carefully moves his phone to see what time it is, trying not to drop it. His eyes can barely focus and his head is throbbing. Twenty-three minutes past seven. He shuts his eyes again, before realising to his dismay that it is almost half past seven in the evening and he's been in bed all day. An impatient delivery driver toots a horn outside, directly under his window and clearly not appreciating some residents in the neighbourhood may be trying to rest. Mitch pulls the duvet back over his head, wanting to hide from the outside world for as long as he can.

As much as he loves to be with him, he is extremely thankful he hasn't got Olly this weekend. If it had been his turn, he wouldn't have had such a late, or indulgent, Thursday night. But it was fun and just what he needed. The badminton club are a good crowd and, after winning their final doubles match of the season, it seemed perfectly acceptable to celebrate in the traditional manner. Plus, it was the first time since his arrest that he had managed to relax.

He had intended to go into the office today, to catch up on the backlog of work. He lost almost two days at the police station and is seriously behind schedule with two tender documents. Then he remembers his bail conditions. Shit. He'd better be quick. He needs to report to them again today, before nine o'clock. He needs to prove he hasn't left the country or done a runner. The irony makes him wince; the chance would be a fine thing.

Emily hasn't replied to any of his texts either. He's sent three now. Every other day, including last weekend when he first got home after being arrested. His eyes, now more accustomed to the screen, come into focus and he can see the most recent message he sent was on Wednesday. He'll try once more today and, if he hears nothing, he'll just have to accept she isn't going to reply. He admires her stoicism. If it had been the other way round, he wouldn't have been able to resist finding out what it was she wanted to talk about.

Fri 20 Jul 19:43
Me again. We really do need to talk. Please give me a ring.

That should do it. A polite message, it sounds important without alarming her too much. Whether or not she wants to discuss their weekend again, or anything else, Emily needs to know about the questions the police have been asking. He has tried his hardest not to say anything, but what if they find out Emily was there too? She'll need to make sure her story is the same as his.

Determined not to wallow in self-pity, Mitch drags himself down to the kitchen; he makes a large mug of tea with a huge teaspoon of sugar and grabs a couple slices of bread. It's at least two days past the use-by date but if toasted and smothered with butter it will disguise the taste of any mould.

The letter confirming his bail conditions is lying on the kitchen table where he threw it down with his keys. He reads it again, shaking his head, although he knows the details by heart. He must report daily to the station. They are allowed to interview him for up to forty-eight hours without charge, after which they must either release him or apply to the court for an extension. He was there for thirty-two so, technically, they have a further sixteen hours available if they want to call him back. *Yippee, aren't I the lucky one.* He thinks to himself as the bread jumps out the toaster.

He'll ring his mum this evening, otherwise word will get out and she'll be mortified if her neighbours hear before she does. She knows he went voluntarily to the police station in Tavistock to help with their enquiries a few weeks ago, after which she became fiercely protective.

"What on earth will everyone say?" she repeated, multiple times. "Nothing like that ever happens around here and it's all since you brought that… that… what's her name here. Emily. That's it, Emily." Then she continued, "I can't believe I let her into my house. She led you astray, she did. Mark my words, Rodney, you're better off without her. Good riddance if you ask me. All this nonsense with the police, you've had nothing but trouble since you brought her here."

And that was it. Whatever it was that happened that weekend, in his mother's eyes, it was all Emily's fault.

Emily.

He isn't entirely sure what to do about Emily but he hopes she does call him. He doesn't want her making things even worse for him. He checks his phone; it doesn't look like she is online at the moment, she must be busy with the kids. He'll give her a bit longer and see what happens.

48

TUESDAY 15 MAY

THREE DAYS AFTER THE REUNION

Tanya hoists a huge lump of clay onto her workbench, ready to work on some new designs. It weighs a ton and she lets it fall back to the floor with a dull thump. She hasn't been for a run today and she's lost her motivation, still fuming about what happened at the reunion.

Try as she might, she cannot let her anger go. It had been a fantastic evening, surrounded by old faces, until Mitch completely ruined it.

As she arrived, 'A Kind of Magic' had been blasting through the speakers, followed by Mental as Anything singing 'Let's Live it Up' and the lyrics had transported her back to her teenage years. A powerful reminder of all her hopes and dreams. Overcoming her initial shyness, it had been wonderful to just lose herself in the music with everyone else on the dancefloor.

A little while later the instantly recognisable David Bowie's 'Little China Girl' filled the room, one of her all-time favourites. She had sipped her drink, closing her eyes to appreciate the lyrics while she gave her feet a rest from dancing. As she did, she sensed someone watching her and when she opened them again there he was, staring at her, after twenty-five long years. A quarter of a century of adulthood, family, jobs and careers; finding their way in the big, wide world after school and college.

Mitch. They had been such good friends. They had shared everything, although he probably had no idea how much she looked forward to their chats on the school bus, debating anything and everything, encouraging each other with their exams and just messing around like teenagers do. She wonders what he *really* thought of her, way back then. Whether he had enjoyed her company as much as she did his.

Enjoying the cheerful, party vibes of the reunion she had wandered over and tapped him on the arm, just as he slopped beer on his sleeve. It made her laugh. She had been catapulted back in time and the trumpet in ABC's 'The Look of Love' soared above the hubbub of noise as she strained her ears to hear what he was saying before The Communards singing 'Don't Leave Me This Way' ensured the dancers remained dancing. It had been such an amazing surprise to see him again after so long.

She has Heart Radio playing now and she throws the clay around in time to Bon Jovi, taking her anger and frustration out on the sticky mass as it gradually becomes more pliable. How she had loved all the music in the charts back then. She still does. Why had she been so foolish as to let Chas pull her away to the dance floor? With hindsight she knows she wouldn't have been able to stop him, he was too insistent, but she never expected Mitch to retaliate in the way he did. Whatever it was that Mr Dodds said to Mitch it must have really cut him up.

Three days have passed and she is still fuming, her fury growing by the day. She can't get the image of Mitch walking away, or the scorn in his eyes, when he said what he did about her and she tried in vain to reason with him.

Tears of sadness and frustration mixed with despair fall onto her potter's wheel, leaving puddles in the clay as she tries to centre it. But it's no good. Instead, she scrapes it up and wallops it on the work top, again and again and again. How dare he think he can humiliate her in front of everyone.

She has to get her revenge. Retribution for all the years she has lost. The life she lost. The life she dreamt of and could have lived – *should* have lived – but didn't. The life he stole from her. She has never been a malicious or vindictive person but this is different, it doesn't make her bad.

She is the victim in all of this.

She is just getting even.

FRIDAY 20 JULY

EMILY

'Mrs Emily Harrison?' The taller of the two officers is brusque.

'Yes, that's me,' she replies nervously, surprised at their curt tone of voice and still holding herself upright with her hand on the doorpost. 'What's happened? Where is Marcus? Please, tell me, what's happened?'

Both officers look directly at her, then the taller one speaks again. 'Mrs Emily Harrison, I am arresting you on suspicion of perverting the course of justice. You do not have to say anything but it may harm your defence if you do not mention, when questioned, something which you later rely on in court.'

'What?' Emily recoils in absolute horror, falling against the door. 'I have absolutely no idea what you are talking about!'

'What's going on?' Marcus has now arrived and is walking up the drive, his eyes wide open in disbelief.

'Is this some sort of joke?' Emily says, convinced it's not for real.

'Mrs Harrison, we need you to accompany us to the local

police station for questioning and we would appreciate it if you would co-operate.'

'But that's daft. What is this to do with?' Emily replies, running her hands through her hair as her mouth struggles to form the words. 'I haven't done anything. Honestly, I haven't... I... I... didn't do anything... I... I've never done anything. It can't be me!'

'Excuse me, I'm Emily's husband. Will someone please explain what is going on?' asks a bemused Marcus, now standing between Emily and the uninvited guests.

'Mr Harrison, we are arresting your wife on the suspicion of perverting the course of justice and we are taking her in for questioning at Thornbury Police Station,' the female officer explains. 'There we will be joined by officers visiting from Devon and Cornwall Police who have all the details.'

This time it is Marcus who is lost for words. As the officer places her hand in the small of Emily's back and guides her deftly but firmly to the patrol car, they are both sat in the back of the vehicle within seconds and the door shuts with a resounding click. Her colleague starts the engine, looks in the rear-view mirror and pulls away sharply, leaving Marcus completely stunned.

Helena appears in the hallway, having heard the commotion, and the children follow closely behind, looking teary-eyed at their dad.

'What's happening Daddy?' Molly asks, her chin wobbling. 'Where has Mummy gone?'

After a few seconds delay, and as the gravity of the situation becomes clear, Marcus runs down the cul-de-sac, waving his arms after the car and shouting at them to stop.

But it has already disappeared from view.

50 SATURDAY 21 JULY

EMILY

It's one thirty in the morning and Emily sits alone in a police cell, forlorn and broken. She can't even cry. She wants to sob her heart out but the tears won't come.

She balances on the edge of the hard, plastic mattress with her arms wrapped around her body. She is shivering with cold, despite it being the middle of July. The walls and floors are bare and a peculiar, unpleasant smell permeates the very back of her nostrils. She couldn't even guess what it is. Probably a mixture of all sorts of things she would rather not know about.

Perverting the course of justice. What the hell, like she would even know how to. When they offered her a solicitor she immediately said yes, there is no way she is going to attempt to answer their questions on her own. She would only make the situation worse.

That's who they are waiting for now. The duty solicitor. She wonders what the logic was, for bringing her in on a Friday night in the middle of the summer. Surely Saturday morning – or afternoon – would have been more practical? Although it will be Saturday afternoon at this rate if the solicitor doesn't turn up soon.

She can't get Marcus's face out of her mind. She only caught a glimpse as she turned around to look out the rear window of the police car as it sped her away, but his expression said it all.

Disbelief.

Shock.

Rage.

Disappointment.

She feels exactly the same. So many emotions churn inside and her mind jumps from what she needs to do and say to rectify the situation, to what has possessed them to arrest her in the first place.

Is it Mitch? Has he said something? Jo said he had been arrested last week. He must have dropped her in it. Maybe he deliberately said something, because he thought she had done the same to him. Then she remembers, he doesn't know she was questioned at home. Nor does he know that she knows that he was arrested. Emily only found out because Jo told her.

What about the anonymous texts? Maybe it was the person who sent them? Bloody hell, that must be it. They were threatening to say something, they must have contacted the police. Why didn't she try harder to find out who had sent them?

Emily can't think straight. Her entire body aches and she wants nothing more than to lie down and go to sleep. Deep, deep sleep. In the hope it will all be a bad dream when she awakes. Surely Marcus will help? Tell the police she is innocent?

*

Emily has no idea what time it is. Every now and then voices echo along the corridor, shouting orders or calling for someone, but no one has walked past her door for what seems like hours. They've taken all her personal belongings, even the belt from her trousers. The Custody Sergeant thought she might be a suicide risk. Seriously? There's no way she would do that, she is too determined to make sure she is exonerated as soon as she can, when they eventually get around to speaking to her.

Emily cannot think straight. What about Molly and Jack? Has anyone explained to them what's happened to her? Are they sleeping? What will be going through their little minds, having seen their mother carted off in a police car? All she wants is to be back home, hugging her precious children as tight as she can and telling them everything is alright. And the neighbours, what will everyone think?

She looks down at her clothes. She's wearing the gorgeous new blouse she bought especially for their celebratory evening. She runs the silky material between her fingers. It is beautiful. She thought it was perfect when she spotted it, an impulse buy. The perfect top to celebrate the perfect evening; to celebrate Marcus moving back home. The vibrant lilac in the pattern goes perfectly with her white, cropped summer trousers, plus it has a fabulous cut that is both flattering and comfy. Win-win. She doubts she will ever wear it again; it would never have the same appeal.

So much for the perfect evening too. Maybe she and Marcus are simply doomed.

She jolts back to earth as there is a noise at the door. The metal cover concealing the little opening is pulled up and a pair of eyes stare at her. Piercing green-blue eyes. For a moment she thinks her time has come, to be escorted to yet another room for questioning, but then, with a loud clunk, the eyes disappear again.

*

It's early morning and daylight is breaking through the tiny square window high above her head. It must be ten feet off the ground. The powerful rays shoot diagonally across the wall and along the floor in dead-straight lines, the shadows of the security bars forming boxes like a game of noughts and crosses. If only this was a game.

Emily is exhausted and her eyes are sore and dry. She still won't allow herself to lie down; as much as she craves sleep, she knows she couldn't if she tried. Twelve hours earlier she had been excited about their evening out and anticipating a fantastic weekend with Marcus, Molly and Jack. Now she is frightened and alone in a police cell. How wrong she had been.

Suddenly, clattering footsteps make their way along the concrete floor of the corridor; echoing off the bare walls, they get louder and louder and then stop. She hears voices directly outside and holds her breath. Hushed at first, the whispers turn into proper voices, followed by someone talking into a radio and a beep as they end the conversation, then a noisy jingle of what sounds like a huge bunch of keys.

At long last.

She had been desperately waiting for someone to come but now they're here and unlocking her door she is shaking with fear.

51

SATURDAY 21 JULY

EMILY

'Interview commenced at 06:32 hours.' DS Fuller breaks the silence.

Emily confirms her name for the umpteenth time and takes a sip of water from the plastic cup that has been placed in front of her. A large blob of water wobbles on the table where it dripped as the DC put it down. Emily can see the detective's face reflected in it. Distorted and grotesque. Upside down.

'Mrs Emily Harrison, you have been arrested on suspicion of perverting the course of justice and we have a number of questions that we need to ask.' DS Fuller's fingers drum annoyingly on the table. He doesn't seem to notice he is doing it. 'You requested the services of the duty solicitor and Ms Smithson is also present as is DC Piper. Please can you confirm you understand?'

'Yes,' she whispers, nodding her head at the three of them.

'Mrs Harrison. The charge relates to the events of the weekend of Saturday the nineteenth of May this year, when you are known to have been visiting Devon. In particular the property known as the Allington Estate.'

Emily gulps. Like before, she had been secretly hoping it would be about something completely different. Something she definitely didn't have anything to do with, so she could put an end to this nonsense and go home. But it's not. The fateful weekend with Mitch has come back to haunt her, yet again. It's like a boomerang that never goes away. The trouble is, each time it returns, it gets more frightening.

'Some of these questions you will have been asked before, by our colleagues on Monday the ninth of July. However, I must explain that for completeness we will need to ask them again. Firstly, can you confirm that you were indeed visiting the area that weekend?'

'Yes.'

'And did you visit the Allington Estate?'

She hesitates. She is scared. Where is all this leading? Of course, she did. She told the officers that before, when they visited her at home.

Lost in her thoughts the detective prompts her once again. 'We have a witness, a mechanic who remembers assessing your car for a fault on the day in question. He also remembers you saying you were on your way to Allington House.'

Emily shakes her head as she silently recalls the events of the afternoon, before she even arrived at the fateful cottage. The lady at the call centre, who made her cry when she called her Mrs Harrison, then the makeshift picnic with Molly and Jack at the side of the motorway and how she told the chatty mechanic all the details about their weekend plans. She remembers it clearly now; but when she and Mitch had thought through all the possibilities of who else knew they were at the Allington Estate she had completely forgotten. What a mess.

'Mrs Harrison, I will ask you one more time. Did you visit the Allington estate?'

'Yes,' Emily whispers.

'How long did you spend at the Allington Estate?'

She looks at her solicitor for guidance and Ms Smithson gives an almost undetectable tilt of her head, which Emily interprets as "*go ahead*".

'I arrived late afternoon. I had made a reservation to stay at one of the holiday cottages.' Emily takes a sip of water as she considers carefully what to say next, to keep it consistent with the information she provided before. 'As I told your colleagues before, when I first got there, I checked my messages and noticed I had received an email from Lady Allington earlier in the day.'

'Thank you. Indeed, you did. And can you please also remind me what the email said?'

'Lady Allington said she had made a mistake with my reservation.' Emily looks up at the DS, who remains silent, clearly wanting her to continue. 'She had messed up the dates of my booking. Basically, it was telling me it was not possible for me to stay there for the weekend after all.'

'So, what did you do next?'

'A friend of mine, Rodney Mitchell, who was there waiting for me, called his mother and he asked her if we could stay with her instead.'

'I see. And who else was with you?'

'Molly and Jack, my children.'

'Please can you confirm what time you arrived and how long you remained at the Allington Estate?'

'I arrived at about quarter past five. We were all hungry and tired. It was probably about fifteen minutes, twenty at most... not long.' Emily fiddles with the sleeve of her blouse, trying to keep her answers short and to the point.

'What did you do next?'

'I drove to Mrs Mitchell's house. Mitch – Rodney – showed me the way.'

The detective stops to take a sip of water and Ms Smithson momentarily puts her pen down. Emily's hands are clammy and she has a sense of dread as DS Fuller leans back in his chair with a look of doubt in his eye. 'The thing is Mrs Harrison, what is concerning me is that I'm not entirely sure your answers tie up with other information we have been given.'

Again, he pauses and Emily can sense they are all watching her closely, to see how she reacts.

'You see, we've checked your mobile phone records and they suggest you were at the property for a significantly longer period of time.'

'What do you mean?'

'They show you arriving at nine minutes past five in the afternoon and leaving at three minutes to nine in the evening.' The detective smirks at her before continuing. 'That means you were at the Allington Estate for almost four hours, not the "twenty minutes at most" you have told us.' He leans back in his chair, now definitely smug. 'In fact, Mrs Harrison, not only do we have reason to believe you were there for almost four hours, you were actually *inside* the building known as The Cowshed. The co-ordinates provided by your mobile phone service provider are extremely precise.'

52

SATURDAY 21 JULY

EMILY

'I am requesting a five-minute break for my client.' Ms Smithson utters her first words in a broad Irish accent, interrupting the silence and taking Emily by surprise, given her manner until now had been verging on perfunctory.

'Interviewed adjourned at 07:24 hours,' DS Fuller replies.

Emily holds her head in her hands. She is under oath. She needs to explain herself clearly, before her already desperate situation gets worse.

Now it makes sense. Perverting the course of justice. They evidently think she was in The Cowshed for the *whole* time her phone was there. When something else, a very sinister something else, was happening, of which she knows nothing.

Think. Think. Think. She tells herself, screwing her eyes shut to help her thought process and block out any distractions.

*

'Interview recommencing at 07:30 hours', announces the detective and Emily summons up the courage to open her eyes. 'Mrs Harrison, I am extremely concerned that you are not telling me the whole truth about what happened.'

Emily hangs her head in shame.

'Please can I ask you one more time to let me know *exactly* what happened after you arrived at the Allington Estate on Saturday the nineteenth of May of this year. In particular, what you did, where you were and who you were with, between 16:00 hours and 21:00 hours.'

Ms Smithson nods in her direction and Emily clears her throat, then takes a deep breath. She must tell them everything, it doesn't matter that she promised Mitch she would keep quiet, she has too much to lose. As she silently collects her thoughts Ms Smithson nods at her once more.

'What I previously told your colleagues was correct. I'm sorry. What I mean to say is, I did arrive at The Cowshed for a weekend with my children, but it was only after I arrived that I read the email from Lady Allington saying my booking was not possible.' Emily takes another sip of water to soothe her dry mouth. 'What I omitted to say before was that I was already inside the property by the time I read the email.'

'I see, please continue.'

'When we opened the safe on the wall there was no key. I was desperate to get inside after our long journey…' Emily stares at the table top. There are now three drops of water. Three grotesque, distorted, upside down faces. '… I started to panic and couldn't understand why the key wasn't there. I was worried about Molly and Jack too; they were tired and hungry. Mitch and I searched everywhere for a key but couldn't find one, that was when I pulled at the patio door, just in case.'

'Just in case what?'

'Just in case it was open,' Emily confirms. 'I didn't expect it to be but, when I pulled it, the door slid open.'

'Please continue.'

'So, I let myself in. I didn't think I was doing anything

wrong.' Emily looks at the detective as she clarifies. 'I had paid to stay there and, at that point in time, I had not yet read her message saying otherwise.'

'What did you do after entering the property?'

'I sat down to check my messages. I thought maybe Lady Allington had provided further details about where to find the key. It was only then that I saw her email from earlier in the day, cancelling my booking.' Emily shuffles in her seat, her legs feel numb. 'By now I was frantic and I was also desperate to use the bathroom.'

'Mrs Harrison, please can you confirm whether anyone else entered the building with you?'

'Yes. Mitch – Rodney Mitchell – entered the property with me. And my two children.'

'And how long were the four of you inside the building?'

'I would say ten minutes actually inside, maybe less.'

'Did you do anything else whilst in the building?'

'I sat down on the armchair to check my phone, that's when I read the email. Mitch had a quick look around; it was such a lovely holiday home, everything looked and smelt brand new.' Emily shuts her eyes again; she has to tell them what happened next. 'Like I said – after I read the message – he said he would call his mum and, while he was on the phone, I decided to use the bathroom as I couldn't wait any longer. When I returned to the lounge Mitch was acting really strange and said we needed to leave, urgently.'

'Why was he in such a rush all of a sudden?'

'I'm not sure. He said he had seen something odd in the bathroom.'

'What do you mean "odd", what did he see?'

'I really don't know. He wouldn't let me look but I told him that if he was *that* worried, he should call the police.'

'It must have been something pretty important if it was necessary to call 999?'

'Like I said, I don't know. I honestly didn't see anything myself.'

'Mrs Harrison, please can you elaborate and tell us what it was your friend Mr Rodney Mitchell saw, or thinks he saw?'

Emily shivers. What does she do? She can't lie. She needs to gain their trust if she wants them to let her go.

'Mrs Harrison?'

'A... body,' Emily whispers. 'Although I'm sure he imagined it. Either way he promised he would call the police when we got to his mum's house. I honestly didn't see anything. All I know is that he said we needed to get out urgently and he started pushing me and the children towards the door.'

All three of them look straight at her as Emily realises the naivety of what she has said.

After a deathly silence the DS articulates what they are all thinking.

'So, let me clarify, Mrs Harrison. You let yourself into a building where, strictly speaking, you shouldn't have been and without a key.'

He pauses for effect.

'You then treat the property as if it were your own; you wander around checking drawers and cupboards and then you even use the bathroom.' He stops again and rubs his chin. 'Then... and this is what I really don't understand... the friend you are with says he has seen a *dead* body and – instead of calling the emergency services or doing anything to help – you just calmly walk out the door?'

53

SATURDAY 21 JULY

EMILY

'No. It wasn't calm, far from it. Mitch pushed me. He literally shoved me out the door and I grabbed Molly and Jack and put them in the car.'

Emily is shaking all over and can't look at them. She feels ashamed of her actions and, staring at the floor, tries to explain.

'Can't you see, I had no idea what was going on. *No* idea. At that point in time, he hadn't told me it was a body, he just told me we needed to get out. He was insistent. He didn't tell me until much later what he thought he saw… when… when we were on our way to his mum's house. That's when I told him he must call the police. He promised me he would.'

'So, if you left the premises, why does your phone record say you were there for almost four hours?'

'I accidentally left my phone there.' Emily can't hold it together any longer. Tears roll down her cheeks, dripping off the bottom of her chin. 'We went to his mum's house; she gave us a cup of tea and while she and I were chatting Mitch went into the kitchen to make the phone call. He said they – the police – had told him they had it all in hand and would deal with it as soon as they could.'

'That was it?'

'Yes, he said it was all sorted. He said they had been really helpful and there wasn't anything else he, or I, could do. Later on, when Mitch went to meet some friends, his mum kindly offered to look after Molly and Jack, so I agreed to join him, just for a little while.'

Emily takes a deep breath.

'The thing is, when I went to phone him to say I was on my way, I couldn't find my mobile. That was when I realised, to my horror, I had left it at The Cowshed.'

'So, what did you do next?' The DC passes her a tissue.

Emily gently holds it against her tired, sore eyes to soak up the tears. Her chin wobbles as she recounts the events of the evening. 'I... I went back on my own... I kept getting lost. I didn't have a clue where I was.'

'What time would you say this was?'

'About quarter past eight, maybe half past. The light was fading but it wasn't completely dark. I was terrified but, equally, I *had* to get my phone back. The trouble was, I thought the patio door would still be open and I would be able to grab it and go.' The tears that had temporarily stopped start flowing again. 'But the stupid door was locked. I shook it and shook it, as hard as I could, but it wouldn't budge.'

'So how did you get in?' DS Fuller asks as Emily falters.

'I sat outside for a bit. Completely exhausted. Then, as a last resort, I tried the code for the safe again and this time there was a key. I was totally gobsmacked. I couldn't understand why – or how – it was in there when it definitely hadn't been before.'

Emily stops to take another sip of water. She's almost told them everything. Perhaps they'll stop asking questions soon.

'Please continue Mrs Harrison.'

'I was frightened to death; I really didn't want to be there, so I ran in to get my phone – which had fallen down the side of the armchair – and left as quickly as I could.'

'Given your companion thought he had seen a *dead* body in the bathroom earlier in the day, did it not cross your mind to look in there?'

'That's the thing, there was nothing there. Absolutely nothing. That was when I assumed he must have imagined it. He was badly hungover from the night before.'

'Were there any signs at all that anything untoward had taken place?'

'No, nothing. The whole place was spotless. Again, that's another reason why I assumed he must have imagined it.'

'What time did you leave?'

'About five to nine, I guess. That's why the phone records say it was there for all that time. I am really sorry I didn't mention going back to The Cowshed when your colleagues visited me, but it wasn't a question I was asked so I had no reason to think it was important.'

'Did you see anyone else on your second visit?' DS Fuller doesn't acknowledge her apology.

'When I first got there, there was a van parked outside the mansion house, it had a ladder tied to the roof, but I didn't see anyone driving it, so other than that, no. The Cowshed was deserted and in darkness. I thought I heard a noise at one point, when I was outside, but it must have been a squirrel or something.'

'And what did you do next, after leaving the property?'

'I drove to the pub – The Moody Ram – to join Mitch and his friends for a drink. It was packed with people enjoying the football match so I squeezed in next to them. I didn't talk much. I was too badly shaken up by everything.'

'Mrs Harrison, thank you for sharing in more detail the events of the date in question. I do, however, have a few more questions that are important to ask.' DS Fuller leans back in his chair and looks kindly at Emily without actually smiling.

Emily nods in response, her chin is still quivering and she fiddles nervously with the sleeve of her blouse, running the material between her fingers.

'What time would you say Rodney Mitchell left his mother's house to meet his friends?'

'I can't remember exactly. I was bathing Molly and Jack. It must have been about half past six.'

'So, you can't account *fully* for his whereabouts between the hours of 18:30 and approximately 21:00 hours when you joined him at the pub?'

'Uh...' Emily thinks what to say.

'Mrs Harrison?'

'No... no... I can't.'

'It's just that we don't have any record of Mr Mitchell calling the police that evening but we *do* have CCTV images that captured what looks like your car travelling past the golf club towards the Allington Estate, and back again, *at least* three times that afternoon and evening.'

Emily flounders. Is that what this is all about? She has been so intent on remembering her own actions that day she hadn't thought about what Mitch had been doing when he was meant to be at the pub. Surely, he didn't go back to The Cowshed as well? No, he couldn't have. They must be mistaken, they must have a record of his telephone call to the police and anyway, she had the car, it was parked outside Yvonne's house. He said he was walking to The Moody Ram.

54

TUESDAY 24 JULY

LEXIE

'Please, take a seat.' The suited lady with red painted nails smiles politely at Lexie and points to a row of chairs in the corridor, their backs pushed up against the wall to leave as much room as possible to walk past. 'The chairman will be with you shortly.'

'Thank you,' Lexie replies demurely as she follows the instruction and the lady disappears behind a solid oak door.

Ten minutes later, she is still waiting. A further twenty minutes pass and she is irritated. The letter had clearly stated the meeting would start promptly at ten o'clock and she had arrived in plenty of time, yet it is acceptable for the board to keep her waiting. Is it part of her punishment?

*

Forty-five minutes later, Lexie sits in front of the poker-faced committee in the middle of the room and stares at the polished wooden floor; she can't stop her right heel bobbing up and down.

'And so it is with deep regret that I hereby inform you, Miss Alexandria Henrietta Williamson, that your position in the 2012 Team GB Modern Pentathlon squad is terminated with immediate effect as of today, Tuesday the twenty fourth of July, at eleven hundred hours.'

The grey haired, bespectacled gentleman peers over his wide rimmed glasses to look Lexie in the eye without any hint of emotion.

'In the interests of the other members of the squad, and for your own privacy, you will be transferred to alternative accommodation within the Olympic Park to organise any necessary travel arrangements and given three days to make your departure.'

FRIDAY 27 JULY

TANYA

The joy of long summer evenings. Tanya has managed to squeeze in a couple hours pottering around in her studio after yet another busy day in the gallery. Sales have been going well, she needs to replenish her stock and is deciding which new pieces to display.

Cleo vies for attention as Tanya collects her post off the mat and she simultaneously picks up the letters and the cat as Cleo purrs approval, nestling into her clay-smeared apron. Tanya's heart sinks. An electricity bill and another handwritten envelope from Lady Allington.

She opens the latter, not certain she wants to read it. She has been pushing her luck, deliberately ignoring the request to move her stand upstairs. Lady Allington visited the gallery today and, knowing she would never make a scene in front of customers, Tanya just smiled when Lady Allington made a polite, but barbed, comment about "that little matter we discussed the other day" followed by "I'll be in touch" and carried on walking past.

Dear Tanya,

It pains me to write again regarding this matter, but further to my letter of last week I am writing to insist you move your stand at the craft gallery, as requested, to Pitch 31 with immediate effect. If this is not done, I will make the necessary arrangements for all your stock to be packed into crates for you to collect when convenient. I know this is a terrible disappointment for you but I have already explained the reasons why and wish you every possible success for the season.

Thank you as always for your support.

Yours faithfully,
Lady Henrietta Allington-Thorpe

WEDNESDAY 25 JULY

EMILY

The kitchen window is a sinister, black rectangle.

It's the middle of the night and Emily can't sleep. Gazing into the void, she sees a disturbing flash of light and her reflexes automatically kick in. Someone must be out there. She ducks down behind the draining board and, in her sleepy stupor, her brain is awash with possibilities.

Bloody hell. It can't be. The person who sent the texts. They've tracked her down. They're in the garden, spying on her. Watching her. They're coming for her. They're going to make her pay, like they said they would.

She scared stiff; biting on her fist, she panics. What will she do if the intruder smashes through the back door? What if they have a knife… or a gun? The children are upstairs, so is Marcus. She opens her mouth to call out, to get Marcus's attention; but nothing comes out.

*

The house is silent, apart from the odd, mysterious creak. All she can hear is her own heart beating rapidly and blood pumping noisily in her ears, swooshing around her head.

After what seems an age, she risks opening her eyes. There are deep teeth marks on her hand and the electronic clock on the microwave says it's half past three; she's been crouching under the worktop for thirty minutes.

Her throat tightens as she sees another flash, reflected in the glass of the eye-level oven door. Then another flash, and another, and another.

She looks again, screwing up her eyes to get a better view. The light is not moving any closer, just rocking side to side.

Feeling a little more courageous, she peeks above the edge of the sink and then falls back on the cold tiled floor with a jolt, laughing hysterically as she realises it is the bird feeder she put in the cherry tree with Molly and Jack, a Christmas present from her sister. It's swinging in the breeze, catching the distant illumination from a street light.

Relieved but still shaking, Emily catches sight of her ghastly reflection in the window as she pulls herself back up. She looks awful. Haggard, pale and tired. She adjusts her dressing gown, pulling it tightly around her waist before retying the belt with a double knot to keep it in place. It's always been too big but, since being arrested last weekend, she has lost so much weight it now looks even more ridiculous.

*

'Jesus, Em. What are you doing? It's four o'clock in the morning.' Marcus puts his head around the door, yawning. 'You'll wake the kids.'

'I couldn't sleep… and… and I thought there was someone in the garden.'

'What do you mean, someone in the garden?'

'I thought they'd come for me…'

'Who?'

'The person who's been sending the texts.'

'Emily, stop it. There's no one coming after you. The police let you go. It's all over,' he tries to reassure her, giving her a hug to stop her shaking.

'But it's so wrong, Marcus. I thought perverting the course of justice was when you do something *deliberately* bad. I honestly didn't do anything.'

There's another creak from upstairs as Marcus pulls his chair to the table, directly opposite where Emily is now sat. He takes both her hands, gently in his.

'It's okay,' he whispers. 'It's only Jack stirring, he'll turn over and drop off to sleep again. He does it all the time.'

'I need your help, Marcus,' she pleads. 'Please. I need your help to clear my name.'

'But they let you go, Em,' he says again, trying to reassure her. 'There's nothing to clear. You haven't done anything wrong.'

'What if the police change their mind? Take me in for questioning again?'

'Why would they?'

'They might still think I know something… and our neighbours, they saw me taken away. What must they think?' Emily's eyes well up and a tear falls silently onto the table between them. 'I dread to think what stories they are making up.'

'Well, let them, Em.' He squeezes her hands even tighter. 'Let them gossip if that's what they want to do. I know you didn't do anything. The police know you didn't do anything.'

'Do you *really* think so?'

'Look, Em, they wouldn't have let you go without a charge if they thought you had. It'll all blow over, trust me. You just need to give it time.'

'I suppose so.' She nods.

*

They sit in silence for a while, as Emily's mind continues to spin.

'What about us? Are you sure you still want to move back in?'

'Well, last weekend wasn't exactly the celebration we had planned, but we'll just have to work our way through it.' Marcus avoids answering the question as he stands up and looks the other way.

'Something did happen though,' Emily whispers, to his back.

'What do you mean?'

'Something *did* happen. That weekend.'

'For God's sake Emily, make up your mind. Did something happen or not?' Marcus spins round.

'I think that is what this is all about.' Emily's voice is weak. 'It's just... *I* don't know what... but somebody, somewhere does. That's why I got the texts.' She takes a deep breath. 'I wasn't involved but, whatever it was that happened, it happened when I was there.'

Marcus turns his back to her once again. The day is breaking; the window now granite grey, rather than black, and Emily catches sight of his puzzled look reflected in the glass. She can tell he is as confused as she is.

'Oh god, Marcus. I've just realised. I never told the police about the texts. When they started asking me loads of questions about Mitch, they completely slipped my mind. They were so busy asking where he was, what he did, could I account for his whereabouts and everything else that I totally forgot.'

Marcus frowns. Deep furrows are etched on his forehead as he wonders how to reply. With a long, deep sigh he rests both hands on the edge of the sink, unable to look at Emily. 'I don't know why you got yourself involved with Mitch.'

Emily shivers. It might be summer but she is stiff and cold. She wraps her hands in the fluffy material of her dressing gown to keep them warm.

'I know. I wish I hadn't too. I'm so, so sorry. Sorry any of this happened, and even more sorry I'm putting you through all this.'

*

After an almost unbearable silence Marcus ruffles his hair and heads towards the lounge.

Emily grabs his arm to pull him back. 'Honestly, I'm sorry.'

Marcus shakes her arm off his. 'It's alright Em, I just need time. I know it's nothing to do with you. Somehow, you were in the wrong place at the wrong time with the wrong person. I'm just trying to get my head around it.'

'I need your help to clear my name, Marcus. I know you aren't Mitch's greatest fan but I need, somehow, to find out exactly what did happen that afternoon at the cottage.'

Marcus still won't look at her. She can tell he is deep in concentration, taking in every word she is saying.

'You know I told you he thought he saw something odd in the bathroom? Well, I'm sure he imagined it, but he said he thought he saw a body.'

'WHAT?!'

'I'm sorry.'

'Sorry?! Bloody hell, Emily. Why didn't you say so before?'

'Because I didn't see anything myself, and because he didn't tell me straight away.'

'So, when did he?'

'On the way to his mum's house. I insisted he call the police, and he told me he had.'

'When?'

'At his mum's. He said they were on their way, that they

would deal with it. The thing is, when I went back to get my phone, there was absolutely nothing there, the whole place was empty. No body. Nothing. That's why I was convinced he imagined it and I didn't say anything to you before.'

Emily wonders briefly if anybody else in their cul-de-sac is having a similar conversation, about imaginary dead bodies, as they get ready for work.

'You honestly think so?'

'He must have, because there is no other logical explanation. But it was really weird; when the police were questioning me, it felt like they were more interested in what Mitch did that day, not me.'

'Why?'

'I don't know. Perhaps he knows something that I don't. Looking back, I wish I had quizzed him harder on what it was he thought he saw.'

'Why?' Marcus throws his arms up in exasperation. 'Why would he say something like that if it wasn't for real?'

'I don't know. I think he was so badly hungover from the night before he wasn't thinking – or seeing – straight.' Emily holds her head in her hands. 'I know I panicked after I found my phone, I was frightened. But there definitely wasn't anything there. Absolutely nothing. The whole place was spotless.'

'Are you certain?'

'Absolutely. One hundred per cent.'

'Was there anyone else around?'

'Not a soul. I got away as fast as I could and went to the pub – the one we went to the other day. It was crazy, packed to the rafters with people watching the football match. I just sat there like a zombie.'

'What did Mitch say when you told him?'

'That's just it, I didn't. He doesn't know I went back…'

'Mum! Dad!' Jack suddenly appears at the kitchen door, clasping his blue blanket and sucking his thumb.

Marcus yawns again. He looks as tired as she feels, with huge, grey bags under his eyes. Emily pulls Jack in for a cuddle and watches Marcus pretend to check their wall planner, rubbing his forehead as if working out what he wants to say or do next. It's annotated with scribbled notes and their childcare plans for the summer holidays.

She can't let him walk away now, she needs to continue this conversation, not leave anything unsaid.

'Hey, Jack, how about you go and get yourself dressed and then we'll have something special for breakfast once Molly is up? Summer camp doesn't start until eight thirty so we've got plenty of time.'

Her incentive does the trick and Jack playfully drags his blue blanket back up the stairs, calling for his sister.

'It's the twenty-fifth of July today,' Marcus announces still staring at the calendar. 'Five months to Christmas.'

Too late.

Emily knows he is deliberately changing the subject; he is frustrated and angry for being thrown head-first into another crazy situation, all because of her. She prays silently that Marcus won't give up on her. That their exciting plans for the summer won't crash and burn before they have even started.

She needs his help more than ever but, as Marcus walks away, Emily can't help wonder what's in store for them between now and Christmas.

57

FRIDAY 27 JULY

LEXIE

Lexie leans against the window of the train, staring through the filthy glass at the passengers rushing up and down the platform. Some drag oversized luggage while others frown intently at the electronic departures board.

She strains to hear the announcements from the public address system over the deafening noise of the trains as they power in and out the station whilst fascinated by a young lady, much her own age, with twin toddlers in tow. The young mum collapses an enormous pushchair in one swift movement, sweeps them up in another and jumps on board. A faultless, choreographed routine, no doubt performed hundreds of times.

Lexie shuffles further into her seat as a bearded man, clasping a half-eaten pasty in his puffy hand, lands heavily next to her while talking loudly on his mobile phone and spraying particles of pastry in her direction. She immediately brushes them off her sleeve.

'Sorry,' he says, only to spray some more.

Lexie was hoping to have a quiet journey, but her aspirations are fading fast. It's the second time in as many months that she is making her way back to Allington House without her grandmother knowing. Only this time she does know for certain where her dear Grammie is and that she won't be there to greet her. She's in London to watch the opening ceremony of the Olympic Games. The one that she is so proud to be a part of. The one that her only granddaughter is taking part in.

Lexie shuts her eyes and wishes she could go back and live the last three months again. She would do it all so differently, if only she could. She has no idea what to tell her Grammie, or how, or when. She is going to be extremely disappointed in her when she finds out what has happened.

At least she has a spare key this time; she found one in her grandmother's study on her last visit so won't need to break in. She'll let her Grammie enjoy the ceremony this evening with her parents and wait for her to return to Allington House. There will be tens of thousands of athletes in the parade and she will never know Lexie isn't among them, she will just assume she is. Plus, her grandmother knows the athletes aren't permitted to mix with spectators once the games have started – not until their events are over – so she isn't expecting to meet up with her tonight, or over the weekend, which buys Lexie a bit of time.

The conductor's shrill whistle permeates her thoughts and she returns to reality with a jolt as the train judders into action. The engine roars and it slowly pulls away, leaving the hubbub and commotion of the station far behind.

The man sitting next to her, having now finished his pasty, screws up the greasy paper bag and tosses it on to the table in front of her. It rolls to the corner, wedged between Lexie's book and the wall of the carriage, its trajectory deflected by another passenger's handbag. He then slurps noisily as he starts drinking his coffee, the polystyrene cup squeaking in his fingers with the vibrations of the carriage.

Lexie is intrigued by the scrunched-up ball of paper. It gradually unfurls with ad hoc, jerky movements as it spontaneously stretches open.

That's me, she thinks to herself. *Defiant. I'm not going to be shoved into a corner, to be discarded like garbage. I'm going to bounce right back and show the world what I'm made of.*

58

FRIDAY 27 JULY

DI SANDS

'Fuller, come take a look. These two reports are *extremely* interesting,' exclaims DI Sands, throwing them on the desk with a grin. 'See what you make of them.'

DS Fuller picks up the first file and reads the contents slowly, to be certain he has interpreted them correctly. 'So, the Mrs Emily Harrison that we arrested and interviewed was also involved in a missing girl case in Cornwall two years ago?'

'Yep. One and the same. Bit mysterious don't you think?'

'Hmmm… there was definitely something about her that I couldn't work out. We'd better check it out, see if there's a history.' DS Fuller picks up the second report, mouthing the words as he absorbs the information.

DI Sands continues to explain as he reads. 'That one's even more intriguing. Think we may need to look a lot more closely at what's been going on.'

'Well, well,' he clarifies, '…forensics are saying the DNA from the blood sample on the broken window at Allington Mansion matches the DNA of the dead guy?'

'No, not a perfect match, but enough of a match to be a close family member.'

'Uh?'

'Exactly. The dead teacher doesn't have any next of kin *per se*. Just an ex-wife who doesn't seem to want much to do with him and a brother who lives in Australia with his wife and son, none of whom have visited the U.K. for well over five years. No kids. No parents – well, none still alive.'

'Perhaps he was adopted and there are blood relations somewhere?'

'Could be, but seems highly improbable. We must be missing something; I just don't know what.'

'What do you mean?'

'Well, it can't just be a coincidence. I mean, someone with a partial DNA match to the dead guy appears to have broken into the mansion just yards from where he was found?' She looks up at him. 'We need to give Lady Allington a ring, let her know. She's been frustrated at the lack of progress and will be pleased we've made some headway, even if we don't have all the answers yet.'

59

SATURDAY 28 JULY

EMILY

Emily checks the foils in her hair. Marcus has taken Molly and Jack to the park and she is enjoying the light-hearted atmosphere in the salon while she has a couple of hours to herself. It is the first time she has relaxed for a week.

It almost feels normal. With hindsight, she wishes she had brought her book to read while the highlighting lotion works its magic; she could have finished it before she goes to her first book club meeting with Sian and she's already exhausted the pile of magazines. They've had the same editions for as long as she can remember and what had been hot, celebrity gossip three years ago is now old news.

She picks up a local paper instead, the *Thornbury Gazette*, and flicks through the pages; an article about the newly installed one-way zone in the town centre and details of "What's On" at the town hall are the main focus, including an art club and a local ramblers' get together. A short paragraph grabs her attention and she clasps her hand over her mouth. The neighbourhood policing team's weekly update. In between various court appearances for shoplifting and speeding fines there's a brief sentence: *"Thornbury resident Mrs Emily Harrison was recently arrested and questioned by police as part of their inquiries into an ongoing investigation relating to a serious incident in Devon in May."*

She is stunned. It's completely wrong. The report doesn't mention she was released without charge, or anything positive. A wave of nausea rises in her throat and Emily swallows hard to get rid of it. Looking around to check no-one is watching she surreptitiously tears the page out of the paper, folds it up, and puts it in her handbag. At least no one else in the salon will read it.

Emily can't believe it. Goodness knows how many people will read the article and be misinformed. Everyone will think she has done something terrible. Something criminal.

Distraught, she attempts to distract herself by checking her phone and is shocked to see four unread messages from Mitch. The nauseous feeling in her throat gets worse. She remembers the text that arrived on the Saturday evening when she and Marcus were at The Piggery – and which she had deliberately ignored – but had completely missed the others.

Sat 14 Jul 22:05
Need to talk. When r u free?

Mon 16 Jul 14:16
Really need to talk. Give me a ring.

Wed 18 Jul 11:29
Still need to talk. Please call.

Fri 20 Jul 19:43
Me again. We really do need to talk. Please give me a ring.

Emily's heart races; the most recent one was a week ago, sent at the very same moment she was being arrested by the police. Would they have seen the message from Mitch when they confiscated all her personal belongings last weekend? Would they have checked her phone and known he was in contact with her?

What is she going to do. Half of her wants to call him, to find out exactly what has been going on. The other half wants to delete every single message and pretend he never existed. Erase him from her phone *and* her life. Forever.

Then she remembers the other texts.

On the spur of the moment, she calls the number again, to see if anyone answers. She might catch them off guard. Surprised when it rings, she holds it close to her ear to block out the noise of the hairdryers which are making it difficult to hear.

'…hello?' answers a familiar female voice.

'Yvonne? Is that you, Yvonne?'

'Who is this? Why are you calling me?'

'It's Emily. I met you a couple of months ago.' Emily can't think what else to say.

'Oh, you don't need to explain, I know who you are alright. You're the bitch who has been messing things up for my son.'

'What do you mean? Messing things up?'

'Where do I start. How about ruining his life? I don't know what you did that weekend but what I *do* know is that you were there. Oh yes, little miss butter-wouldn't-melt-in-my-mouth, I know you were there… in that bloody cottage.'

Emily hears her inhale.

'…and that's when everything kicked off. Rodney told me, after someone I know saw him at the police station. He told me he had nothing to do with it, *nothing*. And now he's in trouble. Big trouble. All because of you and you don't give a shit.'

'But that's crazy! I think you will find it is completely

the other way around, Mrs Mitchell.' Emily wants to shout but can't in front of all the other customers, she hisses her contempt into the phone instead. 'It's actually *my* life that has been ruined since your oh-so-perfect son Rodney decided to mess things up for *me*.'

'Well, perhaps you had better get yourself up to date on what's been happening around here before you go around making accusations. The whole town has been speculating about my Rodney and I'm not going to let you get away with it. Mark my words, you're going to pay for what you did. I am going to tell them everything. *Everything*.'

Confused and upset, Emily ends the call.

'You alright love?' asks her hairdresser, unwrapping one of the silver foil parcels on her head. 'Five more minutes and you should be done.'

60

SUNDAY 29 JULY

EMILY

Emily's worst fears are coming true. Every time the doorbell rings, she gets scared. Every time her phone rings, she gets scared. Every time she receives a text, she gets scared.

'Why the hell did you get involved with that stupid idiot?' Marcus had shouted at her when she told him it was Mitch's mother who had sent the texts. Then, before he had finished – and with immaculate timing – a friend phoned Marcus to say he had spotted Emily's name in the local paper and was it *his* Emily or someone else with the same name?

This morning, after a sombre breakfast, she sits alone, contemplating. Marcus has taken Molly and Jack to the park, yet again, to "give Emily some space". Although she is grateful for some peace and quiet, in reality she knows it is his own "space" he is searching for.

'Are you sure you've told me everything?' he asked before they left. 'How can we ever fully reconcile if you keep things from me?'

'But I have Marcus, don't you see? I can't tell you *everything* because I'm not the person who knows *everything* about what happened that day. I've been innocently caught up in the middle of something, simply through being in the wrong place, at the wrong time.'

He had turned his back on her as she begged him to understand.

'I'm sorry, Marcus, but I'm terrified. Someone, somewhere, knows what happened, but I've no idea who they are. I wish I did. I'd do anything to find out who they are, so I can sort it all out.'

It's a never-ending circle. She's told him that she mistakenly went inside the holiday cottage, before finding out her reservation had been cancelled. She's told him what Mitch thinks he saw. She's told him she went back on her own to retrieve her phone and there was nothing there. She's told him about the missing man. She's told him about the body on the footpath. She's told him the police identified the dead man as a retired teacher who went to the reunion. She's told him about the texts.

In summary, there is absolutely nothing left to tell him. Except Marcus will always think there is. That she is hiding something. That she must have done something. That she must have seen something. That it can't all be a coincidence.

That she's lying.

She opens a letter that had been on the doormat when Marcus left with the children.

Dear Emily,

I am sorry to have to write this, however, having spoken with the others in our book club we have decided that it would be better if, for the time being, you didn't attend. I know you were looking forward to your first meeting next week, but two of our long-standing members have expressed deep concern and are worried your presence may impact the dynamics of the group.

I am sure you understand, this is just until things have calmed down again.

All the best,
Sian

Emily is devastated. She collapses in a heap on the floor and sobs her heart out. Not only is Marcus having second thoughts, she is losing all her friends. How can people be so cruel over something she didn't do?

She is desperate. She needs to completely clear her name *and* save her marriage and that means only one thing.

She has no choice but to find out what really did happen at The Cowshed.

*

Emily calls Mitch. Now is the perfect opportunity, while Marcus is out with the children. It's her starting point. To find out if there is something – anything – that will enable her to make sense about that weekend. She needs to know. She MUST know. However insignificant or trivial or upsetting or frightening it might be. Then, and only then, can she extract herself from this terrible chain of events. None of which has anything, whatsoever, to do with her.

'Took your time, didn't you? I've been messaging and messaging. What kept you?' Mitch is short-tempered, answering his phone before Emily even hears it ring.

'I've been busy, that's what.' Emily replies, determined not to rise to the bait. 'Anyway, I think it's you who owes *me* an explanation. What's going on, Mitch?'

She hears a grunt, followed by silence. 'I'm sorry Emily,' he eventually offers, speaking more gently. 'The last few weeks have been a bit crap, haven't they.'

'To put it mildly. I'm sorry too. Sorry Jo ever introduced us, sorry I went to Devon that weekend and sorry you've got me caught up in this bloody mess!' Emily screams at him. 'I get the distinct impression you know a lot more about what happened than you're letting on, Rodney Mitchell, so if you could do the decent thing and enlighten me, I would very much appreciate it.'

Silence. She knows he is still there but the line has gone deathly quiet.

'I think it all started at the reunion, the week before.'

'You don't say.'

'Stop being so bloody sarcastic Emily. If you want me to tell you what happened, just shut the fuck up and let me explain.'

Emily bites her tongue. The last thing she wants is to rile him. If he stops talking, she doubts he will ever co-operate again.

'The reunion wasn't what I expected.' Mitch starts to speak after another prolonged silence; his words are slow and considered. Emily says nothing, she can sense he is working out what to say next. 'It started off all right…' Mitch sighs and there's a noise in the background; a teaspoon scraping against the side of a mug followed by a metallic chink as he throws it in the kitchen sink. '… it was great seeing everyone again, it's just it seemed to all go very wrong, very quickly.'

'What happened?'

'It's difficult to explain.' There's another deep, painful sigh. 'It's weird, isn't it, meeting up after such a long time. Some faces were familiar, some I didn't even recognise, or they me. Then a girl called Tanya turned up. I wasn't expecting her to be there, I thought she had moved away a long time ago.'

'Then what?' Emily takes a sip of her tepid coffee. It was hot when she called, but she doesn't want to rush him.

'Well, anyway, Tanya showed up, we got talking and it was just like old times,' he continues. 'We used to share homework and chat on the bus. We got on really well. God, Emily, I'm sorry, I'm rambling now.'

'No, carry on, it's fine.'

'If I'm honest, I had a bit of a soft spot for her, but she was always more interested in Chas. When they started dating, I was jealous and tried to hide it. I don't think either of them knew, or understood, how deep my feelings for her were. She just saw me as a friend.'

Emily says nothing. She doesn't want to interrupt Mitch now he is opening up.

'Well, by now there were loads of people there, including Chas, Mr Dodds the biology teacher and the lads I played football with. Everyone was having a great time, but it totally threw me seeing Tanya again after all this time.'

'Go on.' Emily's ears are on stalks. Charles Webber. Mr Dodds. The two people that have made the news headlines for the last eight weeks were actually with Mitch at the reunion, yet he chose not to tell her any of this before?

'Tanya and I chatted for a bit and then I went outside, to get some fresh air. I could see her through the window, standing on her own, so I decided to go back in and ask her to dance. Then, just as I did, Chas came over and said he thought "the honour should be his" – or something equally trite – and whisked her off before I knew what was going on.' Mitch clears his throat before continuing. 'It brought back all the horrible memories of being a teenager. Rejection. Unrequited love. Whatever you want to call it, it really hurt.' Mitch takes a deep breath and she wonders what is coming next. 'I know it's no excuse, but I'd had a few drinks by then and, well, Mr Dodds had obviously been watching and started to mock me.'

'What do you mean?'

'He laughed out loud, saying I had always been incompetent.

A failure. How he always knew I would never make anything of my life. That I would never be able to compete with people like Chas. Ever.'

'That's terrible.'

'But that's not all. I thought I'd show him that I wasn't inferior to the likes of Chas. I lost it… and I mean I *completely* lost it. I ran over to where Chas was dancing with Tanya and punched him in the face.'

'Bloody hell, Mitch, why didn't you tell me this before?'

'Shut up Emily, let me finish. I know I was an arsehole, but it doesn't stop there. People pulled us apart and Chas straightened his shirt, smirked at me and walked away, which only made me even more angry. I stormed off and Tanya ran after me, trying to calm me down. She kept saying Chas hadn't meant to upset me. When I explained it wasn't only Chas, but what Mr Dodds had said as well, it was like a firework going off in my head and I foolishly did something I bitterly regret.'

'Jesus, Mitch, what did you do?'

'I mentioned something that happened, way back in 1987. Something that I should have kept to myself forever. But I opened my big mouth without thinking.'

There is another long, menacing silence.

Emily holds her breath, lost for words. She is fuming. He got into a fight with the missing man after an argument with the dead teacher? No wonder the police have been asking questions.

61

SUNDAY 29 JULY

TANYA

The Sunday crowds at the Allington Estate were slow to start but now they resemble ants. Crawling everywhere, nosing around. Even her early morning run hasn't helped Tanya relax and the therapeutic effect of her studio isn't having the desired result either; any pottery she creates today will be a disaster.

The sound of laughter floats through the open door; happy, contented people visiting the gallery. Distracting her. Buses continually arrive, filled with animated day trippers ready to enjoy the artwork, have a leisurely lunch and then mooch around a bit more, buying gifts and keepsakes, while marvelling at the work on display.

She watches them, peering across the empty back gardens of Meadow View. Annabel is away at the moment and she misses her and the children. She used to enjoy watching them on the trampoline. Not that she blames them for wanting to get away after everything that has happened.

Tanya estimates how many visitors are carrying bags from the gallery. It must be well over fifty per cent. She would have had a bumper day of sales with the school holidays in full swing and Olympic fever gripping everyone.

Her respect for Hattie has waned. She hates herself for it but, right now, she feels nothing but resentment. Last night she had discovered all her beautiful creations stuffed into boxes and hidden behind a curtain in the gallery. It took her at least fifteen minutes to find them.

To add insult to injury, in her rightful place at the bottom of the stairs were some ordinary-looking bowls. Turned wood they may be, and the grain of the ash, beech and walnut very beautiful, but still two-a-penny in her view. Hattie has at least four other woodturners exhibiting, whereas Tanya's stand was far more varied and interesting for the visitors.

Tanya fumes quietly in her studio. She is not in the right frame of mind to set up her new display at the moment, and not entirely sure when she will be. Instead, she can't stop thinking about Lady Henrietta Allington-Thorpe with her posh voice, gilded notepaper and privileged life. Hattie might keep apologising but how dare she think she can pick and choose who she does or doesn't help.

Tanya can't help it; as much as she is fond of Hattie, she is angry with her. She'll spend the day with her bees instead. They will help her relax. She has to be calm around the hives or the bees become agitated and that doesn't do them, or her, any good.

62

SUNDAY 29 JULY

EMILY

'You still there, Mitch?' Emily says quietly. The line has been deathly quiet for a long time.

'Yes… I'm sorry.'

'Why didn't you tell me this before?'

'Because I hate myself, that's why. When I heard Chas had gone missing, I got worried and when Mr Dodds's body was found as well, I became paranoid. People had seen me arguing with both of them and were bound to say something.'

'Exactly, that's why you should have told me.'

'But I didn't know how to. It's not that easy. Plus, apparently, after I left Chas went for Mr Dodds as well, punching him to the floor. It's a bloody mess. All because of what I said to Tanya. That's why I started forwarding the news articles to you. I thought by sharing them, it would help me to rationalise everything. Convince myself it wasn't my fault.'

'What was it that happened all those years ago? It must have been pretty awful?'

'I can't say, it wouldn't be fair on the people involved.'

'Why not? After all these years?'

'I don't know, it just feels wrong. To be honest it wouldn't mean anything to you anyway, you don't know any of them.'

'Bloody hell, Mitch. Do you think they went off and did something stupid because of what you did?'

'Who knows.'

'Is that why the police questioned you?' Emily realises too late what she has said.

'How the hell did you know about that?'

'Jo told me.'

'Shit. What else has she told you?'

'Nothing. She's been annoyingly vague, that's why I wanted to speak to you. I thought it was time you were honest with me. Completely honest. Especially after what your mum said too.'

'What's my mother got to do with any of this?'

'She's been sending me horrible texts. Apparently, she thinks I've ruined your life.'

'Mum? Texting? I find that hard to believe, she wouldn't know how to, she hardly ever switches her phone on, she's too worried the battery will run out.'

'Well, it was definitely her and she was horrid. I thought someone was stalking me.'

'That must be because her nosey neighbour saw me at the police station and won't let it go. Mum is convinced that all the trouble I've had with the police over the last few weeks is because of you.'

Emily hears him rinsing his mug under a tap. Fearing he may have had enough, she decides to probe further, before he ends their conversation. 'Why did they arrest you, Mitch?'

'Arrest me? Come on Emily, hear me out. I know you're pissed off at me but I went voluntarily. They've been contacting everyone who was at the reunion, so I thought I'd do the decent thing. They only took me in for questioning the second time because they're struggling to find out what happened. Mum says it's all that people are talking about; she can't go anywhere without being stared at.'

'But Jo said you had been *arrested*?'

'Okay, okay, they did eventually. But they still don't have anything on me.' Mitch is agitated. 'And you don't need to panic, I haven't told them anything about us at The Cowshed. Just because I had a fight with Chas and Mr Dodds at the reunion doesn't make me guilty. I am simply a person of interest, the same as everyone else who was there. Honestly, Emily, it could have been anyone.' Emily detects a quiver in his voice. 'Trust me Emily, it wasn't me.'

Emily is beside herself. He seems to think none of this has anything to do with him and yet it sounds, remarkably, like it did. Likewise, he didn't tell the police what he saw at The Cowshed to protect her, it was to protect himself. It would have been a gamble. Not only would they know he fought with both men, they would also know he had been in the exact location where Mr Dodds's body was found.

Emily tries to absorb everything he has said. She assumes he doesn't know the police arrested her too, otherwise he would have said something by now. She's certainly not going to tell him she told the police he was at The Cowshed that day *and* what he was doing all evening. He'll be livid if he finds out.

'Are you absolutely certain you don't know anything else, Mitch?' Emily asks. Marcus and the children are making their way up the cul-de-sac and she will need to end the conversation very soon. 'Mitch?'

'Honestly, no, I don't.'

'What about the body you thought you saw at The Cowshed? Was it the teacher?'

'What the fuck Emily. If it was, do you really think I'd be here now, talking to you? Get real.'

'But none of this makes any sense Mitch. It's as clear as mud. I hate the way you've dragged me in to this godforsaken crap and, whilst I appreciate you telling me a little more about what happened, none of it stacks up. None of it. It feels like there is something missing.'

Emily moves away from the window. Marcus and the children are almost at the front door and she needs Mitch to take this seriously.

'Look Mitch, I need to go. Please think about it some more. *Please*. For me. For you. So we can both get out of this stupid mess. Think long and hard about it. I'll give you another call in a day or two so you can tell me the rest.'

63

SUNDAY 29 JULY

TANYA

Tanya spends the afternoon enthralled, sat next to her hives. The sweet smell of the summer flowers and the non-stop buzz of insects flying over the meadow is hypnotic.

She watches the worker bees go in and out, in and out, their hind legs laden with bright yellow pollen as they swoop through the tiny entrance with the precision of an expert fighter pilot. She read in one of her manuals that a bee mixes the pollen with regurgitated nectar to make it stick to their hind legs, like overstuffed saddlebags. It's amazing how they fly at all with so much baggage; not hesitating for a millisecond before squeezing through the narrow gap, depositing their harvest and flying back to the meadow to collect more.

They are such fascinating creatures. She loves all the facts and figures. A single bee can fly as far as eight kilometres for food, but the average is much less, especially if they have an abundance of wild flowers nearby, like hers do. The same manual had calculated that a strong colony – approximately sixty thousand bees – therefore flies the equivalent distance from Earth to the Moon every day. She doesn't know if it's actually true but the enormity of the fact had stuck in her brain. It is phenomenal. It's one of the best things she has ever done, beekeeping. Although they look after themselves really, she just has the privilege of being able to share her life with them and is still chuffed she managed to capture her first swarm a few weeks earlier.

As evening approaches, the warm summer sun cools and her beloved bees slow down. A light has been switched on in the mansion house and she assumes Hattie is home after watching her granddaughter in the opening ceremony.

Tanya had been excited to hear all about it, now she's not so sure. Despite having heard so much about her, in the fifteen months Tanya has lived at Meadow View she has never met her. Lexie has only visited on the odd occasion and they haven't been properly introduced.

She looks again. There's definitely someone in the house. Normally she would pop up straightaway, to check Hattie is okay. Living on her own in such a large property, Tanya knows Hattie appreciates, more than she ever lets on, all her thoughtful gestures. Well, today she might not. Hattie won't know the full extent of her feelings unless she shows her. Hattie will assume Tanya doesn't mind moving her stand. That it's acceptable for "good old Tanya" to just fit in with everyone else.

Polite and respectful. Always happy to do what is expected of her. To put others first. Never question. Never complain.

Tanya reads a book instead, but it's impossible to concentrate. There's a strange feeling in her stomach and far too many lights on. Prudent Hattie never wastes electricity.

Duty beckons and, as night falls, Tanya finds herself walking up the drive. She won't stay long; she'll do what needs to be done, check everything is in order, and leave.

64

SUNDAY 29 JULY

MITCH

Agitated and annoyed, Mitch throws his phone on to the settee. The moment he does, it rings again. He assumes it is Emily calling back, not prepared to leave things where they are, but it's not.

'Mitch, how are you mate?'

'Chas?' Mitch replies, taken aback.

'I'm in the Bristol area next week, just wondered if you fancy meeting up for a beer?'

'You've got a fucking nerve!'

'Hey, steady on. I was only asking if you wanted a beer.'

'I'm surprised you've even considered it.' Mitch is tempted to cut him off. Chas is the last person he wants to speak to right now.

'Thought it would be best if we talk, that's all.'

There's an awkward silence as Mitch decides how best to respond. So much for a relaxed Sunday morning, it's been nothing but grief so far.

'Fuck you Chas. Talk about surprises. You bugger off, after everything that happened at the reunion, leaving me to deal with all the shit on my own… and… and then you phone up again weeks later, out of the blue, as if nothing has happened?' Mitch can't hide his sarcasm as he hisses into his handset.

'That's not exactly true Mitch and you know it.'

'Yes, it is. No one has heard from you in ages – your sister reported you missing two months ago – and all you can say is *"do I fancy a beer?"* and you *"think it's best if we talk"?*'

'What do you mean? Annabel knows where I've been. She asked the police to keep it quiet because she was a bit embarrassed about it all.'

'What do you mean, she was a bit embarrassed about it all? *You* should be embarrassed, not her. She was going insane with worry.' Mitch is fuming now. 'And I won't even begin to tell you about all the police stuff. You're an arsehole Chas, always were. But you aren't going to mess around with me anymore. Not now.'

'Shit, what's got into you mate?' Chas is exasperated. 'Thought you might have learnt it's better to keep your temper under control after everything that happened at the reunion.'

'It wasn't just me.'

'Really?'

'Yes, really.'

'Still fancy a beer though, you sound like you could do with one. How about Thursday, you might have calmed down by then. See you at the White Horse at eight.'

65

SUNDAY 29 JULY

TANYA

Tanya knocks on the door and lets herself in, like she always does. Hattie found her on the doorstep once – soaking wet and shivering with the cold – and made her promise she would never do that again. She has always been so kind; that's why Tanya is finding it hard to understand Hattie's decision to move her stand at the gallery.

Tanya enters quietly, twisting the ornate, circular handle to close the heavy door behind her. There's a voice coming from upstairs and she stands motionless in the hall to concentrate, to see if she recognises it.

One voice becomes two, shouting at each other. Surely it can't be another intruder; the police never found anyone last time, although the pantry window had definitely been forced. A myriad of thoughts whirl in Tanya's head as the heated argument continues and, wondering what to do, she stares at the enormous vase of lilies on the mahogany table at the foot of the stairs; extravagant, colourful and fragrant, it is overpowering in every sense. There are dozens of them. Multiple images upon images, reflected in the antique mirrors hung on the opposing walls, gradually decreasing in size until they disappear from view.

The grand staircase is certainly that. The low risers sweep in a circular motion to the upper floors of the mansion and with her eyes drawn upwards, Tanya creeps up the stairs. There are two large, leather holdalls on the landing, both unzipped and overflowing with sports equipment and clothing.

Still out of sight, the voices get louder. 'But Grammie, please don't be angry. I *was* going to tell you, I *was*.' Tanya's ears prick up. It must be Lexie. She sounds terribly upset. But how can it be, if she is at the Olympics?

'Lexie my love, calm down… I'm not angry with you, I'm confused. Extremely confused. I don't understand what you are doing here, or how you even got here?' Hattie is clearly exasperated.

'I've been kicked out Grammie. That's all there is to it. I won't be taking part after all.'

'But that's nonsense! What's happened?'

'Bullying Grammie, that's what. It's been going on for ages. I came home a few weeks ago to talk to you about it, but you weren't here. You were at the funeral so I broke in. I had to. I didn't know what else to do and I didn't want to upset you.'

Tanya hears Hattie gasp as Lexie explains.

'It was me Grammie, I'm so sorry, I came home to see you, to ask your advice, but you weren't here.'

'NO. Don't you dare say that.' Hattie raises her voice. 'And don't EVER tell your mother either. You don't know the implications of what you are saying.'

'But Grammie, I hate lying to you. I've been meaning to tell you for ages. I just didn't want to do it over the phone.'

'Listen to me, Lexie. Whatever you do, do NOT tell me that it was you who broke in. I won't hear a word of it. You have no idea – absolutely no idea – what you are saying by telling me that.'

A door slams shut and someone appears from Hattie's suite on the first floor. Tanya clears her throat, to make them aware of her presence, then immediately regrets doing so.

'Bloody hell,' Lexie's voice is high pitched as she glares at Tanya, her eyes wide open. 'Who are you?'

'It's okay, I'm a friend of Lady Allington.' Tanya says gently, hoping to dispel the situation. She can tell Lexie is flustered as she looks around for her grandmother, but Hattie is nowhere to be seen.

Lexie's athletic presence towers above Tanya. All Tanya can think to do is hold her hand up as a peace offering, while her brain computes the image before her.

She has seen Lexie before.

She saw Lexie face-to-face on the footpath by the holiday cottages. It comes flooding back. Lexie appeared from nowhere, from behind the builder's skip. The night Tanya watched the person breaking into The Cowshed.

'I said, WHO ARE YOU?' Lexie is impatient.

'I've just told you, I'm a friend of your grandmother,' Tanya replies, calmly, trying to work out what it all means. 'I assume you must be Lexie?'

'Who else would I be?' she sneers. 'Anyway, you haven't answered me, what's your name?'

'Tanya.'

'Well, *Tanya*,' Lexie mocks. 'I don't know what possesses you to think you can let yourself into my grandmother's house unannounced, but you need to leave. NOW.'

'It was you, wasn't it, I saw you on the path by the cottages, I know you were there!'

Tanya is enraged and lunges at her, but Lexie – still at the top of the stairs – has the height advantage and Tanya lands awkwardly at her feet. Lexie kicks Tanya in the ribs, making her yelp in pain, and they scuffle noisily as Tanya, kicking back in self-defence, grabs the handle of one of the holdalls to steady herself and the contents spill untidily down the stairs. Tanya attempts to get back on her feet but, once again, Lexie pushes her over and Tanya smacks her back against the banister as she loses her balance.

With the air violently expelled from her lungs and her ribcage painful from the earlier blow, Tanya struggles to breathe. As she gasps for air, she catches sight of Lexie gathering up some of the spilled items and pulling out a gun.

'Lexie?' Hattie's voice is shrill. 'What on earth is going on?'

Tanya cranes her neck from her position on the carpet as the ancient floorboards creak and, still lying on the floor, she watches Hattie's feet make their way along the landing.

Tanya needs to do something, quickly. Wincing with pain, she pulls herself upright and throws herself towards Lexie who is now just a few steps above her, holding the gun high above her head.

'Let me go, or I'll shoot!' Screams Lexie at the top of her voice, as she struggles to get free of Tanya's tight grip on her ankles.

'Lexie, what are you doing? This is madness!' Hattie screeches, breaking into a run towards her granddaughter. 'Tanya? How long have you been here? WILL SOMEONE TELL ME WHAT IS GOING ON?'

'NO!' Tanya screams, as she realises what is about to happen, still trying to floor Lexie by pulling on her legs.

But it is too late. As Tanya overpowers her, Lexie loses her footing and trips, knocking Hattie over in the process. There is a deafening crack as a single shot is fired vertically into the air and the explosion echoes around the magnificent building. Plaster dust falls like snow in slow motion as the bullet ricochets off the decorative ceiling, then hits an imposing family portrait hanging in the centre of the galleried landing.

Tanya watches in disbelief as Hattie, completely disorientated, tumbles head-over-heels and, with a series of gut-wrenching thuds, rolls down the stairs. Her limp body bounces off each step, one at a time, followed by a blood-curdling scream as she hits the wooden floor at the bottom.

66
TUESDAY 31 JULY

EMILY

Emily repeatedly presses the button on the vending machine. She had no time to make sandwiches this morning because Molly and Jack were arguing and she's doing extra hours to cover for Jo, who is on holiday. To make matters worse all her meetings have overrun, it's almost four o'clock and she is starving. She thought she would have a snack from the self-serve machine rather than dash down the road to get something slightly healthier. Wrong decision. Now she's wasted fifteen minutes instead of five, lost all her spare change and is *still* hungry.

A voice appears from behind. It's Rob the handyman. What a relief, he fixes everything. Leaky taps, light bulbs that have blown, spillages; he even caught a bird once, that had somehow got in through an open window.

'Sorry love,' he says kindly. 'Machine's playing up. It's really temperamental these days; I've come to put a notice on it, to warn people not to put their money in until the engineer mends it tomorrow.'

'Temperamental is one word for it,' Emily replies, resisting the urge to kick it. He may not be too impressed.

'Hey,' he says, staring at the name on her lanyard. 'Are you the Emily Harrison I heard the guys from HR talking about in the lift yesterday? Something about a police investigation and being arrested?'

Emily feels her cheeks burning and, unsure how to reply, turns it so her name is facing the other way. 'I'm sorry, but you must be mistaken because I have no idea what you're talking about. And anyway, even if they did, they should know better than to talk about confidential matters in the lift when they don't know who is listening.'

'Whatever.' He shrugs and smiles.

Determined to keep calm, she walks away with her head held high and reminds herself it's not Rob's fault she was disorganised this morning. She must have an old pack of chewing gum in her desk somewhere if she rummages at the back of the drawer.

*

Multi-tasking, Emily has her desk phone balanced under her chin as she taps away on her keyboard. She found some chewy mints in her drawer but has since realised they must be ancient. They are rock-hard and taste a little weird. It's only Tuesday and she's never going to last another three days at this rate.

Despite the extra work, she's extremely grateful Jo isn't around this week. They've barely spoken since her weekend with Marcus and she's heard nothing more about Mitch being arrested. It's been the elephant in the room; neither of them wanting to say anything. She stretches down to pick up a pen from the floor and the phone, that she had completely forgotten was under her chin, clatters noisily to her desk. Her colleagues gawp to see what all the commotion is and to make matters worse her mobile springs in to life with its *Mission*

Impossible ring tone, vibrating and spinning in circles on the file where she left it a few minutes ago.

She can see it's another news alert. 'Sorry!' she says to her colleagues, self-consciously holding her hand up in mock surrender. 'Thought it was on silent.'

One of them shakes his head and looks back to his screen. Emily will be glad when today is over. She hates to think her colleagues are talking about her behind her back and longs to get home; maybe go for an evening stroll with Marcus and the children to relax, soak up some of the late sunshine.

Shrinking back in her chair she reads the latest message and can't believe her eyes.

DEVON LIVE

** BREAKING NEWS **

Devon and Cornwall Police have confirmed two women are helping them with their inquiries regarding the shooting of Lady Henrietta Allington-Thorpe, who was seriously injured at her home on the Allington Estate on Sunday 29th July.

The women, aged twenty-five and forty-three, are both known to the victim and are said to have witnessed the attack. A police spokesperson said although it is sensible for local people to remain vigilant at all times, they believe it to be an isolated incident and are not currently looking for anyone else in relation to the shooting.

67

WEDNESDAY 1 AUGUST

EMILY

Molly and Jack wave their cheerful goodbyes as Emily walks back to her car. Thankfully, they seem oblivious to her worries and are loving summer camp this year.

Emily yawns. It's twenty to nine and she's exhausted. She was awake all night, yet again, this time thinking about Hattie. She sits in her car and relishes the temporary silence as the laughing children disappear inside and the facilitators sort them into groups for their fun and games. Lucky things. She wishes she could do something more relaxing than a staff appraisal.

Resting her forehead in her hands on the steering wheel she shuts her eyes while she contemplates the day ahead. She feels sick at the thought of going into the office. How ridiculous. She's done it thousands of times, but today her stomach is in knots. She recognises the feeling only too well. Anxiety. Stress. Whatever you want to call it, she knows she is struggling to cope.

She sits there a while longer, in a quandary. Then the scraping noise of plastic wheels on concrete grabs her attention.

An elderly lady shuffles along the pavement, hunched over as she drags her red and green chequered shopping trolley towards the convenience store. It looks like an uphill struggle and Emily's heart goes out to her. Emily doesn't want to grow old. She wants to live her life to the full; laughing and happy. With Marcus, Molly and Jack and all their family and friends. She can't believe how her life is falling apart again, just when she thought they were going in the right direction. The terrible news about Hattie, on top of everything else, has been an awful shock. Emily keeps seeing an image of her lying unconscious on the ground, her silver-grey hair matted with blood and her wicker basket upturned by her side. It's horrible. Hattie, the generous and gregarious host who made them feel so welcome at The Piggery.

The more she thinks about it, the more she can't face going into the office today, especially after what Rob the handyman said about people gossiping behind her back. She feels guilty about the staff appraisal but, if she's not feeling well, it's better to defer it. Better for them and better for her. She rubs her eyes. Five to nine. She needs to make her mind up.

*

'I'm sorry to hear that Emily, but it's no bother, I'll reschedule your meetings for you. Make sure you take it easy and get yourself better.'

Emily turns up the volume on the radio and flops down on a chair at the kitchen table, grateful her manager's PA is so considerate. She can't carry on like this or she will make herself seriously ill. A day at home to get her thoughts together is exactly what she needs. It'll give her time to get to the bottom of all this nonsense. Once she has figured everything out, she can make sure the police don't bother her again *and* make sure all her friends and colleagues know she has done nothing wrong.

*

Grabbing a note pad, she realises it is ten weeks, almost eleven, since her traumatic weekend at The Cowshed. That's ridiculous. More determined than ever, she is not going to waste any time or let anything deter her. She will investigate every possible bit of information to establish *all* the facts and find out what really did happen. Once she has, she will ask Marcus to support her and then she will go back to the police to explain everything and clear her name.

Completely.

Once and for all.

She checks the calendar again. Ten weeks and two days since she watched the Olympic torch parade with Molly and Jack. What a brilliant day that was, even after the terrible events of the weekend. They had literally jumped up and down with excitement.

Now the games are half over, she owes it to them to sort out this mess and the Olympic closing ceremony is on the eleventh of August, just ten days away. That's it then, she promises herself, two hundred and forty hours to stop everyone gossiping. To stop everyone thinking I'm a criminal. To save my marriage. To get my life back.

*

She makes a list. Scribbling ideas down before she starts, otherwise she'll get distracted too easily.

1. The weekend with Mitch / the reunion.
   Any missing details? Did his friends mention anything else at the pub? What about Yvonne? Did she say anything else that might help?
2. The missing man: Charles Webber (Chas).

Schoolfriend of Mitch. Mitch punched him at the reunion. Sister Annabel Tait lives on the Allington estate. Why did he disappear? Where did he go?

3. The dead teacher: Timothy Dodds.
   Went to the reunion. Upset Mitch. Where did he live? Why was he on the footpath? How did he die?
4. Hattie's accident.
   Two women (25 and 43) are being questioned. Who are they? What happened? Why?
5. Anything / anyone else to consider?
   What else did the police say? What else did Mitch say?

Emily stops. None of this makes any sense. Why was Mitch arrested? Why was she arrested? Are the police interested in the missing man or the dead man – or both?

Writing it down helps. She wishes she had done this before, to work out the logic, although there doesn't appear to be any connection at the moment. She remembers reading about the builder, the skip company, Charles Webber and his sister before she went to Devon with Marcus. She didn't make any notes but won't waste time looking at them again. If Charles has been found there would be something in the news and she hasn't seen anything; likewise, there was nothing to indicate the builder or the skip company had any involvement, they just happened to be in the vicinity at the time. Same as her. Talk about being unlucky. No. She'll concentrate her efforts today on the people she *hasn't* yet researched. That way she is more likely to find something new.

Turning to a fresh page in her notebook she starts with the dead teacher. Emily types **Timothy Dodds teacher footpath** in the Google search bar, she can't bring herself to use the word 'dead', it feels morbidly disrespectful. The least she can do is honour his memory and that of his family, if she can actually find out anything about them.

*

Engrossed in her research and blissfully unaware of the time, Emily jumps off her chair as she hears the front door close with a firm push. It must be Marcus. No one else shuts it like that.

'You're home early!' he exclaims, throwing his bag down in the corner of the kitchen.

'I know, the staff appraisal got moved to next week, then the marketing meeting this afternoon got cancelled as well, so I decided to make the most of it and work from home.' Emily thinks on her feet. 'In fact, I've been feeling so exhausted from everything that has been going on I said I might do the same again tomorrow.'

Before she knows it, he is peering over her shoulder. 'God, that looks gory, what are you looking at? I hope you're not skiving. All this working from home malarkey is a bit of a con if you ask me,' he laughs. At least he seems to be in a better mood today.

'Oh, nothing really, just browsing the news while I have a five-minute break.' She replies, getting up to give him a kiss and take his eyes away from her screen. 'You're back early too, we must make the most of it. Let's do something with the kids, go for an ice cream in the park or something? Summer camp will be finishing soon.'

She closes the lid of her laptop discretely behind her.

She's made a good start. She'll carry on tomorrow and tell him everything once she has got to the bottom of it.

68

THURSDAY 2 AUGUST

EMILY

Breakfast seems to last an eternity. Emily, desperate to make the most of her time, impatiently grabs Jack's cereal bowl the instant he finishes his last mouthful and tuts under her breath as a disgruntled Molly, still half asleep, plays with her soggy cornflakes. Counting to ten, Emily tries her utmost to stop her frustration turning into full-blown irritation. That would be completely unfair, given she has the luxury of a whole day at home without interruption once they have left. Plus, it's really thoughtful of Marcus to drop the children off at summer camp on his way to work, even though it is considerably out of his way, so she doesn't have to go out.

Hoping they don't pick up on her rush to get them out the door, the moment they leave she wipes the crumbs from the table, opens her laptop and is typing in her password before Marcus has pulled off the drive, not wanting to waste a precious second. The screen is still there, exactly as she left it the previous afternoon. The results from her Google search eagerly awaiting her return, ready for her to select the pages that interest her the most.

LinkedIn profiles, Wikipedia entries, Facebook, Instagram, websites. Emily doesn't know where to start. There are at least three teachers with the name Timothy Dodds, plus others called Tim Dodson, Timothy Dodwell and numerous, similar variations.

On her third attempt she finds the correct LinkedIn page. The last entry was on the day of his retirement, at the end of the summer term last year. A photograph of him surrounded by colleagues and students, all smiling at the camera.

'After twenty-plus years teaching my favourite subject, I feel very blessed to be able to take early retirement at the grand old age of fifty-three. Exciting times! Looking forward to starting the next chapter of my life. So many happy memories and thank you everyone for such a wonderful send-off!' the caption reads supported by one hundred and thirty-five 'Likes' or 'Congratulations'.

Emily clicks on the text box to open up all the comments, of which there are dozens. It takes a few minutes to scroll through each of them in turn and she feels an overwhelming heaviness in her chest. They are all strikingly similar; thanking him for his amazing teaching skills, wishing him a long and happy retirement, congratulating him on his successful career and grateful former students saying how his support and enthusiasm had been instrumental in their own careers, or enabled them to achieve various accomplishments. "…none of this would have been possible without you," quotes one. How terribly sad. How did such a popular teacher end up dead – and alone – on a deserted footpath?

Emily studies each of the people in turn and thinks it through. This all looks perfectly normal. It certainly doesn't look like anyone in the photo could have held a grudge against him. Plus, he has a kind face. She wonders if he was married; there is no mention of a wife or any children. She adds a few lines to her scribbled notes, before going back to the original search page and methodically working her way through the other results.

They don't bring up anything of significance. He clearly wasn't a social media fan; other than using LinkedIn for professional updates about school related topics, the only other articles are from newspapers when his body was first found, which she reads again to refresh her memory. Emily slumps back in her chair. She doesn't know what she expected to find, but suddenly everything seems far too real. She looks again at the photo on LinkedIn. He looks far too young to have died of a heart attack.

Running out of ideas, she tries another approach and types in the name of his last school, *St Peter's*, followed by his name. A post from a different Facebook group immediately pops up; the photo is the grainy image from the newspaper when he was first identified. Emily starts to read the comments. This time they aren't so complimentary.

MadMax
He was a prat. Rubbish teacher – always gave me the creeps.

FilmBuffy
I agree – he was nasty always picked on me

TaxiMumSue
OMG how can people be so rude about a dead person? Lay off everyone

MinnieMinx
He was horrible. Hated him.

DTT
He was very young at our school, straight out of

teacher training. He taught my sister at St Peters and he was much better there I think

Jonesy
He was evil. EVIL.

BuzzKid
Great teacher, loved his lessons

Chelsea4Ever
No he wasn't, he was a crap teacher. He made my life hell.

MikeW
I liked him, he knew his stuff

Tracy Soames
All very well @TaxiMumSue but he was horrible. He had a nasty streak. I hated his lessons. Everyone is entitled to their opinion. Some people liked him, some people didn't. What's the problem with that?

Emily feels disgusted. Missing people. Dead people. It had previously felt like an imaginary world. A world she had been observing, from the outside looking in. Seeing these comments about a real person who is now dead is awful. She feels guilty for prying. She is just as bad. Searching for information about him, snooping into his life, family and friends.

Her mind is transported back to that fateful Saturday. Emily still doesn't know for sure what Mitch saw that day. She has tried, many times, to convince herself that none of it actually happened. It works for a while; until she reads one of these articles, or remembers her frightful night in the police cell. Then it all becomes horribly real again. If Mitch did see a body in the bath, it can't have been the teacher as she asked him outright just a few days ago – and, if it had been the teacher, Mitch would have recognised him and done something about it. Wouldn't he?

And what about the missing man and the break-in at Allington House? She remembers the landlady at The Moody Ram saying she thought Charles Webber had been found, but Emily hasn't seen anything in the news to confirm he has. Determined to find an answer she types his name on the search bar and about half a dozen links pop up. The third one down looks the most helpful.

DEVON LIVE
MISSING MAN'S SISTER CONFIRMS HE IS SAFE

Annabel Tait, sister of Charles Webber, the man reported missing after a school reunion, has reported him safe and well. She has declined to provide any further updates at this time and has requested privacy for her family.

Emily checks the date. Tuesday 17th July. Two days after she and Marcus stayed at The Piggery. So, the landlady was correct. She reads the article again. Short and to the point, it is the only extract Emily can find anywhere online that mentions his safe return. Clearly the family want it that way. But, how come Mitch never said anything about him being found? Surely, he must know? Once again, Emily thinks Mitch *must* be hiding something and it makes her feel physically sick. Sick to think she trusted him.

Emily's anxiety returns with a vengeance.

Surely the police can't think she has anything to do with either Charles being reported missing or the teacher's death?

Why was she so stupid; stupid to go to Allington House in the first place *and* even more stupid to leave her mobile phone on the armchair?

If only she hadn't gone, then none of this would have happened.

69

THURSDAY 2 AUGUST

EMILY

Her queasy stomach more settled, Emily sits back down. The hours are flying past and she needs to focus. She will look into Hattie next.

Most of the articles that match her search are about Hattie's recent accident. She doesn't want to read about that again but is intrigued by the entry on Wikipedia about her family. She clicks on the highlighted link to her granddaughter.

> **Alexandria (Lexie) Henrietta Williamson** (b. 18 April 1987) is the only daughter of Daniel and Penelope Williamson and the only granddaughter of Lady Henrietta Alexandria Allington-Thorpe. The family seat, the **Allington Estate,** is located in Devon. Lexie is a modern pentathlete and qualified for the 2012 Olympic Games in May this year.

Emily didn't know her surname until now. She calculates Lexie to be twenty-five and wonders if it was her with Hattie the night she was shot. Although common sense tells her it's impossible as she would have been in London at the Olympic Games. She notices her mother was very young when Lexie was born; if Penelope is the same age as Mitch, then she was only eighteen. Emily remembers Yvonne explaining Hattie looked after her granddaughter for her early years. That must be why.

Emily looks at the images for Lexie Williamson. They're not all her, but there are dozens that are. Numerous photographs at various sporting events: holding medals, smiling with team mates, horse riding, swimming, running, fencing and shooting. Wow. She is beautiful, with her long blonde hair pulled back in a ponytail and clearly athletic too. No wonder Hattie is so proud of her.

Her eyes are drawn to another image, one that is definitely not Lexie. The face is vaguely familiar and she studies it carefully, purely out of curiosity. There are four or five people in the photo, including Hattie.

> "*Lady Allington-Thorpe at the official opening of the long-awaited Allington Arts and Crafts Gallery on the family estate with some of the local artists who are exhibiting their work.*" Emily peers closer. "*From L-R: Lady Allington-Thorpe; Mary Secombe (watercolours); Pete Innsley (oils); Terence Baldock (sculpture); Tanya Symonds (Bea's Bees ceramics); Nadia Vetch (pastels).*"

Emily runs her finger from left to right along the faces. Tanya Symonds; Bea's Bees ceramics. Of course, she saw her at the gallery, the stand at the bottom of the stairs. Emily wanted to have a closer look but there was a small crowd of people and the children were getting bored, so Emily picked up her business card instead, intending to look at her website another time.

She dashes upstairs to get her handbag out the wardrobe, the one she took that weekend. Foraging in the side pocket she finds a dog-eared business card. Simple lettering on a pale green background, embellished with drawings of honey bees and wildflowers around the edge.

*** BEA'S BEES ***

Ceramics inspired by the beautiful Devon landscape plus natural, organic beeswax products including luxurious face cream, hand lotion and lip balm.

Tanya Beatrice Symonds, 3 Meadow View, Allington Estate.

Emily is beyond annoyed with herself, why had she not made the connection before? Tanya – the girl Mitch used to know at school, who went out with Charles the missing man – is *also* the person Hattie talked so much about. Emily's head hurts as she computes the information. Tanya Beatrice Symonds. Bea's Bees. Tanya and Beatrice, Hattie's housekeeper, are one and the same. But then she remembers, Hattie's housekeeper was away the weekend she went with Mitch, which was why she couldn't stay in The Cowshed, therefore none of this can be anything to do with her.

Emily stares at the business card, confused. She can't help feeling Mitch has been extremely selective with regard to what he has or hasn't told her. But then, he might be blissfully unaware that Tanya traded under the name of Bea and worked for Hattie, or that she had a stand at the craft gallery and lived on the Allington Estate.

Emily's stomach rumbles and she realises it is already quarter past three. She'll sit in the garden for a few minutes to think things through.

*

The sun is warm on her face and Emily stirs when a car door shuts with a loud clunk. She must have dropped off to sleep as there is a half-eaten sandwich, curled around the edges, lying on her plate. She has no idea how long she has been snoozing.

'Working hard again, eh!' laughs Marcus.

'Hey, cheeky, I just had a late lunch that's all.' She makes light of it despite being annoyed with herself for letting him find her in the garden. He'll never believe she's been working now, even though, technically, she knows she hasn't.

'It's such a lovely afternoon, I decided to surprise you,' Marcus continues. 'It might help us to go for a walk or something, all the stuff that's been going on lately, it's hanging over us.'

'Oh, yes, that's a great idea.' Emily pulls herself up, shaking off the soporific effect of her unexpected siesta, and heads inside.

'So how did you get on today? Have you done everything you wanted to do?'

'I think so. Made good progress, research mainly. How about you?'

'Average. Glad it's Friday though.' Marcus can't resist looking at her screen, still open on the kitchen table. 'That looks interesting, what have you been working on?'

'Oh, nothing really. That wasn't actually work,' Emily confesses as she steps back inside. 'I was curious about Hattie's granddaughter being at the Olympics. I Googled her to find out when her pentathlon heats will be on television so we can watch her. While I was looking another piece came up, all about the craft gallery, and I recognised one of the artists we saw there.'

'Which one?'

'The ceramicist at the bottom of the stairs. I think she must be Hattie's housekeeper, the one we bought our honey from. Bea's Bees. We never met her as we put the money in an honesty box, but I'm sure I remember Hattie calling her that.'

'Why are you so interested?'

'I thought she might know what happened that weekend.' Marcus frowns.

'What?' Emily asks.

'Why should she know?'

'Just because, well, she might.' Emily shrugs.

'That's ridiculous. You're getting obsessed again, clutching at straws. Just like you did before.'

'I am not obsessed!'

'Yes, you are.' Marcus shakes his head. 'I don't think I can do this anymore, Em. It's crazy. *You're* crazy.'

'No, I am not! But I am upset about the police arresting me. I can't get it out of my head. It ruined our special weekend, apart from anything else, and now the neighbours are ignoring me and everyone at work is gossiping about me. I HATE IT!' Emily shrieks at him. 'What if HR raise another disciplinary against me just because I was arrested? I can't go through that again, I can't... and what's more, I WON'T.'

Emily storms out the room and he pulls her back.

'But they let you go, Em. We've talked about this before. You didn't do anything wrong.' The pain in Marcus's eyes is almost too much for Emily to bear.

'I know, but people still think I did and I need to get it sorted.'

'But there is nothing for you to sort.' Marcus raises his voice, frustrated, but still trying to reassure her as he holds her gently.

'But there is, that's the trouble. Something wasn't right that weekend. I just can't put my finger on it.'

'Stop it Em, STOP IT.' Now Marcus walks away. 'I'm not moving back in for you to get all unhinged again. It's not going to work – we're not going to work – if you do that.'

'But I can't lose everything all over again,' Emily shouts after him. 'I really can't. Can't you see it's for us that I'm doing it?'

70

THURSDAY 2 AUGUST

MITCH

It's a drizzly summer evening, distinctly dull and chilly for the time of year. Mitch crawls slowly around the car park and finds the only vacant space, in the furthest corner from the entrance and directly beneath some pine trees. Normally he would avoid it, worried the sap might damage the paintwork on his car, but he doesn't have any choice tonight.

As he gently manoeuvres into the tight space, he only just hears his phone above the noisy beep of the reversing camera.

'Chas?' he asks, surprised at who it is.

'Sorry mate, bit short notice I know, but I can't make tonight after all.'

'Everything all right?' Mitch is disappointed. Having considered it carefully, since their brief conversation a few days ago, he decided it would be sensible for the two of them to talk. Although he is equally dubious about what the outcome of their conversation will be.

Wiping a rectangle of condensation off the inside of the driver's window, Mitch peers out. He's even more disappointed about not having a beer. He may have a quick half anyway, given it's almost the weekend.

'Yeah, sorry. I need to go to Devon to see Annabel, she's still in a bit of a state.'

'Really?' Mitch is sceptical.

'Yeah, really,' he continues. 'Long story short, I had an offer of a television job at short notice because another guy pulled out at the last minute. Anyway, it was a documentary following a group of people living on an uninhabited island for two months; a real-life experiment, with psychologists and loads of other experts and me as one of the guinea pigs. Part of the contract was I had to be totally off-grid – and I mean *totally*.'

'How very convenient.' Mitch can't hide his sarcasm.

'I knew you'd say that. Seriously, it's true. Anyway, Annabel was away with the kids and didn't find my letter until a couple weeks later, it must have fallen down behind the dresser where I left it in her kitchen. We were under strict rules not to use any modern technology, definitely no mobile phones, so, although I had given Annabel the emergency contact details in the note just in case, she didn't know.'

'How long did it take you to think that up Chas?' Mitch is dubious.

'Seriously, I know it sounds ludicrous, but it's true.'

Mitch watches the drizzle form rivulets, running down his windscreen while he decides what to say next.

'What about everything else, Chas?' he sneers. 'Like the dead teacher and the police interviewing everyone? Are you going to run away from all of that too?'

'Look, the police know I'm back and Annabel has asked for privacy. They know it was a misunderstanding. Annabel can't take any more intrusion in her life; it was bad enough when her husband died. I've offered to speak to them – the police – but they haven't got back to me yet.'

Mitch wonders if he can trust anything he says; his explanation sounds completely fabricated. He's done with talking to him.

Chas eventually breaks the silence. 'Look mate, I said I'm sorry. I'm sorry about what happened at the reunion too, even though you were a complete arsehole. Catch up another time, eh? I'll give you a ring when I know my plans.'

Mitch throws his phone down in disgust. It's not just the stress of the last two months eating away at him, it's the exasperation of feeling exactly like he did as a teenager all over again. Living in the shadow of the all-too-perfect Charles Webber. Teacher's pet. The one the girls all swooned over. The best footballer. The fastest runner. The one who could never put a foot wrong, even if he tried.

Nothing has changed. Once again Chas has the upper hand and Mitch knows *exactly* what will happen next. Chas will sweet talk himself out of any trouble, like he always did. He'll pull the wool over the eyes of anyone who cares to listen, whether it's his sister or the police. And then he'll walk away, with that stupid, smarmy grin on his face, leaving Mitch to pick up the pieces.

71
FRIDAY 3 AUGUST

EMILY

Emily is bereft. Marcus is definitely having second thoughts about moving back in after their heated conversation yesterday and the house is far too quiet without Molly and Jack.

Earlier she had watched them drive away, the watery sun promising a better day after the drizzle of last night, and decided to cheer herself up by switching on the radio. The music and chat lift her spirits a little but she needs to make serious progress today and only has four hours before she collects them from summer camp at one o'clock.

Emily starts with Facebook, in particular Bea's Bees and her stand at the craft gallery, and soon finds her business page. Hopeful it will provide more insight into her background, she recalls her conversation with Mitch the previous Sunday. Tanya, who he was great friends with, who went out with Chas, who he upset at the reunion. There definitely seems to be a common denominator here, it's just that Emily can't decide what – or who – it is.

Tanya Beatrice Symonds *Artist and apiarist: Please follow **Bea's Bees** for information about my ceramics business and luxury organic beeswax products.*

It looks interesting and Emily searches through her business posts first. The most recent is the photo from the newspaper showing the official opening of the craft gallery. *"Thrilled to be one of the exhibitors at the brand new Allington Estate Craft Gallery – do come along and say hello!"* the caption reads, then a few posts from the preceding weeks showing the gallery in various stages of renovation including one with her unpacking all her pottery. That's it. It doesn't look like she has had the business for very long.

Emily switches to her personal page. A few of the business posts have been shared but not much else. Working her way back, she has only posted once in the last two years and that was in May; it's a photo of her in a pub with friends.

Tanya Beatrice Symonds is in **The Bay Tree, Cirencester**. *Great to be back for the weekend for some R&R and lots of fresh air!*

There are five smiling friends sat around a table; in the background a barman is serving a frothy pint next to a large television hanging from a rickety bracket on the wall. It looks like horseracing. Not unlikely, given it's a country pub in the middle of the Cotswolds. Emily's curiosity gets the better of her. Six likes and three comments. She clicks on the latter.

Annie
I didn't know you were back? Let me know next time!

Sandy
Really? How?!

Linda
You can't be serious?!

What a shame they missed each other, thinks Emily. She checks the date. Sunday 20th May. That would certainly tie up with what Hattie said about her housekeeper being away when she and Mitch were at The Cowshed.

Emily has another look at her business page. Her beeswax products are beautiful; they would have made a lovely birthday present for her mum.

She stretches back in her chair. Maybe it wasn't such a good idea taking three days off work, pretending to be sick. She hasn't actually achieved anything other than to find out odd bits of information and all she will get in return is a ton of work to catch up on next week.

*

The morning has flown past and, forcing herself to feel more enthusiastic, Emily waves to Molly and Jack as they wait with Dionne the organiser of their summer club. The struggle to clear her name is taking over her life, filling her thoughts day and night, and she hates it. A picnic in the garden and in the sunshine will help, the children love that.

'Hi there, Mrs Harrison, how are you?' Dionne half-smiles, not her usual jolly self. 'Would it be okay to have a quick word? Mary can keep an eye on Molly and Jack while we pop in the office, it's a bit more private in there.'

'Yes, of course, is everything okay?'

'Well, it's a little bit difficult and I feel really awkward having to say this,' Dionne continues, looking at the floor, as she gently shuts the door behind them. 'It's just that some of the parents have said they are a bit concerned.'

'Sorry, I'm not sure what you mean, concerned about

what? Has something happened at summer club?' Emily queries.

'No… goodness no… not at summer club. It's just that… gosh, I don't know how to explain, I haven't heard any of the details myself. However, a few of them are saying that you have been in trouble with the police and… well, the thing is, you see, basically, they're not sure they want their children playing with Molly and Jack.'

Emily is speechless.

'I'm sorry, Mrs Harrison. I know this must be really difficult for you.'

'Difficult? I'll give you difficult. Perhaps *those parents* would like to get their facts straight before they go around casting such terrible allegations.' Emily is livid. 'If you want to know, I helped the police with their enquiries into a tragic event which took place when we were on holiday. I haven't been in trouble with the police, I have *never* been in trouble with the police.'

'Like I said, Mrs Harrison, I really am very sorry.' Dionne winces.

'No, sorry isn't good enough, Dionne. I won't have them – or you – casting aspersions about me. I demand a proper apology, right now, for not checking your facts first and… and… then I am going to take my children home while you explain to all the other parents *immediately* that they are *completely* mistaken and ask them to apologise too.'

Emily storms out, slamming the door.

*

Half an hour later, Emily is still fuming but holding it inside; she doesn't want the children to know how much Dionne upset her or spoil their picnic.

After mini choc-ices for pudding, Emily lies back on the grass and closes her eyes. It's lovely to see them both so happy, playing in the paddling pool, but she is still enraged. How dare the other parents ostracise her. But worse, how dare they ostracise Molly and Jack when they know nothing about what really happened?

Memories from the weekend she was arrested are still vivid. Not just the stale, rancid smell of the police cell that fills her nose whenever she thinks about it, but the overwhelming feeling of loneliness. And hopelessness. She has done nothing wrong and yet here she is, trapped in a situation that is completely beyond her control.

She shudders. Her life is unravelling before her eyes and, on top of everything else, Marcus is definitely having second thoughts. He keeps saying she is getting in too deep, that she needs to trust his judgement, that she needs to let it go. But how can she? If friends, neighbours, colleagues – even strangers – are judging her wrongly, how can she possibly let it go?

Marcus is going to be even more frustrated when she tells him what has happened at the summer club. She knows the police were only doing their job and they shouldn't need to question her again but none of it is helping in the slightest.

Emily gathers up the remains of their picnic. A honey bee has mistakenly settled on a leftover slice of apple, which has turned brown in the sun. She gently puts the insect on a flower to find some pollen. Molly and Jack are still playing so she will finish what she was doing on her laptop and then, when Marcus gets home, they can start their weekend properly. Perhaps watching the Olympics will cheer her up; it has been a welcome tonic each evening since her arrest. The four of them love to watch the highlights. Not only is it a good excuse to sit down as a family and learn about sports they would never usually watch, seeing the incredible athleticism and determination of the competitors is the perfect antidote to the turmoil of the past few weeks. The daily dose of inspiration gives her the stability and comfort she craves and tonight's coverage will be no exception. There are four gold medals up for grabs in the swimming, two in the cycling and one in the women's ten thousand metres.

As she types in her password, five notifications pop up on the screen. The four emails aren't important, just marketing messages about weekend offers for electrical items they won't ever need; the news article, on the other hand, grabs her attention.

DEVON LIVE

** BREAKING NEWS **

Devon and Cornwall Police have confirmed the two women who were helping them with their inquiries regarding the shooting of Lady Henrietta Allington-Thorpe have been released without charge.

A spokesperson for Lady Allington-Thorpe also confirmed she has returned home and is making a strong and speedy recovery and would like to thank everyone for their kind wishes and offers of support. The pistol was accidentally discharged in the incident and she will not be pressing charges against either of the women. It was an isolated and unfortunate accident and an independent review will be carried out to determine how the gun came to be loaded when it should not have been.

72

FRIDAY 3 AUGUST

TANYA

It's been an exceptionally quiet day in the gallery. It must be the glorious sunshine luring tourists elsewhere; a day at the seaside, or a country walk perhaps. Having so many idyllic, sandy beaches *and* Dartmoor on your doorstep is a blessing or a curse, depending on which way you look at it.

Not one to be beaten, Tanya has used the lull in visitors to rearrange her exhibits and stands back to admire them for the fifth, maybe sixth, time. She's lost count. She nods and smiles to herself, feeling proud of what she has achieved. Hattie's accident has been in the news every day and she is now grateful to be tucked away upstairs and out of the limelight, despite her initial misgivings.

Social media is equally bad. The whole town is rife with gossip; the Facebook vultures who preyed over the death of Mr Dodds are now taking delight in pulling Hattie's life apart. When it is about you, or someone you know, it is soul-destroying to read abusive comments from people who have no idea what really happened, or why. The thing is, everyone knows she works for Hattie and her accident was a terrible shock. People always speculate. *"Nothing like that ever happens around here,"* she overheard one person say, to which another replied, *"I didn't really know her, but she seemed like a really nice lady."* Why the past tense? Tanya had almost shouted at them that Lady Allington was still alive and kicking and to leave the poor lady alone, but managed to bite her tongue.

Lost in her thoughts, she can hear Hattie's voice downstairs. Despite her annoyance when she asked her to move her stand, she has to admire the woman as she whizzes around on her crutches. Who else would be able to manage them so well at her age?

Tanya waves and smiles; after the trauma of the last few days, she is delighted Hattie made it public yesterday that she won't be pressing charges. She is also delighted that Hattie said she can keep her job, her cottage and her stand at the gallery. She doesn't want to upset her again. It's simple, really. She – and Lexie – both need to put everything behind them and get on with their lives. How Lexie came to have a loaded gun in her holdall is anyone's guess, but Lexie was mortified. She said it must have been the trauma of being kicked out of Team GB and leaving London in such a rush.

Tanya's still in shock. She can't comprehend that she had met Lexie before, without even knowing. Of course, she had known Lexie's mother, Penelope, when they were both teenagers, but their lives followed very different paths and she never met her daughter.

It all makes perfect sense now, including why Hattie was so distraught when Lexie admitted she was the person who broke in that weekend.

Tanya hadn't put two and two together before. After all, she definitely saw Lexie behaving strangely on the footpath, firstly hiding behind the builder's skip and then sitting in the dark by the pond. All on the very same day she had watched the uninvited visitor snooping around the Cowshed.

73

SATURDAY 4 AUGUST

MITCH

Fists clenched, Mitch strikes the punch bag with all his strength. God, it feels good. He's like a coiled spring, wound up by Chas. Nonchalant, uber-confident, patronising Chas.

Olly is on holiday with Mitch's ex-wife and, having swapped their weekends, he needs to make the most of the free time it's given him. Plenty of exercise and fresh air and whatever else it takes to get the raging resentment and anger out of his system. Chas will no doubt be in touch again when he is good and ready. Mitch is still mulling over Emily's words, too. He really ought to call her back, make sure everything is settled.

"Are you absolutely certain you don't know anything else, Mitch?" she asked. *"None of it stacks up."* He agrees, she is one hundred per cent correct. None of it does indeed stack up. And none of it ever will, unless he tells her the rest. But he's not sure he wants to take the risk. *"Please think some more about it. Please. For me. For you. So, we can get out of this mess. Think long and hard about it. I'll give you another call in a few days so you can tell me the rest."*

Mitch tenses his body again, moves his shoulders in a circular motion to limber up, and pounds the punch bag over and over again.

'Wow, steady on mate,' groans another gym member, as he lies on his back, his face puce, pushing up weights.

Mitch, engrossed in his dilemma, doesn't hear him. It's not just Emily. What is he going to do about Chas? What is he going to do about Tanya? Is he going to spend the rest of his life regretting his actions, feeling guilty for what he did at the reunion – or, equally, what he *didn't* do back in 1987 – unable to live his life how he wants? He despises the thought. He has never let anyone else control his life and he isn't going to start now. He just needs to tackle the problem head on. He'll speak to each of them in turn, to make sure they don't ruin him. Either now or at any point in the future.

Emily first. She should be easy. She doesn't actually know anything about anything. She is suspicious – suspicious of him, suspicious of the reunion, suspicious of their weekend in general – but knows *nothing* that will incriminate him or anyone else. She just wants to get herself out of the mess she has found herself in and move on, so she can get back with Marcus and be a happy family. If he helps her to do that she will be out of his hair and won't even consider getting involved again as she would have too much to lose.

Chas next. He's a loose cannon. He needs careful handling. Extremely careful handling.

Mitch sits on a low bench to get his breath back. He may have overdone it; there's a twinge in his left wrist, but the pain feels good. It makes him feel alive. With salty sweat running down his forehead, he leans his head back against the wall and, in a perverse sort of way, enjoys the roughness of the unrendered brick, like sandpaper against his scalp.

As his heart rate calms, his thoughts return to Chas. Whatever he thinks about Chas, Mitch mustn't let his own concerns stop him from doing what he needs to do. The problem is, the police know Chas is back, so he's definitely going to be questioned at some point about what happened at the reunion, if he hasn't been already. Mitch needs to be prepared.

Chas. His nemesis. Or was he? Maybe Tanya was his nemesis. Maybe it was both of them. Either way he needs to speak to him again. Find out whether he has spoken to the police and, if he has, what he has said.

Then there's Tanya. God, he really messed up this time. But she, like Emily, has far too much to lose. Her cosy, artisan life at the Allington Estate is paramount and she won't do anything to risk having to start all over again. He will have to use all his diplomatic skills to get her on his side with no room for a change of heart but, on the plus side, after all he's done for her recently, she does now owe him a favour.

An extremely big favour.

74

SUNDAY 5 AUGUST

EMILY

A bloodcurdling scream reverberates around the room, and a violent electric shock reverberates through every cell of Emily's body.

She had been dreaming happily about their picnic in the garden; Molly and Jack were laughing as fizzy ginger beer went up their noses and a cheeky robin flew down to inspect the breadcrumbs. Then a honey bee crawled over the slice of apple, just like it did four days ago, except this time it was huge, with iridescent wings that were five times the width of her hand and sparkled gold and silver in the sunshine. Unafraid, she gently moved the giant-sized insect onto a flower, when it unexpectedly stung her. It was like an enormous needle piercing her skin and the searing pain had woken her with a jolt.

She lies still, one hand gripping the edge of the mattress, wondering why she should have such a peculiar nightmare. Blood pulsates through her veins as she tries to focus her eyes sufficiently to read the time on the bedside clock. It looks like a two or maybe a three. Either way, it is the middle of the night and Marcus is in a deep sleep beside her and completely unaware of her distress.

Her brain is in overdrive, her subconscious mind continuously analysing her research even when she is asleep. She feels like a telephone engineer with her head in a box, submerged in a tangle of wires. Thousands of different coloured leads that all need to be connected correctly and in the right sequence or they won't work. Rolling over and snuggling into Marcus, Emily tries to switch off. But he automatically pulls away and she instantly feels rejected.

Rather than fidget and wake him, she pulls on her dressing gown and quietly tiptoes down the stairs and out the back door to sit on one of the garden chairs. The cushion is damp from the night air, but the softness is welcoming on her back, which is stiff from hunching over her laptop so intently all week. Closing her eyes, she enjoys the silence. There is not even the hint of a breeze and the incense-like scent of the nicotiana flower hangs in the air, hoping to attract nocturnal insects. The birds are yet to wake but in just a few hours the calmness will be shattered by children laughing, music playing and lawn mowers mowing. For now, she will simply relish the serenity of the moment and the opportunity to think everything through in peace. If nothing else, she *must* call Mitch again today.

*

Emily rubs her eyes. Tiny rays of sunlight are starting to appear and the blackbirds are beginning to stir. It won't be long before everyone is up. She can hear a car in the distance. Someone leaving for an early shift, or driving home after a late night. Immediately, she thinks of where she was two weeks ago, when the glimmer of daylight shone through the tiny square window in her police cell. Perhaps the vehicle she heard a moment ago is the duty solicitor making her way to the station, having kept someone else waiting while they go insane with worry.

Emily shudders at the memory. Although she must be unusual. Most of the people they have dealings with are not innocent like she is. They are hard-nosed criminals who hate being there as much as she did, but for very different reasons. What if the police take her in for questioning again? Marcus keeps assuring her they won't but the thought of it makes her feel numb. Her life as she knows it would be over, she would lose everything.

That is exactly why she must clear things up.

Tanya. She can't fathom her out. She seems a gentle, kindly soul. She loves to create her ceramics, inspired by nature; she loves her bees and she loves living where she lives. And yet, everywhere Emily searches for an answer, Tanya – or Bea's Bees – seems to be at the heart of it. None of which incriminates her and yet, at the same time, seems very odd.

Then there is Chas: schoolfriend of Mitch and his long-term rival. Theirs is definitely a love-hate relationship. Plus, did he genuinely disappear or was it all just a charade to cover something else up? Emily has serious doubts; the bizarre story is shrouded in mystery with no plausible explanation.

What about Norman the builder and Alistair the skip guy? Were they just unlucky like her and in the wrong place at the wrong time, or are they hiding something too?

Finally, Yvonne. She was incredibly kind when she stayed with her and yet abhorrent when she bumped into her a few weeks later *and* with the threatening texts. Does she know something about Mitch that Emily doesn't, or is she just a mother protecting her child?

She's spinning in circles again, driving herself insane. She wants to shout at the top her voice: shout and scream and holler to her neighbours and anyone else in earshot that she is innocent. That she did nothing. That she saw nothing. That it wasn't her.

*

Emily must have drifted off and gently wakes as her senses fill. The sound of windows being opened and babies crying; curtains being drawn, jingling along metal poles; the whoosh of a distant hose as someone washes their car, a radio playing softly and the smell of bacon cooking.

She hears a familiar squeak. It's the paperboy on his bicycle; his back wheel always needs a bit of oil. It's an indulgence, old-fashioned somehow, having their Sunday newspapers delivered but a habit they haven't yet stopped. She loves trying to complete the crossword, or a sudoku, even if she doesn't get around to it until the following day.

The young lad shoves the thick wadge of paper through the letter box and it lands with a dull thud on the floor. If they aren't already awake, that will rouse Marcus and the children. Emily ties her dressing gown more tightly around her waist while the kettle boils and absentmindedly flicks through the paper, looking for interesting stories. A small paragraph on page eighteen registers in her brain before her eyes have chance to read it and she carefully smooths the paper down on the worktop to get rid of any creases.

Ex-wife of teacher found dead issues statement

Vanessa Dodds, former wife of the retired school teacher found dead on a footpath in Devon, has asked for privacy ahead of his funeral next week. A spokesperson for Ms Dodds said she has been deeply saddened by ridiculous speculation on various social media platforms and this has compounded her grief at such a terrible time.

> Ms Dodds, who had been separated from her husband
> for eleven years, is quoted as saying Timothy Dodds
> was a well-loved, dedicated and respected teacher
> and will always be remembered as such by everyone
> who knew him.
>
> The post-mortem report said his death remains
> unexplained. However, he is believed to have died of
> natural causes while out walking. Most likely a heart
> attack. His funeral will take place in the chapel at
> St. Peter's School, where he last taught, at 11am on
> Friday 10th August 2012.

Emily reads it again. And again. Why has she made herself ill with anxiety about any of this? She had convinced herself that his death was due to something awful, something criminal that she had got herself caught up in. Whereas the truth of the matter is, he died of natural causes and they are allowing his funeral to take place. There can't be any outstanding reason for the police to think his death is suspicious if his funeral is booked for Friday, five days away. On top of which, if Charles Webber has now returned, there can be no remaining mystery about his disappearance either. All of which means she is completely exonerated.

She must let Marcus know. She must let her neighbours know. She must let her book club know. She must let everyone know.

Emily bursts into hysterical laughter; the relief is overwhelming and yet she cringes with embarrassment at her idiocy. All her muddled thoughts and the insecurity she has felt since being questioned by the police. Marcus was right all along. Why had she doubted him? Why had she doubted herself? No wonder he had been on the verge of walking out again.

Whether or not the death of Mr Dodds and the disappearance of Charles were connected, they were both just an unfortunate sequence of events.

SUNDAY 5 AUGUST

EMILY

'That is good news,' agrees Marcus, when Emily shows him the article about the schoolteacher's funeral. 'I guess the police just needed to check everything out, you know, how he came to be there, that sort of thing. They'd do the same for any unexpected death.'

'I know. Perhaps he had an underlying heart condition that he didn't know about. It does happen sometimes, even with young people.'

'Gosh, don't, it's too morbid to think about on a Sunday morning.'

'Okay, but you know what I mean. Anyway, what it *does* mean is that I am definitely off the hook and we can let everyone know.'

'Does it mean you will finally give up all your sleuthing too?' Marcus adds with a hint of sarcasm but making a joke of it. 'Although, I have been thinking about the Facebook post you showed me the other day.'

'Which post?'

'You know the one, the honey lady, this toast has reminded me.'

'You mean Bea's Bees?' Emily is curious. 'I wish I had bought some of her hand lotion for Mum's birthday, it smelt lovely!'

'Yes, that's the one. Well, promise me you won't get all worried again, but I couldn't understand why her post didn't make sense to me.'

'Why not?'

'Didn't you notice? She said she was away for the weekend, but that was the weekend you went down in May.'

'Yes, so what's wrong with that?' Emily is puzzled. 'Lady Allington said her housekeeper was away, that's why I couldn't stay there.'

'I know, but even so, the photo doesn't tie up.' Marcus looks at Emily, he's serious. 'It's been annoying me. The television screen in the background is the Cheltenham Gold Cup, it even had the breaking news banner across the bottom for the horse that won. It was called Long Run with odds of seven to two.'

'So?'

'I'm no detective but I think it's a fake post. The Cheltenham Gold Cup is in March not May, plus that was last year, not 2012. I checked it out, the jockey Sam Waley-Cohen, was the first amateur to win since 1981 so it was definitely that race. I reckon the post was intended to make people *think* she was away that weekend when, in reality, she wasn't.'

'But why would she do that?'

'Oh, come on Em, I don't know, I'm just saying.' Marcus gives her shoulder a squeeze. 'People do funny things sometimes. It was probably the right pub, just the wrong weekend and she selected the wrong photo for her post. A simple mistake. You said it was the first time she had posted for two years, so maybe she got confused.'

'Bloody hell, Marcus, you've got me thinking again. Just

when I thought it was all sorted.' Emily doesn't know whether to laugh or cry. 'Why would she say she was away when she wasn't, other than because she didn't want people to know she was at home? And it's really odd that she should suddenly post again after two years, unless she had an ulterior motive?' Emily flops onto the kitchen chair, exasperated. 'Plus, if she was at home, we could have stayed in The Cowshed and then none of the stuff that's happened over the last two months would ever have happened.'

'Now you are talking nonsense,' he quips. 'Please don't go off on one of your missions again. Honestly Emily, please don't. I wish I hadn't said anything now, I should have kept my thoughts to myself.'

'Oh, don't be like that Marcus,' Emily squeezes his arm. 'I was only thinking out loud. I won't do anything. It's just really odd she should do that, don't you think?'

*

After a long cycle ride, the four of them return home to watch the Olympics. It's awesome. Andy Murray beats Roger Federer in straight sets to take the gold medal in the men's tennis and, buoyed up by his victory, they decide to go for a game of catch in the park before coming back for more. "Super Sunday" they are calling it. It's an amazing line up of events, culminating in the men's one hundred metre sprint final just before ten o'clock with Usain Bolt defending his title.

There's excitement in the air everywhere you go and Emily knows they will all be glued to the television. They've agreed Molly and Jack can stay up extra late to watch it.

But Emily is still on edge. She can't stop thinking about the phoney Facebook post.

MONDAY 6 AUGUST

MITCH

'Hello, Rodney Mitchell speaking.'

'Mitch, it's me, Emily.'

Mitch says nothing.

'Mitch?'

'Sorry, Emily but I'm in the office. I'm just talking with Gabriella and getting ready for a client meeting. Can whatever it is wait?'

'Not really. I said I'd call you again and I need to know. I need to know *now*. Just give me some straight answers.'

'Okay.' He senses the urgency in her voice and decides to deliberately stall her. 'But I'll only do that if you promise to leave me alone and stop bothering me with these inane questions.'

'Fine with me,' Emily says curtly, 'as long as you do.'

'How long will this little game take?'

'If you keep interrupting, who knows? And it's not a game.' She's getting annoyed. 'If you give me simple, honest answers then five minutes.'

'Hmmm. Really?'

'When we last spoke, you said you saw Tanya at the reunion, but she stormed off, after you upset her about something. Correct?'

'Yes.'

'You also saw Charles Webber and Mr Dodds that evening. Correct?'

'Yes.'

'Before I arrived, the following Saturday, did you see any of them again?'

'It depends what you mean.'

'Okay, let me put that differently. Did you see any of them after you got into the fight with Charles and Tanya stormed off?'

'I can't really remember.'

'Not good enough. Did you?'

'Look. No, I didn't. I heard from Trev and Ian that Chas decked Mr Dodds after I left, allegedly because Tanya was so furious with him – and me – but that was it. Happy now?'

'What about the next day… or the following week… or the day I came down?'

'Bloody hell, why the interrogation? I don't think so, why, should I have?' Mitch knows he is wavering. Emily will pick up on his reticence so he adds more detail to convince her that he's being truthful. 'I thought Chas would come to watch the football at the pub but he didn't, so I assumed he was keeping a low profile after the reunion. I didn't give it any other thought.'

Emily is silent.

'Any other questions, or is that it?' Mitch breaks the hiatus. He hasn't got the time, or patience, for this.

'Yes. Why didn't you tell me Tanya was the person who sold the honey?'

'Bloody hell, Emily, why would I? I didn't know she was.'

'And what about your phone call to the police – did you *really* call them?'

'For fuck's sake. Why would I have made it up?'

'You promised the other day to tell me anything else that was important. What else do you have to tell me?'

'I don't remember promising.'

'Don't split hairs. We agreed, when we drove to your mother's house that weekend, to protect each other. To say we weren't there, that we never went.' Then she adds, to clarify. 'That's all I'm trying to do now. Protect you. If you're not honest with me then, quite frankly, I don't see how I can.'

Mitch is bewildered. Emily saw nothing, Emily did nothing. Emily wanted nothing, other than to be out of this. Why is she behaving so oddly?

Then he remembers his thought process at the gym. This is his opportunity to deal with Emily, to make sure she doesn't cause him any problems. She knows none of the *important* details. He simply needs to allay her suspicions once and for all.

'Look, Emily, I'm really sorry about all of this,' he says softly, thinking she'll respond more positively. 'I know it's been horrendous for you. I know you just want to move on. You and Marcus are back together and the most important thing for you is to be a happy family again.'

'I know, you're right. I realise that now, more than ever.'

'I can honestly tell you, hand on heart, that I didn't do anything I shouldn't have done that weekend. Yes, I admit I upset Tanya at the reunion, but I immediately regretted it. Like I said, I didn't see her again that evening.'

'Okay. Thanks, Mitch. I just needed to know. I saw in the paper that the teacher's funeral is this coming Friday and I wanted closure. I know it's just paranoia on my part, but it always felt like there was something you weren't telling me.'

'Don't be so hard on yourself Emily. Neither of us particularly enjoyed that weekend and hindsight is a wonderful thing. We're both strong enough to get through it. Marcus is a lucky man and Molly and Jack are lucky to have you as their mother.'

'Thank you, that is very kind.'

'Look Emily, you've had fifteen minutes of my time now and you said five. I don't mind, but we can't keep going over this. I really do need to go now. My two o'clock appointment has arrived.' Mitch watches as Gabriella asks his client to take a seat. 'You take care Emily, look after yourself and be happy. You deserve it.'

'Thanks Mitch, I'm sorry for how it all turned out. You're a good guy. Hope you get lucky too.'

Mitch puts his handset gently on the desk and draws a long, deep breath through his nose.

Phew. Got away with it. One down, two to go.

TUESDAY 7 AUGUST

EMILY

It's mid-afternoon and Emily is desperate to call Marcus but there's no point; he has an important meeting at work and won't be able to talk. She spent all of yesterday, her day off, going over her notes. The fake Facebook post had played on her mind and while they were watching the Olympics on Sunday evening, she had been completely preoccupied – yet again – with establishing all the facts and deciding what to do. As Usain Bolt sprinted to gold her brain had been racing equally fast, processing all the information.

When she investigated, the post was definitely fictitious. Emily found out the pub had burned down last autumn, so not only had Tanya got the year wrong, it would have been impossible for her to meet her friends there. Which also explains the slightly odd comments she had received too, which Emily hadn't taken any notice of previously.

Then the phone call with Mitch. It helped enormously, even though he had seemed extremely reticent to begin with. In truth, Emily wishes Jo had never suggested the two of them meet, then none of this would have happened. But, on balance, Mitch isn't that bad, she decides. She remembers him being concerned about her when she first arrived at The Cowshed, after she broke down. Then, later, making sure she was okay when she met his old school pals and didn't know anybody. Whatever she thinks about him, she simply needed to know, for certain, that he had absolutely nothing else to tell her about that weekend. Now she is confident he didn't, she can put it out of her mind. That he is as innocent as she is in all of this.

For the first time in weeks, Emily slept well last night. An enormous weight has been lifted from her shoulders. She normally has an energy slump mid-afternoon, but not today. Today she is her old self; focussed and on the ball, it's been the best day she has had for ages. It makes her realise how much the ongoing trauma of the weekend with Mitch has been getting on top of her, even before she was arrested, and that only made everything a thousand times worse.

This morning she woke up refreshed and energised. Able to think clearly again. As she drove to work the roads were quiet and it all fell into place. All the little details; all the little things she had seen but not taken any particular notice of. Each of them insignificant in isolation but so incredibly important when she pieced them together.

As soon as she got to the office, she jotted down the timeline on a large sheet of paper and cross-referenced each of the individual components against her scribbled notes. That was when everything finally made sense. But she can't stop now. There are less than three days to go before the funeral and she needs to tell the police. She doesn't know why they did it, but she definitely knows who. She will be able to get her reputation, her friends and her life back. And stop Marcus walking out on her again.

Emily checks the time; it's gone four o'clock and she is unable to hold off any longer.

'Hey, Marcus, it's me. Sorry to interrupt you at work, but I really need to talk.'

'What, right now? Can't it wait?'

'No, it's important.'

'What is?'

'Since you said about the fake post, I've gone through all the information again and I've worked it out. I know what happened.'

'What do you mean, you know what happened?'

'Exactly that Marcus. I know for sure who did it.' She can hear the uncertainty in his voice and tries to convince him.

'What are you taking about Ems, I thought you agreed not to do anything?'

'I know I did, but I *had* to… and now I know, I *have* to do something about it.'

'What do you mean you have to do something?'

'Exactly that. For us, Marcus. For Molly and Jack. To put everything right.'

'Just wait until I get home, Ems. Don't do anything rash. Please.'

'I won't. I promise. It's just that, if the funeral is on Friday, I've *got* to do something today or it will be too late.'

Marcus is silent.

'I promise I won't do anything stupid. Honest. I just need you to come home,' Emily begs. 'I want to explain everything to you first and then I'll go straight to the police and tell them too.'

'I can't get away yet, Em, there's an IT project meeting in ten minutes. The platform launch is next week so it's going to be a long discussion and there's nothing I can do about that. I'm the programme manager which means I've *got* to be there.'

He's deliberately making this awkward, putting obstacles in her way.

'Please Marcus.' Emily waits. Nothing.

'Ems, I can't believe you're doing this again after everything we talked about.'

'*Please.* I'm doing it for us; for you and Molly and Jack, so they don't lose all their friends at summer camp.'

'Look, Ems, I'm really sorry. I simply can't guarantee to leave on time tonight.' Marcus sighs loudly. 'I know it's not what you want to hear, but, I just can't.'

TUESDAY 7 AUGUST

EMILY

Molly and Jack are fighting noisily over who sits where on the settee to watch the latest Olympic highlights while Emily folds the washing at the kitchen table. The backdoor is open and she can hear the birds chirping outside. It's such a cheerful sound despite her growing frustration as the children argue and she waits for Marcus to return home. It's already half past six and the evening will be gone at this rate.

*

Another hour passes. Time is running out and she needs to do something.

Hi, has your meeting finished yet? Love u xx

Another 30 mins at least. Luv u2 xx

Emily can't believe it. Of all days. Then she has a thought, she'll ask Helena to help.

'I'm sorry, Mrs Harrison, but there's no way my mum will let me come over.'

'Why not?'

'Because of all the stuff, you know, with the police and everything, it's a bit awkward but mum says…'

'But the police got it all wrong, Helena,' Emily interrupts. 'It was all a big mistake. I didn't do anything. Surely you know that?'

'I'm sorry. I just think it's best, you know, if I have a break from babysitting for you for a little while.'

Emily is devastated. She is well aware the last time Helena visited was the evening she was arrested, but surely her neighbours know she didn't do anything? Her eyes well up; it hurts to the core. Helena was the last person she expected to react in this way; she's known Molly and Jack since they were babies and she adores them.

Fighting back the tears, she won't let herself cry. Instead, Helena's reaction has strengthened her resolve. It is *exactly* the reason why she needs to sort this mess out before she not only loses her marriage but all her friends as well.

Desperate times require desperate measures. There is one remaining option: she'll drive to the police station via her parents' house.

Forty minutes later, she lets Marcus know.

Hi M, me again. I know you think I'm crazy but I have got to do something. Have just dropped M&J with Mum and Dad. I can't leave it any longer. Please understand I'm doing this for us, because I love you & M & J with all my heart xxx

*

'I'm sorry, Mrs Harrison. I've just checked and the North Bristol CID team are attending urgent calls this evening. Is it anything in particular you wanted to discuss with them?' the PC on the desk at Thornbury Police station is polite but harassed; a haphazard pile of files sit next to his elbow and another officer is vying for his attention, waving a piece of paper at him.

'It's about an incident in Devon in May this year.' Emily is desperate to sound sane after waiting three quarters of an hour to speak to him. Now she's saying it out loud, she is worried it will sound completely nonsensical and she already knows she is waffling. 'I previously came to this station, to assist with some enquiries. I... I... told them everything I knew... it's just I think I may have some more information, that I've only just thought of, you know, since before.' She looks at him and smiles nervously. 'I'm sorry, this is all garbled. But the thing is, it's urgent. *Really* urgent. There's a funeral taking place on Friday and...'

'I see.' The PC is trying his best to help. 'Let me think. Do you have the name of the person you spoke with before?'

'Yes, it was DS Fuller. He was from Devon and Cornwall Police and his colleague was DI Sands.' Emily is relieved. At least she sounds more in control now.

'Have you tried getting in touch with either of them Mrs Harrison?'

'Not this evening, no.'

'Perhaps that would be your best bet? Even if one of our CID officers is available later, they won't be familiar with the case.'

'I hadn't thought of that.'

'If it is urgent, like you say, DI Sands would definitely be the best person to speak to.' The PC smiles sympathetically. Emily senses she will test his patience if she keeps him from his other tasks any longer and there are two more people waiting in the queue behind her now. One is tutting noisily and the other sniffing, wiping his nose on his sleeve.

'Do you have any contact details for them?' Emily asks, not wanting a wasted journey, before adding out of politeness. 'Please.'

'Let's see. Okay, yes here we are.' He grabs a bit of notepaper, scribbles a few numbers down and hands it over. 'There you go Mrs Harrison. All the best.'

'Thank you.'

Emily moves away from the reception desk and glances down. She is sure she remembers DS Fuller saying they were based at Tavistock Police Station, but it's a mobile number, so that's ideal. She stands in the relative quiet of the porch and taps the digits into her phone.

'This is the answerphone service for DI Sands from South Devon CID, Devon and Cornwall Police. I cannot take your call at the moment, but if you would like to leave a message after the tone, I will get back to you as soon as I can.'

Dithering, Emily cuts off the call. Then, after a moment's deliberation, her determination wins through and she calls back to leave a message.

'Good evening DI Sands, my name is Emily Harrison. We met a few weeks ago when yourself and DS Fuller questioned me at Thornbury police station. Well… there's been a development and I… I need to speak to you urgently. I can't do it over the phone… I'll… I'll come down to see you and call you again when I arrive. Thank you.'

Then she texts Marcus to let him know too.

Hi, me again. Hope your meeting is going well. Local police can't help so driving to Tavistock to see DI Sands who I saw before. Must get there before it's too late. Don't worry, everything OK and M&J still with M&D. Will text when I get there. Love u millions & millions xxxx

WEDNESDAY 8 AUGUST

EMILY

The dark and monotonous motorway had been running smoothly until now. All of a sudden, Emily is surrounded by a menacing army of cones and flashing yellow lights, gradually coercing her to the left of the carriageway and down the slip road.

Damn. She had assumed it would be quiet at this time of night. Instead, it's a scene from a science fiction film. Overnight roadworks; weird, shadowy, alien life forms that don't exist by day.

Emily tunes into a different radio station. A friendly one, with live chat and music, not pre-recorded, artificial entertainment. It reassures her to know there are other human beings still alive in the world. That she is not alone.

*

Diversion signs, held upright with sandbags, illuminate her way and Emily's progress is painfully slow. Amidst a convoy of lorries belching out fumes, she makes her weary way via small country towns that sound familiar, but none she can recall visiting. She realises with a yawn that she has been driving for nearly three hours. It's ridiculous. Quarter past one in the morning and she hasn't even reached Exeter yet.

Emily cranks down the heating to keep her car cool and herself awake. The car, close behind, will be on her bumper before she knows it if she doesn't concentrate. Finally, as the glow of street lights rises over the dark horizon and the motorway reappears in the distance, she almost whoops with delight.

Running on adrenaline, Emily merges with the other traffic. She has at least another hour to go and is thankful she changed her car. The interior still has a reassuring, nearly new smell and just thinking about breaking down at this time of night makes her shiver. The familiar signs to Okehampton are a welcome sight and Emily holds the steering wheel in one hand while she rummages with the other to locate the half-eaten bag of Maltesers she keeps in the pocket on the driver's door. The sweet, sugary taste of the chocolate and honeycomb melting on her tongue is exactly the tonic she needs. Putting two more in her mouth, she settles into a comfortable, steady speed and tells herself she doesn't have much farther to go. She can do it. She *will* do it.

*

Tiredness is setting in and the busy holiday route, normally packed with camper vans and vehicles piled high with luggage in the sunshine, is unrecognisable in the dark. She feels desperately lonely. To make it worse, spots of rain, like spittle, land on the windscreen; not enough for the wipers to work effectively, but more than enough to make her view opaque. It's oppressive, like a shroud. Even in the dark she can tell the cloud is getting lower and heavier the closer she gets to Dartmoor.

Humming along to the radio to keep herself alert, a bright red light illuminates the dashboard and Emily's heart sinks. It's the low fuel indicator. Panicking, Emily tries to calculate how far she can get on what she has left. Running out of fuel in the middle of Dartmoor at three o'clock in the morning sounds like a recipe for disaster and it's not a risk she wants to take.

Thumping the steering wheel in anger, she wishes she had engaged her brain earlier; she could have stopped at the motorway services. Emily bites her lip so hard she makes herself wince in pain. She had been so pleased with herself for coping with the earlier diversion; now she is annoyed and having *serious* doubts about what she is doing. No wonder Marcus told her not to do anything rash.

She recalls a garage near the thatched pub where they were tempted to stop a few weeks ago. She only remembers it because of the name: The First and Last. She had thought it was perfect, whether you are just arriving on Dartmoor or saying goodbye. It must be about two miles away and, crossing her fingers, she wills it to be open as she turns towards the moor.

She's in luck. The forecourt is empty, but the lights are on and she hesitantly pulls up next to the pump closest to the building. Determined not to feel scared, she gets out her car. She definitely feels vulnerable. Exposed. As if she is being watched. It may be summer but the fog is menacing, swirling silently around her head like skeletal, cold fingers on her face. The science fiction film on the motorway has turned into an X-rated horror movie and the breeze blowing through the high beech trees is a vampire, breathing over her shoulder.

The old-fashioned pump takes forever and her hands are shaking so violently it keeps cutting out, but she soldiers on, determined to fill the tank so she doesn't have to stop again. After what seems like an eternity, she replaces the fuel cap and heads to the door of the tiny convenience store. It's locked. She tries again. It is definitely locked. She peers inside, leaning on the glass. The lights are on, but there is nobody there. Surely, they must have seen her? Her relief at finding fuel is rapidly turning to fear, only to be compounded further as the roar of a motorbike echoes eerily in the low cloud. Too scared to turn around, she watches as the headlight becomes increasingly bright until it is immediately behind her, reflected and magnified in the glass door. Blinded, she shields her eyes then suddenly screams; half falling through the door, as a short buzzer sounds and the lock releases.

Emily regains her balance just in time and walks up to the counter. The elderly gentleman looks at her quizzically.

'Pump one?' he says abruptly.

'Yes… yes… please. Thank you,' Emily mumbles, still dazed from almost falling over. 'I wasn't sure if you would be open this late.'

'Lucky for you we are. Only in high summer mind, if you'd been here in three weeks' time, we wouldn't be.'

'Right. Yes… of course… definitely lucky,' Emily stutters.

'What's a young lady like you doing out here at this time of night, anyhow? Don't sound like you're from these parts?'

'No, I'm not. I'm on my way to Tavistock. I've got an appointment, it's urgent.'

'Well, I won't ask. Take it steady out there, mind. The fog's real bad and if you don't know the road it can be harsh. Especially Dead Man's Bend.'

Emily's heart rate quickens further. She takes her receipt and, turning around to leave, collides with the man who was on the motorbike. She bounces off the leather of his jacket so hard the stitching is imprinted on her forehead. He must have been standing *right* behind her and listening to everything she said. Embarrassed, Emily mutters 'Sorry' as she scuttles back to the relative safety of her car.

*

Her legs still shaking, and full of trepidation, Emily pulls away into the darkness. It is reassuring to see the fuel light extinguished but, as her car judders over the familiar cattlegrid and she drives further on to the moor and the altitude increases, the denser the fog becomes. It's impossible to see the side of the road and the warning of "Dead Man's Bend" rings in her ears. Hunched over the steering wheel, the bonnet of her car is barely visible, let alone the tarmac beyond it, and her already tired eyes are struggling to focus.

It's perilous. Progress is excruciatingly slow but a small sign, glinting in her fog lights, catches her attention and she realises it must be the layby where they stopped to watch the ponies. Emily decides to pull over; she needs a few minutes rest and she'll be safer off the road.

Terrified, lonely, and exhausted, she leans back in her seat. She desperately wants to call Marcus, just to hear his voice, but it's half past three in the morning and he'll be fast asleep. She'll text instead, let him know where she is.

Hope u r OK. Diversion on motorway took forever now stopped in layby near the cattlegrid where M&J watched the ponies – do u remember it? Will text again when I get there. Love you with all my heart xxxx

She finishes typing before realising there is no signal and puts her phone back in her bag, dejected; the inability to communicate magnifies the overwhelming sense of isolation and fear. Knowing the only way to escape her predicament is to keep going, she psyches herself up and is about to set off again when an eerie yellow, fuzzy light illuminates the fog. Her heart races. It's moving extremely slowly and it's impossible to tell what, or where, it is until it passes right beside her car and then she realises it's another motorbike. Thank goodness she stopped in the layby and not on the road, or it might have crashed into her.

She watches the bike continue past then, with a sharp intake of breath, she sees the watery atmosphere fill with a blood-red glow.

Brake lights.

They're stopping.

Open-mouthed, Emily stares as a ghostly silhouette props the bike up on the kickstand and walks towards her.

Frozen to the spot, as they reach her car, she recognises the leather jacket. It's the man from the garage. *You stupid idiot. Why did you stop?* Dizzy and weak, as the blood drains from her head, she silently prays the driver's door is locked.

But there is nothing she can do. As the tall, menacing figure taps on her car window, Emily's forehead hits the steering wheel with a thump as she faints.

80

WEDNESDAY 8 AUGUST

EMILY

'Open up, miss, please open up,' says a deep, muffled voice.

Emily is confused; her cheek is numb where it has been leaning on the steering wheel and she doesn't know where she is. It's dark, it's cold and she's strapped in.

'Miss, please, open up. I didn't mean to frighten you.'

It's gradually coming back. It's the middle of the night. She was running out of fuel and she's on Dartmoor, in the worst fog she has ever known, on her way to see DI Sands.

'Look miss, I heard you say you were on your way to Tavistock so, when I saw your car stopped in the layby, I was worried.'

Emily is too scared to talk.

'The fog is really bad. I can show you the way, if you want. If you aren't familiar with the road.'

Emily's head is hurting. She shuts her eyes, too frightened to look, but can sense him standing just inches away, on the other side of her door.

'Honest, miss. I won't hurt you. My parents have a farm not far from where you're heading, I'd been to see a mate in Okehampton and was on my way home when I stopped to fill up ready for work tomorrow and saw you. Old Bernard at the garage can vouch for me.'

Emily reluctantly half-opens her eyes. He sounds genuine, but what does she know? He's hardly going to tell her if he is a madman. Spine-chilling stories of headless horsemen and carjackers on the moor fill her imagination; she is so tired she doesn't know what to think. She wants to trust him. She wants to believe him. If he could show her the way to Tavistock it would be amazing.

She opens the window, just a tiny gap, to make it easier to talk. 'How long will it take?'

'Normally twenty minutes but, in this fog, I'd say forty-five if we take it steady, maybe more.'

'Okay. Thank you.'

'You sure you're okay miss?'

'I've been better but, yes, I'm okay. I think. You scared me.'

'I'm sorry. I didn't mean to.' He opens his visor and Emily can see he is only about eighteen. 'Look, follow behind me. Don't get too close in case I need to brake, but don't lose sight of my bike, either. I know the road and it'll make it much easier for you.'

'Thank you. I mean it, thank you. I don't even know your name.'

'Drew.'

'Emily.'

*

Emily keeps a steady distance behind Drew's bike. She feels more confident but can remember the steep drops on either side of the road from her previous journeys and the thought of rolling over the edge in the fog is a constant worry. Every now and then Drew makes a thumbs up sign and she toots her horn to let him know she is still following him. That she is still awake.

As a new day begins to break, the thick fog gradually turns from charcoal grey to palomino white. Four thirty in the morning. If it wasn't so gloomy, it would be light by now. With each mile that passes, Emily can feel her destination getting closer and hopes the sun will banish the fog as it warms the air. She wonders if Marcus has received her text yet. If not, she will soon be able to let him know she has arrived safely.

Mildly complacent, Emily starts thinking about what she will say to DI Sands; where to start and how to explain everything. But her optimism short-lived. As they clear the brow of a hill, the foggy sky is once again filled with flashing lights.

It is pandemonium. An oil tanker is lying on its side, next to a car that is embedded in the hedge with its bonnet pointing to the sky. There are emergency vehicles everywhere and a police officer is stopping traffic. No wonder they had not passed any vehicles coming the other way.

'Sorry ma'am. The road to Tavistock is closed for investigation work. It's going to take hours. Avoid the lanes if you're not local though, they're already gridlocked. If I were you, I'd go back the way you came, then head west into Cornwall, down to Callington and turn back towards the moor from there.'

Emily is frantic. Tavistock is so close and yet so far. She has been driving since ten thirty. It should have taken her three hours at most; she is now six hours in and has another lengthy detour along winding roads and fogbound hills. Marcus will be going crazy.

*

Two hours later, Emily is almost delirious as she pulls up in the carpark at Tavistock police station. Drew had abandoned her – by mutual agreement – at the road block and, left to her own devices, she ended up getting completely lost.

Somehow, she found herself in deepest Cornwall and way beyond Callington. Then, making her way back across the Tamar Bridge, she drove into Plymouth just as the fog was lifting. Exhausted, she was beeped at, shouted at and cut up by impatient city drivers in the early morning rush hour as she desperately tried to work out the best way back to Tavistock. It must be the craziest journey she has ever made.

Sitting alone in the car park, she finishes the last of the Maltesers and takes a large glug of water, secretly hoping that DI Sands or some kind soul will offer her a huge mug of coffee when she finally gets to speak to her. The station is in darkness, but Emily will give DI Sands a ring to let her know she has arrived. She can't give up now.

'Hello, Mrs Harrison, yes, I did get your message. Thank you. It's very good of you to drive all that way. It's just, I'm really sorry, but I'm not based in Tavistock anymore. We've moved. The CID team all work out of Charles Cross Police Station in Plymouth now.'

'What do you mean?' Emily is distraught, she had been so certain – why didn't she check before she set off?

'We used to be, probably when DS Fuller and I saw you before, but not anymore. I really am sorry. I can give you directions if you like?'

81

FRIDAY 10 AUGUST

DI SANDS

'Bloody hell – talk about cutting it fine! Thank you. Great team work. At least his family can go ahead tomorrow as planned.' DI Sands throws the updated post-mortem report on to her desk after checking it twice, just to be sure, and glances at her watch. 'Actually, make that today, do you realise it's just gone midnight? What a nightmare. I've had to push a funeral back before and it isn't an enjoyable thing to have to do, I can tell you.'

'Yep, the family are bearing up well in the circumstances,' DS Fuller replies, shaking his head in disbelief. 'Really feel for Emily Harrison, though. I can't believe she drove through the night to reach us *and* across Dartmoor; that was the worst fog for months and she didn't even need to go that way, she could have come straight down the motorway and the A38 to Plymouth. No wonder she was scared witless by the time she got here.'

'I agree. I must admit I had serious doubts about her, but she was incredibly thorough with her research. I'm not easily persuaded, but she wasn't going to leave until she knew we believed her... *and* that we would do something about it.'

'I know. She's had it really tough, talk about being in the wrong place at the wrong time. Could happen to any one of us.'

'I feel awful for thinking she was a crank, although we've both had our fair share of those over the years, you simply can't tell from appearances.'

'Too right.'

'I checked out the other case she was involved with too, the one in Cornwall. The DI said she witnessed something aged six in the famous heatwave of 1976. No one believed her at the time, not even her own family, but she was determined to help the missing girl's parents after seeing them on the news thirty-four years later.'

'Really?'

'Absolutely. The elderly mum was terminally ill and desperate to find out what happened to her daughter before she died. Mrs Harrison wouldn't give up on that one, either. She's one tough cookie.'

'Definitely. Amazing how she found the insect research team at Plymouth University too, if they hadn't analysed the DNA so quickly it would never have been possible.'

'Give her a call later will you, check she got back home in one piece? She was genuinely upset *and* exhausted.'

'Yep, will do.' DS Fuller nods. 'Just to let you know, the family liaison officer has been briefed and will be with the family first thing in the morning, the funeral is at eleven. It's been one hell of a shock for them.'

'I know. We still need to get a confession but it's going to be extremely interesting. I bet they think they have committed the perfect murder and that we'd never be able to prove it was them. Little do they know!'

'Wouldn't be surprised at all if this is a first.' DS Fuller smiles in reply, stifling a yawn. 'God, twenty-four hours of ground-breaking forensics – I hope the chief appreciates what we've done.'

'You ready then? We need to make an arrest. No rest for the wicked, eh!' DI Sands grabs her jacket off the back of her chair.

'Who are you referring to – them or us?' replies DS Fuller, grinning.

'Probably both. It's been a long day already and I sense it's going to be a bit longer yet.'

82
FRIDAY 10 AUGUST

DI SANDS

'Interview commenced at thirteen hundred hours at Charles Cross Police Station in Plymouth. I am Detective Inspector Julie Sands and with me are Detective Sergeant Darren Fuller and duty solicitor Mr James Purbeck.'

The suspect confirms their name and the solicitor slides his glasses up his nose with his forefinger, ready to concentrate.

'You have been arrested in connection with the death of Mr Timothy Dodds, a retired teacher whose body was found on a footpath at the Allington Estate. We have reason to believe his death was related to an incident at a school reunion which took place on Saturday 12th May and subsequent events during the week immediately after.' DI Sands looks at the person sat opposite her. 'Please can you confirm you were at the aforementioned reunion.'

'No comment.'

'We have witnesses who have confirmed you were in attendance. Please can you confirm you were.'

'No comment.'

'I'll try a different question. Please, can you to take us

through the events of the evening? In particular, what caused an altercation to take place and what you did immediately thereafter.'

'No comment.'

DI Sands watches as the interviewee rocks from side to side. Their brow is deeply furrowed and their hands wedged under each leg, as if they are not sure what else to do with them. She is finding it difficult to read their expression and tries to gauge what is going through their mind. Regret? Fear? Anger? Most likely all three, mixed with emotions like despair, resentment or hopelessness.

DI Sands almost feels sorry for them. She is experienced enough to know that people react in a myriad of ways when they are first charged. Aggression and belligerence are all too common. Others veer in the opposite direction and will be mute, sad, lonely figures. The one emotion she can't see or feel at the moment with this person is guilt. Maybe that will come later, after they have exhausted all possible explanations. Why it wasn't them.

DI Sands continues to observe; watching as they take a sip of water, barely able to swallow. They haven't yet made eye contact with her, DS Fuller or Mr Purbeck. Instead, they are fixated by a chip on the edge of the table.

DI Sands pushes a grainy photograph across the table. 'Can you confirm this is you, standing on the left-hand side of the image, taken at 2348 hours on the evening of the school reunion? For the purposes of the recording, I am showing the suspect an image taken by the CCTV located just outside The Moon and Sixpence where the reunion was held.'

They lift their eyes for the first time, then look away again, saying nothing.

'As I mentioned a moment ago, a number of witnesses have confirmed you were at the reunion. Can you confirm this is you in the image?'

'No comment.'

'The various witness statements also corroborate in saying you left shortly before midnight after an altercation. Is that correct?'

'No comment.'

'Were you involved in the altercation?'

'No comment.'

'I will ask again, were you involved in the altercation?'

'No comment.'

'Is the altercation the reason you left?'

'No comment.'

DI Sands is beginning to lose patience. She's given them ample opportunity to start talking. It's time to put some hard evidence in front of them. 'The thing is, the same CCTV camera provided images of you arriving at the reunion so it is difficult for you to deny you were there.'

'No comment.'

They finally move their eyes away from the chipped veneer to glance at the photograph and DI Sands swiftly moves another to meet their gaze.

'I am showing the suspect another CCTV image taken at 2349 hours on Saturday 12th May which is in the same location as the first and shows two people having a heated conversation with another standing nearby, observing. One of the two appears to be provoking the other, who is pummelling them in the chest.' She takes a deep breath. 'Can you confirm you are one of the people in the photo?'

'No comment.'

'Please can you confirm you are in both these images?'

'No comment.'

'I repeat, please can you confirm you are in both these images?

'So, what if it is me, none of this proves I did anything.'

'Do you recognise the other people?'

'Why should I?'

'Because one of them is Mr Timothy Dodds, who is now deceased.'

'Like I said, none of this proves I did anything.'

DS Fuller looks across and raises his eyebrows. He doesn't have to say anything, DI Sands already knows. At least they have started to talk, even if they are being deliberately obtuse. She'll up the pressure. It's going to take an extremely long time to get a confession at this rate.

'Given the lack of information you are currently willing to share, and your reticence to answer any questions, I have no choice but to put further evidence before you.' DI Sands wastes no more time. 'The post-mortem for the deceased teacher – found on the footpath at the Allington Estate – shows he did not necessarily die of natural causes, as originally reported. We also have numerous witnesses and pieces of evidence that link you directly to this incident.'

DI Sands pauses temporarily to see if there is any flicker of emotion. A tiny twitch of the jaw, rub of the nose or shake of the head. But there is nothing. No reaction whatsoever.

'We believe you allowed this person to die after making arrangements to meet them at a property known as The Cowshed, a holiday cottage on the Allington Estate. We also have evidence that you returned to The Cowshed on Saturday 19th May to dispose of the body.'

83

FRIDAY 10 AUGUST

TANYA

Tanya can feel DI Sands staring at her, looking smug, but there is no way she or DS Fuller can actually *prove* she did it.

Tanya needs to concentrate. The detective's eyes are burrowing deep into her skin, into her brain; she's been here for hours and she's mentally exhausted.

She assumes they do it every time; asking question after question after question. It doesn't make any difference to them. It's not their life that will be ruined. Only hers. She thought if she kept saying 'no comment' they would give up, but now they are using different tactics. They know she is tired and are trying to trick her into submission by talking about "numerous witnesses" and "pieces of evidence". To frighten her. To weaken her resolve.

'There is no way you can prove I did it,' she says defiantly, sticking out her chin. Then immediately requests fifteen minutes in private with her solicitor.

*

'My advice is to co-operate as best you can with their questions. That way, whatever the outcome, it is likely to be more favourable,' he advises. He has no doubt given the same counsel to hundreds of people before her.

More favourable than what? Tanya can't help but wonder. He constantly plays with his glasses. Taking them off, putting them on. Pushing them up his nose, down his nose. Cleaning the lenses. It is extremely irritating.

'Bear in mind this interview is likely to continue for many hours, until they have got what they need from you. I will request a further adjournment if I think it is necessary or if it will help your situation. However, I must stress again that it is in your best interests to co-operate.'

Co-operate, thinks Tanya. *That's a joke. That's what has got me into this farce in the first place. Always doing what other people want me to do.* She stifles a yawn and takes another sip of water. Weary but still adamant they won't be able to get a confession out of her.

'Interview recommenced at nineteen hundred hours.' DI Sands looks sternly across the table before continuing. 'For the purposes of the tape please can you reconfirm your name and date of birth.'

'Tanya Beatrice Symonds, 22nd March 1969.'

'Ms Symonds, you have declined to confirm you are one of the people in the images. However, we have other evidence to put before you. We have established from your mobile phone service provider that – after attending your school reunion and meeting up with Mr Dodds for the first time in a number of years – you invited him to join you at the holiday cottage known as The Cowshed on Friday 18th May. In a text, which you sent to him on Wednesday 16th May, you said – and I quote – *"it was good to see you again and it would be great to catch up properly, just the two of us. Are you free this Friday?"*. Please can you confirm that you did indeed send this?'

'No comment.'

'I will continue. In reply to your message, Mr Dodds said – and again I quote – *"That would be wonderful and yes I am."* To which you then replied, *"The holiday cottages are free this weekend and Lady A is away. Let's meet in The Cowshed at 7pm, we'll have it all to ourselves for as long as we want."* For the purposes of the recording the message is signed off with a love-heart and a winking face emoji.'

'It was just a joke.'

'Maybe, but given Mr Dodds is now deceased and his body was found in the grounds of the Allington Estate, adjacent to The Cowshed, you can easily understand why we are taking this so seriously.'

'But even if I did send the text, you can't prove anything. No one will ever be able to prove anything because there would have been lots of people in or around The Cowshed that weekend.'

'Ah, but that's where you are wrong, Ms Symonds. Very wrong indeed.' DI Sands is on a roll. 'Now, you may want to think very carefully about what you say next, Ms Symonds. Firstly, we have an updated post-mortem and, secondly, a university research paper. These confirm exactly how Mr Dodds died and the circumstances leading up to his demise.'

Tanya rubs the back of her neck.

'Before I continue, is there anything further you would like to tell us about the events commencing Saturday 12th May and during the following week, up until the date Mr Dodds body was found?'

'Only that it wasn't me. There were other people there. Lexie Williamson for one, and Rodney Mitchell, Charles Webber, Norman Weatherby – lots of people.' Tanya frowns and holds the edge of the table with both hands, her fingers extended, as if they will keep her from toppling over. Her head is spinning. 'There's no way you can prove I did anything. You need to talk to them.'

'Let me explain. We requested a second post-mortem following evidence we received from a person who had, by chance, visited The Cowshed on Saturday 19th May. In the first report, the deceased had been found to have at least three dead insects entangled in his hair; they were originally thought to have ended up there because he had been lying outdoors, on a grassy path in the countryside, for a number of days when his body was found.' DI Sands pauses briefly before continuing. 'However, upon further testing, all of the insects were found to be female worker bees.'

'So what?'

'DS Fuller, please show Ms Symonds and her solicitor the report from Plymouth University Insect Genome Research Project team.'

DS Fuller places a piece of paper in front of them, headed up with the University coat of arms and signed off by a Professor A J Knowles.

'The insect genome project team at the University of Plymouth tested them and found them all to be related. This means – due to the DNA they share – that they are all offspring of the same queen.'

'Like I said, so what?'

'I'll explain. They also tested a sample of Bea's Bees honey – your honey – and not only did the DNA in this show what flowers the bees had visited, it also contained DNA from the bees who collected it. This proved without doubt that the bees found in Mr Dodds's hair were from one of your colonies.'

'So? What difference does that make?'

'It makes a lot of difference, Ms Symonds. It suggests that Mr Dodds didn't die of natural causes, rather, that his death was caused by something far more deliberate.'

'How?'

'When the report is read in conjunction with the post-mortem, it proves he suffered a cruel, tragic end. His heart attack was not an unfortunate medical episode but a deliberate act of torture, caused by someone who knew he had an insurmountable fear of stinging insects.'

'Like I said, what difference does that make?'

'A lot of difference, Ms Symonds, a lot. Please let me continue. He wasn't allergic to bees as he had feared – if he had been the post-mortem would have picked up that he died of anaphylactic shock – what it *did* show was one part of his heart was significantly enlarged and distorted. Ruptured. No, he wasn't allergic to bees, but he was absolutely terrified of them. He was literally scared to death. Petrified. Whatever word you choose to use, he died a terrible, agonising death. Paralysed by fear, due to a swarm of bees he believed were about to sting him. As a result, he died alone and in horrendous pain from a massive heart attack.'

'But, even if they were my bees, that doesn't prove I did it. They might have just been flying past when he happened to be walking along the path.'

'But that, again, is where you are wrong Ms Symonds.' DI Sands clears her throat, her expression serious. 'The thing is, he didn't die on the footpath. Carpet fibres were found lodged in the tread of his shoes, in particular along the back of the heel, meaning his body had been dragged from somewhere else. When examined, they were found to be from a rug in The Cowshed. Furthermore, the forensic team found numerous towel fibres under his thumb and finger nails, and concluded that, in a state of severe panic, he used a towel to protect himself from the bees. When these fibres were tested, they were identical to those of the towels in the bathroom at The Cowshed.'

Tanya takes another sip of water; it tastes stale and unpleasant.

'So, Ms Symonds. I think you owe us an explanation.'

84

FRIDAY 10 AUGUST

TANYA

Tanya sits upright, clenching her fists and determined to prove her innocence.

'But, even if he was dragged from The Cowshed, it still doesn't prove *I* did it. It could have been anyone, lots of people have a key or know the code to the key box.'

'Then, how come a piece of plastic – that had fallen off the sack trolley you use for moving clay – was also found in The Cowshed on the day in question?' DI Sands produces a transparent, labelled bag and empties the contents. 'For the purposes of the recording, I am showing Ms Symonds a circular piece of plastic which has the logo of the brand of trolley she uses, and which we know is missing from the wheel of Ms Symonds's equipment.'

'But that still doesn't prove anything, I'm not the only person to own a trolley like that.' Tanya vigorously shakes her head. She can still deny everything; the evidence is all circumstantial. 'I wasn't even there that weekend, I was away. Lady Allington can vouch for me.'

'Ah yes, we checked that out too. Your deliberate ploy on

Facebook to make it look like you were on holiday. Shame you used an old photo, plus your mobile phone service provider gave us records of your usage that weekend so we know *exactly* where you were. As I said, Ms Symonds, I think you owe us an explanation.'

*

Tanya lets out a strangled sob and slumps onto the table, hiding her face in her arms. The manner in which DI Sands speaks makes it sound like fiction, as if it happened to someone else. Except it didn't. It was her. She thought her bees would make it look natural, cover her tracks.

'I never intended to,' she whispers, sobbing.

'Ms Symonds, for the purposes of the recording please can I ask you to speak louder.'

'I never intended to.'

'Ms Symonds, please elaborate.'

'Please, you have to understand. I'm not a murderer. I just couldn't take any more… you have no idea what he was like… it isn't what you think…'

'I am requesting a break for my client,' Mr Purbeck interjects as Tanya collapses, unable to continue.

*

'Ms Symonds, we know how difficult this is. However, you need to tell us *exactly* what happened. Take as long as you need.' DI Sands places a box of tissues on the table. 'In your own words and in your own time.'

'I thought I had got my life on track again; everything had been going so well. My cottage, my bees, my ceramics, my stand at the gallery. That was, until the reunion.' Tanya raises her head a little, her voice no more than a whisper.

'That's when everything started to go wrong. I wish I had never gone.'

'What went wrong?'

'I don't know. I was a fool to go. It was such a bad idea to meet again, after so long.'

'Please explain Ms Symonds.'

'I shouldn't have gone… I wouldn't have, if I had known they were *all* going to be there.'

'Who?'

'Chas… Mitch… Mr Dodds.'

'Why?'

'It was awkward. Chas and I used to date when we were teenagers. Mitch was always insanely jealous, I mistakenly thought he would have got over it by now.'

'Go on.'

'He – Mitch – was really friendly to begin with and I enjoyed chatting with him, reminiscing. But, as the evening went on, he got more and more drunk and his mood changed.' She goes quiet again. Takes a deep breath. Mr Purbeck adjusts his glasses. 'The more alcohol he drank, the more sarcastic he became, and spiteful.'

'What did he do?'

'He just kept going on and on. He was nasty. About me and Chas, how he had always been second best to Chas, how Chas could never put a foot wrong, how he hated Chas. All that sort of stuff. It had clearly been festering away inside him for twenty-five years and was like vomit, spewing out.' Tanya takes a sip of water.

'Please continue.'

'Well, all of this was going on and I have no idea what he said, but Mr Dodds said something to Mitch and it completely wound him up. In a split second, he turned *really* aggressive. He just flipped and went absolutely mad. Mitch lunged at Chas and punched him in the face.'

'What time was this?'

'Later on. Mitch had just asked me to dance – there were a few slow records towards the end of the evening – but Chas butted in. That's when the fight broke out. The DJ tried his hardest to lighten the mood and stop everyone watching, but it didn't work. The whole atmosphere had changed.' Tanya sobs out loud.

'Take your time,' DI Sands says softly.

'People pulled them apart and I followed Mitch outside; I tried to calm him down but he was in a foul mood. Really, really foul.'

'What did you do?'

'By now crowds were gathering around us but Mitch was beyond reason. I begged him to calm down... I pleaded with him. I told him Chas hadn't meant to upset him, but he didn't take any notice.'

Tanya goes deathly quiet; she is not sure if she can continue but, at the same time, realises she must. She wants to tell DI Sands the whole story now, so she understands how she felt, the depth of her emotions. Why she did it. Surely if she knows the reason, she can't be punished.

Taking a deep breath and closing her eyes, she continues. 'As I tried to reason with him, Mitch swung around with a horrible expression on his face, glaring at me. He shouted "Chas might not have meant to upset me, but Dodds did!" then he laughed a really evil laugh and said, "There. I've said it now – Chas never knew, did he? No, but *I* did. *I* saw you. I know you were there... with Mr Dodds by the photocopier, all those years ago. You thought no one knew. What a sight. Little Miss Perfect wasn't quite as perfect as she liked everyone to think... was she now?". By now everyone was staring at me. Gawping. I felt completely humiliated. So, I hit him, I pummelled him in the chest over and over again... the CCTV image you showed... it... it was me.'

The DS silently tops up Tanya's water as tears roll down her face.

'I didn't know what to do. I was hoping either Chas or Mr Dodds would stick up for me, defend me. But they didn't. Nobody did. The trouble is, it was true. He *did* see me, all those years ago. With Mr Dodds. But it wasn't what he thought it was.' Tanya's head falls and her unkempt hair drags on the table.

'Ms Symonds. I understand this is extremely difficult, but you really must tell us everything.'

'I honestly don't know where to start. I have never confided in anyone before. Ever.'

'Take your time; it will help your situation to tell us everything.'

'He... Mr Dodds... was a popular teacher. He was young and enthusiastic, not long out of college himself. Chas and I both had our futures mapped out. Chas planned to go to Cambridge – which he did – me to Bristol.' Tanya sniffs loudly and DS Fuller pushes the box of tissues in her direction. 'That's when it all started. Mr Dodds was kind and attentive, saying how pretty I was, how clever I was, that I was a model pupil and how he wanted to help me. I must admit I liked the attention. He was exciting, he made me feel special. But then he... he... he started to behave differently. Controlling.'

Tanya stops. Her heart is breaking, she has never spoken about what happened to anyone, anywhere before.

'Go on, Ms Symonds.'

'He... he... blackmailed me. He said if I didn't do what he wanted he would make sure I didn't get the grades I needed to go to university. That he would be invigilating and would sabotage my exam papers, without anyone knowing.' Tanya wipes her nose and dabs at her watery eyes. 'With hindsight I know it wouldn't have been possible for him to manipulate my grades, but I was young and naïve, and I believed him. He made me go into the stationery store with him every Friday afternoon. The noise of the photocopier would disguise what was going on. I can still remember the horrible, acrid smell of the hot ink as he did what he did. He pinned me up against a cupboard and I would bite into his shoulder, as hard as I could. But it just made him worse. He was far too strong for me. It makes me sick just thinking about it.'

DI Sands waits a while then gently encourages. 'In your own time, Ms Symonds. Take as long as you need.'

'He blackmailed me. Made me do things I didn't want to do. When I tried to refuse, he threatened to tell my parents. Either way I was ruined. I honestly didn't know anyone else knew until the night of the reunion. Mitch made it sound sordid and disgusting. It was. I was devastated. Absolutely devastated.' Tanya is inconsolable. She raises her head up, looking straight at DI Sands with red, tear-stained eyes. 'But it didn't stop there. I was livid that he – Mitch – must have seen me with Mr Dodds that day, and yet he didn't do *anything* to help me.'

'In what way, Ms Symonds?'

'Surely, he would have known it was against my will?' she shouts, anger taking over. 'He was my friend, we used to talk about everything, yet the one time I really needed him, he walked away.'

SATURDAY 11 AUGUST

TANYA

Tanya takes a moment. DI Sands and DS Fuller might have known the facts of the post-mortem and *what* happened to Timothy Dodds, but Tanya is certain they would never have imagined *why* it happened.

The tragic events from 1987 that came back to haunt her; that drove her to do something terrible, something unthinkable.

After a brief interlude Tanya summons up the resilience to continue. She remembers Mr Purbeck's words of advice. If she tells them everything, however difficult it is, DI Sands may be more favourable towards her.

'After Mitch said what he did at the reunion, I stormed off. I didn't know what else to do. But, over the next few days, the feelings of humiliation and anger worsened. I couldn't eat. I couldn't sleep.' Tanya's throat is tight, her voice strained. She takes a sip of water but can barely swallow. 'Then, a few days later, I had a stroke of good fortune when my bees started to swarm. I had always dreamt of catching a swarm and it gave me an idea about how to get my revenge, without anyone ever knowing.'

Mr Purbeck pulls at his collar and stretches his neck.

'I can't describe how angry I was with all of them, especially Mr Dodds. So, I decided to teach him a lesson of my own. For ruining my life.'

'How did he ruin your life?'

Silent tears roll down Tanya's face. 'Mr Dodds may have threatened me with bad grades but in the end, he didn't need to. I was so traumatised by what he did to me, I lost all my confidence. I lost my trust in everyone. I finished with Chas, hid myself away and missed all my grades. Instead of going to Bristol, I made do with a London college I had never heard of. I struggled to make friends, was a mediocre student and then just drifted in and out of jobs. All my dreams for the future had evaporated into thin air. *All* because of Mr Dodds and what he did.'

Tanya gulps. She has scarcely taken a breath. She glances up. DI Sands and DS Fuller are both furiously taking shorthand notes although the tape recorder is still displaying the red light. Mr Purbeck is fiddling with his glasses.

'So, what did you do?' DI Sands asks gently as she writes.

'I messaged him. I pretended I wanted to see him again, for old times' sake.' Tanya sobs. 'As if. But he fell for it. I invited him to The Cowshed. I said I knew there were no guests that weekend as Lady Allington was away and it would be special. Just the two of us, together again.' She shuts her eyes, tears now streaming down her cheeks.

'Ms Symonds, do you need a break?'

'No... no, I need to tell you. I didn't mean to, you must believe me, I didn't... I didn't.' She shakes her head, still crying. 'He didn't hesitate for a second, so I said I'd meet him there at seven o'clock on Friday evening. That gave me two days to get everything ready.'

'What do you mean by "get everything ready"?'

'I remembered from a school trip that he was scared of

bees. I can still see him running, screaming, across a field thinking he was going to be stung and all the schoolkids laughing, thinking he was messing around. So, I decided to lure him to The Cowshed. I knew if I played 80's music to get all nostalgic, opened a bottle of wine… that sort of thing… it would lull him into thinking we would get intimate.' Tanya trembles as she remembers. 'It was even easier than I thought. So, so easy. It was all I could do to stop myself laughing at him. Then, when "China in My Hand" started – my favourite song – it was the perfect moment. I can remember as a teenager reading that the lyrics were a reminder of how fragile our dreams are, and how easily they can be broken. It was so very true for me; the song still gives me goosebumps every time I hear it.'

'Perfect moment for what?' asks DI Sands as DS Fuller raises his eyebrows.

'Before he arrived, I had hidden a box of bees in the bathroom, the swarm I caught a couple days earlier. I had temporarily sealed the box and they were placid. The lights were dim and the soft music was sufficiently loud to disguise any gentle buzzing.'

DI Sands clears her throat with a little cough.

'… I pretended to go to the bathroom and, while in there, I removed the sticky tape. I then balanced the box on top of the door, leaving it slightly ajar. He was in the armchair facing the other way so didn't see a thing. I sat back down and we chatted a bit more, sipping our wine.' Tanya takes a deep breath as she recalls the events of the evening, she can't stop now. 'I used to love all the music in the charts when I was a teenager. I would sit in my bedroom for hours on end recording the Top 20 on my cassette player and then listen to them over and over again. The music helped to calm me down while we chatted. He had no idea what was really going on in my head; then, when Phil Collins singing "In the Air Tonight" started playing, I knew it was a sign; it was as if I was being given permission to do what I had planned to do. I had been waiting for this moment, to get my revenge, for all my adult life and I couldn't change my mind at the last minute. I got up, this time pretending to check the front door was locked. Mr Dodds smiled a sickly smile and said *"what a good idea"* and I saw him shut his eyes in anticipation. He was such a creep, it was vile. Absolutely vile.'

'What happened next?' DI Sands asks after a couple minutes silence.

'That was the last thing I heard him say.' Tanya looks at the floor. 'I... I took his mobile phone, which he'd left on the kitchen worktop, slipped out the door, double-locking it behind me, and went home. I had already locked the patio door and all the windows earlier in the day, and taken all the keys, just to be certain there would be no way he could get out.'

Tanya glances up, aware she hasn't stopped talking. DI Sands, DS Fuller and Mr Purbeck are all staring at her, motionless.

'I knew he would be scared stiff. I also knew that, once he realised he was locked in The Cowshed with them, my bees would sense his fear and go after him.' She adds, in case they are sceptical, 'When someone is scared, they release pheromones. Bees can detect this and perceive it as a threat.'

DI Sands looks at her and nods as Tanya collapses, her tears now running uncontrollably as her emotions, stifled and hidden for the last twenty-five years, take over.

'It was perfect; my lovely, loyal bees helped me get my revenge. He was evil. He stole everything from me and felt absolutely no remorse; my future, my career, my life, my relationships, *everything*. He stopped me living the life I wanted to live. The life I *should* have lived. The teacher needed to be taught a lesson of his own.'

86

SATURDAY 11 AUGUST

TANYA

Tanya is past the point of no return. She has to no choice but to tell them what happened the following day.

'Knowing the bees would be active again at sunrise, I returned to The Cowshed at daybreak on Saturday morning in my bee suit, expecting to find him cowering in the corner somewhere.' She swallows the last of her water. 'But he wasn't. I eventually found him in the bath. He had wrapped himself in a large towel and the top of his head was just visible. He must have taken refuge there, in a desperate attempt to escape.'

DI Sands clears her throat and watches Tanya closely. She has never heard a confession like it. 'What did you do?'

'I thought, at first, he was asleep but, when I pulled back the towel, I could see immediately he was cold and lifeless. That's when I panicked. I knew he would be frightened, but I never intended to kill him.'

'And?'

'I tried to move him, but I couldn't. He was far too heavy for me. Instead, using the smoker to calm them down, I worked my way around all the rooms, collecting my bees. Then I tidied away the wine glasses and cleaned up. All the while agonising over what to do with him.' Tanya rubs her hands together. Finding the dead body still haunts her. She had never intended for that to happen.

'How did you move him?'

'I didn't. I couldn't. I'm only five-foot-two and I tried repeatedly, but there was no way I could pull him out the bath without help. I spent the morning in my studio instead, trying to work out what to do.' Tanya sips her water. 'Lady Allington wasn't due back for a few days, so I had time on my side.'

'And did you work out what to do?'

'No. I completely lost track of time. I was in denial. That's when I had the surprise of my life. It was late afternoon when a car pulled up outside and a woman with two children got out.' Tanya is shivering despite the beads of sweat she can feel on the back of her neck. 'She seemed to have the code for the safe, so it was fortunate I hadn't yet replaced the key, otherwise she would have walked straight in. I still had my bee suit on and hid behind the gate, I was scared the children would see me watching.'

'Go on.'

'After fumbling around in the key box she went around the back, by now a man had arrived too but I couldn't get a clear view so I had no idea what either of them looked like. Then I remembered; I had left the patio door unlocked after finding Mr Dodds in the bath. It was wider than the front door and much easier to get through with my box of bees.' She takes a breath. 'Anyway, they were gone for ages, that was when I realised, they must have entered the cottage through the patio door at the back.'

'How long were you watching them?'

'I don't know, it felt like hours. She ran out first – with the kids – then he came after them and they all sped off in the car. I still couldn't see them properly but they were definitely panicking. I assumed they had seen the body and were freaking out.'

'What happened next?'

'I don't really know, it's all a blur. Annabel, my neighbour, and her children were away so I knew there was no one else around and I hid by the gate for a bit then went over to The Cowshed to try and move him, again, in case they phoned the police or something. I thought if I was determined enough I could do it. That's when I got the call.'

'What call?'

'From someone who knew what I had done.'

'Who was it?'

'Mitch – Rodney Mitchell.'

'Go on.'

'All he could say was *"what the fuck have you done"* over and over again. He was almost incoherent. That's when I realised, the man who had been at The Cowshed about half an hour earlier, had been Mitch. He had been meeting a friend there but, somehow, she got the dates of her reservation wrong. Mitch recognised Mr Dodds and immediately knew it had something to do with me.' Tanya starts to sob again as the enormity of what happened begins to register. 'I didn't mean to, please believe me, I didn't mean to.'

DI Sands lets her pause before asking another question. 'Did Mr Mitchell say anything else?'

'No. Nothing that made any sense. That's when I had a thought, karma, whatever you want to call it. I knew he would help me out, to make up for the fact he didn't do anything to help me all those years ago.'

'How?'

'I pleaded with him; I said if he didn't, I would frame him. I would tell the police he had been trespassing at the cottage. I would prove to them – you – it was Mitch who killed Mr Dodds after their fight at the reunion and I just happened to find the body when I went in to clean the cottage, ready for the next guests.'

'And did he agree to help?'

'Yes, eventually. He said he had one hour, no more. He would borrow his friend's car without her knowing, while she was chatting with his mum, and help me get the body out the bath. But that was it.'

DI Sands sits up straight. This ties in with the CCTV images of Mrs Harrison's car going back and forth past the golf club multiple times that evening.

Tanya drinks the last of her water before she continues. 'He said again that he wanted no other involvement. I would have to do everything else on my own.'

'Did he say anything else?'

'No that was it. I wasn't going to get help from anyone else, so I agreed.'

*

'By the time he arrived, he was almost delirious. He said he was only doing it because he loved me, that he had always loved me. Then he shouted at me that I was never to tell anyone about what we were doing or that he was there. He kept repeating himself; making me promise, again and again.'

'Go on.'

'By now I had my sack trolley, I'd fetched it from my studio while I was waiting for him as I thought we could use it as a stretcher and he – Mitch – managed to pull Mr Dodds onto it. It took all his strength to drag him out the bath. We wrapped the body with more towels and tied him to the trolley with some garden twine.' Tanya holds her head in her hands. 'Mitch was desperate to leave by this point but I persuaded him to help me pull Mr Dodds to the door. It was horrendous. It took forever. The wheels caught on the rug and Mr Dodds's feet kept falling over the edge of the sack trolley. When Mitch tried to catch them, he bent his finger back with the dead weight of the body, which made him scream and swear… and even more angry. As soon as we got to the door, he fled, saying that was it. He was done. He could never, ever see me again. He jumped in the car and was gone, literally, in a cloud of dust.'

'What did you do with the body?'

'I really don't know how I managed it on my own, but I heaved the trolley a few centimetres at a time. Bit by bit, I pulled it – him – around the cottage; the wheels kept getting stuck in the soft grass. I struggled as far as I could, then I lost my grip and the trolley overturned next to the skip. I was exhausted. My arms were aching so much I couldn't move them and I left him there, lying face-down on the path. I thought it would look more innocent; a passer-by would find him and assume he had been out walking.'

'That was it?'

Tanya takes another sip of her tepid water. 'It was starting to get dark and I was about to go home when I heard someone on the path. I now know it was Lady Allington's granddaughter, Lexie, but I hadn't met her before then. She was acting really strange, all on edge. I tried to hide but she had already seen me, so I pretended I was tidying up the builder's rubbish, putting stuff in the skip. I thought I had been caught red-handed but, thankfully, she couldn't see the body from where she was standing. She just stared at me for a bit, then climbed over the stile and carried on towards the pond. The next morning, I found her coat. She must have accidentally left it behind where she was sitting next to the pond. I hung it over the stile so it was easy for her to spot, that way she wouldn't go anywhere near the body if she went looking for it.'

'What happened next?'

'I finished unwrapping Mr Dodds and left him there. He was dressed casually, in pale blue chinos and an open-necked shirt, so looked like he could have been out for a stroll. I took my trolley back to the studio, washed and tumbled dried all the towels, and put them back in the bathroom – to make sure The Cowshed was immaculate when Lady Allington returned home. A few days later, when Norman the builder and the skip guy found him on the footpath, it was perfect. I read in the newspaper that the police thought he had died of natural causes – probably a heart attack –which meant everything had gone to plan. I thought I had got away with it.'

87
SATURDAY 11 AUGUST

DI SANDS

'Great work, DS Fuller, what a result. Although I must admit that is the weirdest confession – and murder weapon – I have come across in twenty-five years as a police officer!'

'I know. It's amazing how Mrs Harrison worked out what happened. She felt bad about going in the cottage when she shouldn't have, but just think if she hadn't – and Rodney Mitchell hadn't been there with her – how would Ms Symonds have disposed of the body?' He turns to face her, hands in pockets and rocking back and forth on his heels. 'Would have been a gruesome welcome for the next guests.'

'Imagine that on a Tripadvisor review!' DI Sands shudders at the thought. 'We need to check out the burglar's DNA again, though. I wouldn't be at all surprised if there are more young girls he preyed on, including Lady Allington's daughter, given the DNA match at the burglary. He didn't just teach; he was on the PTA and ran the youth tennis club for many years, so we'll need to do some very sensitive investigations.'

'I've been thinking the same. I feel terrible for Ms Symonds; it was shocking what she did but, whether it's manslaughter or murder, we need to establish exactly what else Mr Dodds got up to back then.' DS Fuller shakes his head. 'We've just had some other results in from the lab too. They've found two distinct DNA results from particles of skin and strands of hair on Mr Dodds's clothing, one of which matches the DNA of a tiny piece of human fingernail that was caught in the hem of the deceased's trousers. I know we need to follow it through but sounds like even more evidence for the prosecution file if it's Ms Symonds and Mr Mitchell's DNA.'

'Great stuff Fuller, too right. Anyway, it's two thirty in the morning, I don't know about you but I am in dire need of some shut-eye. It's time we both went home and got some kip. We just need to contact our colleagues in Avon and Somerset to ask them to arrest Mr Rodney Mitchell. They're going to be pleased this is all sorted too.'

'Sounds like a plan.'

'I'd do it tonight, but we aren't at risk of losing him. He's still on bail so not going anywhere, plus he thinks he's in the clear after denying he used Mrs Harrison's car and all the rest. What a liar. Thought he had pulled the wool over our eyes and everyone else's. It'll be a nice little surprise for him on a Sunday afternoon.'

SUNDAY 12 AUGUST

EMILY

'Do you want a hand with anything?' Emily calls across the garden to Marcus.

'No thanks, just a chilled beer out the fridge please Em, if you're fetching the salad,' he replies. 'Your mum and dad will be here any minute and the barbecue is warming up!'

The closing ceremony for the Olympics is in a few hours and Emily's parents are joining them. Since seeing her name misreported in the paper and Marcus threatening to walk out again, Emily's not sure where the last two weeks have gone but, in contrast, the sport has been incredible and they're looking forward to tonight's extravaganza.

Hattie's granddaughter is up for a medal in the modern pentathlon today too, at least a silver or bronze. Rumour was rife she had been temporarily suspended due to a complaint from another team member. Fortunately, whatever it was about, the case was retracted a few days later and she took part after all, much to her grandmother's enormous relief.

Emily places their garden chairs in a big circle; enough seats for everyone and a couple tables for drinks, nibbles and food. Perfect. The local paper printed an apology on their front page this week, which means everyone now knows she definitely had nothing to do with it, and Sian, Helena and a few other neighbours have been invited this evening too.

'Cheers!' Emily clinks her glass of wine against Marcus's bottle of beer. 'Here's to the Olympics!'

'Here's to 2012 and us too,' replies Marcus, pulling her in close and kissing her gently. '... and to Mrs Harrison for solving yet another mystery and the weirdest crime *ever*.'

'Gosh, don't. I know you always laugh at me, but I knew in my gut that something wasn't right. It just wouldn't go away, however hard I tried, and there was no way on earth I was going to lose everything for something someone else did.'

'You had me sick with worry when I got all those texts from you the other night – they all arrived in one go!'

'Ugh, don't remind me. It was horrendous being lost in the fog. I was terrified. I honestly thought Drew was going to kill me and yet he was only trying to help.' Emily shudders, it still seems so vivid. 'And just think, if we hadn't had a picnic in the garden last week and the bee hadn't crawled onto that slice of apple and made me have that bizarre dream – or you hadn't spotted the fake Facebook post – who knows, she may have got away with it.' Emily's sips her wine and feels truly blessed. She has never been so happy to be in her own garden, with her own family.

'Honestly though Em, how did you manage to work it out?' Marcus kisses her again.

'It was all the little things that started to add up. The dead insects on the windowsill, I realised they were all bees, which is most unusual. Then I remembered the smell of smoke – like burning paper – in The Cowshed that day, I thought it was a bonfire but it must have been the bee smoker. Then the ghost lady, she must have looked really scary to Molly and Jack, yet it was just Tanya in her bee suit.'

'That *was* weird. I couldn't work out what it was they had seen. I thought the place was haunted!'

'And then Peanut – why did he suddenly reappear like that? Even if Cleo the cat took him, she – Tanya – must have known it was me when Hattie rebooked the Piggery for us. Plus the sack trolley I spotted in the photo in the newspaper. I thought the bit of plastic was a jacket button and brought it home to sew back on!' Emily hugs Marcus close, kissing him on the nose and savours another sip of her wine.

'It must be incredibly sad, though. Whatever it was that happened all those years ago.'

'I know – and Mitch never let on – it must have been really, really terrible to make her do that.'

'I must admit, I never felt easy when you were seeing him.'

'Yvonne threw a curve ball sending me those texts though. She was only trying to protect her son, but she made me think he *did* have something to do with it, otherwise why would she have needed to warn me off? It didn't make sense. Either way, I'm truly relieved Mitch wasn't involved.'

'I am too. To think you could have been spending time with a psychopath or a murderer doesn't bear thinking about.'

Emily shudders at the thought. She didn't intend on calling him again, but she might give Mitch a quick call to tell him it's all sorted before their guests arrive. She doesn't need to go into any details but, out of kindness, she thinks it only fair to let him know. Then she doesn't have to speak to him again. Ever.

*

'Hey, Mitch, it's me, Emily,' she says. 'Sorry to bother you again, I know I said I wouldn't ring but I just wanted to share some good news.'

'That's all right, everything okay?'

'Yes, really good thanks. Like I said, that's why I'm phoning. I just want to say thank you again for being so helpful the other day, I really appreciate it.' Emily smiles and waves to her parents as they pull up on the drive. 'Also, to let you know, all the grisly business with the teacher on the footpath is *completely* sorted.'

'Oh, that's great. How do you know?'

'Well, apparently, it was a bit touch-and-go, but his funeral went ahead on Friday and everything got resolved in time.'

'How come?'

'I understand someone has been arrested and charged which means, basically, it's all over. We were simply in the wrong place, at the wrong time. I don't know about you Mitch, but I am beyond relieved. I hadn't realised how much it had been preying on my mind.'

'I know exactly what you mean, thank you for letting me know,' he agrees.

'That's okay, I just thought it only fair to tell you. Anyway, it's a beautiful, sunny Sunday afternoon and I won't hold you up any longer. We're enjoying the last day of the Olympics and I am sure you've got lots to do too.'

Mitch seems distracted and she hears his doorbell ring in the background. 'Look, it's good of you to call, Emily, but I'm really sorry, I've got to go.'

'You sure you're okay, Mitch?'

'Yeah, fine. It's just there are two people at my door and they look a bit official. I'd better see what they want.'

'No problem, and thanks again, Mitch.'

'See you around, Emily, thanks again for everything and for letting me know. Make sure you look after yourself.'

ACKNOWLEDGEMENTS

Heartfelt thanks are owed to so many people it is impossible to name everyone and I am forever grateful to all my family and friends, who have provided encouragement throughout.

In particular Abigail Winfield and Pamela Hudson who read and critiqued numerous versions. Your feedback was amazing and inspired me to keep going. Also, to Nathaniel Cramp, Sarah Bowden and Samantha Radford for your help with adding the final polish to my manuscript and making sure it was completely ready for publication.

Sincere thanks also to Nadine Ledanois-Ikin and Tracey Beal for your unwavering support, it means the world to me, and to Yvonne Bunyan for suggesting – and letting – me use your name for one of the characters. I hope you approve of your namesake!

Last, but certainly not least, to my husband Andy for your never-ending love and support.

I have genuinely loved every second while writing my book but couldn't have done it without you all.

AUTHOR'S NOTE

The story of Emily's fateful weekend was inspired by real life. Indeed, the way in which the victim met their tragic end was based upon by something that happened to me, fortunately not with such a drastic outcome, although it was pretty scary at the time. So – just in case you are reading this before you dive into the story – I won't even hint at what this might have entailed, as to do so would give far too much away!

However, there are some things I can share. Firstly, the unexpected events at Emily's holiday cottage were influenced by the experience of two friends. Luckily for them there was nothing criminal afoot but as soon as they told me about their 'surprise' on holiday, I knew it had the potential with a bit (okay, a lot!) of embellishment, to be turned into something rather more sinister.

Finally, choosing the right setting was vital and this was inspired by childhood memories of my late grandmother's isolated bungalow on Dartmoor, where she lived on her own for many years. Coming from a family with eight children, we took it in turns to stay with her – usually two at a time – and it was always an adventure. I still love the whole area, from exhilarating hikes up and down the tors, with their rugged beauty and magnificent views, to the foreboding sense of isolation. And how it can become terrifying in an instant, when the fog rolls in. A place famous for myth and legend it creates the perfect atmosphere for a suspenseful story that keeps you guessing to the very end.

And so, Emily's second adventure began. Once again, I have loved every single moment while writing; from reliving the music of the 1980's and the excitement of the London 2012 Olympics, to developing believable characters and an intriguing plot full of twists and turns.

My aim was to write a story that anyone could relate to. How a seemingly ordinary family weekend could go horribly wrong, and with long-term repercussions, all because of something someone else – a complete stranger – did twenty-five years earlier. I wanted readers to genuinely care, not only about Emily and her children but all the characters, and ponder long after they finish reading what they would do if it ever happened to them.

*

Finally, a huge THANK YOU for choosing my book. I sincerely hope you enjoyed reading it as much as I did writing it. If you did, please can I ask you to leave a rating and/or review on one (or all!) of the popular websites including Goodreads, Amazon, Waterstones and Troubador Publishing.

Positive comments and personal recommendations really do make a massive difference to a new author like myself and help other potential readers to hear about my books too.

This book is printed on paper from sustainable sources managed under the Forest Stewardship Council (FSC) scheme.

It has been printed in the UK to reduce transportation miles and their impact upon the environment.

For every new title that Troubador publishes, we plant a tree to offset CO_2, partnering with the More Trees scheme.

MORE TREES
LET'S PLANT A BILLION TREES

For more about how Troubador offsets its environmental impact, see www.troubador.co.uk/sustainability-and-community